DATE DUE

DEMCO 38-296

THE COLLECTED STORIES
OF
LOUIS AUCHINCLOSS

REPLICA BOOKS

A DIVISION OF BAKER & TAYLOR
BRIDGEWATER, NJ

)OKS EDITION, APRIL 1998

Published by Replica Books, a division of Baker & Taylor,
1200 Route 22 East, Bridgewater, NJ 08807

Replica Books is a trademark of Baker & Taylor

Copyright © 1994 by Louis Auchincloss

Bibliographical Note

This Replica Books edition, first published in 1998, is an
unabridged republication of the work first published by
Houghton Mifflin Company, New York, in 1994.

Reprinted by special arrangement with
Houghton Mifflin Company

Manufactured in the United States of America

The
Collected
Stories
of
Louis
Auchincloss

THE COLLECTED STORIES
OF
LOUIS AUCHINCLOSS

REPLICA BOOKS

A DIVISION OF BAKER & TAYLOR
BRIDGEWATER, NJ

FOR MY GRANDSON,

ROBERT MOORES AUCHINCLOSS

Contents

Introduction

I WAS DELIGHTED when my editor, Joseph Kanon, agreed to bring
out this volume, for I believe that much of my best work has been in
short stories, and that my best ones have been buried under the bulk of
my now out-of-print fiction. The job of choosing the better tales to
rescue proved surprisingly easy. They simply jumped out at me from
the ranks of their paler brethren. A novel, at least in my experience, can
be enriched by a long gestation and much rumination, but my more
successful short stories have sprung from a single idea or vision. So,
anyway, did those included in this compilation.

The fashion in short stories of the past half-century has tended to
favor those that deal with a single episode, sometimes in a single scene;
the turning on of a light, so to speak, to illuminate a dark room. But I
have stuck to the leadership of Henry James and Edith Wharton, and
at times of Paul Bourget (a master of the short story if not the novel),
in giving my tales the scope of months, even of years. Sometimes,
indeed, such a story, when finished, will seem to appeal for longer
treatment, and on four occasions I have seen fit to develop short pieces
into novels. "In the Beauty of the Lilies" was expanded into *Watchfires*,
"The Money Juggler" into *A World of Profit*, "The Trial of Mr. M"
into *The Rector of Justin*, and "The Great World and Timothy Colt"
into a novel of the same title. Some themes will admit of both major and
minor handling.

"Greg's Peg" and "Billy and the Gargoyles" are examples of subjects
that would wither under longer treatment. The reader would not be
able to abide more than thirty pages of Gregory Bakewell's guileless
fatuity, any more than he could the repetitions of Melville's scrivener
Bartleby. And Peter Wescott's defense of his cousin Billy from little

hazing friends, at sad cost to himself and even against his own misguided faith in a school tyranny, needs only a single pathetic chapter.

"Maud," dear to my heart as my first appearance in print under my own name (it was published in two issues of the *Atlantic Monthly*), could have been a novel, but it seemed to me that a shorter form was more adapted to its message of a life mangled by a neurosis and partially salvaged by the victim's uncommunicated realization that nobody but herself will really care if she insists on throwing away a perfectly good life. Amy Stillman in "The Wagnerians," on the other hand, comes to a different conclusion: she does her damnedest, pathetically enough, to convince herself that she has *not* so disposed of her life, that it has been a cruel fate that has done her in. As does Brooks Clarkson in "The Prince and the Pauper," desperately fantasizing himself as a romantically doomed aristocrat when he is really only a common or garden variety of alcoholic. This tale was a conscious effort on my part to write a story in the manner of John O'Hara. I have often wondered what he would have thought of it.

"The Prison Window" is one of the only three ghost stories I ever wrote. I learned from Henry James's use of ambivalence in "The Turn of the Screw" that one can thus avoid the trap of this genre of fiction, namely, that if the ghost turns out to be real he may be incredible, and if he's a fraud he's ridiculous. My lady curator in the museum is convinced that she is dealing with the ghost of a black slave seeking revenge against the artifacts of the eighteenth-century patroon who allowed him to be burned alive, but she *could* be dealing with a vandal.

"The Single Reader" was first published in a volume of legal short stories, but it is really itself almost a ghost tale. The fact that the obsessed diarist is a tax lawyer is not significant; he could just as well have been a banker or businessman. I have never been a diarist myself, but I am a great reader of them, and I have long been intrigued by their relationship to fiction. Which is which, and can anyone really tell after a hundred years? Did Saint-Simon create the fantastic Versailles of his memoirs? In a French film about the royal château, Sacha Guitry, playing the Sun King, snatches a page from the scribbling little duke, glances through it and exclaims, "No, no, Saint-Simon, you've got it all wrong! It wasn't that way at all!" I decided to encapsulate my fantasies in this tale of a monstrous diary that turns its author into a recording slave.

I have written more stories about lawyers and law firms than on any other theme. I included "The Colonel's Foundation" for its comic relief and "The Fabbri Tape" as my meditation on Watergate and the possible justification of a coverup as sparing the national pride. I put in "The Mavericks" because it was the widest in scope of all the legal tales, probing into the social classifications that can taint even the firms most dedicated to merit and expertise.

"In the Beauty of the Lilies" and "Ares" are rare ventures on my part into the past, in each case the Civil War era. Christopher Lehmann-Haupt pointed out in a review of the former that it contrasted ironically the forced preservation of the union with the forced preservation of an unhappy marriage. Rereading the story after seeing his piece, I was startled but pleased to recognize that it could hardly be construed in any other way, yet his was a construction I had not had the intention or wit to conceive myself! It was a case of brilliantly creative criticism and made me give a hard second look at the whole theory of "deconstruction," in which the writer takes second place to the critic. Needless to say, I followed Lehmann-Haupt's guide when I developed the tale into a novel. "Ares," the second of these historical stories, is a nostalgic ode to the beautiful Lawn of the University of Virginia, in whose law school I spent three happy years.

"Portrait of the Artist by Another" had its seed in my admiration for Philippe de Champaigne's famous portrait of Cardinal Richelieu and my discovery that the great French artist had developed an expertise in painting robes because his Jansenist conscience forbade him the use of the nude. Of course my modern narrator in the story couldn't suffer from any such inhibition; his inability to paint the bare body had to arise from a traumatic experience. This story and "The Reckoning" are examples of the fiction writer's oft-repeated concern with the art of his rival, the painter; James, Wharton, and Bourget made much use of portraitists; the hero of James's "The Tragic Muse" is one. But in the second of these stories I decided to make the viewer and not the artist my subject. What are his or her permissible criteria? Is it possible to build a great collection out of purely subjective, highly personal, even eccentric reactions to paintings?

"The Stoic" and "They That Have Power to Hurt" are my two best efforts in the genre of the long story or novella. It was a form much favored by James, one that is essential for the development of a protagonist not sufficiently sympathetic for a whole novel but too complicated or many-sided for thirty or so pages. My "stoic" was too arid and inner-directed to sustain a reader's interest throughout a whole volume, yet he had to be seen over years and in different situations. And my narrator in the second novella would have fatally antagonized the reader in a longer form. It will be obvious to students of Edith Wharton that this tale was the result of my disgust at the jubilation of literary critics on discovering that she had had her first real love affair at the age of forty-seven and at their instant attribution to such an experience of a "new vein of passion" in her subsequent work. It seemed to me this denigrated her as an artist. It also seemed to me that it wasn't true.

"The Money Juggler" is really more an essay on some of the meaner practices of our financial system than it is a story; I put it in because I couldn't bear to leave it out. And "The Gemlike Flame" is in for the simple reason that Norman Mailer told me he "wouldn't have minded having written it himself." From a fellow writer, and one of such stature, *that* is the ultimate compliment.

LOUIS AUCHINCLOSS

Maud

1949

1

ALL MAUD'S LIFE it had seemed to her that she was like a dried-up spring at the edge of which her devoted relatives and friends used to gather hopefully in the expectation that at least a faint trickle might appear. Their own natures, it seemed, were rich with the bubbling fluid of hearty emotion, and their very repleteness made her own sterility the more remarkable. She gazed back at them; she tried to feel what they felt, tried to respond to their yearning glances. But what was the use? It had been her lot to live alone, surrounded by smiles and love, by sports and games and homely affection, through cold winters with warm fires and long, bright, boisterous summers. To Maud, the Spreddons seemed to be always circling, hand in hand, the bonfire of their own joy in life. Could they mean it? she would sometimes ask herself. Yet in sober truth they seemed to be what they appeared. Daddy, large and hearty, was always spoken of as one of the best lawyers downtown and was certainly a rich man, too, despite his eternal jangle about being the average father of an average American family. Mummie, stout and handsome, bustled with good works, and the morning mail was always filled with invitations to accept the sponsorship of worthy drives. Brother Fred was captain of his school football team; brother Sam was head of his class; Grandpapa was the good old judge whom all had revered, and beautiful Granny one of the "last" of the great ladies — there was no end to it.

But why did they always think that they had to draw *her* in, make *her* part of it? Why did they all turn to her on those ghastly Christmas Eves, when they gathered around the piano to bray out their carols, and cry: "Maud, sing this," and "Maud, isn't it lovely?" And why, when, with the devil in her soul, she raised her uncertain voice to sing the page's part in "Good King Wenceslaus," did they say: "That was *really* nice, Maud. You do like Christmas, don't you, after all?" It was the "after all" that gave them away. They smelled her out, spotted her for what she was, a rank intruder in their midst; but at the same time, with inexhaustible generosity, they held open the gate and continued to shout their welcome.

"Damn you! Goddamn all of you!"

There. She had said it, and she had said it, too, on Christmas Eve, one week after her thirteenth birthday. Not as long as she lived would she forget the shocked hush that fell over the family group, the stern amazement of her father, the delighted animosity of the boys. It was out at last.

"Maud!" her father exclaimed. "Where did you ever pick up language like that?"

"From Nannie," she answered.

"From Nannie!"

"Darling!" cried her mother, enveloping her with arms of steel. "Darling child, what's wrong? Aren't you happy? Tell Mummie, dearest."

"Maud's wicked," said brother Sam.

"Shut up, Sam," his father snapped.

Pressed to the lacy warmness of her mother's bosom, Maud felt welling up within herself the almost irresistible tide of surrender, but when she closed her eyes and clenched her fists, her own little granite integrity was able, after all, to have its day. She tore herself out of her mother's arms.

"I hate you all!" she screamed.

This time there was no sternness or hostility in the eyes around her. There was only concern, deep concern.

"I'll take her up to her room," she heard her mother tell her father. "You stay here. Tell Nannie, if she hasn't already gone out, to stay."

Her mother took her upstairs and tried to reason with her. She talked to her very gently and told her how much they all loved her and how much they would do for her, and didn't she love them back just a little, tiny, tiny bit? Didn't she really, darling? But Maud was able to shake her head. It was difficult; it cost her much. Everything that was in her was yearning to have things the way they had always been, to be approved and smiled at, even critically, but she knew how base it would be to give in to the yearning, even if everything that stood for resistance was baser yet. She was a bad girl, a very bad one, but to go back now, to retrace her steps, after the passionately desired and unbelievably actual stand of defiance, to merge once more with that foolish sea of smiles and kisses, to lose forever her own little ego in the consuming fire of family admiration — no, this she would not do.

Alone in the dark she flung herself upon her pillow and made it damp with her tears, tears that for the first time in her life came from her own causing. Why she was taking this dark and lonely course, why she should have to persist in setting herself apart from all that was warm and beckoning, she could only wonder, but that she *was* doing it and would continue to do it and would live by it was now her dusky faith. "I will. I will. I *will!*" she repeated over and over, until she had worked herself into a sort of frenzy and was banging her head against the bedpost. Then the door opened, swiftly, as though they had been standing just outside, and her mother and father and Nannie came in and looked at her in dismay.

2

Mrs. Spreddon had certainly no idea what had possessed her daughter. She was not without intelligence or sympathy, and responsibility sat easily with the furs on her ample shoulders, but there was little imagination and no humor in her make-up, and she could not comprehend any refusal of others to participate in that portion of the good of the universe which had been so generously allotted to herself. The disappointments that resulted from a failure to achieve an aim, any aim, were well within her comprehension, and when her son Sammy had failed to be elected head monitor of his school she and Mr. Spreddon had journeyed to New England to be at his side; but misery without a cause or misery with bitterness was to her unfathomable. She discussed it with her husband's sister, Mrs. Lane, who was in New York on a visit from Paris. Lila Lane was pretty, diminutive, and very chatty. She laughed at herself and the world and pretended to worship politics when she really worshiped good food. She dressed perfectly, always in black, with many small diamonds.

"It isn't as if the child didn't have everything she wanted," Mrs. Spreddon pointed out. "All she has to do is ask, and she gets it. Within limits, of course. I'm not one to spoil a child. What could it be that she's dissatisfied with?"

Mrs. Lane, taking in the detail of her sister-in-law's redecorated parlor, heavily Georgian, all gleaming mahogany and bright new needlework, reflected that Maud might, after all, have something to be dissatisfied with.

"Is she ever alone?" she asked.

"Why should she be alone?" Mrs. Spreddon demanded. "She's far too shy as it is. She hates playing with other children. She hasn't a single friend at school that I know of."

"Neither did I. At that age."

Mrs. Spreddon was not surprised to hear this, but then she had no intention of having her Maud grow up like Lila and perhaps live in Paris and buy a Monet every fifth year with the money that she saved by not having children.

"But Maud doesn't like *anybody*," she protested. "Not even me."

"Why should she?"

"Oh, Lila. You've been abroad too long. Whoever heard of a child not liking her own family when they've been good to her?"

"I have. Just now."

Mrs. Spreddon frowned at her. "You seem to think it's my fault," she said.

"It isn't anyone's fault, Mary," Mrs. Lane assured her. "Maud didn't choose you for a mother. There's no reason she should like you."

"And what should I do about it?"

Mrs. Lane shrugged her shoulders. "Is there anything to be done?" she asked. "Isn't the milk pretty well spilled by now?"

"That's all very well for you to say," Mrs. Spreddon retorted. "But a parent can't take that point of view. A parent has to believe."

"I don't mean that she's hopeless," Mrs. Lane said quickly. "I just mean that she's different. There's nothing so terrible about that, Mary. Maud's more like her grandfather."

"The Judge? But he was such an old dear, Lila!"

Mrs. Lane placed a cigarette carefully in her ivory holder and held it for several seconds before lighting it. She hated disputes, but the refusal of her sister-in-law to face any facts at all in the personalities around her other than the cheerful ones that she attributed to them, a refusal that Mrs. Lane felt to be indigenous to the stratum of American life that she had abandoned for Paris, irritated her almost beyond endurance.

"My father was not an 'old dear,' Mary," she said in a rather metallic tone. "He was a very intellectual and a very strange man. He was never really happy until they made him a judge, and he could sit on a bench, huddled in his black robes, and look out at the world."

"You have such a peculiar way of looking at things, Lila," Mrs. Spreddon retorted. "Judge Spreddon was a great man. Certainly, I never knew a man who was more loved."

Mrs. Lane inhaled deeply. "Maybe Maud's daughters-in-law will say the same about her."

"Maybe they will," Mrs. Spreddon agreed. "If she ever has any."

Mr. Spreddon worried even more than his wife, but he knew better than to expose himself to the chilly wind of his sister's skepticism. When he sought consolation it was in the sympathetic male atmosphere of his downtown world where he could always be sure of a friendly indifference and an easy optimism to reassure his troubled mind. Mr. Spreddon at fifty-five showed no outward symptoms of any inner insecurity. He was a big man of magnificent health, with gray hair and red cheeks, who had succeeded to his father's position in the great law firm that bore his name. Not that this had been an easy or automatic step, or that it could have been accomplished without the distinct ability that Mr. Spreddon possessed. He was an affable and practical-minded man whose advice was listened to with respect at directors' meetings and by the widows and daughters of the rich. But it was true, nevertheless, that beneath the joviality of his exterior he carried a variegated sense of guilt: guilt at having succeeded a father whose name was so famous in the annals of law, guilt at having leisure in an office where people worked so hard, guilt at being a successful lawyer without having ever argued a case, guilt at suspecting that the sound practical judgment for which he was reputed was, in the last analysis, nothing but a miscellany of easy generalities. It may have been for this reason that he took so paternal an interest in the younger lawyers in his office, particularly in Halsted Nicholas, the prodigy from Yonkers who had started as an office boy and had been Judge Spreddon's law clerk when the old man died.

"I tell you she's all right, Bill," Halsted said with his usual familiarity when Mr. Spreddon came into the little office where he was working surrounded by piles of photostatic exhibits, both feet on is desk. "You ought to be proud of her. She's got spunk, that girl."

"You'll admit it's an unusual way to show it."

"All the better. Originality should be watered." Halsted swung around in his chair to face the large ascetic features of the late Judge Spreddon in the photograph over his bookcase. "The old boy would have approved," he added irreverently. "He always said it was hate that made the world go round."

Mr. Spreddon never quite knew what to make of Halsted's remarks. "But I don't want her to be abnormal," he said. "If she goes on hating everybody, how is she ever going to grow up and get married?"

"Oh, she'll get married," Halsted said.

"Well, sure. If she changes."

"Even if she doesn't."

Mr. Spreddon stared. "Now, what makes you say that?" he demanded.

"Take me. I'll marry her."

Mr. Spreddon laughed. "You'll have to wait quite a bit, my boy," he said. "She's only thirteen."

3

Mr. and Mrs. Spreddon were not content with the passive view recommended by Mrs. Lane and Halsted Nicholas. Conscientious and loving parents as they were, they recognized that what ailed Maud was certainly something beyond their own limited control, and they turned, accordingly, in full humility and with open purses, to the psychiatrist, the special school, the tutor, the traveling companion. In fact, the whole paraphernalia of our modern effort to adjust the unadjusted was brought to bear on their sulking daughter. Nobody ever spoke to Maud now except with predetermined cheerfulness. She was taken out of the home that she had so disliked and sent to different schools in different climates, always in the smiling company of a competent woman beneath whose comfortable old-maid exterior was hidden a wealth of expensive psychological experience, and whose well-paid task it was to see if somehow it was not possible to pry open poor tightened Maud and permit the entry of at least a trickle of spontaneity. Maud spent a year in Switzerland under the care of one of the greatest of doctors, who regularly devoted one morning a week to walking with her in a Geneva park; she spent a year in Austria under equally famous auspices, and she passed two long years in Arizona in a small private school where she rode and walked with her companion and enjoyed something like peace. During visits home she was treated with a very special consideration, and her brothers were instructed always to be nice to her.

Maud saw through it all, however, from the very first and resented it with a continuing intensity. It was the old battle that had always raged between herself and her family; of this she never lost sight, and to give in because the struggle had changed its form would have been to lose the only fierce little logic that existed in her drab life. To this she clung with the dedication of a vestal virgin, wrapping herself each year more securely in the coating of her own isolation. Maud learned a certain adjustment to life, but she lost none of the bitterness of her conflict in the process. At nineteen she still faced the world with defiance in her eyes.

When she returned from the last of her many schools and excursions and came home to live with her family in New York, it was just six years from the ugly Christmas Eve of her original explosion. She had grown up into a girl whose appearance might have been handsome had one not been vaguely conscious of a presence somehow behind her holding her back — a person, so to speak, to whom one could imagine her referring questions over her shoulder and whose answer always seemed to be no. She had lovely, long, dark hair which she wore, smooth and uncurled, almost to her shoulders; she was very thin, and her skin was a clear white. Her eyes, large and brown, had a steady, uncompromising stare. She gave all the appearance of great shyness and reserve, for she hardly spoke at all, but the settled quality of her stare made it evident that any reluctance on her part to join in general conversation did not have its origin in timidity. Maud had established her individuality and her prejudices, and it was felt that this time she had come home to stay. Her parents still made spasmodic efforts to induce her to do this thing or that, but essentially her objectives had been attained. Nobody expected anything of her. Nobody was surprised when she did not kiss them.

She adopted for herself an unvarying routine. Three days a week she worked at a hospital; she rode in Central Park; she read and played the piano and occasionally visited the Metropolitan Museum. Mrs. Spreddon continued the busy whirl of her life and reserved teatime every evening as her time for Maud. What more could she do? It was difficult to work up any sort of social life for a daughter so reluctant, but she did make occasional efforts and managed once in a while to assemble a stiff little dinner for Maud where the guests would be taken on, immediately upon rising from table, to the best musical comedy of the season, the only bait that could have lured them there. Maud endured it without comment. She was willing to pay an occasional tax for her otherwise unruffled existence.

At one of these dinners, she found Halsted Nicholas seated on her right. She remembered him from earlier days when he had spent a summer with them as her brothers' tutor, and her memories of that summer were pleasanter than most. He was, of course, no longer a boy, being close to thirty-five, and a junior partner now of her father's; but his face had lost none of the sensitivity and charm, none of the uncompromising youth that she dimly remembered. He seemed an odd combination of ease and tension; one could tell that his reserve and even his air of gentle timidity were the product of manners; for when he spoke, it was with a certain roughness that indicated assurance. This was reinforced by the intent stare with which he fastened his very round and dark eyes on his plate and the manner in which his black eyebrows seemed to ripple with his thick black hair. She would have liked to talk to him, but that, of course, was not her way, and she watched him carefully as he crumbled his roll on the thick white tablecloth.

"You've certainly been taking your own sweet time to grow up, Maud," he said in a familiar tone, breaking a cracker into several pieces and dropping them into his soup as Maud had been taught never to do. "This makes it six years that I've been waiting for you."

"Six years?" she repeated in surprise.

He nodded, looking at her gravely. "Six years," he said. "Ever since that wonderful Christmas Eve when you told the assembled Spreddon family to put on their best bib and tucker and jump in the lake."

Maud turned pale. Even the heavy silver service on the long table seemed to be jumping back and forth. She put down her spoon. "So you know that," she said in a low voice. "They talk about it. They tell strangers."

He laughed his loud, easy laugh. "I'm hardly a stranger, Maud," he said. "I've been working as a lawyer in your father's office for twelve years and before that I was there as an office boy. And you're wrong about their telling people, too. They didn't have to tell me. I was there."

She gasped. "You couldn't have been," she protested. "I remember it so well." She paused. "But why are you saying this, anyway? What's the point?"

Again he laughed. "You don't believe me," he said. "But it's so simple. It was Christmas Eve and I was all alone in town, and your old man, who, in case you don't know it, is one prince of a guy, took pity on me and asked me up. I told him I'd come in a Santa Claus get-up and surprise you kids. Anyway I was right in here, in this very dining room, sticking my beard on and peering through the crack in those double doors to watch for my cue from your father when — bingo! — you pulled that scene. Right there before my eyes and ears! Oh, Maud! You were terrific!"

Even with his eyes, his sure but friendly eyes, upon her as he said all this, it was as if it were Christmas again, Christmas with every stocking crammed and to be emptied, item by item, before the shining and expectant parental faces. Maud felt her stomach muscles suddenly tighten in anguished humiliation. She put her napkin on the table and looked desperately about her.

"Now Maud," he said, putting his firm hand on hers. "Take it easy."

"Leave me alone," she said in a rough whisper. "Leave me be."

"You're not going to be angry with me?" he protested. "After all these years? All these years that I've been waiting for the little girl with the big temper to grow up? Maud, how unkind."

She gave him a swift look. "I've been back home and grown up for several months," she pointed out ungraciously. "If you know Father so well, you must have known that. And this is the first time you've been to the house."

He shrugged his shoulders. "Lawyers are busy men, Maud," he said. "We can't get off every night. Besides, I'm shy."

She was not to be appeased so lightly. "You didn't come to see me, anyway," she retorted. "You came because Daddy begged you to." She smiled sourly. "He probably went down on his knees."

"Nothing of the sort," he said coolly. "If you must know, I came because I heard we were going to *Roll Out the Barrel.*"

Maud stared at him for a second and then burst out laughing. "Then you're in for a sad disappointment, Mr. Nicholas," she said, "because

Daddy couldn't get seats. We're going to *Doubles or Quits*. I do hope you haven't seen it."

He covered his face with his napkin. "But I have," he groaned. "Twice!"

Maud, of course, did not know it, but Halsted Nicholas was the partner who, more than any other, held the clients of Spreddon & Spreddon. Mr. Spreddon increasingly accepted positions of public trust; he was now president of a museum, a hospital, and a zoo, all the biggest of their kind; he represented to his partners that this sort of thing, although unremunerative and time-consuming, "paid dividends in the long run." If anyone grumbled, it was not Halsted, whose industry was prodigious. What drove him so hard nobody knew. He never showed ambition of the ordinary sort, as, for example, wanting his name at the top of the firm letterhead or asking for paneling in his office. He felt, it was true, the deepest gratitude to Mr. Spreddon and to his late father, the Judge, who had seen promise in him and who had sent him to college and law school, but this he had already repaid a hundredfold. He loved the law, it was true, but he was already one of the ablest trial lawyers in the city and could certainly have held his position without quite so liberal an expenditure of energy. No, if Halsted was industrious it was probably by habit. He may have lacked the courage to stop and look into himself. He was a man who had met and undertaken many responsibilities; he had supported his friends with advice and his parents with money; he was considered to be — and, indeed, he was — an admirable character, unspoiled even by a Manhattan success; but whatever part of himself he revealed, it was a public part. His private self was unshared.

He left the theater that night after the second act to go down to his office and work on a brief, but the following Sunday he called at the Spreddons' and took Maud for a walk around the reservoir. A week later he invited her to come to Wall Street to dine with him, on the excuse that he had to work after dinner and could not get uptown, and after she had done this, which he said no other girl would have done, even for Clark Gable, he became a steady caller at the Spreddons'. Maud found herself in the unprecedented situation of having a beau.

He was not a very ceremonious beau; he never sent her flowers or whispered silly things in her ear, and not infrequently, at the very last moment, when they had planned an evening at the theater or the opera, he would call up to say that he couldn't get away from the office. Maud, however, saw nothing unusual in this. What mattered to her was that he expected so little. He never pried into her past or demanded her agreement or enthusiasm over anything; he never asked her to meet groups of his friends or to go to crowded night clubs. He never, furthermore, offered the slightest criticism of her way of living or made suggestions as to how she might enlarge its scope. He took her entirely for granted and would, without any semblance of apology, talk for an entire evening about his own life and struggles and the wonderful things that he had done in court. She was a slow talker, and he a fast one; it was easier for both if he held forth alone on the subjects closest to his heart. In short, she became accustomed to him; he fitted in with her riding and her hospital work. She had been worried at first, particularly in view of his initial revelation, never thereafter alluded to, of what he had once witnessed, but soon afterwards she had been reassured. It was all right. He would let her be.

4
—
꽃

Mr. and Mrs. Spreddon, in the meantime, were holding their breath. They had almost given up the idea that Maud would ever attract any man, much less a bachelor as eligible as Halsted. It was decided, after several conferences, that what nature had so miraculously started, nature might finish herself, and they resolved not to interfere. This, unfortunately, they were not able to do without a certain ostentation, and Maud became aware of an increasing failure on the part of her family to ask their usual questions about what she had done the night before and what meals she expected to eat at home the following day. If she referred to Halsted, her comment received the briefest of nods or answers. Nobody observing the fleeting references with which his name was dismissed at the Spreddon board would ever have guessed that the parental hearts were throbbing at the mere possibility of his assimilation into the family.

Maud, however, was not to be fooled. The suppressed wink behind the family conspiracy of silence was almost lewd to her, and it brought up poignantly the possibility that Halsted might be thinking of their friendship in the same way. It was true that he had said nothing to her that could even remotely be construed as sentimental, but it was also true, she realized ruefully, that she knew very little of such things, and the effusive, confiding creature to whom her brother Sammy was engaged, who frequently made her uncomfortable by trying to drag her into long intimate chats "just between us girls," had told her that when men took one out it was never for one's society alone and that this went for a certain "you know who" in the legal world as well as anyone else, even if he *was* somewhat older. Maud seemed to feel her breath stop at this new complication in a life settled after so many disturbances. Was this not the very thing that she had always feared, carried to its worst extreme? Was this not the emotion that was reputedly the most demanding, the most exacting of all the impulses of the heart? She had a vision of bridesmaids reaching for a thrown bouquet and faces looking up at her to where she was standing in unbecoming satin on a high stair — faces covered with frozen smiles and eyes, seas of eyes, black and staring and united to convey the same sharp, hysterical message: Aren't you happy? Aren't you in love? Now, then, didn't we *tell* you?

The next time Halsted called up she told him flatly that she had a headache. He took it very casually and called again about a week later. She didn't dare use the same excuse, and she couldn't think of another, so she met him for dinner at a French restaurant. She nibbled nervously on an olive while he drank his second cocktail in silence, watching her.

"Somebody's gone and frightened you again," he said with just an edge of roughness in his voice. "What's it all about? Why did you fake that headache last week?"

She looked at him miserably. "I didn't."

"Why did you have it then?"

"Oh." She raised her hand to her brow and rubbed it in a preoccupied manner. "Well, I guess I thought we were going out too much together."

"Too much for what?"

"Oh. You know."

"Were you afraid of being compromised?" he asked sarcastically.

"Please, Halsted," she begged him. "You know how people are. I like going out with you. I love it, really. But the family all wink and nod. They can't believe that you and I are just good friends. They'll be expecting you — well, to say something."

He burst out laughing. "And you're afraid I won't. I see."

She shook her head. "No," she said gravely, looking down at her plate; "I'm afraid you will."

He stopped laughing and looked at her intently. Then he gave a low whistle. "Well!" he exclaimed. "So that's how it is. And this is the girl whose father used to say that she had no self-confidence! Well, I'll be damned!"

Maud blushed. "You mustn't think I'm conceited," she said with embarrassment. "It's not that at all. I just don't understand these things. Really." She looked at him, imploring him not to take it amiss.

"Look, Maud," he said more gently, taking her hand in his. "Can't you trust me? I know all about it. Honest."

"All about what, Halsted?"

"What you're afraid of. Listen to me, my sweet. Nobody's going to make you do any falling in love. Nobody could. Yet. Do you get that? It's just possible that I may ask you to marry me. We'll see. But in any case I'm not going to ask you how you feel about me. That's your affair. Is that clear?"

She looked into his large and serious eyes and felt her fears subside. It was true that he was completely honest. He did not even tighten his grip on her hand.

"But why should you ever want to marry me?" she asked. "Nobody likes me."

"Give them time, darling," he said, smiling as she withdrew her hand from his. "They will. You want to know why I should be thinking about marrying you? Very well. That's a fair question. I'm thirty-four. There's one reason. It's high time, you'll admit. And I'm not so attractive that I can pick anyone I want. I have to take what I can get." And again he laughed.

"But don't you feel you could do better than me?" she asked seriously. "I'm really a terrible poke. Besides, Sammy says you make all sorts of money. That should help."

He shrugged his shoulders. "Oh, I haven't quite given up," he said cheerfully. "Don't get your hopes too high."

This time she smiled too. "You mean I'm only a last resort?"

Again he put his hand on hers. "Not quite. There's another point in your favor, Maud," he said. "If you must know."

"And what's that?"

He looked at her for a moment, and she suddenly knew that they were going to be very serious indeed.

"I wasn't going to mention it," he continued, "but I might as well now. I'm in love with you, Maud."

She could only shake her head several times in quick succession as if to stop him. "Why?" she asked. "What do you see in me?"

He shrugged his shoulders. "Who knows?" he said. "Call it the desire to protect. Or the mother instinct. Or just plain middle-aged folly. It might be anything. But, Maud, you wouldn't believe it. I can even catch myself thinking about you in court."

They looked at each other gravely for several seconds.

"Well, I suppose that does it," she said, smiling. "I'll have to marry you now."

He raised his hand. "Wait a moment!" he warned her. "First you've got to be asked. And after that you've got to think it over. For several days. I want no fly-by-night answer."

Halsted did things in his own way, and he adhered strictly to a program laid down by himself. Three days later she received a telegram from Chicago, where he had gone on business, saying: "This is the formal offer. Think it over. See you Friday."

Maud did think it over. In fact, she had thought of nothing else since it had first occurred to her that he might do this. She examined the state of her heart and asked herself if her feeling for Halsted could, even by the watered-down standards of her own emotions, be called love, and she decided that it probably could not. She then tried to analyze what it was that she did feel for him; it was certainly the friendliest feeling that she had ever experienced for another human being. She asked herself if she was not lucky indeed — miraculously lucky — to have run into the one man, probably in the whole country, who wanted her as she was. She visualized the joy of sudden and final liberation from her family. And then too, undeniably, she felt stirring within her the first faint manifestations of a new little pride in her own self that she could pull this off, that she could mean so much to a man like Halsted, a good man, an able man, a man whom people looked up to; she thought of Sammy and his silly little fiancée, and of her worried parents and their hopelessness about her; she pictured the amazement of the family friends. She stood before her mirror and pushed the hair out of her face and tossed her head in sudden resolution.

When Halsted called for her on Friday night she was waiting for him in the front hall with her hat and coat on. She was so nervous that she didn't even allow him to speak.

"Halsted," she said, and the words tumbled out. "I've decided. I will. Definitely."

He walked slowly across the front hall to the bottom step of the circular stairway where she was standing and took both her hands in his. For a long tense moment he looked at her.

"Darling," he said and then laughed. "I thought you'd never make up your mind!"

5

Halsted's courtship occurred during the winter of the first year of the war in Europe. It was the period of the "phony war," which, however much it may have bothered Halsted, was of little concern to Maud. For her the fall of France had as its immediate consequence the precipitous return of her father's sister, Lila Lane, from Paris. Aunt Lila took up her residence, as was to be expected, with her brother, and family meals came to be held in respectful silence while she expounded in her own graphic fashion on her hasty departure from Paris, the forced abandonment of her Renault in a roadside ditch, and her successful arrival, half-starved but with all her diamonds, in an unfamiliar and unfriendly Madrid.

It was not an easy time for her unenthusiastic sister-in-law. Mrs. Spreddon was hardly able, in the untroubled safety of her New York home, to debunk these experiences, simply because they had happened to Lila. She was obliged to give lip service to the family idea that Lila for once in her life had come up against the fundamentals, things that in the Spreddon mind loomed as vast round bollards on the long dock of a routine existence. Maud's mother could only bide her time, provoking as it might be, and stop for a bit to listen to Lila's tales.

Maud, as might have been expected, did not think as her mother did. Feeling as she had always felt about the restricted atmosphere of her family life, she thought of this aunt in Paris, with perfect clothes and no children, as the desired antithesis of the boisterous and the vulgar. The vision of Lila's garden and the marble fountain surrounded by the bit of lawn, so closely cut and brightly green, which Maud had seen as a child from the grilled balcony of the exquisite house on the rue de

Varenne had always lingered in her mind as the essence of everything that was cool and formal and wonderfully independent. It was no wonder that she hovered expectantly before the exotic gateway of her aunt's existence. And Lila, in her turn, appreciating this silent devotion, particularly from a Spreddon, and having always regarded Maud's troubles as the result of a life spent in the limelight of her sister-in-law's exuberant wealth and bad taste, turned as much of her attention as she could spare from hats to Maud and her singular love life. There were long morning conferences in Lila's littered room over a very little toast and a great deal of coffee.

She had, of course, insisted on meeting Halsted; they lunched, the three of them, one Saturday noon at a small French midtown restaurant, and, as poor Maud could clearly see, it had not gone well. Lila had spent the meal telling Halsted the well-known story, already published in a women's magazine, of her arduous escape from the Germans. Halsted, taciturn and obviously unimpressed, had said almost nothing. But it was later, when Maud was having tea and an early cocktail alone with her aunt, that the important conversation occurred.

"I hope you like him, Aunt Lila," Maud said timidly. "Mother and Daddy do, but, of course, they would. He's a wonderful lawyer. But you've lived abroad and know about people."

Lila Lane inserted a cigarette in her holder and surveyed her niece's almost expressionless face. She prided herself on being the one member of the family who had a kindred sense of the deep antipathies that had gone into Maud's make-up, and she saw her niece's solution along the lines of her own life. "I certainly like him, my dear," she said in a definite tone. "He's obviously a very fine and a very intelligent man. In fact, I shouldn't be surprised if I'm not a little afraid of him. He's *un peu farouche*, if you see what I mean. But attractive. Undeniably."

"Oh, he is, isn't he?"

Lila hesitated a moment before trying a stroke of sophistication. To clear the air. "All in all, my dear," she said with a smile, "an excellent first marriage."

"Oh, Aunt Lila!" Maud's eyes were filled with protest. "What do you mean?"

Her aunt reached over and patted her hand. "Now there, dear, don't get excited. You must let the old Paris aunt have her little joke. You see,

Maud, as you say, I've lived abroad. A long time. I've been used to people who are, well — to say the least — stimulating. Your young man, who isn't, by the way, so frightfully young, is more of your father's world. Of course it was my father's world, too. But it's certainly a world that I myself could never be happy in. And I hope you'll forgive me for saying so, my dear, but I have my doubts if you ever could, either. It's a dull world, Maud."

"But I'm dull, Aunt Lila!" Maud protested. "I'm a thousand times duller than Halsted!"

Her aunt looked suddenly stern. "Don't let me ever hear you say that again!" she exclaimed. She got up and took Maud to the mirror over the mantel. "Take a good look at yourself! Your skin. Those eyes. They're good, my dear. Very good." She took Maud's long hair and arranged it in a sort of pompadour over her forehead. "You haven't tried, Maud. That's all. You could be beautiful."

Maud stared at her reflection with momentary fascination, and then turned abruptly away. She shrugged her shoulders. "I'd still be dull."

"Beautiful women are never dull," Lila said, sitting down again at the tea table. "But now I'm sounding like a rather bad Oscar Wilde. Tell me, my dear. In all seriousness. Are you in love with this wonderful lawyer?"

Maud's face was filled with dismay as she stared down at the floor. Neither her mother nor Halsted had presumed to ask her such a question, but there was no escaping it. Now she had to hear it from the lips of Aunt Lila, who spoke, she felt, with an authority that could not be resented. Whatever love may have been to the Spreddons — and Maud, when she thought of it, had a sense of something thick and stifling like a blanket — to Aunt Lila it was a free and glorious emotion that knew not restraint and graced those whom it touched. She was not sure that Aunt Lila had been one so graced, but she had infinite faith in her aunt's ability to observe. Venus had risen, so to speak, on a shell from the sea and was awaiting her answer.

"I really can't say that I am," she answered at last in a low voice. "The way you use the word, anyway."

"The way I use the word, Maud! But there's only one way to use it. Either you are or you aren't."

"Oh, Aunt Lila." Maud's eyes filled with tears.

"Listen to me, Maud." Lila had moved over to the sofa and put her arm around her niece. "You know that I love you dearly. Do you think I'd have asked you such an impertinent question if I hadn't been sure that the answer was no?"

Maud shook her head. "Everyone knows about me," she said despairingly. "What should I do?"

"Do?" Lila queried. "You don't have to *do* anything at all. You certainly don't have to marry Halsted because you're *not* in love with him. Maud, darling, if you only knew how I understood! You think you're always going to be bottled up like a clam and that this is the way to make the best of it. But it's not. You're just beginning to stick your head out and peer around. It's absurd to be snapped up by the first one of your father's partners who comes along! Before you've even had a chance to take your bearings!"

But if Maud accepted her aunt as an expert in love, it did not mean that she accepted her as a judge of her own character. She had no interest in her own future, but a very deep interest in her duty to Halsted. Getting up, she went to her room. She sat there by herself for an hour. Then, for the first time in her life, she went to her mother for advice. Mrs. Spreddon was sitting at her dressing table, getting ready for dinner.

"Mother, I'm going to break my engagement to Halsted," she said abruptly.

Mrs. Spreddon eyed her closely in the glass as she fastened a pearl bracelet on her wrist. "May I ask you why?"

"I'm not in love with him."

Mrs. Spreddon was silent for a moment. Then she nodded. "Let me ask you one thing," she said. "Have you been talking to your aunt?"

"I have. But it's not her fault. She said nothing I didn't know already."

"I see."

There was a pause. Then poor Maud blurted forth her appeal. "Mother, what should I do?"

Mrs. Spreddon stood up, very slowly, and turned around. She faced her daughter with dignity, but her voice was trembling. "I'm sorry, Maud," she said. "I'd give anything in the world to be able to help you. You know how your father and I love Halsted. We think he'd be the perfect husband. But this is your life, my dear. Not mine. If we'd had more of a relationship, you and I, we might have been able to work this thing out. God knows I've tried. But parents can take only so much, Maud, and then they're through. You've always wanted to work things out your own way. I'm afraid that now it's too late for me to butt in."

For a long moment they looked at each other, almost in surprise and a little in fear at the sudden reclarification of the gulf between them.

6
—
※

It was dark and cool inside the little restaurant where she was to meet Halsted for lunch. When her eyes were adjusted to it, she saw him sitting at the bar talking to the bartender. She went up and sat on the stool beside him, and he smiled and ordered her a drink. Then she told him, straight away. She did it very clearly and rather coldly; she was sure as she looked into his large hurt eyes that she had been convincing.

"But Maud," he protested in a tone almost of exasperation, "we've been through all this before! You know I don't expect anything of you. We can leave that to the future."

"I don't trust the future," she said. "I want to know more about it first."

"Maud, have you gone crazy?"

"It may well be."

There was a pause.

"How can you talk that way, Maud?" he asked suddenly. "How can you be such a smug little — ? Good God! Maud, have you really never given a damn about me? Even one little damn?"

She looked at him steadily. From way back in her past she felt the stirrings of that almost irresistible tide of surrender, the tide that she had dammed so desperately and so decisively on that long ago Christmas Eve. But once again she was the mistress of her fate. "Not in that way, Halsted," she said.

He turned to his unfinished cocktail. "Well, I'll be damned," he said, almost to himself. "I'll be damned."

"You believe me, Halsted, don't you?"

He turned back to her. "I guess I'll have to, Maud," he said. "Maybe I had you doped out all wrong." He shrugged his shoulders. "Lawyers can be persistent," he continued, "but even they know when the game's really up. You'd better go home, Maud. I'll get you a taxi."

He got up and left her, and she knew, as she stared at her reflection in the mirror across the bar, that she was at last doing penance for what she had done that Christmas Eve.

Halsted disappeared from her life as suddenly as he had come into it. Shortly after the fateful meeting, he came into Mr. Spreddon's office, sat down, and putting one leg as usual over the arm of the chair, asked, "Got another litigator around here, Bill? You'll be needing one."

"Oh, Halsted. You too?"

"Me too. I've decided to take that War Department job, after all. Maybe after I've been around there a few months they'll give me a commission. Just to get rid of me."

"Can't you get a commission now?"

"Eyes."

Mr. Spreddon looked broodingly at the photograph of his daughter which stood on his desk between him and Halsted. His heart was heavy. "You must do what you think best, of course," he said sadly. "We'll make out. I'm not trying to hide the fact that it'll be difficult. You know how we stand. This is your firm, Halsted."

Halsted's face clouded with embarrassment. "Cut it out, will you, Bill!" he protested. "You're the whole business around here, and that's the way it should be."

Mr. Spreddon shook his head. "Just a name, my boy. But I won't embarrass you. There's only thing I'd like to know. Your going to Washington isn't because of Maud, is it?"

Halsted stood up and sauntered around the big office. "Like everyone else," he said in a rather rough tone, while his back was turned to Mr. Spreddon, "I have my own feelings about this war. And they happen to have nothing under the sun to do with your daughter."

"I'm sorry," Mr. Spreddon said meekly. "I shouldn't have mentioned it. But you know how I feel about that. It was the hope of my life."

Halsted shrugged his shoulders and left the room.

Mrs. Spreddon said nothing to Maud when the engagement was broken. She gave her a kiss and offered to send her on a trip. She was seething, however, against her sister-in-law, who, she felt, had betrayed her hospitality. She determined to break openly with her and debated for two days how most cuttingly to accomplish it. Then she went, without consulting her husband, to her sister-in-law's room.

"I hope, Lila," she said in a voice that trembled slightly, "that it gives you some satisfaction to reflect that in all probability you've ruined whatever slight chances Maud may have had for a normal and happy life."

Lila flushed deeply. "I wouldn't expect you to understand, Mary," she answered in a hurt but lofty tone. "All I can say is that anything I may have said to Maud was with her best interests at heart. We differ too fundamentally to make explanations worthwhile. Under the circumstances I think it would be best if I moved to the Pierre."

"Under the circumstances, I must agree with you."

And so it ended. Halsted wrote Maud from time to time, amusing, impersonal letters, but he never called at the Spreddons' when he came to New York. Then we entered the war, and he got his commission and was one of the first to be sent overseas. Lila tried to cheer Maud up by giving a cocktail party for her at her hotel, but Maud would not even go. Despite what her aunt had said about beautiful women, she still knew that she was dull.

7

Maud joined the Red Cross shortly after the attack on Pearl Harbor. She worked for two years in New York, after which she was sent to Southampton, England. She worked hard and well, serving coffee to literally thousands of young men. When she looked back over her time in uniform she pictured a sea of faces, young and healthy faces; it seemed to her as if there would never be an end to the pressure of youth and vigor and courage upon the barred doors of her heart. But she never yielded, never opened — and anyway, she sometimes wondered, did it matter? They kept passing her tumultuously, and if she had opened the door, just the tiniest crack, and peered out for a glimpse of the surging throng, would anyone have stopped to look or listen, to reach out a hand to her and cry: "Maud, come on! Can't you see us? We're on our *way!*"

If Maud, however, was uncompromising in her attitude towards the future, she was learning, nonetheless, a new latitude in the examination of her past. She was perfectly willing, even eager, to entertain the possibility that she had, after all, been in love with Halsted from the beginning and still was, but she was afraid to fall into the oversimplifications of wishful thinking. She still had no referent by which to judge love, and though she realized from time to time that she might be losing herself in the forests of introspection, she was capable, in spite of her doubts, of a fierce single-mindedness. There could be no question of other men. If Halsted had been dead she would still have felt an obligation to resolve the incomprehensible problem of her own determination.

Halsted, however, was far from dead. He was in London, and she actually had his address, though she dared not go to see him. She had not even let him know that she was in England. Their correspondence, in fact, had entirely ceased. Now she could see dimly that life might be offering her that rarest of all things, a second and final chance, and she hardly dared face the fact that, in her usual fashion, she was going to let it pass.

Her brother Sammy's destroyer had put in to Southampton at this time, and she was seeing a good deal of him. They had had little enough to say to each other before the war, but now that they were both three thousand miles from their family, they met in the evening in pubs and exchanged confidences with some of the excitement that is shared by new and congenial friends. They drank gin when they could get it and ale when they couldn't, and discussed their parents and themselves with detachment and impartiality. Sammy and his wife were not getting on, and this lent to his conversation the flavor of a superior disillusionment.

"The trouble with you, Maud," he told her one night, "is that you take everything too seriously. You're always analyzing your own emotions. Hell. The thing to do is to grab fun where you can get it. You ought to write Halsted and tell him you're crazy about him."

She looked skeptically at his blond, undoubting face. "But do you really think I am?" she asked.

He shrugged his shoulders. "I think you want to be," he said. "Which is just as good."

"But is that honest, Sammy?"

He laughed. "Do you want to be an old maid, Maud?" he demanded. "A sour, bitter old maid?"

She shook her head. "Not particularly," she answered.

"Well?"

"But I am what I am, aren't I, Sammy?"

"Sure. And you will be what you will be."

He was essentially indifferent, of course, but it was only the indifference of one adult for another. It filled her nonetheless with a bleak loneliness.

"I'm an idiot, Sammy," she said abruptly. "And I'm an idiot to think anyone cares whether or not I'm an idiot. I'll go to London. I'll be like the rest of you."

"That's better, Maud. Much better."

8

When she got her next leave she actually did go to London. She left her bag at the Red Cross on Grosvenor Square and walked down the street to Army Headquarters. It was some time before she found Halsted's office, and then she was unable to send a message to him because he was in conference. She waited in the main hall for an hour and a half.

"He may not even come out for lunch," the sergeant told her.

"I'll wait," she said, and he smiled.

When Halsted, now a lieutenant colonel, looking thinner and serious, walked through the hall he was with several other officers, and there was a preoccupation about their quick stride that made her suddenly feel small and unwanted. She was shrinking back in her chair when he spotted her and stopped.

"Maud!" he exclaimed in astonishment. "Well, I'll be damned!"

He went up to her, holding out both arms, and there was a funny little smile on his face.

"I just dropped in to see you," she stammered.

"Been waiting long?"

"Oh, no."

"Like to go out on the town tonight?" he asked. "For auld lang syne?" He looked at his watch. "I guess I can make it."

She nodded eagerly.

"You're at the Red Cross?" he said. "I'll pick you up at ten."

And he was gone. During the rest of the afternoon, as she wandered through the great and empty rooms of the Victoria and Albert Museum, she speculated in vain on the significance of his smile. He did not pick her up that night until long after ten, for he was again in conference. They drove in his jeep to an officers' club which had formerly been a private house, and a rather elaborate one, and sat at a table in a corner of the large Tudor front hall near the stairway, under which a bar had been installed. Halsted did not seem at all nervous, as she was, but he looked tired and older. He talked about the general aspects of the war in a rather learned way and drank a good deal, but she was too excited to take in a word that he said. He was speculating on the possibilities of a revolution within Germany when she interrupted him.

"Halsted, aren't you going to ask about *me?* And the family? I'm dying to tell. And to hear all about you. But not about the war. Please."

He smiled, just a bit wearily. "How have you been, my dear?" he asked.

"Well, not so terribly well," she began nervously. "But better now. Oh, much better, Halsted. I'm not the fool I was."

It was perfectly evident that he had caught the full import of her words, for he frowned and looked away from her. "When you say you're not the fool you were, Maud," he said in a distant, even a superior tone, "does it by any chance mean that you've changed your mind about me?"

She felt the chill in his voice and hesitated. She held her breath for a moment. "Yes," she said.

He turned and looked at her fixedly, but she could not read the expression in his eyes. "Then as far as you're concerned," he said, "it's on again?"

"Oh, no, Halsted," she said hastily. "Of course not! What do you take me for? It's not 'on' again. I have no claim on you. I've had my chance. Making a mess of things hardly entitles me to another."

"Oh, 'entitles.' " He shrugged his shoulders, almost in irritation as he repeated her word. "When women say they're not 'entitled' to something, what they usually mean is that any man who's not an utter heel would make sure that they get it."

The tears started to Maud's eyes. It was the tone that he had sometimes used in court, or to people whom he thought little of, like Lila, or to the world. Never to her.

"Halsted," she protested in a low voice. "That's not fair."

He looked down into his glass. "Maybe not."

"And it's not like you to be unfair," she continued. "It isn't as if I were expecting you to fall all over me. I know it would be a miracle if you had any feeling left."

He looked even more sullen at this. "But you still feel sorry for yourself," he retorted.

Maud put her napkin on the table and reached for her cigarettes. "Good night, Colonel," she said crisply. "There's nothing like auld lang syne, is there?"

"Nothing."

She got up. "You needn't worry about taking me back," she said. "I can find my way."

"Oh, sit down," he said roughly, but in a more human tone. "We've got a whole bottle of whiskey here. I don't suppose you expect me to get through it alone?"

"I'm sure," she said with dignity, "that I don't care how you get through it. There must be plenty of other officers with desk jobs in London who can help you out."

He caught her by the arm and pulled her back into her chair. "Desk jobs, hell," he muttered and poured her a drink. "Now drink that and shut up. I wish to hell I did have a desk job. Would you like to know where I was last week?"

"We're warned," she said, "not to encourage officers who drink too much and start revealing military information."

He finished his drink in a gulp and leaned his head on his hands. "Oh, Christ, Maud," he said.

She said nothing.

"I don't know why you had to come back," he continued. "The same prim little girl. Just a bit older, that's all. I'd gotten over you, you know. I mean it, God damn it. And I was enjoying my melancholy. I liked feeling a hero and thinking of the little girl back home who didn't give a rap about me, and wouldn't she be sorry now? Oh, I could spit." He reached again for the bottle and poured himself another drink. "Now I don't know what I feel. I wish like hell, Maud, that I could say it's all the way it was, but I'm damned if I know."

She believed him, believed him absolutely, but there was no humiliation or pain in it. For her the long uncertainty had ended. In her excitement his doubts seemed almost irrelevant.

"You needn't worry about it, Halsted," she said. "It seems so fair."

He looked at her suspiciously. "Fair?" he repeated. "You must be an icebox, Maud. How else could you talk that way?"

"It's just that I don't know how to talk," she said humbly. "You know that."

He smiled at her. "Oh, you can talk, Maud."

"You can make your life very difficult by being complicated," she went on. "I ought to know something about that. You can think you ought to be feeling all sorts of things that you don't. The people around you don't help. I've been through that. I was a fool."

He stared hard at her for a moment, but as if he were concentrating on something else. He opened his mouth as if he were about to say something and then closed it.

"Maud," he said finally, looking down again at the table, "would you marry me? If I were to ask you again?"

She nodded gravely. "I would."

"After all I've said?"

"After all you've said."

There was a pause, an interminable pause. Then he suddenly smiled and put his hand on hers. "Well, nobody would be able to say," he said, "that we were rushing into this thing without having given it thought. And yet, somehow, I feel that's just what we would be doing."

She took out her handkerchief at last and wiped her eyes. "We've tried waiting," she pointed out. "And that didn't work."

He laughed.

"Well, I'm game," he said. "I'm always taking chances with my future in these days. I might as well take a fling with my past." He put his hand suddenly around her shoulder. "Poor little Maud," he said, smiling. "Poor helpless little Maud. This is only the second time you've trapped your victim. But don't worry. You won't be able to get out of it this time."

"The only thing I'm worrying about," she observed, with an eye on the diminished bottle, "is getting you back to your quarters sober."

"I see you're starting right," he agreed more cheerfully. "Well, I asked for it. Or did I?"

How it would have worked out they never were to know, for Halsted was killed two days later when his reconnaissance plane was shot down over Cherbourg. They had met only once in the interval, at lunch, for Halsted had been in conference or flying day and night in preparation for the great invasion of France that took place only a week after his death. Into the blackness of Maud's heart there is no need to penetrate.

It was fortunate for her that her work increased in intensity during those days.

A few weeks later her club mobile unit crossed to France, where it operated just below the front. A friend of Halsted's sent her a note that he had placed in an envelope marked "Maud Spreddon, Red Cross" just before he had taken off on his last flight. It was simply a line: "Maud, dearest, never forget. You're all right, and you're going to be all right. With me or without me." She had folded the note and placed it in a locket which she wore around her neck and which she never afterwards reopened. She did not tell her parents or even Sammy that she had seen Halsted again before his death, or what had passed between them. Such a tale would have made her a worthy object of the pity that she had so despised herself for seeking. It was her sorrow, and Halsted would have admired her for facing it alone.

Greg's Peg

1950

1

I T W A S in the autumn of 1936 that I first met Gregory Bakewell, and the only reason that I met him then was that he and his mother were, besides myself and a handful of others, the only members of the summer colony at Anchor Harbor who had stayed past the middle of September. To the Bakewells it was a period of hard necessity; they had to sit out the bleak, lonely Maine September and October before they could return, with any sort of comfort, to the Florida home where they wintered. To me, on the other hand, these two months were the only endurable part of Anchor Harbor's season, and I had lingered all that summer in Massachusetts, at the small boarding school of which I was headmaster, until I knew that I would find the peninsula as deserted as I required. I had no worries that year about the opening of school, for I was on a sabbatical leave, long postponed, and free to do as I chose. Not, indeed, that I was in a mood to do much. I had lost my wife the year before, and for many months it had seemed to me that life was over, in early middle age. I had retreated rigidly and faithfully to an isolated routine. I had taught my courses and kept to myself, as much as a headmaster can, editing and re-editing what was to be the final, memorial volume of her poetry. But during that summer I had begun to look up from the blue notepaper on which she had written the small stanzas of her garden verse to find myself gazing out the window towards the campus with a blank steadiness that could only have been symptomatic, I feared, of the heresy of boredom. And thus it was with something of a sense of guilt and a little, perhaps, in that mood of nostalgic self-pity that makes one try to recapture the melancholy of remembered sorrow, that I traveled up to Anchor Harbor in the fall.

My wife and I had spent our summers there in the past, not, as one of her obituary notices had floridly put it, "away from the summer resort in a forest camp, nestled in that corner of the peninsula frequented by the literary," but in the large rambling pile of shingle, full of pointless rooms and wicker furniture, that belonged to my mother-in-law and that stood up on the top of a forest-covered hill in the very heart of the summer community. In Anchor Harbor, however, the poets' corner and the watering place were akin. Each was clouded in the haze of unreality that hung so charmingly over the entire peninsula. It was indeed a world unto itself. Blue, gray and green, the pattern repeated itself up and down, from the sky to the rocky mountaintops, from the sloping pine woods to the long cliffs and gleaming cold of the sea. It was an Eden in which it was hard to visualize a serpent. People were never born there, nor did they die there. The elemental was left to the winter and other climes. The sun that sparkled in the cocktails under the yellow and red umbrella tables by the club pool was the same sun that dropped behind the hills in the evening, lighting up the peninsula with pink amid the pine trees. It was a land of big ugly houses, pleasant to live in, of very old and very active ladies, of hills that were called mountains, of small, quaint shops and of large, shining town cars. When in the morning I picked up the newspaper with its angry black headlines it was not so much with a sense of their tidings being false, as of their being childishly irrelevant.

By mid-September, however, the big summer houses were closed and the last trunks of their owners were rattling in vans down the main street past the swimming club to the station. The sky was more frequently overcast; there was rain and fog, and from the sea came the sharp cold breezes that told the advent of an early winter. I was staying alone in my mother-in-law's house, taking long walks on the mountains and going at night to the movies. I suppose that I was lonelier than I cared to admit, for I found myself dropping into the empty swimming club before lunch and drinking a cocktail on the terrace that looked over the unfilled pool and the bay. There were not apt to be more than one or two people there, usually the sort who had to maintain a residence in Maine for tax purposes, and I was not averse to condoling with them for a few minutes each day. It was on a day when I had not found even one of these that a youngish-looking man, perhaps in his early thirties, approached the table where I was sitting. He was an oddly shaped and odd-looking person, wide in the hips and narrow in the shoulders, and his face, very white and round and smooth, had, somewhat inconsistently, the uncertain dignity of a thin aquiline nose and large owl-like eyes. His long hair was parted in the middle and plastered to his head with a heavy tonic, and he was wearing, alas, a bow tie, a red blazer, and white flannels, a combination which was even then out of date except for sixth-form graduations at schools such as mine. All this was certainly unprepossessing, and I shrank a bit as he approached me, but there was in his large gray eyes as they gazed timidly down at me a look of guilelessness, of cautious friendliness, of anticipated rebuff that made me suddenly smile.

"My name is Gregory Bakewell. People call me Greg," he said in a mild, pleasant voice less affected than I would have anticipated. "I hope you'll excuse my intrusion, but could you tell me if they're going to continue the buffet lunch next week?"

I looked at him with a feeling of disappointment.

"I don't know," I said. "I never lunch here."

He stared with blinking eyes.

"But you ought. It's quite delicious."

I shrugged my shoulders, but he remained, obviously concerned at what I was passing up.

"Perhaps you will join me for lunch today," he urged. "It's *suprême de volaille argentée*."

I couldn't repress a laugh at his fantastic accent, and then to cover it up and to excuse myself for not lunching with him I asked him to have a drink. He sat down, and I introduced myself. I confess that I expected that he might have heard of me, and I looked into his owl eyes for some hint that he was impressed. There was none.

"You weren't up here during the season?" he asked. "You've just come?"

"That's right."

He shook his head.

"It's a pity you missed it. They say it was very gay."

I murmured something derogatory in general about the summer life at Anchor Harbor.

"You don't like it?" he asked.

"I can't abide it. Can you?"

"Me?" He appeared surprised that anyone should be interested in his reaction. "I don't really know. Mother and I go out so little. Except, of course, to the Bishop's. And dear old Mrs. Stone's."

I pictured him at a tea party, brushed and combed and wearing a bib. And eating an enormous cookie.

"I used to go out," I said.

"And now you don't?"

Even if he had never heard of me I was surprised, at Anchor Harbor, that he should not have heard of my wife. Ordinarily, I hope, I would not have said what I did say, but my need for communication was strong. I was suddenly and oddly determined to imprint my ego on the empty face of all that he took for granted.

"My wife died here," I said. "Last summer."

He looked even blanker than before, but gradually an expression of embarrassment came over his face.

"Oh, dear," he said. "I'm so sorry. Of course, if I'd known —"

I felt ashamed of myself.

"Of course," I said hurriedly. "Forgive me for mentioning it."

"But no," he protested. "I should have known. I remember now. They were speaking of her at Mrs. Stone's the other day. She was very beautiful, wasn't she?"

She hadn't been, but I nodded. I wanted even the sympathy that he could give me and swallowed greedily the small drops that fell from his meager supply.

"And which reminds me," he said, after we had talked in this vein for several minutes, "they spoke of you, too. You write things, don't you? Stories?"

I swallowed.

"I hope not," I said. "I'm an historian."

"Oh, that must be lovely."

I wondered if there was another man in the world who could have said it as he said it. He conveyed a sense of abysmal ignorance, but of humility, too, and of boundless admiration. These things were fine, were wonderful, he seemed to say, but he, too, had his little niche and a nice one, and he as well as these things existed, and we could be friends together, couldn't we?

I decided we were getting nowhere.

"What do you do?" I asked.

"Do?" Again he looked blank. "Why, good heavens, man, I don't do a thing."

I looked severe.

"Shouldn't you?"

"Should I?"

"You haven't got a family or anything like that?"

He smiled happily.

"Oh, I've got 'something like that,' " he answered. "I've got Mother."

I nodded. I knew everything now.

"Do you exercise?"

"I walk from Mother's cottage to the club. It's several hundred yards."

I rose to my feet.

"Tomorrow morning," I said firmly, "I'll pick you up here at nine-thirty. We're going to climb a mountain."

He gaped at me in horror and amazement as I got up to leave him, but he was there when I came by the next morning, waiting for me, dressed exactly as he had been the day before except for a pair of spotless white sneakers and a towel, pointlessly but athletically draped around his neck. He was very grateful to me for inviting him and told me with spirit how he had always wanted to climb a mountain at Anchor Harbor. These "mountains" were none higher than a thousand feet and the trails were easy; nonetheless I decided to start him on the smallest.

He did well enough, however. He perspired profusely and kept taking off garments as we went along, piling them on his arm, and he presented a sorry figure indeed as his long hair fell over his face and as the sweat poured down his white puffy back, but he kept up and bubbled over with talk. I asked him about his life, and he told me the dismal tale of a childhood spent under the cloud of a sickly constitution. He had been, of course, an only child, and his parents, though loving, had themselves enjoyed excellent health. He had never been to school or college; he had learned whatever it was that he did know from tutors. He had never left home, which for the Bakewells had been St. Louis until the death of Mr. Bakewell and was now St. Petersburg in Florida. Greg was thirty-five and presented to me in all his clumsy innocence a perfect *tabula rasa*. His mind was a piece of blank paper, of white, dead paper, on which, I supposed, one could write whatever message one chose. He appeared to have no prejudices or snobbishnesses; he was a guileless child who had long since ceased to fret, if indeed he ever had, at the confinements of his nursery. I could only look and gape, and yet at the same time feel the responsibility of writing the first line, for he seemed to enjoy an odd, easy content in his own placid life.

We had passed beyond the tree line and were walking along the smoother rock of the summit, a sharp cool breeze blowing in our faces. It was a breathtaking view, and I turned to see what Greg's reaction would be.

"Look," he said pointing to an ungainly shingle clock tower that protruded from the woods miles below us, "you can see the roof of Mrs. Stone's house."

I exploded.

"God!" I said.

"Don't be angry with me," he said mildly. "I was just pointing something out."

I could see that decisions had to be made and steps taken.

"Look, Greg," I said. "Don't go to St. Petersburg this winter."

He stared.

"But what would Mother do?"

I dismissed his mother with a gesture.

"Stay here. By yourself. Get to know the people who live here all the year round. Read. I'll send you books."

He looked dumbfounded.

"Then you won't be here?"

I laughed.

"I've got a job, man. I'm writing a book. But you're not. Give one winter to being away from your mother and Mrs. Stone and the Bishop, and learn to think. You won't know yourself in a year."

He appeared to regard this as not entirely a happy prognostication.

"But Mrs. Stone and the Bishop don't go to St. Petersburg," he pointed out.

"Even so," I said.

"I really don't think I could leave Mother."

I said nothing.

"You honestly think I ought to do something?" he persisted.

"I do."

"That's what Mother keeps telling me," he said dubiously.

"Well, she's right."

He looked at me in dismay.

"But what'll I do?"

"I've made one suggestion. Now it's your turn."

He sighed.

"Well, it's very hard," he said, "to know. You pick me up, and then you throw me down."

I felt some compunction at this.

"I'll write you," I said. "To St. Petersburg. You can keep me informed of your progress."

He beamed.

"Oh, that would be very kind," he said.

During the remaining two weeks of my visit to Anchor Harbor I walked with Greg almost every day, and we became friends. It was agreeable to be with someone whose admiration was unqualified. He listened to me with the utmost respect and attention and forgot everything I said a moment afterwards. But I didn't mind. It gave me a sense of ease about repeating myself; I talked of history and literature and love; I set myself up as counsel for the forces of life and argued my case at the bar of Greg's justice, pleading that the door might be opened just a crack. Yet whoever it was who represented the forces of his inertia was supplying very cogent arguments against me. I decided that it must be his mother, and I stopped at the Bakewells' one day after our walk to meet her.

Mrs. Bakewell I had made a picture of before I met her. She would be a small grim woman, always in black, mourning the husband whose existence one could never quite believe in; she would be wearing a black ribbon choker and a shiny black hat, and she would never change the weight or the quantity of her clothing, equally inappropriate for St. Petersburg or Anchor Harbor, for any such considerations as seasons or weather. I saw her thus as small, as compact, as uncompromising, because in my imagination she had had to wither to a little black stump, the hard remnants of the heaping blaze of what I visualized as her maternal possessiveness. How else could I possibly explain Gregory expect in terms of such a mother? And when I did meet her each detail of her person seemed to spring up at me to justify my presupposition. She *was* a small, black figure, and she *did* wear a broad, tight choker. She was old, and she was unruffled; her large hook nose and her small eyes had about them the stillness of a hawk on a limb. When she spoke, it was with the cold calm of a convinced fanatic, and beyond the interminable details of her small talk that dealt almost exclusively with Episcopal dogma and Episcopal teas I seemed to catch the flickering light of a sixteenth-century *auto-da-fé*. But a vital element of my preconceived portrait was missing. She showed no weakness for her only child. Indeed, her attitude towards him, for all one could see, demonstrated the most commendable indifference. He had hatched from her egg and could play around the barnyard at his will. I discovered, furthermore, that, unlike her son, she had read my books.

"It's very kind of you to take time off from your work to walk with Gregory," she said to me. "I don't suppose that he can be a very stimulating companion for an historian. He never reads anything."

Gregory simply nodded as she said this. She brought it forth without severity, as a mere matter of fact.

"Reading isn't everything," I said. "It's being aware of life that counts."

She looked at me penetratingly.

"Do you think so?" she asked. "Of course, I suppose you would. It's in line with your theories. The Bishop and I were interested in what you had to say about the free will of nations in your last book."

"Did you agree with it?"

"We did not."

Gregory looked at her in dismay.

"Now, Mother," he said protestingly, "you're not going to quarrel with my new friend?"

"I'm going to say what I wish, Gregory," she said firmly, "in my own house."

No, she certainly did not spoil him. Nor could it really be said that she was possessive. It was Greg who kept reaching for apron strings in which to enmesh himself. He seemed to yearn to be dominated. He tried vainly to have her make his decisions for him, and even after she had told him, as she invariably did, that he was old enough to think things through for himself, he would, not only behind her back but to her very face, insist to those around him that she ruled him with an iron hand. If I asked him to do something, to take a walk, to go to a movie, to dine, he would nod and smile and say "I'd love to," but he would surely add, and if she was there, perhaps in a lower tone, behind his hand: "But I'll have to get back early, you know. Mother will want to hear all about it before she goes to bed." And Mrs. Bakewell, overhearing him, with her small, fixed grim smile, did not even deign to contradict.

2

During that winter, when I was working on my book in Cambridge, I forgot poor Greg almost completely, as I usually did Anchor Harbor people. They were summer figures, and I stored them away in camphor balls with my flannels. I was surprised, therefore, each time that I received a letter from him, on the stationery of a large St. Petersburg hotel, protesting in a few lines of wretched scrawl that he had really met a number of very nice people, and could I possibly come down for a visit and meet them? One of them, I remember, he thought I would like because she wrote children's plays. I wrote him one letter and sent him a Christmas card, and that, I decided, was that.

I was in a better frame of mind when I went up to Anchor Harbor towards the end of the following July to stay with my mother-in-law. I was still keeping largely to myself, but the volume of my wife's poems was finished and in the hands of the publishers, and I no longer went out of my way to spurn people. I asked my mother-in-law one afternoon while we were sitting on the porch if the Bakewells were back in Anchor Harbor.

"Yes, I saw Edith Bakewell yesterday at Mrs. Stone's," she said. "Such an odd, stiff woman. I didn't know you knew them."

"Was her son there?"

"Greg? Oh, yes, he's always with her. Don't tell me *he's* a friend of yours?"

"After a fashion."

"Well, there's no accounting for tastes. I can't see a thing in him, but the old girls seem to like him. I drew him as a partner the other night at the bridge table."

"Oh, does he play bridge now?"

"If you can call it that," my mother-in-law said with a sniff. "But he certainly gets around. In my set, anyway. I never go out that I don't run into him."

"Really? Last fall he knew nobody."

"And Anchor Harbor was a better place."

Little by little I became aware that my friend's increased appearances in the summer-colony world were part of some preconceived and possibly elaborate plan of social self-advancement. He was not, I realized with a mild surprise, simply floating in the brisk wake of his mother's determined spurts; he was splashing gaily down a little backwater on a course that must have had the benefit of his own navigation. At the swimming club he had abandoned the lonely couch near the table of fashion magazines, where he used to wait for his mother, for the gay groups of old ladies in flowered hats who gathered daily at high noon around the umbrella tables and waited for the sun to go over the yardarm and the waiters to come hurrying with the first glad cocktail of the day. I was vaguely disgusted at all of this, though I had no reason, as I well knew, to have expected better things, but my disgust became pointed after I had twice telephoned him to ask him for a walk and twice had to listen to his protests of a previous engagement. I wondered if he fancied that his social position was now too lofty to allow of further intimacy between us, and I laughed to myself, but rather nastily, at the idea. I would have crossed him off my books irrevocably had I not met him one day when I was taking my mother-in-law to call on old Mrs. Stone. We had found her alone, sitting on the porch with her back to the view, and were making rather slow going of a conversation about one of my books when her daughter, Theodora, came in with a group of people, including Greg, who had just returned from what seemed to have been a fairly alcoholic picnic. I found myself caught, abandoned by my fleeing mother-in-law, in the throes of a sudden cocktail party.

"My God!" cried Theodora as she spotted me. "If it isn't Arnold of Rugby!"

I had always been rather a favorite of Theodora's, for she had regarded, in the light of the subsequent tragedy, her very casual friendship with my wife, of the kind that are based on childhood animosity and little more, as the deepest relationship that she had ever known. And in all seriousness it may have been. Theodora had had little time, in her four marriages, for friendships with women. At the moment she was in one of her brief husbandless periods, and her energy, unrestrained, swept across the peninsula like a forest fire. She drew me aside, out on the far end of the huge porch, hugging my arm as she did when she had had one drink too many, and hissed in my ear, with the catlike affectation that purported to be a caricature of itself and which, presumably, a minimum of four men had found attractive:

"Isn't he precious?"

"Who?"

"Little Gregory, of course." And she burst into a laugh. "He tells me that you were kind to him. Great big you!"

"Where on earth did you pick him up?"

"Right here." She indicated the porch. "Right here at Mummie's. I found him in the teapot. The old bitches were stuffing him into it, as if he were the dormouse, poor precious, so I hustled right over and caught him by the fanny and pulled and pulled till he came out with a pop. And now he's mine. You can't have him."

I glanced over to where Gregory was talking to two women in slacks. His white flannels looked a tiny bit dirtier, and he was holding a cocktail rather self-consciously in his round white hand.

"I'm not sure I want him," I said gravely. "You seem to have spoiled him already."

"Oh, precious," she said, cuddling up to me. "Do you think Theodora would do that?"

"Is he to be Number Five?"

She looked up at me with her wide serious eyes.

"But could he be, darling? I mean, after all, what sex is he? Or *is* he?"

I shrugged my shoulders.

"How much does that matter at our age, Theodora?"

She was, as always, a good sport. She threw back her head and howled with laughter.

"Oh, it matters!" she exclaimed. "I tell you what, darling. Greg will be Number Seven. Or maybe even Number Six. But not the next one. No, dear. Not the next one."

I found it in me to speculate if I had not perhaps been selected on the spot for that dubious honor. Anyway, I decided to go. Conversation with Theodora, who believed so patently, so brazenly, in nothing and nobody, always made me nervous. As I reentered the house and was crossing the front hall I heard my name called. It was Greg. He ran after me and caught me by the arm at the front door.

"You're leaving!" he protested. "And you haven't even spoken to me!"

"I'm speaking to you now," I said shortly.

To my dismay he sat down on the stone bench under the porte-cochère and started to cry. He did not cry loudly or embarrassingly; his chest rose and fell with quiet, orderly sobs.

"My God, man!" I exclaimed.

"I knew you were mad at me," he whimpered, "by the way you spoke on the telephone when I couldn't go on a walk with you. But I didn't know you wouldn't even speak to me when you saw me!"

"I'm sorry," I said fretfully.

"You don't know what you've meant to me," he went on dolefully, rubbing his eyes. "You have no idea. You're the first person who ever asked me to do anything in my whole life. When you asked me to go for a walk with you. Last summer."

"Well, I did this summer too."

"Yes," he said, shaking his head, "I know. And I couldn't go. But the reason I couldn't go was that I was busy. And the reason I was busy was what you told me."

I stared down at him.

"What the hell did I tell you?"

"To do things. See people. Be somebody." He looked up at me now with dried eyes. There was suddenly and quite unexpectedly almost a note of confidence in his tone.

"And how do you do that?"

"The only way I can. I go out."

I ran my hand through my hair in a confusion of reluctant amusement and despair.

"I didn't mean it that way, Greg," I protested. "I wanted you to see the world. Life. Before it was too late."

He nodded placidly.

"That's what I'm doing," he said.

"But I wanted you to read big books and think big thoughts," I said desperately. "How can you twist that into my telling you to become a tea caddy?"

His wide thoughtless eyes were filled with reproach.

"You knew I couldn't read books," he said gravely. "Or·think big thoughts. You were playing with me."

I stared.

"Then why did you think you had to do anything?"

"Because you made me want to." He looked away, across the gravel, into the deep green of the forest. "I could feel your contempt. I had never felt that before. No one had ever cared enough to feel contempt. Except you."

As I looked at him I wondered if there were any traces of his having felt such a sting. I was baffled, almost angry at his very expressionlessness. That he could sit and indict me so appallingly for my interference, could face me with so direct a responsibility, was surely a dreadful thing if he cared, but if he didn't, if he was simply making a fool of me . . .

"I hope you don't think," I said brutally, "that you can lessen any contempt that you think I may feel for you by becoming a social lion in Anchor Harbor."

He shook his head.

"No," he said firmly. "Your contempt is something I shall have to put up with. No matter what I do. I can't read or think or talk the way you do. I can't work. I can't even cut any sort of figure with the girls. There aren't many things open to me. You're like my mother. You know that, really, but you think of me as if I was somebody else."

I took a cigarette out of my case, lit it and sat down beside him. From around the corner of the big house came a burst of laughter from Theodora's friends.

"Where are you headed, then, Greg?" I asked him as sympathetically as I could.

He turned and faced me.

"To the top of the peninsula," he said. "I'm going to be a social leader."

I burst into a rude laugh.

"The *arbiter elegantiarum* of Anchor Harbor?" I cried.

"I don't know what that means," he said gravely.

Again I laughed. The sheer inanity of it had collapsed my mounting sympathy.

"You're mad," I said sharply. "You haven't got money or looks or even wit. Your bridge is lousy. You play no sports. Let's face it, man. You'll never make it. Even in this crazy place."

Greg seemed in no way perturbed by my roughness. His humility was complete. The only thing, I quickly divined, that could arouse the flow of his tears was to turn from him. As long as one spoke to him, one could say anything.

"Everything you say is true," he conceded blandly. "I'd be the last to deny it. But you watch. I'll get there."

"With the old ladies, perhaps," I said scornfully. "If that's what you want."

"I have to start with the old ladies," he said. "I don't know anyone else."

"And after the old ladies?"

But he had thought this out.

"They all have daughters or granddaughters," he explained. "Like Theodora. They'll get used to me."

"And you're 'cute,' " I said meanly. "You're a 'dear.' Yes, I see it. If it's what you want." I got up and started across the gravel to my car. He came after me.

"I'm not going to hurt anyone, you know," he said. "I only want to be a respected citizen."

In the car I leaned out to speak to him.

"Suppose I tell them?"

"About my plans?"

"What else?"

"Do. It won't make any difference. You'll see."

I started the motor and drove off without so much as nodding to him.

3

Gregory was good to his word. Every ounce of energy in his small store was directed to the attainment of his clearly conceived goal. I had resolved in disgust to have no further dealings with him, and I adhered to my resolution, but curiosity and a sense of the tiny drama latent in his plans kept me during the rest of that summer and the following two with an ear always alert at the mention of his name for further details of his social clamber.

Little by little Anchor Harbor began to take note of the emergence of this new personality. Greg had been right to start with the old ladies, though he had had, it was true, no alternative. The appearance of this bland young man with such innocent eyes and wide hips and such ridiculous blazers would have been followed by brusque repulse in any young or even middle-aged group of the summer colony, intent as they were on bridge, liquor, sport and sex. In the elderly circles, however, Greg had only to polish his bridge to the point of respectability, and he became a welcome addition at their dinner parties. His conversation, though certainly tepid, was soothing and enthusiastic, and he could listen, without interrupting, to the longest and most frequently repeated anecdote. He liked everybody and every dinner; he radiated an unobtrusive but gratifying satisfaction with life. Once he became known as a person who could be counted upon to accept, his evenings were gradually filled. The old in Anchor Harbor had an energy that put their descendants to shame. Dinner parties even in the septuagenarian group were apt to last till two in the morning, and in the bridge circles rubber would succeed rubber until the sun peeked in through the blinds to cast a weird light on the butt-filled ashtrays and the empty, sticky highball glasses. The old were still up when the young came in from their more hectic but less prolonged evenings of enjoyment, and Gregory came gradually, in the relaxed hours of the early morning, to meet the children and grandchildren of his hostesses. Friction, however, often ran high between the generations, even at such times, and he found his opportunity as peacemaker. He came to be noted for his skill in transmitting messages, with conciliatory amendments of his own, from mother to daughter, from aunt to niece. Everyone found him useful. He became in short a "character," accepted by all ages, and in that valuable capacity immune from criticism. He was "dear old Greg," "our lovable, ridiculous Greg." One heard more and more such remarks as, "Where but in Anchor Harbor would you find a type like Greg?" and "You now, I *like* Greg." And, I suppose, even had none of the foregoing been true, he would have succeeded as Theodora's pet, her "discovery," her lap dog, if you will, a comfortable, consoling eunuch in a world that had produced altogether too many men.

That Mrs. Bakewell would have little enough enthusiasm for her son's being taken to the hearts of Theodora and her set I was moderately sure, but the extent of her animosity I was not to learn until I came across her one hot August afternoon at the book counter of the stationery store, which was a meeting place second only in importance to the club. She was standing very stiffly but obviously intent upon the pages of a large volume of Dr. Fosdick. She looked up in some bewilderment when I greeted her.

"I was just looking," she said. "I don't want anything, thank you."

I explained that I was not the clerk.

"I'm sorry," she said without embarrassment. "I didn't recognize you."

"Well, it's been a long time," I admitted. "I only come here for short visits."

"It's a very trivial life, I'm afraid."

"Mine? I'm afraid so."

"No," she said severely and without apology. "The life up here."

"Greg seems to like it."

She looked at me for a moment. She did not smile.

"They're killing him," she said.

I stared.

"They?"

"That wicked woman. And her associates." She looked back at her book. "But I forgot. You're of the new generation. My adjective was anachronistic."

"I liked it."

She looked back at me.

"Then save him."

"But, Mrs. Bakewell," I protested. "People don't *save* people at Anchor Harbor."

"More's the pity," she said dryly.

I tried to minimize it.

"Greg's all right," I murmured. "He's having a good time."

She closed the book.

"Drinking the way he does?"

"Does he drink?"

"Shockingly."

I shrugged my shoulders. When people like Mrs. Bakewell used the word it was hard to know if they meant an occasional cocktail or a life of confirmed dipsomania.

"And that woman?" she persevered. "Do you approve of her?"

"Oh, Mrs. Bakewell," I protested earnestly. "I'm sure there's nothing wrong between him and Theodora."

She looked at me, I thought, with contempt.

"I was thinking of their souls," she said. "Good day, sir."

I discovered shortly after this awkward interchange that there was a justification in her remarks about Greg's drinking. I went one day to a large garden party given by Mrs. Stone. All Anchor Harbor was there, old and young, and Theodora's set, somewhat contemptuous of the throng and present, no doubt, only because of Theodora, who had an odd conventionality about attending family parties, were clustered in a group near the punch bowl and exploding periodically in loud laughs. They were not laughing, I should explain, at the rest of us, but at something white-flanneled and adipose in their midst, something with a blank face and strangely bleary eyes. It was Greg, of course, and he was telling them a story, stammering and repeating himself as he did so to the great enjoyment of the little group. It came over me gradually as I watched him that Mrs. Bakewell was right. They *were* killing him. Their laugher was as cold and their acclaim as temporary as that of any audience in the arena of Rome or Constantinople. They could clap hands and cheer, they could spoil their favorites, but they could turn their thumbs down, too, and could one doubt for a moment that at the first slight hint of deteriorating performance, they would? I felt a chill in my veins as their laughter came to me again across the lawn and as I caught sight of the small, spare, dignified figure of Greg's mother standing on the porch with the Bishop and surveying the party with eyes that said nothing. If there were Romans to build fires, *there* was a martyr worthy of their sport. But Gregory. Our eyes suddenly met, and I thought I could see the appeal in them; I thought I could feel his plea for rescue flutter towards me in my isolation through the golden air of the peninsula. Was that why his mother had come? As I turned to her I thought that she, too, was looking at me.

He had left his group. He was coming over to me.

"Well?" I said.

"Come over and meet these people," he said to me, taking me by the arm. "Come on. They're charming." He swayed slightly as he spoke.

I shook my arm loose.

"I don't want to."

He looked at me with his mild, steady look.

"Please," he urged.

"I said no," I snapped. "Why should I want to clutter my summer with trash like that? Go on back to them. Eat garbage. You like it."

He balanced for a moment on the balls of his feet. Evidently he regarded my violence as something indigenous to my nature and to be ignored.

"Theodora's never been in better form," he held out to me as bait.

"Good for Theodora," I said curtly. "And in case you don't know it, you're drunk."

He shook his head sadly at me and wandered slowly back to his group.

4
—
發

Gregory went from glory to glory. He became one of the respected citizens of the summer colony. His spotless white panama was to be seen bobbing on the bench of judges at the children's swimming meet. He received the prize two years running for the best costume at the fancy dress ball. On each occasion he went as a baby. He was a sponsor of the summer theater, the outdoor concerts, and the putting tournament. He was frequently seated on the right of his hostess at the very grandest dinners. He arrived early in the season and stayed into October. What he did during the winter months was something of a mystery, but it was certain that he did not enjoy elsewhere a success corresponding to his triumph at Anchor Harbor. Presumably, like so many Anchor Harbor people whose existence away from the peninsula it was so difficult to conceive, he went into winter hibernation to rest up for his exhausting summers.

That he continued to drink too much when he went out, which was, of course, all the time, did not, apparently, impair his social position. He was firmly entrenched, as I have said, in his chosen category of "character," and to these much is allowed. Why he drank I could only surmise. It might have been to steady himself in the face of a success that was as unnerving as it was unfamiliar; it might have been to make him forget the absurdity of his ambitions and the hollowness of their fulfillment, or it might even have been to shelter himself from the bleak wind of his mother's reproach. Theodora and all her crowd drank a great deal. It was possible that he had simply picked up the habit from them. It would have gone unnoticed, at least in that set, had it not been for a new and distressing habit that he had developed, of doing, after a certain number of drinks, a little dance by himself, a sort of jig, that was known as "Greg's peg." At first he did it only for a chosen few, late at night, amid friendly laughter, but word spread, and the little jig became an established feature of social life on Saturday night dances at the club. There would be a roll of drums, and everybody would stop dancing and gather in a big circle while the sympathetic orchestra beat time to the crazy marionette in the center. Needless to say I had avoided being a witness of "Greg's peg," but my immunity was not to last.

It so happened that the first time that I was to see this sordid performance was the last time that it ever took place. It was on a Saturday night at the swimming-club dance, the festivity that crowned the seven-day madness known as "tennis week," the very height, mind you, of Anchor Harbor's dizzy summer of gaiety. Even my mother-in-law and I had pulled ourselves sufficiently together to ask a few friends for dinner and take them on to the club. We found the place milling with people and a very large band playing very loudly. I noticed several young men who were not in evening dress and others whose evening clothes had obviously been borrowed, strong, ruddy, husky young men. It was the cruise season, and the comfortable, easy atmosphere of over-dressed but companionable Anchor Harbor was stiffened by an infil-tration of moneyed athleticism and arrogance from the distant smart-ness of Long Island and Newport. All throbbed, however, to the same music, and all seemed to be enjoying themselves. Theodora, in a sweater and pleated skirt and large pearls, dressed to look as though she were off a sailboat and not, as she was, fresh from her own establishment, spotted me and with characteristic aplomb deserted her partner and came over to our table. She took in my guests with an inclusive, final and undiscriminating smile that might have been a greeting or a shower of alms, took a seat at the table and monopolized me.

"Think of it," she drawled. "You at a dance. What's happened? Well, anyway," she continued without waiting for my answer, "I approve. See life. Come for lunch tomorrow. Will you? Two o'clock. I'll have some people who might amuse you."

Since her mother's death Theodora had begun to take on the at-tributes of queen of the peninsula. She dealt out her approval and disapproval as if it was possible that somebody cared. Struggling behind the wall of her make-up, her mannerisms and her marriages one could sense the real Theodora, strangled at birth, a dowager, with set lips and outcasting frown, a figure in pearls for an opera box. I declined her invitation and asked if Gregory was going to do his dance.

"Oh, the darling," she said huskily. "Of course he will. I'll get hold of him in a minute and shoo these people off the floor."

"Don't do it for me," I protested. "I don't want to see it. I hear it's a disgusting sight."

She snorted.

"Whoever told you that?" she retorted. "It's the darling's precious little stunt. Wait till you see it. Oh, I know you don't like him," she continued, wagging her finger at me. "He's told me that enough times, the poor dear. You've hurt him dreadfully. You pretend you can't stand society when the only thing you can't stand is anything the least bit unconventional."

I wondered if this were not possibly true. She continued to stare at me from very close range. It was always impossible to tell if she was drunk or sober.

"Like his old bitch of a mother," she continued.

"That's a cruel thing to say, Theodora," I protested sharply. "Do you even know her?"

"Certainly I know her. She's sat on poor Greg all his life. Lord knows what dreadful things she did to him when he was a child."

"Greg told you this?"

"He never complains, poor dear. But I'm no fool. I can read between the lines."

"If she's a bitch you know what that makes him," I said stiffly. "I was going to ask you tonight to give him back to his mother. She's the one person who knows what you're doing to him. But now I don't want to. It's too late. Keep him. Finish the dirty job."

"You must be drunk," she said and left me.

It was not long after this that the orchestra suddenly struck up a monotonous little piece with a singsong refrain and as at a concerted signal the couples on the floor gathered in a half-circle around the music, leaving a space in which something evidently was going on. The non–Anchor Harborites on the floor did not know what it was all about, but they joined with the others to make an audience for the diversion. I could see nothing but backs from where I was sitting, and suddenly hearing the laughter and applause and an odd tapping sound, I was overcome with curiosity and, taking my mother-in-law, we hurried across the dance floor and peered between the heads that barred our view.

What I saw there I shall never be able to get out of my mind. In the center of the half-circle formed by the crowd Gregory was dancing his dance. His eyes were closed and his long hair, disarrayed, was streaked down over his sweating face. His mouth, half open, emitted little snorts as his feet capered about in a preposterous jig that could only be described as an abortive effort at tap dancing. His arms moved back and forth as if he were striding along; his head was thrown back; his body shimmied from side to side. It was not really a dance at all; it was a contortion, a writhing. It looked more as if he were moving in a doped sleep or twitching at the end of a gallows. The lump of pallid softness that was his body seemed to be responding for the first time to his consciousness; it was only thus, after all, that the creature could use it. I turned in horror from the drunken jigger to his audience and noted the laughing faces, heard with disgust the "Go it, Greg!" It was worse now than the hysterical arena; it had all the obscenity of a striptease.

As I turned back to the sight of Gregory, his eyes opened, and I think he saw me. I thought for a second that once again I could make out the agonized appeal, but again I may have been wrong. It seemed to me that his soul, over which Mrs. Bakewell had expressed such concern, must have been as his body, white and doughy, possessed of no positive good and no positive evil, but a great passive husk on which the viri of the latter, once settled, could tear away. I turned to my mother-in-law, who shared my disgust; we were about to go back to our table when I heard, behind us, snatches of a conversation from a group that appeared to feel even more strongly than we did. Looking back, I saw several young men in flannels and tweed coats, obviously from a cruise.

"Who the hell is that pansy?"

"Did you ever see the like of it?"

"Oh, it's Anchor Harbor. They're all that way."

"Let's throw him in the pool."

"Yes!"

I recognized one of them as a graduate of my school. I took him aside.

"Watch out for your friends, Sammy," I warned him. "Don't let them touch him. Remember. This is his club and not yours. And every old lady on the peninsula will be after you to tear your eyes out."

He nodded.

"Yes, sir. Thank you."

This may have kept Sammy under control, but his friends were an-

other matter. When Greg had finished his jig and just as general dancing was about to be resumed, four young men stepped up to him and
quietly lifted him in the air, perching him on the shoulders of two of
their number. They then proceeded to carry him around the room.
This was interpreted as a sort of triumphal parade, as though students
were unhorsing and dragging a prima donna's carriage through enthusiastic streets, and everybody applauded vociferously while Greg, looking rather dazed, smiled and fluttered his handkerchief at the crowd.
Even I, forewarned, was concluding that it was all in good fun when
suddenly the four young men broke into a little trot and scampered with
their burden out onto the porch, down the flagstone steps and across the
patch of lawn with the umbrella tables to where the long pool shim-
mered under the searchlights on the clubhouse roof. People surged out
on the terrace to watch them; I rushed out myself and got there just in
time to see the four young men, two holding the victim's arms and two
his legs, swinging him slowly back and forth at the edge of the pool.
There was a moment of awful silence; then I heard Theodora's shriek,
and several ladies rushed across the lawn to stop them. It was too late.
There was a roar from the crowd as Greg was suddenly precipitated into
the air. He hung there for a split second in the glare of the searchlights,
his hair flying out; then came the loud splash as he disappeared. A
moment later he reappeared and burbled for help. There were shouts
of "He can't swim" and at least three people must have jumped in after
him. He was rescued and restored to a crowd of solicitous ladies in
evening dress who gathered at the edge of the pool to receive him in
their arms, regardless of his wetness. At this point I turned to go. I had
no wish to see the four young men lynched. I heard later that they
managed to escape with their skins and to their boats. They did not
come back.

5
—
卍

Gregory appeared to have developed nothing but a bad cold from the
mishap. He spent the next two days in his bed, and the driveway before
his mother's little cottage was jammed with tall and ancient Lincoln and

Pierce-Arrow town cars bringing flowers from his devoted friends. When he recovered Theodora gave a large lunch for him at the club. Everybody was very kind. But it became apparent after a little that, however trivial the physical damage may have been, something in the events of that momentous evening had impaired the native cheerfulness of Greg's sunny disposition. On Saturday nights he could no longer be prevailed upon to do his little dance, and at high noon his presence was frequently missed under the umbrella tables when the waiters in scarlet coats came hurrying with the first martini of the day. Theodora even spread the extraordinary news that he was thinking of going with his mother to Cape Cod the following summer. He had told her that the pace at Anchor Harbor was bad for his heart.

"That old witch of a mother has got her claws back into him," she told me firmly. "Mark my words. You'll see."

But I suspected that even Greg could see what I could see, that despite the sympathy and the flowers, despite the public outcry against the rude young men, despite the appeal in every face that things would again and always be as they had been before, despite all this, he had become "poor Greg." What had happened to him was not the sort of thing that happened to other people. When all was said and done, he may have known, as I knew, that in the last analysis even Theodora was on the side of the four young men. And perhaps he did realize it, for he was never heard to complain. Silently he accepted the verdict, if verdict it was, and disappeared early that September with his mother to St. Petersburg. I never heard of him again until several years later I chanced to read of his death of a heart attack in Cape Cod. I asked some friends of mine who spent the summer there if they had ever heard of him. Only one had. He said that he remembered Greg as a strange pallid individual who was to be seen in the village carrying a basket during his mother's marketing. She had survived him, and her mourning, if possible, was now a shade darker than before.

The Colonel's Foundation

1955

RUTHERFORD TOWER, although a partner, was not the Tower of Tower, Tilney & Webb. It sometimes seemed to him that the better part of his life went into explaining this fact or at least into anticipating the humiliation of having it explained by others. The Tower had been his late Uncle Reginald, the famous surrogate and leader of the New York bar, and the one substantial hope in Rutherford's legal career. For Rutherford, despite an almost morbid fear of clerks and courts, and a tendency to hide away from the actual clients behind their wills and estates, had even managed to slip into a junior partnership before Uncle Reginald, in his abrupt, downtown fashion, died at his desk. But it was as far as Rutherford seemed likely to go. There was nothing in the least avuncular about Uncle Reginald's successor, Clitus Tilney. A large, violent, self-made man, Tilney had a chip on his shoulder about families like the Towers and a disconcerting habit of checking the firm's books to see if Rutherford's "Social Register practice," as he slightingly called it, paid off. The junior Tower, he would remark to the cashier after each such inspection, had evidently been made a partner for only three reasons: because of his name, because of his relatives, and because he was there.

And, of course, Tilney was right. He was always right. Rutherford's practice didn't pay off. The Tower cousins, it was true, were in and out of his office all day, as were the Hallecks, the Rutherfords, the Tremaines, and all the other interconnecting links of his widespread family, but they expected, every last grabbing one of them, no more than a nominal bill. Aunt Mildred, Uncle Reginald's widow, was the worst of all, an opinionated and litigious lady who professed to care not for the money but for the principle of things and was forever embroiled with landlords, travel agencies, and shops. However hard her nephew worked for her, he could never feel more than a substitute. It was Clitus Tilney alone whose advice she respected. Rutherford sometimes wondered, running his long nervous fingers over his pale brow and through his prematurely gray hair, if there was any quality more respected by the timid remnants of an older New York society, even by the flattest-heeled and most velvet-gowned old maid, than naked aggression. What use did they really have for anyone whom they had known, like Rutherford, from his childhood? He was "one of us," wasn't he — too soft for a modern world?

The final blow came when Aunt Margaretta Halleck, the only Tower who had married what Clitus Tilney called "real money," and for whom Rutherford had drawn some dozen wills without fee, died leaving her affairs, including the management of her estate, in the hands of an uptown practitioner who had persuaded her that Wall Street lawyers were a pack of wolves. The next morning, when Rutherford happened to meet the senior partner in the subway, Tilney clapped a heavy hand on his shrinking shoulder.

"Tell me, Rutherford," he boomed over the roar of the train. "Have you ever thought of turning yourself into a securities lawyer? We could use another hand on this Smilax deal."

"Well, it's not a field I know much about," Rutherford said miserably.

"But, man, you're not forty yet! You can learn. Quite frankly, this Halleck fiasco is the last straw. I'm not saying it's anyone's fault, but the family business isn't carrying its share of the load. Think it over."

Rutherford sat later in his office, staring out the window at a dark brick wall six feet away, and thought gloomily of working night and day on one of Tilney's securities "teams," with bright, intolerant younger men who had been on the *Harvard Law Review*. The telephone rang, startling him. He picked it up. "What is it?" he snapped.

It was the receptionist. "There's a Colonel Hubert here," she said. "He wants to see Mr. Tower. Do you know him, or shall I see if Mr. Tilney can see him?"

It was not unusual for prospective clients to ask for "Mr. Tower," assuming that they were asking for the senior partner. Rutherford, however, was too jostled to answer with his usual self-deprecation. "If I were the receptionist," he said with an edge to his voice, "and somebody asked for Mr. Tower, I think I'd send him to Mr. Tower. But then, I suppose, I have a simple mind."

There was a surprised silence. "I'm sorry, Mr. Tower. I only meant —"

"I know," he said firmly. "It's quite all right. Tell Colonel Hubert I'll be glad to see him."

Sitting back in his chair, Rutherford immediately felt better. *That* was the way to deal with people. And, looking around, he tried to picture his room as it might appear to a client. It was the smallest of the partners' offices, true, but it was not entirely hopeless. If his uncle's best things, including the Sheraton desk, had been taken over by Mr. Tilney, he at least had a couple of relics of that more solid past: the large framed signed photograph of Judge Cardozo in robes, and his uncle's safe, a mammoth green box on wheels with REGINALD TOWER painted on the door in thick gold letters. The safe, of course, would have been more of an asset if Tilney had not insisted that it be used for keeping real estate papers and if young men from that department were not always bursting into Rutherford's office to bang it open and shut. Sometimes they even left papers unceremoniously on his desk, marked simply "For Safe." Still, he felt, it gave his room some of the flavor of an old-fashioned office, just a touch of Ephraim Tutt.

An office boy appeared at the doorway, saying "This way, sir," and a handsome, sporty old gentleman of certainly more than eighty years walked briskly into the office.

"Mr. Tower?"

Rutherford jumped to his feet to get him a chair, and the old man nodded vigorously as he took his seat. "Thank you, sir. Thank you, indeed," he said.

He was really magnificent, Rutherford decided as he sat down again and looked him over. He had thick white hair and long white mustaches, a straight, large, firm, aristocratic nose, and eyes that at least tried to be piercing. His dark, sharply pressed suit covered a figure whose only fault was a small, neat protruding stomach, and he wore a carnation in his buttonhole and a red tie with a huge knot.

"You are in the business of making wills?" the Colonel asked.

"That is my claim."

"Good. Then I want you to make me one."

There was a pause while the Colonel stared at him expectantly. Rutherford wondered if he was supposed to make the will up then and there, like a sandwich.

"Well, I guess I'd better ask a few questions," he said with a small professional smile. "Do you have a will now, sir?"

"Tore it up," the Colonel said. "Tore them all up. I'm changing my counsel, young man. That's why I'm here."

Rutherford decided not to press the point. "We might start with your family, then. Do you have a wife, sir? Or children?"

"My wife is dead, God bless her. No children. She had a couple of nieces, but they're provided for."

"And you sir?"

"Oh, I have some grandnephews." He shrugged. "Nice young chaps. You know the sort — married, live in the suburbs, have two children, television. No point in leaving them any money. Real money, I mean. Scare them to death. Prevent their keeping down to the Joneses. Fifty thousand apiece will be plenty."

Rutherford's mouth began to feel pleasantly dry as he leaned forward to pick up a pencil. He quite agreed with the Colonel about the suburbs. "And what did you have in mind, sir, as to the main disposition of your estate?"

"I don't care so much as long as it's spent," the Colonel exclaimed, slapping the desk. "Money should be spent, damn it! When I was a young man, I knew Ward McAllister. I was a friend of Harry Lehr's, too. Newport. It was something then! Mrs. Fish. The Vanderbilts. Oh, I know, people sneer at them now. They say they were vulgar, aping Europe, playing at being dukes and duchesses, but, by God, they had something to show for their money! Why, do you know, I can remember a ball at the Breakers when they had a footman in livery on every step of the grand stairway. Every step!"

"I guess you wouldn't see that today," Rutherford said, impressed. "Not even in Texas."

"Today!" The Colonel gave a snort. "Today they eat creamed chicken and peas at charity dinners at the Waldorf and listen to do-gooders. No, no, the color's quite gone, young man. The color's entirely gone."

At this, the Colonel sank into a reverie so profound that Rutherford began to worry that he had already lost interest in his will. "Perhaps some charity might interest you?" he suggested cautiously. "Or a foundation? I understand they do considerable spending."

The Colonel shrugged. "Only way to keep the money out of the hands of those rascals in Washington, I suppose. Republicans, Democrats — they're all alike. Grab, grab." He nodded decisively. "All right, young man. Make me a foundation."

Rutherford scratched his head. "What sort of a foundation, sir?"

"What sort? Don't they have to be for world peace or some damn-fool thing? Isn't that the tax angle?"

"Well, not altogether," Rutherford said, repressing a smile. "Your foundation could be a medical one, for example. Research. Grants to hospitals. That sort of thing."

"Good. Make me a medical foundation. But, mind you, I'm no Rockefeller or Carnegie. We're not talking about more than twelve or fifteen million."

Rutherford's head swam. "What — what about your board?" he stammered. "The board of this foundation. Who would you want on that?"

The Colonel looked down at the floor a moment, his lips pursed. When he looked up, he smiled charmingly. "Well, what about you, young man? You seem like a competent fellow. I'd be glad to have you as chairman."

"Me?"

"Why not? And pick your own board. If I want a man to do a job, I believe in letting him do it his own way."

Rutherford's heart gradually sank. One simply didn't walk in off the street and give one's fortune to a total stranger — not if one was sane. It was like the day, as a child at his grandmother's table, when she suddenly gave him a gold saltcellar in the form of a naked mermaid with a rounded, smooth figure that he had loved to stroke, only to be told by his mother that it was all in fun, that "Granny didn't mean it." It had been his introduction to senility. Projects like the Colonel's, he had heard, were common in Wall Street. It was a natural place for the demented to live out their fantasies. Nevertheless, as the old Colonel's imagined gold dissolved like Valhalla, he felt cheated and bitter. Abruptly, he stood up. "It's a most interesting scheme, Colonel," he said dryly. "I'd like a few days to think it over, if you don't mind. Why don't you leave me your name and address, and I can call you?"

The Colonel seemed surprised. "You mean that's all? For now?"

"If you please, sir, I'm afraid I have an appointment."

After the old man had placed his card on the desk, Rutherford relentlessly ushered him out to the foyer, where he waited until the elevator doors had safely closed between them. Returning, he told the receptionist that he would not be "in" again to Colonel Hubert.

That night, Rutherford tried to salvage what he could out of his disappointment by making a good story of it to his wife as she sat knitting in the living room of their apartment. Phyllis Tower was one of those plain, tall, angular women who are apt to be tense and sharp before marriage and almost stonily contented thereafter. It never seemed to occur to her that she didn't have everything in the world that a well-brought-up girl could possibly want. Limited, unrapturous, but of an even disposition, she made of New York a respectable small town and believed completely that her husband had inherited an excellent law practice.

She followed his story without any particular show of interest. "Hubert," she repeated when he had finished. "You don't suppose it was old Colonel Bill Hubert, do you? He's not really mad, you know. Eccentric, but not mad."

Rutherford felt his heart sink for the second time as he thought of the card left on his desk — "William Lyon Hubert." He watched her placid knitting with a sudden stab of resentment, but closed his lips tightly. After all, to be made ridiculous was worse than *anything*. Then he said guardedly: "This man's name was Frank. Who is Colonel Bill?"

"Oh, you know, dear. He's that old diner-out who married Grandma's friend Mrs. Jack Tyson. Everyone said she was mad for him right up to the day she died."

Again his mouth was dry. It was too much, in one day. "And did she leave him that — the *fortune?*"

"Well, I don't suppose she left him all of it," she said, breaking a strand of yarn. "There were the Tysons, you know. But he still keeps up the house on Fifth Avenue. And *that* takes something."

"Yes," he murmured, a vast impression of masonry clouding his mind. "Yes, I suppose it must."

"What's the matter, dear?" she asked. "You look funny. You don't suppose you could have been wrong about the name, do you? Are you sure it was Frank?"

"Quite sure."

Buried in the evening newspaper, he pondered his discovery. And then, in a flash, he remembered. Of course! Mrs. Jack Tyson had become Mrs. W. L. Hubert! What devil was it that made him forget these things, which Phyllis remembered so effortlessly? And fifteen million — wasn't that just the slice that a grateful widow *might* have left him?

The next morning, after a restless night, Rutherford looked up Colonel Hubert's number and tried to reach him on the telephone, but this, it turned out, was far from easy. The atmosphere of the great house, as conveyed to him over the line, was, to say the least, confused. Three times he called, and three times a mild, patient, uncooperative voice, surely that of an ancient butler, discreetly answered. Rutherford was obliged to spell and respell his name. He was then switched to an extension and to a maid who evidently regarded the ring of the telephone as a personal affront. While they argued, a third voice, far away and faintly querulous, was intermittently heard, and finally, on the third attempt, an old man called into the telephone "What? What?" very loudly. Then, abruptly, someone hung up, and Rutherford heard again the baffling dial tone. He decided to go up to the house.

When he got out of the cab, he took in with renewed pleasure the great façade. He knew it, of course. Everyone who ever walked on the east side of Central Park knew the eclectic architecture of the old Tyson house, rising from a Medicean basement through stories of solemnified French Renaissance to its distinguishing feature, a top-floor balcony in the form of the Porch of the Maidens. To Rutherford, it was simply the kind of house that one built if one was rich. He would have been only too happy to be able to do the same.

Fortunately, it proved as easy to see Colonel Hubert as it was difficult to get him on the telephone. The old butler who opened the massive grilled door, and whose voice Rutherford immediately recognized, led him without further questions, when he heard he was actually dealing with the Colonel's lawyer, up the gray marble stairway that glimmered in the dark hall and down a long corridor to the Colonel's study. This was Italian; Rutherford had a vague impression of red damask and tapestry as he went up to the long black table at which an old man was sitting, reading a typewritten sheet. He sighed in relief. It *was* the right colonel.

"Good morning, Colonel. I'm Tower. Rutherford Tower. Do you remember me? About your will?"

The Colonel looked up with an expression of faint puzzlement, but smiled politely. "My dear fellow, of course. Pray be seated."

"I wanted to tell you that I've thought it over, and that I'm all set to start," Rutherford went on quickly, taking a seat opposite the Colonel. "There are a few points, however, I'd like to straighten out."

The Colonel nodded several times. "Ah, yes, my will," he said. "Exactly. Very good of you."

"I want to get the names of your grandnephews. I think it advisable to leave them more substantial legacies in view of the fact that the residue is going to your foundation. And then there's the question of executors . . ." He paused, wondering if the Colonel was following him. The old man was now playing with a large bronze turtle — the repository of stamps and paper clips — raising and lowering its shell. "That's a handsome bronze you have there," Rutherford said uncertainly.

"Isn't it?" the Colonel said, holding it up. "I'd like Sophie to have it. She always used to admire it. You might take her name down. Sophie Winters, my wife's niece. Or did she take back her own name after her last divorce?" He looked blankly at Rutherford. "Anyway, she's living in Biarritz. Unless she sold that house that Millie left her. Did she, do you know?"

Rutherford took a deep breath. Whatever happened, he must not be impatient again. "If I might suggest, sir, we could take care of the specific items more easily in a letter. A letter to be left with your will."

The Colonel smiled his charming smile. "I'd like to do it the simple way myself, of course. But would it be binding? Isn't that the point? Would it be binding?"

"Well, not exactly," Rutherford admitted, "but, after all, such a request is hardly going to be ignored —"

"How can we be sure? Do you see?" the Colonel said, smiling again. "Now, I tell you what we'll do. I'll ring for my man, Tomkins, and we'll get some luggage tags to tie to the objects marked for the different relatives."

Rutherford sat helpless as the Colonel rang, and told Tomkins what he wanted. When the butler returned with the tags, he gave them to the Colonel and then took each one silently from him as the old man wrote a name on it. He then proceeded gravely to tie it to a lamp or a chair or to stick it with Scotch tape to the frame of a picture or some other object. Both he and the Colonel seemed quite engrossed in their task and entirely unmindful of Rutherford, who followed them about the study, halfheartedly writing down the name of the fortunate niece who was to receive the Luther Terry *Peasant Girl* or the happy cousin who was to get the John Rogers group. By lunchtime, the study looked like a naval vessel airing its signal flags. The Colonel surveyed the whole with satisfaction.

"Well!" he exclaimed, turning to Rutherford. "I guess that's that for today! All work and no play, you know. Come back tomorrow, my dear young man, and we'll do the music room."

Rutherford, his pockets rustling with useless notes, walked down Fifth Avenue, too overwrought to go immediately back to the office. He stopped at his club and had an early drink in the almost empty bar, calculating how long at this rate it would take them to do the whole house. And what about the one on Long Island? And how did he know there mightn't be another in Florida? It was suddenly grimly clear that unless he managed to get the Colonel out of this distressing new mood of particulars and back to his more sweeping attitude of the day before, there might never be any will at all. And, looking at his own pale face in the mirror behind the bar, he drew himself up and ordered another drink. What was it that Clitus Tilney always said was the mark of a good lawyer — creative imagination?

At his office, after lunch, he went to work with a determination that he had not shown since the Benzedrine weekend, fifteen years before, when he took his bar examinations. He kept his office door closed, and snapped "Keep out, please!" to each startled young man who banged it open to get to the real estate safe. He even had the courage to seize one of them, a Mr. Baitsell, and demand his services. When Baitsell protested, Rutherford asserted himself as he had not done since his uncle's death. "I'm sorry. This is an emergency," he said.

Once obtained, Baitsell was efficient. He dug out of the files a precedent for a simple foundation for medical purposes and, using it as a guide, drafted that part of the will himself while Rutherford worked out the legacies for the grandnephews. This was a tricky business, for the bequests had to be large enough to induce the young Huberts not to contest the will. There were moments, but only brief ones, when he stopped to ponder the morality of what he was doing. Was it *his* responsibility to pass on the Colonel's soundness of mind? Did he *know* it to be unsound? And whom, after all, was he gypping? If the old man died without a will, the grandnephews would take everything, to be sure, but everything minus taxes. All he was really doing with his foundation was shifting the tax money from the government, which would waste it, to a charity, which wouldn't. If that wasn't "creative imagination," he wanted to know what was! And did anyone think for a single, solitary second that in his position Clitus Tilney would not have done what he was doing? Why, he would probably have made himself residuary legatee! With this thought, Rutherford, after swallowing two or three times, penciled his own name in the blank space for "executor" on the mimeographed form he was using.

The following morning at ten, Rutherford went uptown with his secretary and Mr. Baitsell to take the Colonel, as he now knew was the only way, by storm. While the other two waited in the hall, he followed the butler up the stairs and down the corridor to the study. Entering briskly, he placed a typed copy of the will on the desk before the astonished old gentleman.

"I've been working all night, Colonel," he said, in a voice so nervous that he didn't quite recognize himself, "and I've decided that it doesn't pay to be too much smarter than one's client — particularly when that client happens to be Colonel Hubert. All of which means, sir, that you were right the first time. My scheme of including in the will all those bequests of objets d'art just isn't feasible. We'll accomplish the same thing in a letter. And in the meanwhile here's your will as you originally wanted it. Clean as a whistle."

The Colonel watched him, nodding vaguely, and fingered the pages of the will. "You think it's all right?"

"Right as Tower, Tilney & Webb can make it," Rutherford said, with the smile and wink that he had seen Clitus Tilney use.

"And you think I should sign it now?"

"No time like the present." Rutherford, who had been too nervous to sit, walked to the window, to conceal his heavy breathing. "If you'll just ring for Tomkins and ask him to tell the young lady and gentleman in the hall to come up, we'll have the necessary witnesses."

"Is Tomkins covered all right?" the Colonel asked as he touched the bell beside him.

"He's covered with the other servants," Rutherford said hastily. "In my opinion, sir, you've been more than generous."

The witnesses came up, and the Colonel behaved better than Rutherford had dared hope. He joked with Baitsell about the formalities, laughed at the red ribbon attached to the will, told a couple of anecdotes about old Newport and Harry Lehr's will, and finally signed his name in a great, flourishing hand. When Rutherford's secretary walked up to the table to sign her name after his, he rose and made her a courtly bow. It was all like a scene from Thackeray.

In the taxi afterward, speeding downtown, Rutherford turned to the others. "The Colonel's a bit funny about his private affairs," he told them. "As a matter of fact, I haven't even met his family. So I'd rather you didn't mention this will business. Outside the office *or* in."

Baitsell looked very young and impressed as he gave him his solemn assurance. He then asked, "But if the Colonel should die, sir, who would notify us? And how would the family know about the will?"

"Never mind about that," Rutherford said, with a small smile, handing him the will. "I don't think the Colonel is apt to do very much dying without my hearing of it. When we get to the office, you stick that will in the vault and forget it."

It was risky to warn them, of course, but riskier not to. He couldn't afford to have them talk. There was too much that was phony in the whole picture. He had no guaranty, after all, that the Colonel had either the money or the power to will it. It was the kind of situation where one had to lie low, at least until the old man was dead, and even after that, until it was clear that one had the final and valid will. How would he look, for example, rushing into court to probate the document now under Baitsell's arm if the family produced a later will, or even a judicial ruling that the old man was incompetent to make one? Would he not seem ridiculous and grabby? Or worse? And Clitus Tilney! What would *he* say if his firm was dragged into so humiliating a failure? But no, no, he wouldn't even think of it. He could burn the will secretly, if necessary; nobody need know unless — well, unless he won. And his heart bounded as he thought of the paneled office that Tilney would have to assign to the director of the Hubert Foundation.

A new office was only the first of many imaginative flights in which he riotously indulged. He saw himself dispensing grants to universities and hospitals, called on, solicited, profusely thanked. He calculated and recalculated his executor's commissions on increasingly optimistic estimates of the Colonel's estate. In fact, his concept of the old man's wealth and his own control of it, the apotheosis of Rutherford Tower to the position of benefactor of the city, *the* Tower at long last of Tower, Tilney & Webb, began, in the ensuing months, to edge out the more real prospect of disappointment. The fantasy had become too important not to be deliberately indulged in. When he turned at breakfast to the obituary page, he would close his eyes and actually pray that he would not find the name there, so that he would have another day in which to dream.

When the Colonel did die, it was Phyllis, of course, who spotted it. "I see that old Colonel Bill is dead," she said at breakfast one morning, without looking up from her newspaper. "Eighty-seven. Didn't you say he'd been in to see you?"

For a moment, Rutherford sat utterly still. "Where did he die?" he asked.

"In some lawyer's office in Miami. So convenient, I should imagine. They probably had all his papers ready. Why, Rutherford, where are you going?"

He didn't trust himself to wait, and hurried out. In the street, he bought copies of all the newspapers and went to a Central Park bench to read them. There was little more in any of the obituaries than the headlines: "Former Army Officer Stricken" or "Husband of Mrs. J. L. Tyson Succumbs." He could find nothing else about the Miami lawyer. After all, he reasoned desperately as he got up and walked through the Mall, wasn't it only natural for the Colonel to have Florida counsel? Didn't he spend part of the year there? But, for all his arguments, it was almost lunchtime before he gathered courage to call his office. His secretary, however, had to report only that Aunt Mildred Tower had called twice and wanted him to call back.

"Tell her I'm tied up," he said irritably. "Tell her I've gone to the partners' lunch."

For, indeed, it was Monday, the day of their weekly lunch. When he got to the private room of the Down Town where they met, he found some twenty of them at the table, listening to Clitus Tilney. Rutherford assumed, as he slipped into a chair at the lower end of the table, that the senior partner was telling one of his usual stories to illustrate the greatness of Clitus and the confounding of his rivals. But this story, as he listened to it with a growing void in his stomach, appeared to be something else.

"No, it's true, I'm not exaggerating," Tilney was saying, with a rumbling laugh. "There are twenty-five wills that they know of already, and they're not all in by a long shot. Sam Kennecott, at Standard Trust, told me it was a mania with the old boy. And the killing thing is, they're all the same. Except for one that has forty-five pages of specific bequests, they all set up some crazy foundation under the control of — guess who — the little shyster who drew the will! Sam says you've never seen such an accumulation of greed in your life! In my opinion, they ought to be disbarred, the lot of them, for taking advantage of the poor old dodo. Except the joke's on them — that's the beauty of it!"

Rutherford did not have to ask one of his neighbors the name of the deceased, but, feeling dazed, he did. The neighbor told him.

"Did any of the big firms get hooked?" someone asked.

"Good Lord, we have *some* ethics, I hope!" Tilney answered. "Though there's a rumor that one did. Harrison & Lambert, someone said. Wouldn't it be wonderful?" Tilney's large jowls positively shook with pleasure. "What wouldn't I give to see old Cy Lambert caught like a monkey with his fist in the bottle!"

Rutherford spoke up suddenly. His voice was so high that everyone turned and looked at him. "But what about the man with the *last* will?" he called down the table to Mr. Tilney. "Why is it a joke on him?"

"You mean the man in Miami?" Tilney said, flashing at Rutherford the fixed smile of his dislike. "Because the old guy didn't have that sort of money. Not foundation money. The big stuff was all in trust, of course, and goes to the Tysons, where it should go."

Rutherford concentrated on eating a single course. It would look odd, after his interruption, to leave at once. When he had emptied his plate, he wiped his mouth carefully, excused himself to his neighbors, and walked slowly from the room.

Back at the office, however, he almost dashed to Baitsell's room. Closing the door behind him, he faced the startled young man with wild eyes. "Look, Baitsell, about that will of Colonel Hubert's — you remember." Baitsell nodded quickly. "Well, he died, you see."

"Yes, sir. I read about it."

"Apparently, he's written some subsequent wills. I think we'd better do nothing about filing ours for the time being. And if I were you I wouldn't mention this around the office. It might —"

"But it's already filed, sir!"

"It's *what?*"

"Yes, sir. I filed it."

"How could you?" Rutherford's voice was almost a scream. "You haven't had time to prepare a petition, let alone get it signed!"

"Oh, I don't mean that I filed it for probate, Mr. Tower. I mean I filed it for safekeeping in the Surrogate's Court. *Before* he died. The same day he signed it."

Rutherford, looking into the young man's clear, honest eyes, knew now that he faced the unwitting agent of his own devil. "Why did you do that?" he asked in a low, almost curious tone. "We never do that with wills. We keep them in our vault."

"Oh, I know that, sir," Baitsell answered proudly. "But you told me you didn't know the relatives. I thought if the old gentleman died and you didn't hear about it at once, they might rush in with another will. Now they'll find ours sitting up there in the courthouse, staring them right in the face. Yes, sir, Mr. Tower, you'll have to be given notice of every will that's offered. Public notice!"

Rutherford looked at the triumphant young man for a moment and then returned without a word to his own office. There he leaned against Uncle Reginald's safe and thought in a stunned, stupid way of old Cy Lambert laughing, even shouting, at Clitus Tilney. Then he shook his head. It was too much — too much to take in. He wondered, in a sudden new mood of detachment, if it wasn't rather distinguished to be hounded so personally by the furies. Orestes. Orestes Rutherford Tower. His telephone rang.

"Rutherford? Is it you?" a voice asked.

"Yes, Aunt Mildred," he said quietly.

"Well, I'm glad to get you at last. I don't know what your uncle would have said about the hours young lawyers keep today. And people talk about the pressure of modern life! Talk is all it is. But look, Rutherford. That blackguard of a landlord of mine is acting up again. He now claims that my apartment lease doesn't include an extra maid's room in the basement. I want you to come right up and talk to him. This afternoon. You can, can't you?"

"Yes, Aunt Mildred," he said again. "I'm practically on my way."

The Mavericks

1962

1

HARRY REILLEY occupied a peculiar status among the associates of
Tower, Tilney & Webb. He had not been netted by the hiring committee in its annual Christmas canvas of the editors of the Harvard, Yale
and Columbia law reviews. He was thirty-two and clerking for a small
firm of real estate lawyers in Brooklyn when Clitus Tilney had decided
to bolster Tower, Tilney's small department in that field by hiring a
young man, already trained, from the outside. Harry understood that he
was being employed as a specialist with little chance of ultimate partnership, and he had not minded until he had discovered the tight little
social hierarchy into which the firm was organized. Then he decided
that working in his status was like climbing the stairs in a department
store while alongside one an escalator carried the other customers
smoothly and rapidly to the landing.

The real estate department of Tower, Tilney had for years been run
by an old associate, Llewellyn Buck, a dry, scholarly gentleman who
spent most of his time studying Plantaganet law reporters through thick
glasses and who was referred to about the office, with a mild and affectionate contempt, as one who had made nothing of a brilliant start.

"Real property, my dear Reilley, was the golden field of the common
law," he had told Harry at the beginning. "Everything else grew out of
it. That's why everything else is warped, and only the law of convey-
ances is pure. Stay with purity, my boy. Also, it's a wonderful field in
which to study your fellow mortals. There's something about a deed or
a lease that brings out the meanest and the pettiest in them. I've seen
a man lose a ten-million-dollar corner property over a difference of
opinion about the reading of an oil meter!"

Harry cared little for legal philosophy and less for the opportunity to observe his clients at their less becoming moments, but he liked the salary and stuck to the job. He was used to the small print of deeds and mortgages and was not bothered by detail; his mind, like his body, was tough. He was a big man with big shoulders, and he walked in a stiff, blocky fashion that was yet consistent with a fine muscular coordination. He had a large round head and a bull neck, thick blond hair that he wore in a crew cut and small, grayish-blue eyes with a habitual expression of reserve that bordered on suspicion. His nose was straight and wide, his jaw square, and the slanting lines of his unexpectedly delicate upper lip were almost parallel to his cheekbones. Harry was handsome with the handsomeness of a hundred-and-ninety-pound Irishman in the prime of life, but the danger of overweight already hung about him.

He would have got on well enough with the other clerks had he been less sensitive about real or imagined condescension. When Bart French, Tilney's son-in-law, the rich young man who worked harder than all the others simply because he was rich, paraded down the corridor to go out to lunch, followed by the little group with which he was working on a corporate indenture, and paused at the door of Harry's office to ask cheerily: "Care to join us —" Harry would wonder if he was not performing an act of charity to the poor slave in real estate. But he would join them and listen, bored, while they discussed in tedious detail the problems of their current indenture until Bart, towards the end of the meal, would turn to him with a perfunctory show of interest and ask in that same maddening, cheery tone: "What's new in the metes and bounds department? Have you caught any covenants running with the land?"

Harry had been a prickly soul since the age of fourteen when his father, a seemingly successful Brooklyn building contractor, had gone to jail for looting his company. Harry, the youngest of seven, had been the one to feel it most keenly and, in the ensuing years of retrenchment and hardship, had been his mother's primary consolation. After his father had been released, and when he had taken to whiskey and self-pity, Harry had been passionately and articulately bitter in his resentment of him. But fathers like Angus Reilley always win in the end, and his death of cancer in Harry's freshman year at Fordham had so crushed the latter with remorse that he had seemed doomed for a time to the paternal alcoholic course. Indeed, his older brothers and sisters, including Joseph, the priest, had gloomily prognosticated that Harry would go to the dogs, but Harry seemed to have a stabilizer built into his character which, when he tipped too close to the fatal angle, suddenly, if with a great deal of churning and throbbing, succeeded in righting the lurching vessel. He had finished Fordham and Fordham law in the first third of his classes; he had fought as a marine in Korea and been decorated, and he had supported himself creditably in the law ever since. It was a disappointment to his mother that he preferred a room in Manhattan to the family home and a dissolute bachelor existence to the safer joys of early matrimony, but when he came to the Reilleys' Sunday lunch he always looked hearty and well, and he was charming with all the little nephews and nieces. The family had to concede that when Harry wanted to put his best foot forward, he had a very good foot to offer.

In Tower, Tilney, however, this foot was seen more by the staff than by the lawyers. Harry blandly ignored the elaborate etiquette laid down by the late Judge Tower. He called the stenographers by their first names and went out to lunch with the men in the accounting department. He maintained an easy, joking, mock-flirtatious relationship with the older women — Mrs. Grimshawe, as head of stenographic, Mrs. Lane, the librarian, and Miss Gibbon, the chief file clerk — as a result of which he got as good service as Clitus Tilney himself. In fact, Mrs. Grimshawe, "Lois" as he impudently called her, had been known to leave her desk on the little dais from which she supervised her department, grab a pencil and pad from one of her girls and go to Mr. Reilley's office to take dictation herself!

Among the law clerks his only two friends were the two whom he considered, like himself, to be mavericks: Lee Ozite, the managing clerk, who handled the court calendars and arranged for the service of papers, and Doris Marsh, the single woman lawyer in the office. Doris's interest in Harry was immediate and lively, aroused by nothing greater than his merely civil appreciation of herself as a woman. To the other clerks she might as well have been neuter, a tall, pale, tense, awkwardly moving figure of near thirty in a plain brown suit, distastefully associated with taxes, whose black hair was lightly flaked with a premature gray. But Harry did not, like many working men, relegate sex to nonworking hours. A woman to him was always a woman, and, without finding Doris particularly his type, he could perfectly see that her skin, if chalky, was nonetheless smooth and soft, her breasts full and fine and that, without the glasses and the nervous smile, her face might reveal the firm, rounded lines of a Greek statue. Harry could picture Doris sitting on a rock naked, looking out to sea, her hair blown in the wind, and he deplored the fate which had confined her to a city desk.

The first time they lunched together, he discovered that she was a great talker. She drank a martini before her meal and a glass of ale with it and complained at length of the difficulties of being a woman lawyer in Tower, Tilney. She gave instances of discrimination in the tax department: of how she was paid less than associates who had come in after her and not asked to the office outings at the Glenville Beach Club. What just saved her from being a bore was the dry accuracy of her observation and her evident sense of the foolishness of the whole show.

"Now, don't ask me why I don't get another job," she concluded, taking off her glasses and gazing at him with a stare of bland seriousness. "It would be very ungentlemanly because I wouldn't have a thing to say. Let's put it that I have a persecution complex."

"I thought perhaps you hoped to marry one of the partners."

"Which?"

"Why not Madison? He's single, isn't he?"

"That he is." She maintained all her air of gravity. "He might be just mean enough to do it to save the pittance he now pays me."

"And think of the income tax deduction you'd bring him! For a man in his bracket that might even make up for a wife who reads herself to sleep with the Revenue Code."

Doris startled him by throwing back her head and uttering a long, rather wild laugh. But she cut it off with equal abruptness. "I *crave* you, Harry Reilley. You're human. One of the few people in the whole damn shop who is. Do you realize you're the first of the associates who's ever asked me to lunch? The very *first?*" She paused to reflect. "Except Ozey, and they treat him, poor man, like the janitor."

For the rest of lunch they took apart, one by one, the partners of the firm. Doris, of course, had more to say, because she knew them better. At first she showed some slight degree of reticence, but she rapidly lost it as she drank her ale, and by dessert she was speculating freely that Waldron Webb was a sublimated homosexual and that Morris Madison had a neurotic fear of women. It was the most obvious kind of female revenge against a male community: she simply denied that they were men.

"It must be a sorry prospect for a single woman," Harry observed as they walked back to the office. "You should have gone into advertising."

"But things have looked up since they started hiring big Irishmen. I may stick around a bit."

They both laughed and went back to work as easily as if there had been nothing between them but a common employer. Yet Harry was faintly ashamed of his little game of coaxing the woman out from behind the tax computer. It took so little to do it. Doris developed the habit of dropping into his office once a day to smoke a cigarette and "reset her sights," as she put it. She pretended that it was essential, after a certain number of hours of work at Tower, Tilney, to become "rehumanized." Together they laughed at things and people, and he found her office gossip amusing, but basically the world in which he lived began outside the doors of the office while hers ended on the same threshold. The little bites of the legal hierarchy raised small red welts in his sensitivity which he could afford to ignore, or at the most irritably scratch, but in her they seemed to secrete a subtle poison which by dint of the constant application of antitoxins had become a necessity to her nature.

He had had too much to do with women not to be aware that the least advance on his part would be immediately and gratefully misinterpreted, and he was determined that no such advance would be made. She had asked him to two cocktail parties at the apartment which she shared in Greenwich Village with another woman lawyer, and he had declined both. Doris had chosen to accept his lame excuses literally and had had the sense not to betray any disappointment that she might have felt. But when the approach was made by a third person, Harry's plan of action, or inaction, was upset, and so he came to be committed to a weekend with Doris in a cottage in Devon, a small sandy summer settlement on the south shore of Long Island.

It was Lois Grimshawe's cottage, and the invitation came from her. Nobody knew better than Lois the incongruity, under Judge Tower's rules, of such a bid from even a senior staff member to a junior associate, and her sense of the indecorum was pasted all over her round, smiling, pink and yellow countenance when she came into Harry's office.

"You may think it very bold of me, but you have been so very friendly — not at all like the other associates — that I wondered — if you were going to be stuck in town over next weekend — whether you might not like . . ." She paused here, still smiling, and stuck a finger in the high pile of her dyed auburn hair. "Oh, no, but you wouldn't, of course."

"Wouldn't what, Lois?"

"Wouldn't want to spend that weekend with me in my little place in Devon. Oh, it's just a shack, you know. We do all our own cooking and everything, but there's plenty of whiskey and nice neighbors and lots of sun and sea, and if I say so myself we do have fun." Here Lois giggled.

"Of course I'll come. I'd love to."

"Oh, goody!" Lois clapped her hands in excitement. "There'll be just you and me and Doris Marsh and Henry Barnes, an old friend of mine. He's a senior cashier at Standard Trust. Really a lovely person. And Marjorie Clinger — you know, Mr. Tilney's secretary — has the cottage next door, so you'll see some familiar faces!"

Harry sighed when she had gone and debated how best to get out of it, but this, he finally decided, was unworthy. It was insulting to attribute too much design to Doris and absurdly weak of himself to be afraid of being able to resist it, if design there was. He had taken care of himself on the beaches of Korea; he could certainly do so on those of Devon. The way to take life was as it came.

And, indeed, it seemed to come easily enough. The cabins of Lois Grimshawe and Miss Clinger, like dozens of others along the dunes of Devon, were small weatherbeaten shingle structures, like overgrown bathhouses, each with a back porch facing the sea on which drinks were constantly mixed. There was a great deal of laughing and joking on arrival, and much shouting back and forth between cabins and many hilarious references to last weekend's hangovers, but one could do, apparently, as one pleased, and Harry, after changing to a pair of red bathing trunks and sitting for a few minutes with the group on the beach, took off alone down the dunes at a pace that was no invitation to any woman to join him. He walked for miles, past larger cabins, past huge summer palaces, past swimming clubs, and every half-hour he would run down into the water and plunge in the hissing surf. It was glorious exercise, and he did not return until eight that night, when he found a noisy picnic of some twenty people going on in front of Lois's cabin. Lois had already drunk too much to be cross at his disappearance, and when he had changed to a shirt and blue jeans and joined the group, he felt better than he had felt all summer and in a mood to drink deeply.

Which he did. Much later in the evening, when the others were singing songs, he was sitting above the group on a ridge of dune with Doris Marsh. She looked very well in the moonlight and in the flicker of the fire below. Her hair blew in the wind, and her figure was well accentuated by her long velvet pants. Harry was reminded of his earlier vision of her naked by the sea. Yet Doris seemed absorbed in a melancholy and reflective mood. She, too, was interested in drinking.

"You know, Harry, on a night like this, under all those stars, it just doesn't seem possible that Monday will find me back in that sweatshop writing a memorandum on Miss Johanna Shepard's capital loss carryovers."

"Why go back, then?"

Doris squinted at the moon. "Just a little matter of bread and butter."

"Oh, can it, Doris. You could make more money for half the work. What about Uncle Sam? Ever think of the Collector's Office? As a matter of fact, I've been turning the idea over myself."

"Oh, no, Harry, don't you dare!" Very solemn now, she turned to shake her head at him. "You're not like me, you know. You *could* make the grade."

"What grade?"

"You could be a partner. No, dear boy, don't grunt and throw sand. I know exactly what I'm talking about. And I know all about the real estate department not being the best place to start. Sure, it's a dead end. But you don't have to stay in it. You could go to Mr. Tilney and ask for a transfer. And with your personality, you'd get it. Believe me, Harry!"

"Oh, bosh. They don't want my kind in their paneled offices. Give me that cup and let me get you a drink."

"Here's that cup and by all means get me a drink, but I still know what I'm saying." As he took her empty cup she turned away and hugged her knees, facing the soft breeze. "And I'm a fool to tell you, too."

"Why?"

"Because when you *do* make the grade, you certainly won't come down to spend weekends in Devon with Lois Grimshawe and Doris Marsh."

"Dry up, will you, Doris?"

"I *am* dry," she said without turning. "Why don't you get me my drink?"

When he returned with the full cups he was determined not to let the conversation get back to Harry Reilley, even if it had to become sentimental about Doris Marsh. "How did you ever get into this racket?" he asked her. "Why aren't you living in the suburbs with a station wagon and three children? With one eye on your husband and one eye on somebody else's?"

"Would you really like to know?" she asked rhetorically. "Would you really like to hear my dreary tale? I went to law school because of a guy. I went into practice because of a guy. I molded my whole life into a particular twisted shape to please one guy, and I didn't even catch him." She turned to give Harry a friendly little push on the shoulder. "It's your fault if I bore you with my love story, old man. You asked for it. You shouldn't be so goddamn sympathetic with your questions."

Harry listened with mild interest, as he sipped his drink and watched the moonlight on the waves, to her tale of "Phil," who was now practicing law, still unmarried, in Hawaii. It seemed that Phil was one of those men who could not live with or without Doris. She had waited for his mother to die, then his father, but these events had brought him no closer. And finally had had left the country.

"It was all I could do not to follow him to Honolulu," she concluded mournfully. "I suppose I might have, had I thought there was really any chance. The trouble with Phil was that he couldn't face up to the fact that he was in love with me."

"You were well out of it," Harry said curtly. "Phil sounds to me like a first-class heel."

"You say that because you didn't know him. You'd have liked Phil."

"The hell I would."

"What about *you*, Harry? What's kept you single this long?"

"I haven't found anyone who would have me."

"Don't look too hard." He knew there had to be a meaningful gleam in her eyes, but he could not make it out in the darkness. "Of course, I was a fool to think you'd tell me anything," she continued with a grunt. "You're a real Irishman. You speak with blarney and raddle out all my sordid little secrets. And what do I get in return? Nothing. What will anybody get? Nothing."

"Maybe there's nothing to get."

Lois Grimshawe came stumbling up the dune to whisper in Doris's ear. Then she hurried off with a "Thanks, dearie" and went to the cabin. It was very late, and the party was breaking up.

"What's on old Lois's mind?"

"She told me to ask you not to notice if Henry Barnes wasn't sleeping in the living room," she replied with a slow and careful articulation.

"You can imagine where he *will* be sleeping. Evidently, she's not 'old Lois' to him."

Lois's cabin contained two small bedrooms over the living room. The plan had been that she and Doris would occupy these while the men slept on a sofa and daybed below. "I don't give a damn where Barnes sleeps," Harry retorted. "Except I'm glad it won't be with me. He looks like a snorer."

"You're not hopelessly disgusted at our sordid little ménage?"

"Be your age, Doris!"

They finished their drinks and rose to walk back over the now deserted beach to the cabin, which was dark. Doris stumbled in the sand, and he put an arm around her waist, and as she leaned heavily against him, he knew that he was not going to resist any further. He had had many drinks, but he was not drunk, and he saw clearly that what he was going to do he might regret, but he doubted that he would regret it very much. And, anyway, what the hell? There was a touch of fall wind in the air which reminded him that he had been chaste since June.

"Oh, Harry, please come up with me," she whispered as they reached the outside stairway. She clung to him in sudden desperation. "Please, *please!* I'll be so lonely if you don't, I can't stand it."

"I'm coming, don't worry," he said and chuckled. "Go on up, scat!" And he turned her around and gave her a slap on the buttocks to send her stumbling up the stairs.

It was not so much that night that was the mistake as the following night. Doris and Lois spent all Sunday on the beach, in a hazy mood between the pleasures of remembered satisfaction and the misery of their hangovers, while Mr. Barnes slept and Harry took another of his hikes. When he returned, late again, the others were drinking cocktails, and again he drank too many, and again he slept with Doris. But this time she was soberer and more demanding, and when he rose at five, for he had to drive to a real estate closing in Jamaica, leaving the girls to come in by train, and contemplated the gently snoring figure with the messy graying hair on the bed, he knew that he was never going to share a room with Doris Marsh again.

He did not get to the office until noon, but he had not been at his desk ten minutes reading his mail when he looked up to see her in the doorway, gazing at him with limpid eyes.

"Good morning, Harry," she said softly and then continued her way down the corridor. That she did not even wait for him to return her greeting was all the proof he needed that she regarded him now as her own. Harry sighed and prepared himself for the job that had to be done.

Nor did he have much time. In ten minutes Doris was back in his doorway to ask: "How about lunch?"

"Sorry, Doris, I've got to write up a closing memo. I may just have a sandwich sent in."

"Why don't you order two, then? I'll come in and eat it with you."

"I said I was working."

"My, my, aren't we busy all of a sudden? Are you trying to avoid me?"

Her tone was light and teasing; it was obvious that she did not take his truculence seriously. Harry rose. "Step in, Doris, will you, please?" he asked abruptly and closed the door behind her. "Now let's get one thing straight," he continued, looking directly into her startled eyes, "and then everything will be easier. What happened this weekend was great fun, but it was *just* a weekend and *just* fun. Is that clear?"

"You mean you're not coming next weekend? Lois told me to ask you."

He noted how quickly she tried to shift the discussion from the general to the particular. "I'm sorry. I don't believe in repeating these things."

"It's a question of kiss and run?" She laughed with sudden harshness.

"I'm not running, Doris."

She gasped. "Do you think, Harry Reilley, that I'm the kind of girl who behaves that way every weekend?"

"Not every weekend, no."

"*Oh!*"

"Well, you don't expect me to believe I was the *first*, do you?"

The tears jumped into her eyes as she exclaimed: "What a brute you are! I should have known better than to have had anything to do with you!"

Harry was uncomfortable when she had gone, but he knew that it was better and kinder to put things in their proper setting at the earliest possible moment. Whatever Doris should say about him in the future, she would not be able to bracket him with Phil.

It had required a certain flexing of the muscles to stand up to Doris, but no similar exertion was required with Lois Grimshawe when she came to his office that afternoon.

"May I see you a minute, Mr. Reilley?" she asked from the doorway in her high, sweet, synthetic tone.

"Why, certainly, Mrs. Grimshawe."

She sat in the chair before his desk and darted her head forward so that her chin was over the edge of his blotter. "What's wrong, Harry? Doris says you won't come down next weekend. I thought we all had such a good time. Didn't you enjoy it?"

"I enjoyed it very much."

"Doris Marsh is one of the kindest, sweetest creatures that ever drew breath!"

"Exactly a reason for giving her fair warning. Before she begins to get proprietary ideas."

"You might have thought of that *before*."

"I don't see why. A good time was had by all. Can't we leave it at that?"

"But I'm not thinking of Doris. I'm thinking of you, Harry. Isn't it time you settled down? And where in the world would you find a better wife than Doris?"

"Wife!" Harry laughed, but his laugh was not pleasant. "I hardly think your role last weekend, Lois, was one that justifies your playing the outraged father with the shotgun!"

Lois's comprehension was slow, as manifested by the gradual deepening of her color behind a disconcerted stare. "I think that's a very nasty way for you to talk."

"I think you've brought up a very dangerous topic."

"Then you have no morals?"

"I have those of Devon."

At this Lois Grimshawe took her dignified departure, and Harry's popularity with the staff was over once and for all. What vicious tales she spread about him he was never to know, but Miss Gibbon only grunted now when he went to the file room and Mrs. Lane in the library gave him cursory nods in exchange for his cheerful greetings. And, needless to add, the stenographers sent to him from Lois's pool were the greenest she could find. Doris never spoke to him now and seemed to want others to observe her coolness. When they passed in the corridor, she averted her face in an unmistakable cut.

Harry's effort to convince himself that he did not care was not altogether successful. He had formed so few friendships in the firm that the loss of his easy bantering relationship with the girls on the staff made the office a cold place. Had he loved his work, it might have made the difference, or had he had any reasonable hope of a transfer to a more interesting department. He decided that if he was going to stay, he would have to reexamine his position, and to do this he determined upon an interview with the senior partner.

As he turned the corner of the corridor on his way to Clitus Tilney's office, he almost collided with the large, broad-shouldered, tweeded figure coming out.

"Hello, Harry." Tilney made a point of addressing each associate by his first name. He was about to walk on when he stopped suddenly. "Oh, Harry."

"Yes, sir?"

"Mrs. Tilney and I have never had the pleasure of seeing you in our home. I wonder if you'd care to take family supper with us next Saturday. Quite informally. At seven o'clock?"

"Why, I should like to very much. Thank you, sir."

"Good. We'll expect you, then."

Harry had heard of the Tilney suppers and had always assumed that only "disciples" were asked. Now, as he gazed in surprise after that retreating figure he grunted in self-derision at his own fatuousness for remembering what Doris had said about his future in the firm.

He would never have believed that home life in New York could be as attractive as he found it that night at the Tilneys'. The house had a dark, cool, leathery, masculine comfortableness. One felt that Mrs. Tilney had done it all, but had done it with her husband in mind. It was an ordinary brownstone in size, but the ceilings were higher than average, and the walls were covered with landscape paintings of the Hudson River school and photographs of bar groups and judges. The chairs were low and deep and hard to get out of, and the big low mosaic tables invulnerable to spilt drinks. Clitus Tilney himself turned out to be an excellent host. He moved cheerfully about the room with a big silver cocktail shaker from which he poured very cold dry martinis into chilled silver mugs. He was evidently not a man who confined his perfectionism to the law. Mrs. Tilney was attractive, in a large, serene way, but she let her husband take the lead, which Harry liked.

There were a dozen people in the room, mostly associates and their wives. Harry looked suspiciously about to see with whom Tilney had classed him, half expecting to find Doris Marsh and Lee Ozite. Would it be a pickup party for all the oddities in the office hitherto neglected by the great man? But he had immediately to admit that his suspicion was unfair. All the other men were "disciples," and as he was putting this together, Bart French, who had married the oldest Tilney girl, came up to him.

"Good to see you, Harry. You'll find my father-in-law makes a *very* dry martini."

"Is that a warning or a compliment?"

"Both, I guess."

Harry was not sure that he liked being made to feel at home by French, and he looked stiffly at that long oval brown face with the tired eyes that Doris Marsh had once described as charming. French was what Harry called a "boy scout." He was always pretending that, like the other clerks, he had to live on his salary.

"Quite a place your old man's got here."

"Isn't it?" French responded eagerly. "What I think of as a real lawyer's house. I hope someday I'll be able to afford one like it."

"Can't you now?'

"On what they pay us clerks at 65 Wall? Fat chance!"

"But I thought you had a large private income."

"I don't know what you call large," French muttered, and moved away, obviously put out by such bad form.

Harry was delighted to have ruffled him so easily. Besides, there was someone far better to contemplate, as he finished his drink, than Bart French, and that was the youngest Tilney daughter, who had just entered the room. He learned that her name was Fran from the nice old gray woman passing cheese and that she taught English at Miss Irvin's School. She was thin and pale, with soft long auburn hair and small brown eyes that had an odd shine, almost a glitter. Her face was the least bit long and features very delicate, her nose turned up and her skin, Harry observed as he moved closer, almost translucent. Despite the slightness of her frame and the quick nervous gesticulations of her arms, she conveyed, in the rapid, soft tone that he could just hear across the room, the sense of a brittle, bright intelligence. Taking his refilled drink to a corner by a globe of the world that he could pretend to be turning, he resumed his contemplation of Miss Tilney. Suddenly she turned, as if aware of his gaze, and walked over to him.

"You must be Harry Reilley. I'm Fran Tilney. We're going in to supper now, and you're next to me. Can you bear it?"

Harry would not have thought, as he followed her down the narrow stairway to the dining room, that anything could have spoiled that evening, and yet her very first question at the table did so.

"What do you do in the office? Are you in 'green goods,' too?"

This was a term used downtown, always with a perfunctory snicker, to describe the department which dealt with corporate securities. Every other lawyer at the party was in "green goods."

"No, I'm an untouchable," he said gruffly. "I'm in real estate."

"But that must be interesting, too. Or at least basic."

"As interesting as anything else, I guess."

"That doesn't sound as if you had a very high opinion of the law."

He shrugged. "It's a living. If it was too much fun, people wouldn't pay you to do it."

Miss Tilney looked at him more closely. She was a very serious girl. "But Daddy *loves* his work."

"I daresay. But he's on top of the heap."

"It's not a question of his being on top, Mr. Reilley. It's a question of his caring about his profession."

"I beg your pardon, Miss Tilney. It's a question of his having hired help to take care of the boring details."

"I never heard anything so cynical," she exclaimed, obviously shocked. "In a learned profession none of the details should be boring."

"But they are. Writing up all that small print so the client can get out of a bad bargain." Harry paused, marveling that the urge to be unpleasant at the expense of his superiors could be stronger than the urge to make friends with a beautiful girl. "Your father's a very clever man, you know. He knows he has to idealize the law for the benefit of all those young men who follow him around like faithful hounds. If he didn't make them feel like Jesuit missionaries, they wouldn't be happy, and if they weren't happy, they wouldn't work so well."

It was clear that no such heresy had been talked in the Tilney house before. "You mean Daddy says things he doesn't *mean?*"

"Let's put it that he counts on different interpretations at different levels."

"Of which mine must be the lowest!"

He saw that he was making her really angry and bitterly regretted his course. But it seemed like a one-way street; he had to go to the end to turn around. "You're not a lawyer," he tried to explain. "But your dad certainly knows that the greater part of securities work is jamming as many ads into a prospectus as one can slip under the nose of the Securities Exchange Commission."

"I think you'll find the facts to be otherwise if you take the trouble to look into them," she said in a chilling tone. "My father cares passionately that only the exact truth be stated in his prospectuses."

"What is truth? Pilate asked."

"I really can't understand, if you feel that way, why you work for Tower, Tilney at all."

"I told you, it's a living."

"Surely there must be an easier one."

"Let me know if you hear of it."

She turned away abruptly to the man on her other side, and Harry was graced with her back for the rest of the meal. After dinner, too, she avoided him, and it was only when he was leaving and had the excuse to bid her goodnight that there was an opportunity for further interchange.

"I guess you only talk to green goods. The poor 'basic' real estate man has hardly had a word with you all evening."

"It's not that at all, Mr. Reilley. I haven't talked to you because it seemed to me you had such a poor opinion of us all."

"Of you all? Not of you, surely."

"Oh, I don't pretend to set myself apart."

Something tore now in his heart at the stupidity of it. Particularly when he sensed, in the very tensity of her anger, that she, too, was aware of something in the atmosphere between them. "Look, Miss Tilney. No, let me call you Fran. I've been an awful ass tonight, saying a lot of things I didn't mean at all. Playing the cheap cynic. The only thing I really wanted to tell you was what a beautiful, bright girl I think you are. Give me another chance, will you? Let me take you out to dinner some night. Any night you say. I'd like to show you I'm not a complete hick." They were standing alone, by the door to the living room, and she was staring at him with intent, startled eyes. "How about it? Tuesday night?" She still said nothing. "Are you too mad at me? Or are you engaged to be married, or something like that?"

"No, nothing like that," she said at last and laughed flatly. "I'll be glad to go out with you on Tuesday, Mr. Reilley. Harry, I mean."

He had to walk home that night to work off his excitement. What he marveled at most, as he looked back over the evening, was the miracle of his own apology at the last moment. If she had gone to bed early, if she had slipped out of the house for a later engagement, or if she had even been standing with her father when he came up to bid her good-night, all would have been lost. She would have gone out of his life forever. It would have been simply another closed chapter in the long wasteful history of his truculence. Never before could he remember having experienced so sudden an attraction. He had not even dared to shake her hand in leaving. And she had been glad he hadn't, too. Oh, yes. She had felt some of the same pull. It was a pity that she should be quite so identified with her father's firm, but that was something he could not help. The whole evening, for that matter, was showing signs of developing into something that he could not help. And where, after all, had helping things got him?

She was waiting in the front hall when he called on Tuesday night. Not for her was the pose at the piano, the startled look at the clock, the "Good heavens, is it seven already?" She tucked her arm under his as they went down the steep stoop and suggested an Italian restaurant on Third Avenue.

"I see you have my pocketbook in mind," he said as they got into a taxi.

"Well, I hate to see a lot of money spent on ravioli. And ravioli is what I've been looking forward to all day."

Harry reflected that to some men her abruptness in taking the lead might have been slightly offensive. But he felt no need to assert himself in the matter of the choice of restaurants. As he watched her, he saw her shoulders twitch, in a sudden involuntary spasm. Was she afraid of what she was doing, afraid of going out with him? Because he wasn't the right type of young man? He wondered if she had told her father.

At the restaurant he ordered a cocktail and she a glass of Dubonnet. She ordered it with the promptness of a habitual nondrinker who knows that a man likes her to have something in her hand. He guessed that she would not finish it, which turned out to be correct. He guessed later that she would drink one glass of red wine with her ravioli, and this, too, turned out to be right.

"I behaved very badly at your family's the other night," he apologized again. "When I'm faced with people whom I basically admire, or even

envy, like your father, I have a tendency to revert to the nasty little boy
I once was. I try to tear them down. My father went to jail when I was
fourteen, and I suppose a psychiatrist would say that I can't admit that
anyone else's could be any better."

He watched her carefully as he said this to see if she would set her face
in the mask of the young lady determined to show that she can't be
shocked. But she was quite natural. "Your father went to jail! How
perfectly horrible for you."

"It wasn't fun."

"What had he done? Or what did they say he'd done? Or would you
rather not talk about it?"

"No, I was the one who brought it up. Of course I'll talk about it. My
dad was guilty of the dullest of crimes. He was caught with his hand in
the company till. And it wasn't to get money for his wife and kiddies,
either. It was for more exotic pleasures."

"Poor man, I hope he enjoyed them."

"Don't feel too sorry for him. He felt sorry enough for himself. In
fact, he died of self-pity. Not to mention the unkind cracks of his
youngest born."

"Was that you? You mustn't mind. We always exaggerate our meanness to the dead."

"Not I," Harry retorted with a bitter laugh. "I won't horrify you by
giving particulars."

She was too wise to insist. "When I hear about other people's hard
lives, I realize how easy my own has been," she said ruefully. "I've been
very spoiled. Or blessed, as they call it."

"My life hasn't really been hard. But I was banking on your thinking
it was. I figured, if I shot off my mouth about my old man, you'd forgive
me for being such a crumb the other night."

"You don't mean you made it all up?"

"Oh, no, it's true enough," he reassured her, smiling at her instant
spurt of indignation. "God knows, it's true enough. My father was
always sentimental about ideals. That's what made me distrust them."

"Daddy's not unlike you, you know. He has his black moods, too.
The days when he describes Tower, Tilney & Webb as 'Shyster, Beagle
and Shyster.' "

"As *what*?"

"It was the name of the law firm in an old Marx Brothers comedy.

Mother can always tell Daddy's mood by the sound of his step in the hall. If she looks up from her needlepoint when he comes in and asks: 'How's Shyster, Beagle and Shyster?' then I know it's one of *those* days."

"You make your old man sound almost human."

"Oh, Daddy's the most human person in the world! You'd love him, Harry, if you got to know him."

Harry smiled at the incongruity of such a verb to describe any potential relationship between himself and the senior partner. "Of course, he asked me to dinner," he allowed. "I owe him a lot for that, no matter how snooty his green goods boys are."

"Are they snooty?"

"Well, I think they are," Harry said with a shrug. "But maybe it's just because I'm not one of them. Does your father know you're out with me tonight?"

She looked away. "I didn't tell him."

"Why not?"

"Because I don't tell Daddy everything I'm doing," she retorted with an edge of irritation. "Why should I?"

"Not because he'd hate to have his daughter going out with a mick?"

"Oh, *Harry!*"

"I'm serious. Do you know that I have a brother who's a priest? And two first cousins who are nuns? How would that sit in his Presbyterian soul?"

"My father is above religious prejudice," Fran said with dignity. "Besides, he'd never have asked you to the house if he'd objected to our being friends."

"Oh, so that's it. You wouldn't have gone out with me if I hadn't been asked to the house?"

"Really, you're too ridiculous. I wouldn't have known you if you hadn't been asked to the house. But if you can't get that log off your shoulder, I'm going to take myself straight home."

"No, no, Fran, please don't do that. I promise to be good." He took her hand calmly and folded it in both of his, but, although obviously surprised, she made no motion to pull it away. "Don't worry about the church. I haven't been to mass in a year. Only you probably mind that even more. All right, I'll go. Next Sunday. Or with you to your church."

"I don't know where you got the notion that either I or Daddy are such bugs on religion. Honestly, I don't care if you're a Moslem."

"Be careful now or *I'll* be shocked. That's the way with bad Catholics. We want all you Protestants to be good as gold."

It was now apparent that they were going to be the best of friends. There had been talk in the taxi of a movie, but they went instead to a bar where they sat in a booth and she drank gingerale while he drank beer. He talked an outrageous amount about himself, even working in the Korean war and the wound in his leg. She listened perfectly, but she talked, too. For the Korean war he had to hear about the girls in her Shakespeare class at Miss Irvin's. It was all very fair. In the taxi afterwards, as they drew up at her door, he kissed her. It was a very light and gentle kiss, and like the Dubonnet there was only one of them, but he did not press her for a second. He had made enough botches for one lifetime. Something had intervened in his destiny, and he was learning to be wise enough to give it a free hand.

2
—

Lee Ozite, "Ozey," as he was known to all, received a tense, minute-to-minute satisfaction, during the working hours of the day, in his merited reputation for efficiency. "Have you asked Ozey about that?" or "Has anyone put Ozey on the job?" was the first question a partner would ask when brought to a halt by any kind of procedural snag. As managing clerk it was his duty to see that the court calendars were answered, the papers served on time and the litigators notified of their dates for oral argument, but his jurisdiction, spurred by his own eagerness, had spread to cover traffic tickets, tips to court clerks, detectives in morals cases, any field, in fact, where the right word to the right person could solve the difficulties of the individual in conflict with the minor officers of organized society. To assist him he had three night law students who worked a six-hour day running his errands over the city and calling in every hour, when he would give them a further task or else cry: "Head in!" in the bark of an operations officer sitting over a map. It made for a busy and satisfying day, but sometimes during the long evenings in Queens, where he lived in an apartment with his old mother and aunt, he would suffer doubts about his position in the office. Were the jocular compliments of the partners sincerely meant? Or was he just poor old Ozey with his panting law students and his ringing telephones? Like a mouse on a treadwheel?

At such moments he would become absolutely still except for his almond eyes, which moved furtively from side to side. His aunt would glance up from her detective story and comment that he was looking like a Buddha again. And Miss Ozite was right; there was something synthetically Oriental about her nephew, something of Charlie Chan, something grinning and hand rubbing and faintly sinister. Fortunately, at just the right moment, somebody always laughed, and Ozey laughed with them.

"But someday I won't," he would tell himself grimly. "Someday I'll have the last laugh."

His fear of being laughed at had a natural counterpart in his fear of being unattractive to women. He realized, intellectually, that this fear was a foolish one. Ozey was bald on the top of his head and inclined to be fleshy, but his round head and face and firm, well-formed features went well with baldness, and his extra weight was evenly distributed over a short but muscular body. He liked to think of himself as the bald, sexually potent Siamese monarch in *The King and I*. But he could never get over the apprehension that women, particularly "ladies," would find him somehow unpalatable, perhaps, dreadful thought, even "greasy," and his sexual experiences — up to his present and thirty-sixth year — had all been purchased.

But Ozey had one great hope, and that was marriage. He knew that women were more interested in marriage than in anything else and that they gave even unlikely proposals their most serious consideration. Ozey felt that allied to a handsome, good-tempered woman of size — he always pictured her as larger than himself — he would be surer of the respect of the world that he had to face. He had another vision of Lee Ozite, again as the Siamese potentate but this time drawn in fiercer lines, a touch of Tamburlaine added, leading a large white naked Christian slave girl by a slender cord about her neck. Of course he would be nice to her, very nice to her. And the more he entertained this vision, the more he saw Doris Marsh in the role of the docile captive.

In real life, however, and as a tax associate, she ranked the managing clerk, and he would never forget her cool, justified reproach when one of his boys had filed a tax return at the wrong bureau. Yet on all other occasions she had been perfectly friendly, perfectly democratic. Unlike some of the associates, she gave herself no airs and would linger in his office after checking the calendar for a few minutes of chat and jokes. When she leaned over his desk to read the law journal that was always spread out there, the proximity of her breasts and the sound of her breathing excited him uncomfortably. She was just the height of his Christian slave and had the same white soft skin. He would have preferred blond hair to black and gray, but, after all, the real world could never match fantasy. Was she aware of the effect upon him? Was she tantalizing him? When he had asked her once to lunch, she had agreed readily enough, and they had had a pleasant hour of shop talk, but when he had tried to push away the money that she handed him for the check, she had simply laughed and said: "Come now, Ozey. This isn't a date."

Did she mean she wouldn't have had one with him? Ozey brooded furiously all that afternoon. But when he left the office, she happened to be going down in the same elevator and told him: "I enjoyed our lunch, Ozey. Do you realize not one of the other lawyers except Harry Reilley has ever asked me? You might think I was some kind of pariah." Ozey was too thrilled to sit, in the subway, and all the way home he hung on a strap in a half-empty car, calculating the wisdom of a sudden proposal. She would be startled, to be sure. It might be fun to see just how startled she would be. There would be something titillating about marching into her office and suggesting the most intimate of relationships without a single preliminary. Right there and then, before the set of Prentice-Hall tax services and before she had had time to take off her glasses. Could she *afford* to turn him down? Shrewdly, rather meanly, he assessed her. She was near thirty; she would never be a partner; she was an orphan of obscure origin. Yet as Mrs. Ozite all these liabilities would immediately become assets. She would not be too much younger than her husband or too much more successful a lawyer, and she would bring no tiresome in-laws. Besides, since she was a professional woman, his mother and aunt were bound to dislike her, which would make the inevitable break with his own family a cleaner, neater thing.

If Ozey, however, was precipitate in his thinking, he was cautious in his actions, and it was a good two months from the day of their lunch to the day of his decision to ask her for a date. But as he stood in the doorway of her office with a sheepish smile, the question fluttering about his lips, she anticipated him.

"Ozey! I was just coming to see *you*."

"Well, that's nice."

"Can you lunch with me? Or rather *on* me. I want to take you out and buy you a cocktail and pick your brains. It's a personal matter."

He grinned broadly. "You mean a date?"

"Would it were anything so pleasant." She frowned and shook her head. "The fact of the matter, Ozey, is that I'm in a bit of trouble, and I need your advice."

"What are we waiting for? Let's go!"

In the restaurant Doris drank a martini rapidly and then, to his surprise, ordered another. She seemed very agitated, as if she were finding it cruelly difficult to bring out whatever was on her mind. He watched her closely.

"You'd just better spit it out, Doris. Try to pretend I'm not here."

She turned to him with a sudden defiance as if he had merged with his whole sex into a single enemy. "Very well, I'm pregnant," she declared. "I'm having a baby, and I've got to get rid of it. It's very early, so it shouldn't be too hard." She seemed to sense now from his gaping face that he, at least, was without responsibility for her plight. "I've come to you, Ozey," she continued in a humbler tone, the tears starting to her eyes, "because I don't know where else to turn. They all say you can do anything. I thought you might be able to get me a decent doctor."

Pregnant! Ozey was transfixed. For a few moments he could not swallow, so thick was his throat, so wild and overwhelming his mental pictures. So *that* was what his tall, cool tax girl had been up to while he was blushing for the fantasies of what he had wanted to do with her! At first this new idea of her moral abandonment made her even more desirable, and he felt himself swooped up by the dizzy thought that he could have been the father of her child. But then the truth and jealousy, like a team of plowhorses, came crashing into the fragile barn of his illusions.

"Who is the man? Do I know him?"

Ozey's aggressive tone took her by surprise. "What does that matter?"

"A lot. If he's in the office, I don't want the risk of speaking to him. Much less of shaking his filthy paw!"

"But, Ozey, he doesn't even know!"

"Then he *is* in the office?"

Doris seemed helpless before this new complication. "All right, he is.

But what good will a quarrel between you and him do me? Please, Ozey, can't you help me?"

"Of course I can help you. I can get you the best doctor in the business this afternoon. It won't be cheap, but what's that when your life might be at stake? And if you can't raise the money, I'll lend it to you."

"Oh, Ozey." Her tears fell freely now. "What a friend you are. What a kind, true friend. What a man. What a real man."

"You needn't worry," he said with a swelling heart. "I shan't make a scene with your friend. I shall go to him quietly and firmly and see that he pays your doctor, if nothing else."

Doris looked at him with murky eyes. "I'm in your hands, Ozey. I must do as you say. I must trust to your discretion. It was Harry Reilley."

"Harry Reilley!"

Reilley was the associate whom Ozey most admired in the office. He was not only large and blond and easily sure of himself, qualities notably lacking in Ozey, but he was somehow above, or at least aside from, the petty rivalries of the hierarchy. There was absolutely no difference in the way Reilley spoke to Ozey and in the way he spoke to Clitus Tilney. Ozey had been pleased, rather than soured, by the current office rumor that Reilley was taking out the senior partner's daughter. But now!

"I thought he was after the Tilney girl," he said in a flat voice.

"No doubt he is," Doris said bitterly. "Dear Harry makes a brave show of being one of the people when all he really wants is to marry the boss's daughter. I was just a rung in his ladder. And a fool not to have known it."

Ozey wondered from what level to what Doris's "rung" had conducted her ruthless lover, but she was obviously in no mood for analytic inquiry. Besides, the maddening idea that Harry's open, candid front had all along been only the mask of a mercenary ambition made him want to believe her. What did Reilley really think of Ozey? As a poor sap, grateful for a smile and a clap on the shoulder, who would still be managing clerk (if he was lucky) when the firm was known as Tower, Tilney & Reilley?

"I guess we've both been rungs in Mr. Reilley's ladder," he said bitterly. "But Mr. Reilley hasn't reached the top of that ladder yet. And rungs can break, you know. And send him toppling down."

"He's a cheap, lying Irishman! And if that's what Miss Tilney wants, with all *her* advantages, all I can say is that I congratulate her on a splendid match!"

For the rest of their lunch they tore Harry to pieces, but over the coffee they turned to the matter in hand. It was agreed that Doris, who had still a week of vacation due her, would take it starting the following Monday and that Ozey would get hold of his doctor that afternoon.

Everything proceeded as smoothly as matters ordinarily did in Ozey's department. It took him only two discreet telephone calls to secure the doctor, and on Monday the abortion was successfully performed. Ozey had visited the doctor on Sunday and paid him a thousand dollars in cash. It had contributed not a little to his excitement that he had obviously been regarded as the father. When he called on Doris at her apartment on his way home from work, three days after the operation, he found her in a dressing gown, a bit pale and teary, but very grateful and glad to see him. She threw her arms around him and gave him a hug.

"Oh, Ozey, you old darling, how good of you to come. Do you know I haven't even told Madge?" Madge was the girl with whom she shared the apartment. "She thinks I've just got some woman's trouble. Which God knows I have! But what a friend *you've* been, Ozey. Sometimes I think my only friend!"

She insisted on moving about the room to mix him a drink, to get him an ashtray, although he begged her to sit still, and when they were settled at last, she kept staring at him with eyes of poignant humility. Ozey was pleased with the change from the easy, assured professional woman, and it somehow seemed, because he had produced the money and the doctor, because he was sitting there in the full armor of a business suit while she was vulnerably attired in an old blue dressing gown and a pair of soiled pink slippers, that it was he and not Reilley who had brought her to this sorry pass. He shuddered with excitement at the idea that one good tug at that dressing gown could transform her into his Christian slave.

"I *want* to be your friend, Doris," he muttered. "You can't imagine how much I've always wanted to be your friend."

The next morning, at half past nine, Ozey went to Harry Reilley's office and demanded in a barking tone the price of the abortion. Harry's face hardened as he listened.

"Assuming that all you say is true and that I was responsible, why should I deal with you?"

"Because I'm acting for Doris. And because I paid the money."

"Why don't you get it from her, then?"

"Do you mean to tell me, Reilley, that you'd put all the expense on her?" Ozey's voice became high and shrill. "Is that the kind of guy you are?"

"Now wait a minute, wait a minute," Harry said angrily, "before we start the name-calling. Since you seem to know so much about it, you may as well get it all straight. Doris and I spent a weekend together. She was just as keen on the idea as I was. But a girl her age who's been smart enough to be admitted to the bar ought to be smart enough to take precautions. I don't see why I should be stuck with the whole cost of that weekend — always assuming, of course, that it *was* that weekend . . ."

"You cad!" Ozey cried, jumping to his feet.

Harry was on his feet at the same moment, and with a heavy hand on Ozey's shoulder, he pushed him roughly back into his chair. "Now let's take it easy, shall we? Let's not get ourselves hurt. I don't know why you're involved in this, and I'm not going to ask. But in return for my tact, I insist that you appreciate my position. I do *not* know that I'm the guy who knocked Doris up. But I admit I might be. And considering all the factors in the situation — and a few that you don't know about — I think I'm doing a hell of a lot more than most men would do in offering you five hundred bucks."

Ozey debated the beautiful gesture of spurning this, but when he left Harry's office he had the check in his billfold, postdated to give Harry time to raise the money. As he passed Mr. Tilney's office on his way back to his own, he felt that the dragging weight of his hatred for Reilley was what brought him to a halt. He took a quick step past Miss Clinger's desk and pushed his head boldly in the open doorway.

"May I see you a minute, Mr. Tilney?"

Tilney looked up in surprise. His dealings with the managing clerk were infrequent and usually handled through Miss Clinger. "What can I do for you, Mr. Ozite?"

Even with his present preoccupation, Ozey had a sour moment to reflect that Tilney made a point of calling the other associates by their first names. "It's a personal matter, sir. May I close the door?"

Tilney stared. "Oh, I hardly think that will be necessary."

"I mean personal to you, sir," Ozey explained. "It's about your daughter."

Tilney's eyes flashed forbiddingly, but he rose, walked quickly to close his door and then turned to face Ozey with his full height and presence. "Now, Mr. Ozite," he said softly, "will you be good enough to tell me what's on your mind?"

"It's about Mr. Reilley, sir. Harry Reilley."

"You said it was about my daughter."

"I mean that it concerns your daughter, sir. I doubt if you will wish her to have any more dates with Mr. Reilley when you hear what I have to say."

"Hearing about my daughter in one thing," Tilney said irately. "Hearing tales by one associate about another is a different matter. You may go, Mr. Ozite."

Ozey, dazed with anger and humiliation, almost ran to the door. To his surprise, Tilney continued to bar his way.

"Pray excuse me, sir."

But Tilney remained there, motionless. Then he suddenly rubbed a hand over his broad brow. "I'm sorry, Mr. Ozite," he said, blinking. He walked slowly back to his desk. "I spoke too rapidly. Please be good enough to forgive me and tell me what you know about Mr. Reilley."

He resumed his seat and bent his shaggy gray head over his desk as Ozey, standing in the middle of the room, told him in a high, clear, excited tone of the iniquities of Harry Reilley.

"I see," Tilney said gravely when he had finished. "Thank you very much. Of course, we don't know what degree of enticement Miss Marsh may have exercised."

"Miss Marsh is a lady, sir!" Ozey exclaimed. "As much of a lady as any member of your own family."

Tilney looked up and regarded Ozey with a quizzical expression. "Did she behave as ladies behave?"

"When they're seduced, sir, yes!"

Tilney looked back down at his desk, and Ozey had the uneasy suspicion that he might be hiding a smile. "If you have Miss Marsh's interests so much at heart, Mr. Ozite, it occurs to me that you might have considered the damage to her position in the firm of such a revelation to me."

"I *have* considered it, sir!" Ozey exclaimed in triumph. "Miss Marsh will no longer have a position in the firm. She is planning to resign at the end of the year."

Tilney glanced up again quickly. "Oh, see here, I don't say anything like that is going to be necessary."

"It's not for the reason you think, sir."

"Oh? Has she been offered a better job?"

"Yes. As Mrs. Lee Ozite!"

As Tilney, after a rather blank stare, smiled and rose to congratulate him, Ozey felt with pride that the senior partner was for once overwhelmed. He, Ozey, had taken the lead in their short interview and had held it to the end. It was only much later that it occurred to him that Mr. Tilney's predominant reaction might have been simple embarrassment.

3
—

Clitus Tilney was sick at heart. He was sure that he would never again be able to think of Harry Reilley except in reference to the shabby tale told him by his smirking managing clerk. Harry's assets and liabilities had barely balanced before this splashing entry had dyed his statement in irredeemable red. Tilney had liked the young man well enough and had admired his forthright manner and seeming straightness, but when Fran had taken him up, in her own determined way, he had reflected ruefully on the Irish Catholic background and the criminal parent which, for all his sincere efforts to overcome his upstate, small-town prejudices, seemed still to have a natural connection. And now Miss Marsh! To have seduced a bespectacled, pathetic old-maid tax lawyer! For Tilney irritably brushed aside the memory of flitting moments, passing her in the corridor and greeted by her low, pleasant "Good morning, sir," when he had thought of her as something else. And, for Reilley to have come from the sweaty pleasures of Miss Marsh's couch to flirt with his own daughter at the dinner table! And then to chisel on the cost of the abortion and send poor Miss Marsh to the arms of such a one as Ozite. No, the man was obviously a lecher of the coarsest sort who was after Fran for whatever promotion he could get out of her father.

How far had things gone with Fran? Alas, Tilney was almost sure that she was in love with him. He knew that she had been out with him half a dozen times at least, and she was perfectly frank now about her interest in him. Only that morning at breakfast she had begged him to try Harry in green goods, and her face had been radiant when he had said he would consider it. Of course Reilley had put her up to it. And then Ada, too, had been all for Reilley, and had lectured him roundly when he had muttered his doubts about the Reilley background. Ada, whose instinct about people he had always considered so flawless! He groaned aloud as he thought of his Fran, his youngest and favorite child, as pure and fine and good as God had ever made a woman, with a power of sympathy and love to raise a man to greatness, wasted on such a cynical wretch. And a Catholic to boot. Even if she woke up to what he was, he would probably refuse her a divorce!

After a miserable hour of these considerations he summoned Harry to his office and, turning his chair away to the window, he dryly reported the facts that he had learned from Ozite, ending with the terse question: "I suppose it's all so?"

"Yes, sir. It's so."

Tilney whirled around in his chair to face the stiff, truculent young man whose hands, he at once noticed, were clenched. "If you have anything to add to that statement," he snapped, "I'd be glad to hear it."

"I have nothing to add."

"In these matters I like to think I'm not a complete Victorian," Tilney grumbled, but in a more reasonable tone. "I realize a young man can be inveigled into situations."

"I'm not that young a man, sir."

Tilney surveyed him critically. He liked the fact that Harry sought no excuses. "What pains me most about the whole wretched business is how recent it was."

"I'll say only this, sir. It was all over *before* I met your daughter."

"Yet it can't have been more than a matter of days." Harry was silent. "Well, Fran's not a child," Tilney continued with a sigh. "She can make up her own mind about it. You realize, of course, I'll have to tell her?"

Some of the obstinacy faded from Harry's eyes. "Would you have to tell her if I didn't see her anymore?"

"No, I don't suppose I would," Tilney said slowly, surprised. "Of course, I don't know how things are between you. Or how much of a shock it would be to her."

"That's not for me to say, sir. But I'm sure it's not anything she won't get over. There's been no engagement between us." Harry flushed as he added: "Or anything else you need worry about."

"Thank you, Harry," Tilney responded in a kinder tone than he had ever expected to use again to the young man. "Well, suppose we try it that way? And see what happens?"

"As you wish, sir."

Tilney felt worse when Reilley had left than before he had come. He tried to interpret Reilley's willingness to give up Fran first as indifference and then as simple sullenness, but he was not successful. He had an uncomfortable suspicion that the young man's feelings for his daughter were of a very different variety from those (if any) that he had entertained for Miss Marsh. And the very fact that the latter had so rapidly consoled herself with such a man as Ozite was evidence that she had not been too deeply involved with Reilley. But where Tilney remained adamant was in his conviction that he would still be acting in his daughter's best interests to get Reilley out of her life.

He did not dare tell Ada, for he was afraid that she would disagree, and he wondered how he was to bear alone Fran's silent unhappiness — for he knew it would be silent — in the terrible breakfasts that were bound to follow. The next morning and the one after were without incident, but on the third Fran asked him: "Daddy, tell me. Did you ever move Harry to green goods?"

"Not yet, dear. But I have it in mind."

"Do you happen to know if he's working particularly hard at the moment?"

"Well, most of the boys *are* pretty busy. I don't happen to know about him. Why?"

"Oh, nothing. I just thought he might have called me about something. It doesn't matter."

When she had left for school, Ada turned to him.

"You don't suppose Harry's lost interest, do you?"

"I haven't the faintest idea," Tilney retorted irritably. "And I'm not at all sure I care if he has. Fran can do a lot better than Harry Reilley."

"But she *cares*, Clitus. I'm warning you. She cares!"

"I'll be seeing him tonight at the firm dinner. *If* he comes," he added, remembering Harry's truculent face. "I'll find out if he's been working nights."

"Why don't you bring him home for a drink afterwards?"

"Because I shall be tired and want to go to bed," he said snappishly, and raised his paper between them to run his eye down the obituary column.

The firm had a semiannual men's dinner at the University Club where it was customary for certain of the partners to speak on the highlights of the season's practice. Tilney sat in the middle of the principal table, between Chambers Todd and Waldron Webb, and was grateful that he did not have to speak that night, for he could think only of Fran. The image of her pale face and of the glimmer of pain in her eyes had ejected every other from his mind. He noticed Harry Reilley at a far table and heard the sound of his loud laugh. It was too loud, that laugh, too defiant. Tilney wondered if he was drinking too much and regretted the custom of having bottles of whiskey on the table.

Chambers Todd was the last speaker and discussed a committee of the City Bar Association of which he was chairman and whose other members he was trying to persuade to recommend to the State Legislature the abolition of an excise tax that was particularly onerous to a trucking client. There was nothing in the subject to distract Tilney from his speculations on the effect of Harry's defection. Would it kill Fran, as sometimes happened in Victorian novels? Would she droop and pine away? Or would she master her sorrow and never show it, but remain for the rest of her days a bright, brittle, useful, dryly smiling old maid, a sacrifice to her father's prejudice? Tilney suddenly leaned forward and put both hands over his face, and Waldron Webb whispered in his ear: "Are you all right, Clitus?"

"Oh, yes, yes."

The speeches were over, and he rose to indicate that the meeting was adjourned. As he lingered to light a cigar and to let the firm file out of the doorway, he saw Harry Reilley walk over to Todd. What followed he could not help but overhear as both men had carrying voices.

"May I ask you a question, Mr. Todd?"

"Go right ahead, my dear fellow." Todd was mellow with the evening's whiskey and the sense of a successful address.

"In your speech tonight you spoke of using your position on a bar association committee in favor of a client. Isn't it the duty of committee members to render unbiased opinions on behalf of the association?"

Todd's heavy features congealed as he took in the unexpected attack. "You speak like a first-year law student," he said curtly. "If you ever have the good fortune to secure a big company as a client, you will learn that the word 'unbiased' has no further meaning for you. A good lawyer doesn't forget his clients when he closes his shop. A good lawyer eats, lives and breathes for his clients. A good lawyer represents his clients even in his sleep!"

Harry laughed unpleasantly. "I had been wondering what the difference was between your kind of lawyer and a lobbyist. Now I see there's none!"

Tilney stepped forward to touch the young man on the arm. "I want to talk to you, Harry." He turned abruptly and walked to a corner to get away from the now livid Todd. "I can't let you commit suicide like that," he continued. "Come back to my house and have a drink with me."

"Won't Fran be there?"

"I don't know. It doesn't matter."

Harry stared. "You mean the ban's off?"

"Must you tie me down? I mean I won't fight you anymore."

The glitter in the young man's eyes went far to convince Tilney that he had done the right thing. "She'll be sore as hell I haven't called her."

"Tell her you were out of town. Invent a business trip. I'll back you up. That's easy. The guy who has the really tough job is the guy who's going to have to save your neck from Chambers Todd. And that guy is me!"

In the taxi Tilney tried to reduce some of the constraint between them by reverting to Harry's interchange with Todd. "Actually, I agree with what you said. I wish we could return to the old days of greater integrity. When a lawyer could argue one interpretation of a statute in the morning and its opposite in the afternoon. Before we were captured by the corporations. Before we became simple mouthpieces."

"It doesn't worry me as much as I made it appear," Harry replied with a candid laugh. "I'm used to politicians in my family. My old man knew so many. What I can't stand is sanctimoniousness. And your partner, Mr. Todd, is sanctimonious."

Tilney wondered if he shouldn't object to such familiarity. "You don't like Mr. Todd?"

"I don't like any of them, to tell the truth, Mr. Tilney. Except yourself. I've just about decided that your firm is not the place for me."

"Well, don't let's make the decision tonight," Tilney said hastily. "If you and I get along, it's always possible to work something out. The partners aren't all Chambers Todds. Wait till you know them better."

"It's up to you, sir. If you say stay, I'll stay." He laughed again. "I guess it's pretty clear that I want to see Fran."

Tilney had figured out that Ada would wait up for him on the chance that he might have learned something about Harry, and he was correct. Yet with her usual control she did not manifest the least surprise at seeing his companion. When Fran came in from the library, where she had been correcting homework, she was equally impassive.

"Good evening, Mr. Reilley."

Harry got up and took her by the hands. "I'm sorry, Fran. I was sent up to Boston on a rush closing. I haven't had a minute."

"Not even to telephone?"

"You know how things are. Ask your father."

Fran looked around at her father and then shook her head dubiously. "You both look so foxy. What have you been up to? Sometimes I think I hate lawyers."

"Perhaps you should get them a drink, Fran," her mother suggested.

"I think it's the last thing either of them needs."

But when she turned to go to the dining room, Tilney knew that the damage had already been repaired. It was only the tiniest shadow on the sky of his relief that Harry should have lied so convincingly. There were things about that young man that he was obviously never going to understand. But, as Ada would have said, *he* was not going to marry him. There had to be a point where he stopped playing senior partner at home.

4
—
꿎

In the large square room decorated with light blue wallpaper and French travel posters showing the châteaux of the Loire Valley, Fran stood by a window, gazing down at the East River, while her class of tenth graders wrote their ten-minute theme on *Cymbeline*. In her mind she was writing a theme of her own, for she had to do something to keep within bounds the agitation of her happiness. Her theme was about the heroines of the romantic comedies, Imogen, Helena, Portia, Rosalind, those noble, radiant, resourceful women, so finely intelligent, so pure and yet so gay, so graceful in men's clothing and yet so innately feminine, who come to us somehow embellished even by the fulsome encomiums of Victorian admirers, somehow in the images of tall, golden-toned actresses on old postcards. She was too happy to be in the least ashamed of her own exuberant conceit in likening herself to them.

"Miss Tilney?"

"Yes, Gretchen." Gretchen Kay was always the first to ask a question after the theme. She was the serious girl of the class, nervous, dark and disliked by the others.

"Wasn't it very bad of Posthumus to make a wager on Imogen's virtue? And then to let her be tested?"

"Very bad."

"And to want to kill her afterwards?"

"No, I don't think that was as bad," Fran answered, turning from the window. "After all, he thought her faithless."

"Yes, but even if she had been, was that a reason for *killing* her?"

"Perhaps." Fran shrugged lightly. "In those days. People were more violent then."

"Would it have been all right for her to kill him if *he'd* been faithless?"

"Oh, no." Fran was very sure about this. "That would have been altogether different. None of the comedy heroines have men who are worthy of them. Except perhaps Rosalind. Bassanio was after Portia's money, and Bertram had to be trapped into loving Helena. And Posthumus — well, we've seen how *he* behaved. But I sometimes think the goodness of the heroines depends on their having to put up with such things. If the men were as good as the women, wouldn't the women seem a bit dull?"

"Do you think that's true in real life, Miss Tilney? Is it better for a girl to go with a boy who's mercenary or faithless or unkind?"

The other girls laughed mockingly, but Fran did not join them. "It may be, Gretchen," she said gravely. "It may indeed."

She was troubled for the rest of the morning, as well as surprised, by her own ready acceptance of what had seemed at first the idlest of speculations. She was afraid that she had been disloyal to Harry. While none of the girls in her class knew that she was engaged, they would find out in two weeks' time when it was announced. And then would they speculate that he was a Posthumus or a Bertram or a Bassanio? It made matters worse that Harry in the three months following the night of the office dinner had been the gentlest, the most considerate of lovers. Lovers, she noted mentally, as if one of the girls might read her thoughts, in the Shakespearean sense. Why then did she want to represent him as someone hard or callous? Was it part of his appeal that he had seemed so on the night of their first meeting? Was she so debased that she wanted a man who, as Gretchen might have put it, would "kick her around"? Or would she all her life be a schoolgirl who wanted to play Imogen, or rather who wanted to play Ellen Terry playing Imogen?

Her mood darkened as the day progressed, and by the time school was out, she was deeply depressed. She had dreaded to face the real origin of her trouble, but at home in her room, looking at her own startled eyes in the mirror, she made herself do so. Had not Harry, in a single quarter of a year, become rather too much what her father had set out to make him? He worked in green goods now, along with Jake Platt and Bart French and the other "disciples," and he seemed to be thoroughly content. Certainly, her father did not share her misgivings — if "misgivings" was not too strong a word. He was even demonstrative in his pleasure at how Harry had "taken hold" and hinted to Fran that he might still — despite the unhappy scene with Todd — have a future in the firm. Was it all too early? Did she respect less the more conservative Harry, in darker suits with darker ties, in white shirts only now, who tried to get on with Bart and laughed so roundly at her father's jokes? How contemptible of her!

That evening her father telephoned to say he was bringing Bart and Harry and Jake Platt home for supper and that they were going to work in the library afterwards. It was a primary rule in the household that he could always do this. Ada would be ready, at an hour's notice, to supply hot soup and beans and cold cuts, salad and beer to any number of young men from the office. It was the only way, at times, that she could get her husband home. She always invited the wives, too, if they could leave their children, and the ladies could play cards or knit and chat during the long evening.

They had a buffet supper that night, and Fran sat in a corner of the dining room with her brother-in-law, Bart, watching Harry, who was talking to her sister across the room. She could see that he was trying to make a good impression by the rather dainty way that he held his fork in scooping up the last of his beans. She despised herself for noticing this. After all, he didn't really hold his fork any more daintily than the others. It was simply that he held it more daintily than he had used to. Daintily! The very word was a dye strong enough to discolor the image of any man. She had to watch herself.

"Harry fits right into the groove now, doesn't he?"

There was no mistaking the antagonism in Bart's tone, and Fran turned to him in surprise. Bart was so rarely antagonistic. "What groove?"

"That of the smooth young associate of Tower, Tilney."

"The Bart French?" she asked crisply.

"If you will." He shrugged. "It doesn't seem so very long ago that he was telling off partners at firm dinners and wearing silver ties with green bubbles on them."

Fran found that she was trembling all over and knew that it was less because Bart had remembered that tie than because she remembered it herself. "You don't like him, do you?" she asked softly.

"No," he answered with a strained little smile that did not in the least disguise his awareness that they were having a very important discussion. "And I guess it's about the last chance I'll have to tell you so. I should have done it earlier, but you've moved so fast."

"That's all right, Bart. Tell me why you don't like Harry."

"I hate people who say somebody's not their type. Okay, I hate myself. Harry's not my type. Or yours either."

"I guess I'm the best judge of that."

He shook his head. "The worst. A girl in love is the very worst. But anyone in Tower, Tilney can tell you about Harry. He's the guy who was the great rebel until he found it was worth his while to make sheep's eyes at the senior partner's daughter."

Fran closed her eyes for a moment. "Thank you, Bart," she half whispered. "I know it wasn't easy for you to say that."

"It wasn't. And the ridiculous thing is I'm not even sure that I want to influence you." Bart's long face was strangely alive with his perplexity. "I just thought you ought to know."

"I think I ought. And I assure you that it will *not* influence me." She even managed to smile now at her brother-in-law. "But go and talk to someone else for a bit, Bart. One may appreciate candor, but it's impossible not to resent the candid. For a day or so, at least. Don't worry. It won't last forever."

Fran went to her room after supper, on the excuse of correcting school papers, and sat alone in the dark to hug her misery. What an absurdly fragile thing happiness was! When she thought of how she had felt only that morning! Yet as small a thing as the memory of an ugly tie — no, more than that, a *vulgar* tie — was enough to blow away all the shining cobwebs of her good humor and leave her alone in as drab a mental chamber as was ever occupied by Bart French. It might have been a judgment for the hubris of likening herself to Imogen and Helena. It was not easy to imagine *them* being distressed by a lover's way of holding a fork or by a silly tie. They were not petty snobs. Middle-class snobs. There was at least the expiation of knowing that she could make up for a part of her meanness by being a good wife to Harry. But happiness, where was happiness?

When she answered the knock at her door and saw Harry, she suddenly threw her arms around his neck. "Oh, darling, how wonderful! Are you through already?"

"The boss broke up school early tonight. Come on, I'm taking you out for a drink."

At the Third Avenue bar where they had gone on their first evening together he stared a moment into his beer and then looked up at her with an embarrassed smile. "I have something to tell you. Something about myself. Unless your father's already told you."

"Daddy knows? It can't be so bad, then."

She listened in fascinated silence as he told her, in brief, bleak sentences, without embellishment or apology, the story of his affair with Doris Marsh. At first she found herself thinking of Imogen again and the hero whose defects threw into greater relief the virtues of the heroine. The she found herself thinking that Bart French could never have done such a thing. That at least he would have paid the doctor's full bill. And all the while, from a wonderful shivering within, she knew that the full glow of her morning ecstasy had been restored.

"Has she really married Mr. Ozite?" she asked when he had finished.

"Oh, yes. Weeks ago."

"Perhaps you should give her the other five hundred as a wedding present."

He saw in her eyes that his cause was undamaged, perhaps even curiously enhanced, and he laughed. "Is that all you have to say? I sometimes think women have no morals."

"Not where other women are concerned, anyway." She cleared her throat with a little cough. "And now I have something to tell *you*. Something much worse." When she saw the hard, bright instant gleam of alarm in his eyes, she added quickly: "Oh, not what you're thinking. It's not about another man. It's about you. I was criticizing you in my mind tonight. For seeming too much like Bart and Jake."

He looked confused. "But how?"

"By being too much the smooth young Tower, Tilney associate."

"You mean a toady?"

"Oh, no. It was just that you seemed less like Harry Reilley."

"And now I'm old Harry again? Because I'm the hero of a dirty story?"

She laughed at the absurdity of it. "I guess so. That's the kind of illogical thing a woman is."

But Harry was not in the least amused. He was suddenly very angry, and two bright red spots appeared just under his cheekbones. "It gave you a thrill that I wasn't a gentleman, is that it? You only cared about the mick? You don't want me in the same dancing class with Bart French — I look too pathetic in those silk tights and black pumps? Is that it?"

"Oh, *Harry*," she whispered, appalled.

"Do you think I give a goddamn about those precious little disciples of your father? Do you think I give a goddamn about his sacred firm? Do you know that I was going to resign the day he asked me for dinner? Every case I've worked on since then, every shirt and tie I've bought, every drink I've passed up, every snotty partner I haven't told off, has been because of you. And what a sweet ass that makes me! When all you wanted was a tough mick to give you a black eye!"

In the suffocation of her shame Fran felt a sudden terror that he would leave the bar and walk out of her life before she had found her voice. "Oh, my darling," she gasped, "forgive me!"

His anger faded to exasperation as he looked into her desperately pleading eyes. "Well, you needn't make a soap opera of it."

"I love you, darling!" She reached across the table to seize his hand. "Does anything else matter?"

"For Pete's sake, Fran!"

"No, listen to me, Harry. *Please.* It's only fair to give me a chance to explain. You see, I've always had a fetish about the office. Because it was Daddy's world, that shining man's world that I could never get into. And then when you came along, and without even caring about it, without in the least admiring it, made it yours, I began to wonder if it could have been so great a world, after all. And because that idea was painful to me, I had to accuse you of conquering it unfairly!"

"I haven't conquered it yet. By a long shot."

"But you will! I know you will. And all the while I should have been telling myself that it's not because Daddy's world was weak but because you were strong!"

"Tower, Tilney doesn't mean that much to me," he grumbled, and she saw that she had said enough. More than enough.

"Of course it doesn't, darling! Why should it? And in the future it's only going to mean to me what it means to you. Is that a bargain?"

When she saw him smile at last, if reluctantly, she could only pray that the crisis had been averted and swear an inward vow that she would never play Imogen again.

The Single Reader

1963

NONE OF HIS law partners or clients, or even the friends who considered themselves closest to him, knew the secret of Morris Madison. They saw the tall, thin, smooth, urbane tax expert, at the height of his career in his early fifties, the thick, graying hair parted in the center and rising high above a tall forehead, the long, strong, firm nose and the long oblong face, the melancholy but un-self-betraying eyes. They heard the soft, precise voice, the slow, clear articulation; they marveled at the ease with which he could explain the thorniest tax principle and at the profundity of his general information, from politics to social gossip. Morris, they all agreed, was not only the ideal extra man for the grandest dinner party; he was the perfect companion for the Canadian fishing trip. But they had no idea that he was a dedicated man. They suspected all kinds of lacks in his life, besides the obvious ones of a wife and children, and in the free fashion of a psychiatrically minded era they attributed his reserve and good manners to every kind of frustration and insecurity. But none of them suspected that he had a passion.

He kept a diary. He had started it twenty-five years before, when his wife had left him, a horsy country girl who had never relaxed her attitude that the city was full of "snobs and toadies," of whom her husband was one of the worst. Madison had resented her for a year; then in his mind he had forgiven her; ultimately he had even admitted that he might have mishandled her. He had taken her too seriously, too literally, too reasonably. She had wanted domination rather than understanding. The only person who cared about understanding was himself. And for himself he started a diary.

How he could have lived without it in the years that followed, he would not have known. As a rising young lawyer and a single man he was at everybody's mercy. The wives of the older partners expected him to fill in at their dinner parties and listen respectfully to widows and matrons who talked about their servants and children. Clients with personal problems, knowing that he had no family, felt entitled to help themselves to his nights as well as his days for greater self-revelation. Married friends in domestic trouble poured out their woes to him, ostensibly to profit from his experience, but actually for the heady delights of indiscreet confession. Single women regarded him as fair game for every imaginable confidence, and even happy husbands in summertime, when their wives were at the seashore, sought out the congenial company of "old Morris" to relate to him, in alcoholic profusion at the bars of their clubs, the business worries that no sensible spouse would dream of listening to. It began to seem to Madison, in the words of Emily Dickinson, that "all the heavens were a bell and being but an ear" and that the only way for him to talk was to talk to himself.

At first the diary was, naturally enough, primarily the vehicle for his resentment. His circle of acquaintance appeared in it in all the banality of their unsolicited communication, with huge heads and eyes and bigger mouths; their talk was lampooned rather than reported. But on a reading at the end of its first year Madison had been struck by the fact that the most illuminating passages were those where he had dryly set down scenes and conversations that had not seemed of particular interest at the time. For example, a lunch with Clitus Tilney in which the latter had discussed his own prospects of partnership in the firm contained in a dozen lines the very portrait of downtown ambition. Madison now became more selective in his entries. His ears were alerted for the right confidence, the right complaint, even the right phrase that would convey the essential quality of the speaker. And as his people began to breathe and chatter like themselves in his pages, he realized the first great joy of re-creation.

He began to raise his sights. He decided that he wanted to paint a picture of life in New York for a subsequent generation. He began to note the razing of buildings and the erection of new ones. He watched ticker tape parades and dined in the newest restaurants. He marked fashions and fads and even attended fires. He read exhaustively in the great diarists of the past, Pepys, Evelyn, Saint-Simon, and paid many visits to the New York Historical Society to pore over the unpublished pages of Mayor Hone. His conservative friends were surprised to find themselves deserted for Elsa Maxwell's frolicsome balls, as was café society in turn to find itself abandoned for the dullest bar association dinners. Madison would leave a reception at the Archdiocese to go to a late party at Mrs. Cornelius Vanderbilt's and slip away from there to a gathering at Sardi's. He was widely regarded as a snob, but it was rare for two people to agree on what kind.

Inevitably, he came to think of his people as they would one day appear in his diary. If a judge was rude to him while he was arguing a case, if a government official was quixotic or arbitrary, Madison would reflect with an inner smile that they were marring their portraits for posterity. Yet he took great pains to avoid the prejudices which he suspected even in his idol, Saint-Simon. Most of the people whom he knew, like many of Saint-Simon's, would survive to posterity only in his own unrebuttable pages. If he succumbed to the temptation of "touching them up," of making them wittier or nastier or bigger or smaller than they were, nobody in a hundred years would be any the wiser. But his work would have become fiction, and he had no intention of being a mere novelist.

When he was fifty-three, the great set of red morocco on the shelves of his cedar closet totaled more volumes than the years of his age, for there were sometimes three or four to a single year. The diary was now insatiable. It not only demanded its daily addition; it demanded footnotes, appendices, even illustrations. Madison found that he spent as much time editing it as he did writing it, but the former task had the advantage of requiring a constant rereading of his work, a constant reabsorbing of his own glowing, crowded, changing picture of the city, now a Bruegel, now a Hogarth, now a quiet, still Vermeer. Was it not as near as he might ever come to the joys of having an audience? Friends were surprised to find him asking for snapshots of themselves or of their deceased relatives or even of long destroyed houses. They decided that he was becoming sentimental with age. His dinner partners were sometimes piqued to find the "perfect listener" interrupting their confidences with such questions as: "Do you happen to remember what year your father sold the house in Seventieth Street?" or "Is it true that your Aunt Gisèle refused to swim in a pool if there were men in it?"

But only Clitus Tilney seemed to suspect the existence of an avocation. At lunch one day at the Down Town Association, Tilney rubbed his cheeks, his elbows on the table, for several long silent moments, reminding Madison of a great sleek lazy bear, bored in a zoo.

"Morris, do you know something?" he began, folding his hands on the table and contemplating them with an air of mild surprise. "I worry about you. Oh, I know, downtown we never talk personally. We live and work, cheek by jowl, year after year, and never know a thing about each other. And never seem to want to, either. But once in a while I have to break that rule. With people I like, anyway. And I like you, Morris. But if you don't want to hear me, just tell me to shut my big mouth."

"No, please, Clitus. I'd love to hear you."

"That's what you always say: 'I'd love to hear you.'" Tilney shook his large head as if Madison's response were the very symptom that most troubled him. "But anyway. I've never had a doubt that, after my own, yours was the best legal head in the office." He smiled to show that his boast was humorous. "Yet you and I both know that we can go just so far in life as lawyers. We don't kid ourselves. I'm a securities expert, and you're a tax wizard. We've mastered our respective fields of gimmickry. But that's not enough for us. Rutherford Tower can be perfectly happy with his wills and trusts, and Waldron Webb with his lawsuits. But you and I . . . well, our souls need more."

"What does your soul need, Clitus?"

"There you go again, throwing the ball right back at me. Will you hang on to it a moment, for pity's sake? I want to talk about *you*."

Madison stirred uneasily. "But I could answer better if you told me first."

"Oh, very well," Tilney answered with an impatient shrug. "Only you know it, anyway. I've got the Washington bug. Ever since I had that job with Bob Lovett. And sometimes I even think I'd like to go back to Ulrica and teach."

"The firm will never let you go."

"Ah, well," said Tilney with a sigh, "that's another matter, isn't it? But to get back to you. You see? I can be very persistent. I've noticed in the past year that you've delegated more work."

"Is that a reproach?"

"Not in the least, my dear fellow. You know how I feel about that sort of thing. If a man can't delegate most of his work at fifty, he's either a dunce or a Napoleon. No, I'm wondering what you *do* with your life. Do you have any hobbies? Are you a Sunday painter? Or do you simply gaze at the sky and think great thoughts?"

The bantering tone of Tilney's question did not in the least conceal its genuine friendliness and concern. Madison was surprised to feel, for the first time in many years, that sharp pricking little urge to confide in another human. As he gazed back into his partner's sympathetic gray eyes, he moistened his lips and after a silence that was beginning to be embarrassing, began: "Well, as a matter of fact, I have what you might call a hobby —"

But he stopped. He stopped, frozen, on the edge of this new precipice. Talk about his diary? It was appalling; it was unthinkable. He shook his head quickly several times, as if to awaken himself. "It's my social life," he concluded lamely.

"Great Scott, man!" Tilney exploded. "You don't mean to sit there and tell me that all you care about is to dress up in a monkey suit and exchange banalities with stupid women?"

Madison wondered if he had ever wanted anything so much as he now wanted to have Tilney read the diary. But it was out of the question. Tilney would have been scandalized at the entries about his partners and clients, about the innermost workings of the firm, about Tilney himself. Besides, his personality was too powerful. Even if he *liked* the diary, in some bullying fashion he would try to put his own stamp on it.

"I take a broader view of social life than you do, Clitus," Madison said meekly. "To me it's more than a matter of monkey suits and stupid women. I like to think I'm observing a microcosm of the world. Everything, you know, can be contained in everything else. Isn't it a question of the power of one's lens?"

"I suppose it is, of course," Tilney said gruffly, and, giving up, he turned the conversation to office matters.

꽃

Madison discovered in the weeks that followed that the seeds which Tilney had so officiously scattered were growing with tropical speed into the jungle of his own uneasiness. His evening delight of dipping into the old volumes of the diary was now curtailed by the most agitating speculations. What would Tilney think of it? What would his other partners think? What would his ex-wife, long since remarried and contentedly living in Pasadena? Would they laugh? Or would they be impressed? Even dazzled? Was it enough to be thought all one's life a mere clever lawyer and diner-out and only to be posthumously appreciated at one's true worth? If there were no life hereafter, what would it gain him to have his diary acclaimed? Madison began to feel that he had to have at least one reader. At least one judge in his lifetime. But whom? Nobody seemed to have just the right qualifications. They were all too close to him or too distant, too ignorant or too terrifyingly knowing, too kind or too malicious. He started thumbing the Social Register and ended with the Manhattan Directory.

There was, however, one name that reoccurred on every list that he jotted down, and that was Aurelia Starr. Mrs. Starr was a widow, without children or other visible appendages, a few years younger than himself, with a small but adequate income, a trim and well-clad figure, who managed, for the proverbially unwanted extra woman, to get herself asked out nearly as widely as Madison himself. She was very decorative, with her dark, sleek hair, her long eyebrows rising to her temples, her widely parted blue eyes, her straight Egyptian nose. She might have had some of the elegance of a Nefertiti had she not trembled with an American widow's insecurity. But Aurelia, for all her nervous charm, was "safe." She was supposed, like all the unattached of her sex, to be after a husband, but she was so kind, so considerate, so understanding, such a good sport, that no man felt there was any danger of a dinner-table flirtation being taken too seriously. It was probably for just this reason that poor Aurelia had not re-wed. Like Madison himself, she was too good a listener.

When he sat beside her at dinner the next time, in the penthouse of a theatrical designer, he for once had no eyes or ears for the other guests. All he could think of, as he listened to her quiet, tense, pleasant chatter, was the question of showing her the diary. When the party was over, he took her home in a taxi, and she asked him up to her apartment for a drink. It was the kind of invitation that as a prudent single man he ordinarily declined, but now he hesitated.

"Oh, do come up, Morris," she urged him. "You and I meet and talk so often, and I love it, of course, but what do we ever really *say?* What do any of us ever really say in social life? Couldn't we try to talk for once, just you and me?"

"We could try."

In her tiny white and gold living room, which gloried in an Aubusson rug and Hubert Robert panels, he took a long draft of whiskey and relaxed.

"It's true that people talk banalities at parties," he agreed. "They like it that way. They think any real communication would be too much work. And then they complain of loneliness." He snorted in derision.

"Are you never lonely?"

"I think I can honestly say I'm not."

Aurelia laughed. "You sound very superior. With whom do *you* communicate? Or don't you?"

"I communicate with the future."

When she paused to consider this, he hoped that she would not try too hard to be sympathetic. But she was simplicity itself. "And how do you do that?"

"By keeping a diary. Or a journal. I'm not sure which you'd call it."

"I can see the advantage to *you*. But how does the poor future get its word in?"

"That's exactly what I was going to ask you. How can I arrange to let it?"

She mused. "Does it go back far, your diary?"

"Twenty-five years."

"My goodness. And it's complete?"

"As you can't imagine."

"Oh." She seemed to be looking through him, her lips apart, as if she could dimly make out those red volumes in the cedar chest. "And now you want someone to see it. For an opinion? Do you want a historian or a professor of literature?"

"Hardly. I think I just want someone to tell me if it's . . ." He paused to swallow and moisten his lips. "Well, if it's real. I mean, if it really exists. I sometimes wonder. But I think I've found the person who can tell me. Do you suspect who it is, Aurelia?"

"Of course I do! But I'm doubling back and forth in my tracks. I'm scared stiff! Why should *I* be the one so honored?"

"Because you never appear in it." He had not realized that this was so until the second before he said it, and immediately he understood that it might hurt her. "I don't mean by that that there's nothing to say about you. I mean that I must have always planned that you should be my reader."

"But I can't!" she protested, and the way she touched her middle fingers to the ends of her long eyebrows conveyed some of her tenseness. "It's not simply that I'm scared of such a responsibility. I think you're making a mistake. Once it's shared, it isn't really a diary any-more. There wouldn't still be that special intimacy between you and it. Be careful how you play with that!"

"Oh, but I *know*," he exclaimed. "This has been no light decision, believe me. You should be very proud. My diary and I are choosy!"

"I *am* proud, dear Morris. But I'm not foolhardy."

Nor was she. He was baffled and at length irritated to find that he could not move her. The most that he could obtain was her promise to discuss it on another occasion, and to do this he took her out for dinner the following week in a new Javanese restaurant. Aurelia had quite recovered her equanimity and was able to talk about the diary in a lively, even a facetious manner. She asked him all kinds of questions and seemed particularly fascinated by the mechanical details of its typing and storage. He told her about the safe deposit vault where one copy was always kept and described his plans for its posthumous publication and the trust to effect them that he had established in his will.

"But we can't talk all evening about my diary," he interrupted him-self, with perfunctory courtesy, when the dessert was placed on the table.

"You mean you'd rather talk about mine?"

"Do you keep one?" The sudden sharpness of his tone reflected the instant crisis of his jealousy. "But of course you do! It's too obvious. How could I not have guessed it?"

"It's just a line-a-day."

"Just a line-a-day!" he retorted with a snort. "But, obviously, you love it. Obviously, you have visions of it being published."

"Oh, Morris," she protested, laughing. "You're too absurd!"

"Am I?" His tone was almost plaintive. "I see it all too clearly. Your diary will come out the same year as mine and put it completely in the shade. Oh, I can read those reviews as if they were written on that wall! 'Although Mrs. Starr may not have the thoroughness of Mr. Madison, neither does she have his pedantry. Hers is the woman's hand, the light touch that illuminates her era. The universities and the scholars will undoubtedly be grateful for Mr. Madison's painstaking observations, but for that train trip, for that hospital gift, or even for reading aloud at the family hearth, we recommend Aurelia Starr.'"

"My dear friend, I promise you my diary is simply to keep track of dentist appointments and cleaning women." Aurelia had stopped laughing and was serious again. "I'm in no way a writer. I like to talk. And, like a mirror, to reflect."

"What do you reflect?"

"Well, at the moment, you. Or perhaps your diary. I'm not always quite sure which. I'm like a confidant in a French tragedy. I may not exist when the hero's offstage, but he tells me his thoughts. Or maybe just the ones that aren't worthy of his diary. I wouldn't have the presumption to compete with *yours*."

She was very elusive, but she was equally charming. Their dinner was repeated the next week and then the following and soon became a Friday night habit. It was agreed that neither would accept another invitation, no matter how exalted, for that evening. Madison had never enjoyed the regular companionship of a sympathetic woman, and he was beginning to understand what he had missed. They discussed other things besides the diary, yet it continued to have significance in their relationship as a starting point, a link, as the leitmotif that symbolized their rare intimacy. Aurelia always raised her first cocktail of the evening with a little nod across the table that meant she was drinking to it.

At times he would think back ruefully over the crowded years in which he had lived so constantly with people, so rarely with friends, and wonder if he had not wasted his life by being so private. But then it would strike him that he could never have met another Aurelia, for Aurelia was unique. She seemed to have no self at all. She listened; she laughed; she sympathized, and when she talked it was always about the subject that he had raised. He had never imagined that another human could be so intuitively understanding.

"You realize, of course, that you're spoiling me horribly," he pointed out. "Shouldn't we ever talk about your life?"

"I don't have one. Or rather, this is it."

"But you make me feel such a fatuous ass!"

"Do I? I'm sorry."

"Not really, of course. Only when I stop to think what an egotist I'm becoming."

"Don't." She was very clear about this. "My theory has nothing to do with egotism. I simply believe that communication can only exist between a man and a woman and then only when the man takes the lead. Don't worry about me. I think I'm doing rather nicely."

One result of their friendship was that his diary entries were becoming shorter and more matter-of-fact. He knew now that Aurelia would ultimately consent to read it, and his words no longer flowed when subject to her imagined scrutiny. It was like writing with her looking over his shoulder. This was not because he thought of her as necessarily critical; it was more that he could not imagine, well as he now knew here, just what her reaction would be. Once he went so far as to insert a flowery compliment to her in his description of one of their dinners, but he then ripped out the page. Perhaps as a diarist he needed a vacation. Perhaps he needed to do less observing and more thinking. For the first time in twenty-five years he let a week go by without a single entry. He was conscious at night of that neglected cedar closet from which he could imagine a mist of reproach emanating, but he resolutely turned over in his bed, saying aloud: "You've had the best years of my life. It's time you let *me* do a little living."

Matters came logically to a head one early spring afternoon on a bench under the rustling trees of Bryant Park after a matinee of *Tristan und Isolde*. When Aurelia told him it was her favorite opera, he accused her jokingly of harboring a secret death wish.

"It's better than being dead, anyway," she retorted. "You, my dear, are dead and living in a downy heaven where you see your published diary having the greatest success imaginable."

For once she had gone too far. "It seems to me that I live very much in the world," he said gruffly.

"Yes. As a spy."

"You say that because you know I keep a diary," he protested. "People always assume that whatever a man does, he does at the expense of something else. I guess there's only one way a diarist can persuade a beautiful woman that he's more than that."

She looked up quickly. "Oh, Morris," she warned him.

"Only one," he reiterated, firmly, his eyes fixed upon her.

"Be careful."

"What are you afraid of?"

"That you're going to propose to me!"

Madison was so startled that for a moment he could do nothing but shout with laughter. "But that's exactly what everyone thinks you want!" he cried. "The world is always wrong, Aurelia."

"The world is always libelous," she said, flushing.

"Oh, my dear, forgive me. Forgive me and marry me!"

Her face immediately puckered up into what struck him as a curious blend of gratification and near panic. She looked like a child who wanted to cry and couldn't.

"Do you mean it?"

"Of course I mean it."

"Do you swear?"

"I swear! By . . . by my diary!"

Aurelia's countenance cleared at this; already she resumed her mask. "My goodness, as serious as that? Then you must give me time."

"Time for what?"

"Well, for one thing, to read the diary."

"*All* of it?"

"That won't be necessary. Give me one early volume and one in the middle and . . . the current one."

Madison looked at her suspiciously. "You want to read where you come in?"

"What woman wouldn't?"

"You'll be disappointed. There's very little about you."

"Ah, but that's just what I want to see!"

卐

That night, perched on a high stool in the big cedar closet, Madison pulled volume after volume from the shelves and skimmed their pages. The mild pique occasioned by Aurelia's failure to accept him right away vanished with the exuberance of choosing the volumes for her inspection. There was no longer any real question of the outcome; he could trust his faithful diary to plead his cause. And the thrill of thinking of her reading his choicest pages! It made for a giddy night. As a sample of his early work he picked the volume that covered the winter months of 1936. He had been working night after night on a big tax case, which gave to his entries a wonderful unity of mood. Madison liked to conceive of his diary pictorially, and this volume seemed to him a Whistler nocturne, with its dull gray foggy atmosphere of exhausting work, streaked here and there with the golden flashes of ambition. For the middle period he chose a little gem of a divorce story in high circles with which he had been professionally involved. And for the last . . . well, of course, he had to be honest and submit the latest volume, though he hated to have Aurelia end on a flat note. He dated the blank page following the final entry and wrote: "My diary is to have its first reader. May she and it be friends!"

The next Friday night they were to meet as usual at their restaurant, and Madison, who arrived first, ordered a cocktail to dull the edge of his now almost unbearable excitement. As he was raising the glass to his lips, however, he saw Aurelia crossing the room towards their table, carrying the three red volumes which he had sent to her. He noted with instant dismay that she looked pale and haggard, as if she had not slept in two nights, and her eyes avoided his as she slipped into his seat. She pushed the books towards him, without a word, and he placed them carefully on the bench beside him.

"Is something wrong?"

"Oh, Morris, my friend, I don't know how to tell you. Please order me a drink. No, let me have yours." She took his glass and drank from it quickly. "I can't stay for dinner. I'm all done in. I'm going to bed. I only came to return the books. I know how precious they are."

"Are you ill?"

"No, just tired."

"Was my poor diary so tedious?" he asked, with death in his heart.

She took another sip of his cocktail. "I tell you what," she said abruptly. "I'll have my little say, and then I'll be off." She paused, and when she spoke again there was a tremble of deep feeling in her voice. "Dear Morris, I hope that you and I will always be the best of friends. But I cannot marry you."

"Because of the diary?"

"Because of the diary."

"Is it so terrible?"

She seemed to consider this. "It's a monster," she said in a hushed, low tone. Again she paused and then relented a bit. "Though I suppose there's nothing wrong with a monster if you don't happen to be on its bill of fare."

"And you are?"

"Oh, my dear, you should know that. Don't you send a tribute of men and maidens each year to the labyrinth? No, I'm *serious*, Morris," she exclaimed when he smiled. "You've created a robot! He's grown and grown until you can no longer control him, and now he's rampaging the countryside. I dared to face him. I tried to give you time to get away. I was even able to stand him off a while. But now my stones are gone, and Goliath is stalking towards me!"

"How fantastical you are. Really, Aurelia, I wouldn't have thought it of you. You've seen for yourself that the entries stop with our friendship. If anyone's won, it's you."

"But I tell you I'm out of ammunition!" she exclaimed shrilly. "I have to take my heels while I can. For don't think Goliath wouldn't get his revenge for all those missing entries. I should be made his slave, like you. I should be harnessed and put to work. After all, he has missed the woman's touch, hasn't he? The woman's point of view? Isn't that the one thing he needs? Didn't Pepys have a wife? Wasn't there a Mrs. Saint-Simon?"

"There was a duchess," Madison said dryly.

"Exactly. And your diary wants a Mrs. Madison. But it won't be me. And if you're wise, Morris, it won't be anyone. You and your diary can be happy together. But, I beg of you, don't listen to it when it points its long, inky finger at another human being!"

Madison was beginning to wonder if she was sober. "You must think me demented."

"Well, I don't suppose you'd burn down New York to make a page for your diary." She laughed a bit wildly. "After all, you might burn the diary with it. But, no, you have copies in a vault, don't you?" Here she seemed at last to remember herself, and she placed a rueful hand on his. "Forgive me, my dear, for being so overwrought. Let me slip away now and get a good night's sleep. I'll take a pill. And next week we'll talk on the telephone and see if we can't put things back on the nice old friendly basis."

"Aurelia —"

But she was gone. She was hurrying across the room, between the tables, and he had actually to run to catch up with her, clutching his three volumes.

"Aurelia!" he cried in a tone that made her turn and stare. "Wait!"

"What is it, Morris? What more is there to say?"

"You haven't told me what you *think* of the diary."

She seemed not to comprehend. "I haven't?"

"I mean what you think of it *as* a diary."

"Oh." She treated this almost as an irrelevance. "But it's magnificent, of course. You know that."

"It's just what I *don't* know! It's just what I've spent the past several months trying to find out!"

"Oh, my dear," she murmured, shaking her head sadly, "you have nothing to worry about *there*. It's luminous. It's pulsating. It's unbelievable, really. I doubt if there's ever been anything like it. Poor old Saint-Simon, his nose *will* be out of joint. Oh, yes, Morris. Your diary is peerless."

She turned again to go out the door, and he let her go. For a moment he stood there, dazed, stock-still by the checkroom, until the headwaiter asked him if he wished to dine alone. He shook his head quickly and went out to the street to hail a taxi. It was only seven-thirty; he had still time to dine at the Century Club. When he got there, he hurried to the third floor and glanced, as he always did, through the oval window to see who was sitting at the members' table. There was an empty seat between Raymond Massey and Ed Murrow. Opposite he noted the great square noble face and shaggy head of Learned Hand. He must have just finished one of his famous anecdotes, for Madison heard the sputter of laughter around his end of the table. It would be a good night. As he glided forward to take that empty seat he knew that he was a perfectly happy man again.

Billy and
the Gargoyles

1952

SHIRLEY SCHOOL in appearance was gloomy enough to look at, but it was only when we returned there in later years that it seemed so to us. As boys, we took its looks for granted. The buildings were grouped in orderly lines around a square campus; they were of gray stone and had tall, Gothic windows. The ceilings inside were high, making large wall spaces which were covered with faded lithographs of Renaissance paintings. There was a chapel, a gymnasium, a schoolhouse, several dormitories and, scattered about at a little distance from the campus, the cottages of the married masters. No fence separated the school from the surrounding New England countryside, but none was needed. Shirley was a community unto itself; its very atmosphere prohibited escape or intrusion. The runaway boy would know that he was only running from his own future, and a trespasser would immediately feel that he was intruding on futures never intended for him. For Shirley, even through the shabby stone of its lamentable architecture, exuded the atmosphere of a hundred years of accumulated idealism. You were made as a boy to feel that great things would be expected of you after graduation; you would rise in steady ascent on the escalator of success as inevitably as you rose from one form to another in the school. Life was a pyramid, except that there was more room at the top, and anyone who had been through the dark years of hazing and athletic competitions, who had prayed and washed and conformed at Shirley, should and would get there. It was good to be ambitious because, being educated and God-fearing, you would raise the general level as you yourself rose to power, to riches, to a bishopric or to the presidency of a large university. At the end there was death, it was true, but with it even greater rewards, and old age, unlike Macbeth's, would be sweetened by a respectful lull broken only by the rattle of applause at testimonial dinners. I find that I can still look at life and feel that it ought to be this way, that I can still vaguely wonder why one year has not put me farther ahead than its predecessor. There were no such doubts at Shirley, unless they were felt by Billy Prentiss.

Billy was my cousin and the only other boy at school whom I knew when I went there first at the age of thirteen. The contrast between us, however, was not one to make me presume on the relationship. Billy came of a large and prosperous family, and I was an only child whose mother gave bridge lessons at summer hotels to help with my Shirley tuition. Billy, though thin and far from strong, was tall and fair and had an easygoing, outgiving personality; I was short, dark and of a truculent disposition. But these contrasts were as nothing before the overriding distinction between the "old kid" and the "new kid." Billy and I may have been in the same form, but he had completed a year at the school before my arrival, which gave him great social prerogatives. By Shirley's rigid code there should have been only the most formal relations between us.

Billy, however, did not recognize the code. That is what I mean when I say that he had doubts at Shirley. He greeted me from the first in a friendly manner that was entirely improper, as if we had been at home and not at school. He helped me to unpack and showed me my gymnasium locker and supplied me with white stiff collars for Sunday wear. He talked in an easy, chatty manner about how my mother had taught him bridge and what he had seen during the summer with his family in Europe, as if he believed that such things could be balanced against the things that were happening at Shirley, the real things. He was certainly an odd figure for an old kid; I think of him now as he looked during my first months at school, stalking through the corridors of the Lower Forms Building on his way to or from the library, running the long fingers of his left hand through his blond hair and whistling "Mean to Me." He lived in a world of his own, and, with all my gratitude, I was sufficiently conservative to wonder if it wasn't Utopian. It embarrassed me, for example, when he was openly nice to me in the presence of other older kids.

"How are you getting on, Peter?" he asked me one morning after chapel as we walked to the schoolhouse. Nobody else called me by my Christian name. "Have you got everything you need? Can I lend you any books or clothes?"

"No, I'm fine, thank you."

"You're a cousin, you know," he said, looking at me seriously. "Cousins ought to help each other out. Even second cousins."

I didn't really believe that anyone could help me. Homesickness was like cutting teeth or having one's tonsils out. I nodded, but said nothing.

"If you have any trouble with the old kids, let me know," he continued. "I could speak to them. It might help."

"Oh, no please!" I exclaimed. Nothing could have more impressed me with his otherworldliness than a suggestion so unorthodox. "You mustn't do that! It wouldn't be the thing at all!"

We were interrupted by voices from behind us, loud, sneering voices. It was what I had been afraid of.

"Is that Prentiss I see talking to a new kid? Can he so demean himself?"

"Do you pal around with new kids, Billy?"

"What's come over you, Prentiss?"

The last voice was stern; it was George Neale's.

"Peter Westcott happens to be my cousin," Billy answered with dignity, turning around to face them. "And there's nothing in the world wrong with him. Is there a law that I may not talk to my own cousin?"

He turned again to me, but I hurried ahead to join a group of new kids. I'm afraid I was shocked that he should speak in this fashion to a boy like George Neale. George, after all, was one of the undisputed leaders of the form. He was a small, fat, clumsy boy who commanded by the sheer deadliness of his tongue and the intensity of his animosities. He also enjoyed an immunity from physical retaliation through the reputation of a bad heart, the aftereffect, it was generally said, of a childhood attack of rheumatic fever. He had chosen for his mission in school the persecution of those who failed to meet exactly the rigid standards of social behavior that our formmates, represented by himself, laid down. I sometimes wonder, in trying to recollect how George first appeared to me, if he derived the fierce satisfaction from his activities that I believed at the time. It seems more probable, as I bring back the straight, rather rigid features of his round face and his tone of dry impatience, that he looked at nonconformists as Spanish Inquisitors looked at heretics who were brought before them, as part of the day's work, something that had to be done, boring and arduous though it might be. Why George should have been chosen as the avenging agent of the gods it was not for him to ask; what mattered only was that they required, for dim but cogent reasons of their own, a division of the world into the oppressed and their oppressors. He and his victims were the instruments of these gods, caught in the ruthless pattern of what was and what was not "Shirley," a pattern more fundamental and significant in the lives of all of us than the weak and distant humanitarianism of the faculty, who brooded above us, benevolent but powerless to help, like the twentieth-century Protestant God whom we worshiped in the Gothic chapel.

George was in charge of the program of hazing the new kids, and Billy's ill-considered kindness only resulted in bringing me prematurely to his attention. Custom required that each new kid be singled out for a particular ordeal, and I was soon made aware, from the conversation of the old kids who raised their voices as I passed, that mine had been decided on. Apparently I was to have my head partially shaved. I lived from this point on in such apprehension that it was almost a relief to discover one Sunday morning, from the atmosphere of huddles and whispers around me, that George had chosen his moment. I retreated instinctively to the library to stay there until chapel, but the first time I looked up from the book I was pretending to read, it was to find George and the others gathered before me.

"Won't you come outside, Westcott?" George asked me in a mild, dry tone. "We'd like to have a little talk with you."

"It won't take a minute, Westcott," another added with a leer.

No violence was allowed in the library; it was sanctuary. I could have waited until the bell for chapel and departed in safety. George knew this, but he knew too, as I knew, and he knew that I knew it, that the fruition of his scheme was like the fall of Hamlet's sparrow: if it was not now, it would be still to come. I got up without a word and walked out of the library, down the corridor and out to the back lawn. There I turned around and faced them.

There was a moment of hesitation, and then someone pushed me. I went sprawling over on the grass, for George, unnoticed, had knelt beside me. They all jumped on me, and I struggled violently, too violently, destroying whatever sympathy might have been latent in them by giving one boy, whose heart was not really in it, a vicious kick in the stomach. In another moment I was overwhelmed and held firmly down while George produced the razor. I closed my eyes and felt giddy with hatred.

Then the miracle occurred. I distinctly heard a window open and a voice cry:

"Cheese it, fellows! Mr. O'Neil!"

And in a second twenty hands had released me, and I heard the thump of retreating feet in the earth under my head. I sat up dazedly and looked around. Nobody was there but Billy; he was standing inside the building looking out at me through an open window. He smiled and climbed over the low sill. He was actually helping me to my feet.

"Where did they go?" I demanded.

"They beat it."

"But why?"

He laughed.

"Didn't you hear me?"

I stared at him in perplexity.

"Then where's Mr. O'Neil?" I asked.

He laughed again.

"How should I know?"

I rubbed my head.

"Why did you do it, Billy?" I asked.

He helped me brush the grass off my blue suit.

"Because you're my cousin," he said cheerfully. "And because they're down on you. Isn't that enough?"

I felt for the first time since I had come to Shirley that I might be going to cry.

"They'll be back," I pointed out, "when they find out."

"Then let's clear out."

"You go," I said. "They're not after you."

Incredibly, he laughed again.

"They will be now."

Again we heard the stamping of feet, this time from within the building. The door burst open, and they surrounded us.

"What's the idea, Prentiss?" George snarled, stepping out of the circle toward him. "Where's Mr. O'Neil?"

Billy shrugged his shoulders and put his hands in his pockets.

"Didn't you see him? He and his wife were coming over by the hedge on their way to chapel."

He flung this off coolly, as if to him it was a matter of the utmost indifference whether or not he was believed. Then he gave his attitude a further emphasis by turning to me, quite casually, and smiling.

"We saw them, didn't we, Peter?" he said.

"Well, *we* didn't!" George cried.

"I can't be bothered with what you see and don't see," Billy retorted.
"If you didn't, you didn't."

"Are you siding with Westcott, Prentiss?" George demanded. "Are
you on the side of the new kids? Is that where you stand, Prentiss?"

He glanced from side to side at the others as he said this.

"What about it, Billy?"

"Are you with the new kids, Billy?"

"Let's *get* Prentiss!"

But just then the bell for assembly, at long last, jangled sharply from
within the building, and the crowd burst apart and rushed up the steps
to the door. I can still remember the fierce joy with which, as George
Neale leaned down to pick up the comb that had slipped from his
pocket, I stamped on it and broke it in two. He didn't even bother to
look at me, but turned and hurried after his friends.

George was not a boy to let an assembly bell stand between him and his
victim, and I lived for days in dread of a renewed effort to execute the
head-shaving plan. I soon found out, however, that I had nothing personally to be afraid of. George, it was rumored, had put the new kids
quite out of his mind; he was concentrating his energies on a project
against the person whose basic challenge of authority he had so immediately recognized. One Sunday after chapel, when Billy was waylaid by
the gang and pelted with the icy snowballs of the season's first snow, his
books flung in the mud and the lining ripped from his hat, we knew that
George's campaign had begun in earnest.

"I don't know if I'm quite as popular as I supposed," Billy told me,
with a sort of desperate gaiety, as he and I engaged in the sorry task of
collecting his books and rubbing them off. "I would suggest that I might
be a good person to stay away from for a while."

"Cousins should help each other," I said tersely. "You told me that."

Every persecution has a pattern, and George soon revealed the nature
of his. It was to establish that Billy was really not a boy at all, not even
an effeminate boy, but a girl. This was carried out with the special vindictiveness which old kids reserved for other old kids who had been disloyal. George devised not one but several nicknames for his victim; Billy
became known as "Bella," then as "Angela" and finally, with a venom-
ous simplicity, as "Woman." George trained his boys to carry through

the identification with a completeness that would have done credit to a secret police. He knew at an early age that the way to break a human being is never to relax, to follow him through the day and into the night until he lets down his guard for just a moment, a private moment, alone in his cubicle, in the lavatory, in his seat at chapel, and then to strike hardest. If George and the others found Billy taking a shower in the morning when they came into the lavatory, they would act like men who have stumbled into a ladies' room. "Eek!" they would shriek. "It's Angela! Excuse me." And they would leave the lavatory and insist in waiting outside even when the prefect on duty came by and ordered them in to take their showers, shouting in voices clearly audible to poor Billy: "But we can't go in! There's a naked woman in there," until the bewildered prefect would go in and find Billy and order them in, but not without a leer to show that he sided with the conspirators, grinning at their joke and looking the other way when, upon entering, they pelted Billy with pieces of soap, crying, "Cover her up! For the sake of decency cover her up!" George was careful to carry the use of the female pronoun into every department of life at school; if commenting on a translation of Billy's in Latin class he would say, even if reprimanded, "She left off the adjective in line ten, sir," or filing into the schoolroom for prayers he would always step aside, pushing the others with him, on Billy's arrival and cry, "Ladies first!" Even in chapel, the sacred chapel, where the headmaster, lost in illusion, believed that freedom of worship existed, I have seen Billy, intensely religious as one can only be at thirteen, interrupted from his devotions by having a hat jammed on his head by George, crouching in the pew ahead, and hearing him hiss: "Ladies always wear hats in church. Didn't Saint Paul say so?"

Billy's reaction to all of this seemed designed to bring out the worst in George. He simply appeared to ignore the whole thing. He would stare blankly, at times even pityingly at the crowd that baited him and then turn on his heel, carefully smoothing back the hair which they would inevitably have rumpled. He never seemed to lose his temper or strike back except when he was physically overwhelmed and pinned to the ground and then in a sudden galvanization of wheeling arms and legs, with closed eyes, he would try to fight himself free with an ineffective frenzy that only aroused laughter. But such moments were rare. For the most part he was remote and disdainful, like a marquise in a tumbrel looking over the heads of the mob.

The very fact that I think of a marquise and not a marquis shows the effectiveness of George's propaganda. I saw it all, for I stayed close to Billy throughout this period. The fact that he was in trouble on my account overcame, I am glad to say, my instinctive, if rather sullen, deference to the majority. And then, too, I should add, there was a certain masochistic pleasure in sacrificing myself on the altar of Billy's unpopularity. My real difficulty came less in sharing his distress than in sharing his attitude of superiority to it, for I believed, superstitiously, in all the things that he sneered at. I believed, as George believed, in the system, the hazing, in the whole grim division of the school world into those who "belonged" and those who didn't. The fact that I was one of the latter, partly at my own election, was not important; I was still a part of the system. It bothered me that Billy, on our Sunday walks in the country, insisted on discussing faraway, unreal things — home and his mother and her friends and what they did and talked about. He would never talk about George Neale, for example. One afternoon I made a point of this.

"Do you suppose there will always be people like Neale in life?" I asked him as we walked down the wooded path to the river. "Will we always have to be watching out for them?"

"George?" Billy queried, as if not quite sure to whom I had referred. He paused. "Why, people like George simply don't exist in my parents' world." He shrugged his shoulders. "After all, you can't spend your time throwing snowballs at people and expect to be invited out much. You don't make friends by going up to your host at a party and calling him by a woman's name."

"But he might learn to do other things, mightn't he?" I persisted. "Spread lies and things like that?"

"My dear Peter," Billy said with an amiable condescension, "George will be utterly helpless without his gang. And his gang, you see, will have grown up."

But he couldn't quite dispel my idea that some of the ugliness that was George might survive the grim barriers of our school days. Billy's faith in the future was a touching faith in a warm and sunny world where people moved to and fro without striking each other and conversed without insults, a world where the idea was appreciated, the mannerism ignored. I could feel the attraction of this future, so different from the Shirley future of struggle and success; I could even yearn for it, but try as I would, I could never quite bring myself to believe in it. As the sky grew darker and we turned back to the school and saw ahead over the trees the Gothic tower of the chapel, my heart contracted with a sense of guilt that I had been avoiding, even for an afternoon, the sober duty of facing Shirley facts.

"I don't know if the world will be so terribly different from school," I said gloomily. "I bet it's very much the same."

Even Billy's face clouded at this. It was as if I had voiced a doubt that he was desperately repressing, a doubt that if admitted would have made his troubles at school too much to bear. He gazed up at the tower, anticipating perhaps all that we were returning to, the changing of shirts and collars, the evening meal, the long study period amid the sniggering, the note-passing, the sly kick from the desk behind.

"It should have gargoyles, like cathedrals in Europe," he said suddenly. "Grinning little gargoyles like George Neale."

Even George could not keep a thing going forever, and the persecution of Billy at length became a bore to his gang. We had been through the long New England winter, and in the spring of second-form year we were beginning to emerge as individuals from the gray anonymity of childhood. We were even forming friendships based on something besides mutual insecurity and joint hostility to others, friendships more intense than any relationships that we were to know for many years. It was a time in our lives that the headmaster viewed with suspicion, conducive, as he believed it to be, to a state of mind which he darkly described as "sentimental," but it was nonetheless exciting to us to be aware of ourselves for the first time as something other than boys at Shirley. We were beginning to discover, in spite of everything, that there were not only blacks and whites, but reds and yellows in the world around us and that life itself could be something more than a struggle.

It seems clear to me now that George must have resented our maturing and the breakup of the old hard line between the accepted and the unaccepted. He tried to maintain his waning control over his group by reminding boys of their ungainliness and ineptitudes of a few months before, by reviving old issues and screaming the battle cries that used to range the group against the individual. He sought new victims, new scapegoats, but public opinion was increasingly unmanageable. George represented the past, or at most the passing; he was like an angry Indian medicine man who finds his tribe turning away to the attractions of a broader civilization. Though he could beat his drum and dance his dance, though he could even still manage to burn a few victims, essentially his day was over. But if George had been left behind, so, oddly enough, had Billy. Instead of stepping forward to take his place among the boys who would now have received him, he preferred to remain alone and aloof. He seemed tired, now that the ordeal was over, discouraged, just when there was hope. It was as if, in the struggle, he had received a small, deep wound that was only now beginning to fester. George, deprived of other victims, seemed to sense this, for he pressed the attack against Billy all alone, with a desperate vindictiveness, as if to deliver the last and fatal blow of which his declining power was capable. Their conflict had come to be an individual thing, almost a curiosity to the rest of us. They stood apart, fighting their own fight, quaint if rather grim reminders of a standard of values that had passed.

Toward the middle of spring Billy developed the habit of reporting sick to the infirmary. He would go there for two or three days at a time, using the old trick of touching his thermometer to a lamp bulb when the nurse was out of the room. The infirmary had its pleasant side; like the library it was sanctuary, an insulated white box where one could stay in bed and read the thick, rebound volumes of Dickens and Baroness Orczy. It so happened that we were both there, I with a sinus infection and he with the pretense of one, on the day of the game with Pollock School, the great event of the baseball season. I hated to miss the game, for it involved a half holiday, a trip to Pollock and a celebration afterward if we won. Billy, less regretful, was sharing a room with me on the empty second floor.

Late in the afternoon of the game, as we were working on a picture puzzle, Mrs. Jones, the matron's assistant, hurried in, greatly excited. One of the masters had just telephoned from Pollock to report that we had won the game. I gave a little yell of enthusiasm, partly sincere, partly perfunctory. Billy looked at me bleakly.

"Now we'll have that damn celebration," he said curtly. "Drums and cheers, drums and cheers, all night. God! And for what?"

He lost all interest in what we were doing and refused to discuss it with me. He lay back in bed and simply stared at the ceiling while I turned back to the unfinished puzzle.

It was late in the afternoon, about six o'clock, when the buses which had taken the school to Pollock began to return. We could hear the crunch of their wheels on the drive on the other side of the building and the excited yells of the disembarking boys. From across the campus came the muffled roll of the drums. Already the celebration was starting. The entire school and all the masters would now assemble before the steps of the headmaster's house. He would come out in a straw hat and a red blazer and be raised to the shoulders of the school prefects on a chair strapped to two poles. Waving his megaphone, he would be borne away at the head of a procession to a martial tune of the fife and drum corps on a circuit of all the school buildings. Before each of these the crowd would stop and in response to the headmaster's deep "What have we here?" would shout the name of the building followed by the school cheer. As the slow procession wended its way around the campus it would become noisier and the cheers more numerous; wives of popular masters would be thunderously applauded and would have to appear at the windows of their houses to acknowledge the ovation; statues, gates, memorial fountains would be cheered until the procession wound up by the athletic field, where a bonfire would be built and the members of the triumphant team tossed aloft by multitudinous arms and cheered in the flickering light of the flames. And all the while the "outside," the big bell over the gymnasium which sounded the hours for rising, for going to chapel, for attending meals, a knell that brought daily to the countryside the austere routine of Shirley School, would toll and toll, symbolizing in its shocking unrestraint the extraordinary liberty of the day.

The atmosphere pervaded even the infirmary. Mrs. Gardner, the matron, and her assistant watched from the dispensary window. The infirmary cook gave Billy and me an extra helping of ice cream. I moved my bed over to the window and listened to the distant throb of the band. When it stopped we would know that the headmaster was speaking and a moment later would come the roar of the school cheer. Glancing at Billy, after one of these roars, I noticed that he looked pale and tense.

"Listen to that damn bell," he complained, when he saw me looking at him. "It gets on my nerves. It's like Saint Bartholomew's Day, with everyone coming after the Huguenots."

I said nothing to this, but there was something contagious about his tensity. As the shouts grew louder and more distinct, as we finally made out the stamp of feet, I got out of my bed and pushed it away from the window.

"What are you doing?" Billy asked me sharply. "Are you ashamed of being in the infirmary?"

He sat up suddenly and got out of bed. He walked to the open window and stood before it, his hands on his hips. From behind him, looking into the courtyard below, I could see the first boys arriving, waving school banners and blowing horns.

"Billy, get back," I begged him. "They'll see you! Please, Billy!"

Then I spotted the headmaster's chair coming around the corner of the adjacent building and ducked out of sight. Billy ignored me completely. From below, through the open windows, almost unbelievably close now, came the din of the assembling school. The drums kept beating, and laughter and jokes, often from recognizable voices, came to our ears. It seemed to me, as I shrank against the wall near the window, pressing my spinal cord against its white coldness, as though every shout and drumbeat, every retort, detaching itself from the general roar and suddenly coherent, every laugh and cheer, each sound of feet on gravel, was part of some huge reptilian figure surrounding the infirmary and our very room with the cold, muscular coils of its body. Fear pounded in me, sharp and irrational.

"Billy!" I called again at him. "Billy!"

There was a sudden silence outside, and we heard the rich, assured tones of the headmaster's voice, starting his classic interrogatory to the crowd.

"What is this building that I see before me?"

"The infirmary!" thundered the school.

"And who is the good lady who runs the infirmary?"

"Mrs. Gardner!"

"And does Mrs. Gardner have an assistant?"

"Mrs. Jones," roared the crowd.

This would have been followed immediately, in normal procedure, by the headmaster's request for cheers for the infirmary and for the good women who ran it. Instead there was an unexpected pause, a silence, and then, as my blood froze I heard the headmaster's other voice, his disciplinary voice, directed up and into the very window at which Billy was standing.

"Who is that boy in the window? Go away from that window, boy, and get to bed." It then added, with a chuckle for the benefit of the crowd: "Good gracious me, anyone might think he wasn't sick." There was a roar of laughter.

Billy, however, continued to stand there as if he hadn't heard, and the momentary hush that followed was broken by the sharp, clear tones of George Neale.

"Go back to bed, Angela! Can't you hear? Take the wax out of your ears!"

Once again there was a startled quiet. The amazement must have been as much at George's impudence as at Billy's immobility; it was unheard of for a boy to second the headmaster's order. The old struggle between George and Billy hung like a lantern in the darkening air before the upturned eyes of three hundred boys. It may have been the use of his nickname, the bold, casual, unconventional use of it before the boys and the faculty, before Mrs. Gardner and Mrs. Jones watching from the window of the dispensary, before the townspeople from Shirley who had come to watch the celebration, that broke Billy down. It was as if he had been stamped "Angela" unredeemably and for the ages. The future, in spite of all his protest, would be a Shirley future. He suddenly waved his arms in a frenzied, circular fashion at the mob.

"Three cheers for Pollock!" he screamed in a harsh voice that did not sound like him at all. "Three cheers for Pollock School!" he screamed. "I wish they'd licked us! I wish they had!"

What I remember feeling at this unbelievable outburst, as I pressed my back harder against the wall, was its inadequacy to express the outrage with which Billy was throbbing. It was too hopelessly disloyal, too hurt, too puerile to do more than dismay or shock. Yet he had said it. He had actually said it! Then the door opened and Mrs. Gardner came in, followed by Mr. O'Neil. I was moved at once to another room, and Billy at last was left alone.

He was taken out of school for good a few days later. His parents drove up from New York and had a long conference with the headmaster. Immediately afterwards his things were packed. I was out of the infirmary by then and went to see his mother at the parents' house. She wept a good deal and talked to me as though I were grown up, which flattered me. She said that Billy had had a little "nervous trouble" and would be going home. She added that he was tired and would not be able to see anyone before he left. Then she kissed me and tucked a five-dollar bill in my pocket. I'm afraid that I rather enjoyed my sadness over the whole catastrophe.

At school, after Billy had gone, I did much better. In the ensuing years I rose to be manager of the school press, head librarian and even achieved the dignified status of rober to the headmaster in chapel. Billy diminished in retrospect to a thin, shrill figure lost in the past darkness of lower-school years. But it was only a part of me that felt this way. There was another part that was always uneasy about my disloyalty to the desperate logic of his isolation. It was as though I owed the warmth and friendliness that I later found at Shirley to a compromise that he had not been able to make. Whether or not I was justified in any such reservation can only be determined for himself by each individual who has passed as a boy through that semi-eternity which begins with homesickness and hazing and snowballs and ends, such seeming ages afterwards, with the white flannels and blue coats of commencement in the full glory of a New England spring.

The Gemlike Flame

1953

W HEN I LOOKED UP Clarence McClintock that summer in Venice it was partly out of curiosity and partly out of affection. He had long ceased to be anything but a legend to the rest of our family, the butt of mild jokes and the object of perfunctory sympathy, a lonely, wandering, expatriate figure, personally dignified and prematurely bizarre, rigid in his demeanor and impossibly choosy in his acquaintance. It was universally agreed among our aunts and uncles that he had been an early casualty in the terrible battle that his mother, my ex-aunt Maud, a violent, pleasure-loving woman with a fortune as large as her appetites, had waged over his custody with my sober, Presbyterian uncle John. Yet I had remembered the Clarence of those early years and how, for all the sobriety of demeanor that had so amused our older relatives, there had also been a persistent gentleness of manner that had gone hand in hand with kindness, particularly to younger cousins. Clarence as a boy had been scrupulously fair, invariably just, in his personal dealings with me. The fact that I choose such words may imply that he set himself up as a judge, and there may have been a certain arrogance or at least fatuity in this, but it is the impression of his integrity and not his pretentiousness that lingers. If Clarence was magisterial to my childish eyes, he was also loyal.

When we met at the appointed café on St. Mark's Square I felt more like a nephew than a cousin. Clarence, tall and bonily thin, with small dry lips and a small hooked nose, with thin receding hair and dark, expensive clothes, did not seem a man of only thirty-seven. I did feel, however, that he was glad to see me.

"So at last one of the family comes to Europe!" he exclaimed with a small, shy, yet hospitable smile of surprise. "And is writing a novel, too!

Let us hope that Venice will do for your fiction what it did for Wagner's music. You're very good to look me up, Peter. No one does anymore, you know. No one, that is, but Mother. She cannot, in all decency, quite neglect the sole fruit of her many unions." He smiled bleakly at this. "But give me the news," he continued in a brisker tone. "About all the good aunts and uncles and all the cousins like yourself."

News, however, was the last thing that he seemed to wish to hear. He interrupted me when I started on Aunt Clara's stroke with a sudden rush of reminiscence about the secret gift drawer that she had kept for us as children. When I tried to tell him about Uncle Warren's lawsuit, he broke in with apostrophes about the nursery rhymes which the old man used to write for us. What obviously intrigued him about me was the fact of our cousinship; it provided him with a needed link to the past which still seemed to occupy so many of his thoughts. His memory was extraordinary. It was almost as if he had spent his early years carefully collecting this series of vivid images which he somehow knew even then were to be his only companions in the self-imposed loneliness which the future held for him. My turning up after so many years must have given him a sense of reassurance, a proof of the facts on which these images were based, whose very existence he may have come to doubt.

We dined together the following night and the one after. He helped to get me settled in a hotel that he recommended and which turned out to be just right for my needs. He attached himself to me with all the pertinacity of the very shy when they do not feel rebuffed, and I began, perhaps ungraciously, to see that he might become a problem. For, as far as I could make out, despite the fact that he spent every summer in Venice and had an apartment there, he not only had no friends in the city but no inclination to make any. He was too stiff and too reserved, and his Italian, although accurate, was too halting for native circles. He loved Italy and its monuments, but he would have preferred it unpopulated. Americans abroad, on the other hand, he had even less use for. He divided them into four categories, all equally detestable. There were the diplomats, who alarmed him with their polish; the strident tourists, who reminded him of the business world in New York that he had found too competitive; the women who had married titles, whom he thought pretentious, and finally the artists and writers, whom he regarded with a chaste suspicion as people of unorthodox sexual appetite who had come to the sunny land of love in search of a tolerance that was not to be found in the justly censorious places of their origin. And he himself?

Clarence McClintock? Why, he had simply come to Italy to admire it and be left alone. The noisiest Italians could be noisy without making demands on him. That was their great virtue. It was as if they had a self-assurance that his fellow Americans lacked, which enabled them to pass by the lone observer from across the seas without the compulsion to turn and make him part of them.

On the third night after our meeting I dined out with Italian friends and was a bit discouraged, I confess, on returning to my hotel, to find Clarence waiting for me in the lobby. He seemed upset about something and wanted to talk, so we went over to St. Mark's Square for a *cinzano*. There he told me that he had had a letter from his mother. She was coming to Venice at the end of the following month to attend the fancy-dress ball at the Palazzo Lorisan.

"You mean she'll fly all the way from New York to go to a ball?" I asked in mild surprise. "All those expensive miles for one party?"

Clarence nodded grimly. "She's even proud of it," he affirmed. "Mother's not afraid to face the absurdity of her own motivations. I'll say that for her."

"But I rather admire that, don't you? I hope I have that kind of spirit when I'm seventy."

There was a disapproving pause while Clarence sipped his *cinzano*.

"Sixty-eight," he corrected me dryly. "You forget, Peter," he continued more severely, "that someone always pays for a woman like Mother. I don't mean financially because, obviously, my grandfather left her very well off. But emotionally. She is quite remorseless in the pursuit of pleasure."

"Oh, come, Clarence, I'm sure you're being hard on her," I protested. "How do you know she isn't really coming over to see you?"

He smiled sourly.

"The Lorisan ball is far more important than I," he replied. "Though I won't deny," he conceded, "that seeing me may provide a subsidiary motive for her coming. She knows how I feel about Olympia Lorisan and that set of international riffraff."

"You mean she's coming here to *annoy* you? Don't you think that's going rather far?"

He shrugged his shoulders.

"Not altogether to annoy me, of course not. But it adds the icing to the cake. Oh, she's up to no good. You can be sure of that."

I had to laugh at this.

"Do you honestly think she cares that much?"

Clarence had to pause to think this over.

"We are the two most different people in the world," he said more reflectively, "and we know it. We each know in our heart that the other will never change. Yet we go on as if there was a way, or as if the other must be made to see the way even if he won't take it. In any event," he continued, changing to a brisker, more deliberate tone, as if embarrassed by his reverie, "she will not find me this time. I shall be safely in Rome while the Princess Lorisan's friends are debauching the bride of the Adriatic."

"You won't even stay to see your mother?"

"She can meet me, if she cares, in the eternal city. Will you go with me?"

I told him I had to stay in Venice and work, ball or no ball.

"I suppose you might even go to it?" he speculated.

"I might. If I'm asked."

"I see, Peter, that I must not overestimate you," he said regretfully, shaking his head. "You are essentially of that world, aren't you? Yet I wonder how any artist could really prefer to dance and drink with those shallow people than walk in Hadrian's Villa or in the moonlit Colosseum. Mind how you reject me, Peter. Haven't I told you that I burn with a 'hard, gemlike flame'?"

As a matter of fact, he had. He had told me the first night that we had dined together and in that same mocking tone. He had said that most people saw only the "brownstone front" side of his nature, the austere, stiff, conservative side, but that there was another, a truer side, a romantic, loyal, idealistic one. This was what he meant when he quoted Walter Pater, but the disdainful smile that accompanied his phrase made me wonder if any gemlike flame within him had not been smothered or at least isolated so that it burned on invisibly, a candle in a crypt.

"Well, some of us have to do more than burn for a living," I was saying, rather crudely, when looking up I saw Neddy Bane crossing the square alone.

"Why, it's Neddy Bane!" I exclaimed.

Clarence looked up too, immediately alarmed at the prospect of a stranger.

"And who, pray, is Neddy Bane?"

"And old friend of mine," I said promptly, feeling for the first time that he was. "We went to school and college together. Let me ask him over, Clarence. You'll like him."

"Yes, why don't you do that?" he said in a dry, suddenly hostile tone. "But if you'll excuse me," he continued, glancing down at his watch, "I think it's time that I was on my way."

"Now, Clarence, wait. Don't be rude." I put my hand firmly on his arm. "It's not that late."

I turned and waved at Neddy, who stared for a moment and then smiled and started toward our table. It was suddenly important to me that Clarence should make this concession. The sight, as he approached us, of Neddy's friendly smile made me feel that the last three evenings had been a lifetime. It was as if I had been locked in a small dark library with the windows closed and Neddy Bane, of all unlikely people, was life beating against the panes.

"Neddy!" I called to him. "How are you, boy? Come on over and drink with us." And as he came up to the table I put my hand on Clarence's shoulder. "Do you remember my cousin, Neddy? Clarence McClintock?"

Neddy was my age, about thirty-three, but he was not as tall as Clarence or myself, and this, together with his gay sport coat and thick, brown, curly hair, made him seem like a smiling and respectful boy at our table. He had large blue eyes that peered at one with a hesitant, almost timid friendliness, but when they widened with surprise, as they were apt to if one said anything in the least interesting, their blue faded almost into gray, the puffiness above his cheekbones became more evident and he seemed less boyish. He was weak, and he was supposed to be charming, but I have often wondered if his charm was not rather assumed by people who had been told that it was a quality that went with weakness. He had been a stockbroker in New York with an adequate future, married to a perfectly adequate wife, the kind of nice girl of whom it was said that she would bloom with marriage, that even her rather pinched features would separate into better proportions and glow when love had touched her. Conceivably something like this could have happened had another husband been her lot. She wanted only what so many girls wanted, a house in the suburbs in which to bring up her children and a country club whose male members were all doing as well or better than her husband. But Neddy was constitutionally unable to find content in any regular life. He could not even commute. He would get to Grand Central and drink in a bar until he had missed his train and every other reasonable one and had to spend the night with his widowed mother in the city. He was fond of rather dramatic collapses, of simply lying back and doing nothing when he felt pressure, refusing to answer questions or to give explanations, and his poor wife, lacking the maturity or the understanding to be able to cope with him, gave vent to her deep sense of injustice that he was not as other husbands and nagged him until he walked out on her and the children and fled to Europe.

It was like Neddy that he had made no arrangements for divorce or separation or for his own or anyone else's support. All this he left to his mother, who, far from rich, sent him a check when she could, at great sacrifice. He professed to be an artist, but he did condescend to take various jobs. He worked for a travel agency, for the French edition of a New York women's magazine, as secretary and guide to a Pittsburgh industrialist. Now, he told Clarence and me, his money had really given out and he was going back to New York.

"Well, it's been fun while it lasted," he said with his disarming smile, raising the drink I had ordered for him, "and I'm never one to regret things, as you, Peter, ought to know. Peter has never really approved of me, Mr. McClintock," he continued turning his attention suddenly to Clarence. "Peter is the greatest bourgeois I know. Despite his writing and despite his being over here. Fundamentally, his heart has never left Wall Street."

I glanced at Clarence and noticed to my surprise that he no longer seemed bored.

"But you're quite right, Mr. Bane," he said seriously. "Peter isn't really willing to give himself to the European experience. I'm interested that you see that."

I could hardly help laughing at this unexpected alliance.

"Perhaps it's because I don't burn with a hard, gemlike flame," I retorted. "Do you, Neddy?"

Neddy glanced from me to Clarence and saw from the latter's quick flush whom my reference was aimed at.

"Do I? Of course I do!" he exclaimed. "And I'll bet your cousin here does too. Every true artist or art lover burns with a hard, gemlike flame." He turned back to Clarence. "Naturally Peter doesn't understand. What would a novelist of manners, bad manners at that, know of the true flame? I can see, Mr. McClintock, that you're a person who cuts deep into things. You have no time for surfaces. It's the only way to be. Oh, I've batted around a lot myself, as Peter here knows; I've wasted time and energy, but none of that's the real me. The real me is a painter, first and last!"

"Is it really?" Clarence asked. "But how sad then that you have to go back. People who can paint Italy should stay here. It's the only way we can contribute."

"Do you paint yourself, Mr. McClintock?"

"Alas, no. I'm a bit of a scholar, that's all. I hang my head before a real artist."

"But why!" Neddy cried. "The artist and the scholar, weren't they the team of the Renaissance?"

They continued to talk in this vein, Neddy putting himself out more and more to please Clarence. I knew his habit in the past of trying to placate the kind of disapproving figure that Clarence initially must have seemed to him at the expense of familiar and hence less awesome figures like myself. I had never, however, seen him carry it so far. When he talked about painting he deferred with humility to Clarence's amateur yet aggressively old-fashioned judgment and sought his opinion on recent exhibits. When he elicited the fact that Clarence's last monograph, on the art collection of Pius VII, was to be published in *Via Appia*, he praised the discrimination of Princess Vinitelli, its publisher. I knew that he must have heard me describe Clarence in the past as my "rich" cousin, and decided that he was simply after a loan. What really surprised me, though, was Clarence's reaction. At first he glanced at me from time to time while Neddy was talking to see if I shared his interest, but after a couple of rounds of drinks he forgot me entirely and kept his eyes riveted on Neddy. I had noticed on our previous evenings that he had drunk almost nothing, which was evidently because of a light head, for now under the influence of the mild *cinzanos* he became almost as loquacious as Neddy.

"It's wonderful to find someone who really *feels* Italy," he said, looking around at me again, but with a reproachful look. "I had begun to be afraid that the whole world was a Lorisan ball."

When I glanced at my watch and saw how late it was and got up to go, Clarence only squinted up at me, his usually sallow features softened with what struck me as an air of rather smug satisfaction, and said that he and "Neddy" would sit on a bit and have "one for the road." I left them together, amused at their congeniality, but slightly irritated at being made to feel like an elderly tutor after whose retiring hour the young wards, released, may frisk in the dark of a forbidden city. Really, I said to myself, with a sneer that surprised me, what an ass Clarence can be.

I didn't see either of them again until I ran into Neddy a week later when I was getting my mail at the American Express.

"I thought you were going home," I said.

"Well, no," he said, looking, I thought, slightly embarrassed. "I'm not exactly. Not for a while anyway."

"Where are you staying?"

He hesitated a moment and then stuck his chin forward in a sudden gesture of defiance.

"I'm staying with Clarence."

"With Clarence!" I exclaimed. "In his apartment? Why, I thought nobody ever stayed with Clarence."

"Maybe he never found anyone he wanted to ask," Neddy said in a superior tone.

"But how did it happen?" I asked. "How did you ever pull it off?"

Neddy was like a child in his obvious pleasure at my interest. All his pores opened happily under the reassuring sunshine of curiosity.

"Well, after you left us the other night," he said eagerly, "Clarence and I sat on and had a few more drinks. He became very reminiscent and told me about his mother and how dreadfully she had treated him when he was little. She must have been awful, don't you think, Peter? Except rather wonderful at the same time." He looked at me questioningly, afraid that his speculation was bold. I shrugged my shoulders. "Well, anyway, when I finally got up to go, just when I thought I was saying goodbye to him for good, he suddenly seized my arm and blurted out: 'If you really want to stay here and paint, you can, you know. You can set yourself up in my apartment. I'm quite alone.' Don't you think that was marvelous, Peter? From someone who looks just as cold as ice?"

"Marvelous," I agreed dryly. "And you accepted, of course?"

"I moved in the very next day! Wouldn't you have?"

"What does that matter?"

I thought over what Neddy had told me, and two days later I called on Clarence at his small, chaste, perfect apartment. He received me alone, as Neddy was out sketching. I noted that the somber living room with its carved-wood medieval statues and red damask curtains had already been turned into a studio.

"I suppose you've been wondering," he told me in his cool formal tone, "whether or not I've taken leave of my senses."

"No, Clarence. I'm just interested, that's all."

"As a cousin or as a novelist?"

"As a friend."

He looked at me suspiciously for a moment and then, nodding his head as if satisfied, proceeded in his own slow, measured pace to give me the story of what had happened. I had the feeling as he went along that his formality concealed a sort of defiance, a smug, rather cocky little satisfaction that he should have captured Neddy. It didn't matter what I thought; I was simply a person to whom an accounting had to be rendered, a visiting parent at the school where Clarence was headmaster. He admitted, to begin with, that he had been terrified at what his unprecedented impulsiveness might have led him into. Never before, he assured me, had he assumed so much responsibility for a fellow human being. But Neddy, it appeared, had soon set his mind at rest. He had proved as docile and pliable as a well-brought-up child, not only applauding the quiet and orderly routine of Clarence's life, but earnestly adapting it to his own. Clarence had found himself the preceptor of a serious and dedicated art student.

"What Neddy needs," he told me gravely, "happens to be exactly what I can offer: order and discipline. I get him up every morning at eight and send him off with his sketchbook. In the afternoons he paints in here." He pointed proudly to an easel in the corner of the living room on which stood an unfinished painting of a canal after the manner of Ziem, colorful and dull. "In the evenings we relax, but in a tempered way. We dine out in a restaurant and drink a bottle of wine. But that's all. Bed by eleven is the rule."

"I see that it's wonderful for Neddy," I said at last. "But what, Clarence, is there in it for you?"

He stared at me for a moment and then shook his head thoughtfully.

"Well, if you don't see that, Peter, what *do* you see? It's what I have always waited for."

When I walked back to my hotel I reflected with some concern on these words of his. I couldn't help feeling a certain responsibility at having been the agent who had brought him and Neddy together. Yet who was I to say that it was a bad thing? I had seen Clarence before he had met Neddy and I had seen him after, and I wondered if I could honestly say that the irritation which I felt at his blind enthusiasm for so fallible a young man was anything more than the irritation that we are apt to feel when an outsider helps one of our family for whom we have given up hope. If such was the case my doubts were the doubts of a dog in the manger.

Having established myself on a friendly basis in Clarence's new ménage, I was asked there from time to time, but by no means constantly, during the rest of the summer. It was apparent that both Clarence and Neddy were slightly on the defensive with me. The mere fact that I had previously known both of them without losing my head over either may have seemed an implied reproach to the extravagance of their mutual admiration. When two weeks passed in August without my hearing from either of them, I assumed that Clarence had carried Neddy off to Rome to avoid the pollution of the city by the influx of guests for the Lorisan ball. It was with surprise, therefore, that I received a card one morning from Aunt Maud, Clarence's mother, telling me that she had arrived at the Grand Hotel and asking me to come in that afternoon for a drink with her and Clarence and "Clarence's friend."

Aunt Maud Dash, as she now called herself, having resumed her maiden name after the last of her marriages, had done me the dubious honor of singling me out from the other members of her first husband's family on the theory that I was not "stuffy," or at least, as she sometimes qualified it, not quite as stuffy as the rest. There was also, of course, the fact that I was comparatively young, male, unattached, and last but not least, a writer. When I came into her sitting room at the hotel I found her on a chaise longue, her large round figure loosely covered by a blue silk negligee, examining with a careful, almost professional interest a wide ruff collar that was obviously a part of her ball costume. Her hair was pink, a different shade than when I had last seen her, and her skin, dark and freckled, was heavily powdered. Propped up in her seat she looked as neat and brushed and clean as a big doll sitting in the window of an expensive toy store. There was nothing, however, in the least doll-like about her eyes. They were small and black and roving; they seemed to make fun, in an only half goodhearted fashion, of everything about her, even of her own weight and of the stiff little legs that stuck out before her on the chaise longue and the wheezing, asthmatic note of her breathing.

"Why, Peter," she called to me, "you've got a corduroy coat! We'll make a bohemian out of you yet."

"Maybe it's time I went home."

She turned away now from the ruff collar and examined me more critically.

"Not yet, dear. Wait a bit. You're almost presentable now. I always said there was a chance for you."

"It's what has given me hope."

She snorted.

"Tell me about Clarence," she said abruptly. "I know I can count on you. They say he has a boyfriend."

"Neddy Bane is not exactly a boy," I replied with dignity. "He's my age. As a matter of fact I introduced them. Neddy's wife used to be a friend of mine." I hoped by this to change the direction of her thinking. It was a vain hope.

"Now look here, Peter Westcott, if you think you can put me off with some old wives' tale at my time of life and after all I've seen —" She stopped as we heard steps in the corridor and then a light, authoritative knock on the door.

"Mother?" I heard Clarence's voice.

"Come in, darling, come in," she called, and the door opened to admit Clarence followed by a rather sheepish-looking Neddy. "How are you, my baby," she continued in a husky voice that seemed to be making fun of him. "Give your old ma a kiss."

Clarence bent down gingerly and touched his cheek to hers, emerging from her embrace with a white powder spot on his face that he immediately, without the slightest effort at concealment, proceeded to rub off with a handkerchief.

"And is this your Mr. Bane?" Aunt Maud continued in the same voice. "What sort of man are you, Mr. Bane? Are you as severe and sober as my Clarry?"

"No, but I try," Neddy answered shyly. "Clarence is my guide and mentor."

Aunt Maud looked shrewdly from one to the other and grunted.

"Are you going to the ball, Mother," Clarence put in quickly, with a bleak glance at the ruff collar, "as the Virgin Queen?"

"Clarry, dear, your *tone*," she reproached him. "But since you ask, child, I am. I've always liked the old girl." She turned suddenly back to Neddy. "Do you believe in the theory that she was really a man, Mr. Bane? Nobody ever saw her, you know, with her clothes off."

Neddy was fingering the red velvet hoop skirts of the costume spread out on the chair beside him.

"Oh, never!" he protested with unexpected animation. "You don't think so, do you?" Then he appealed to her suddenly, with a rather sly little smile that I had not seen before. "You mean she was really a queen?"

Aunt Maud put her head back and roared with laughter.

"But I *like* your friend, Clarry!" she exclaimed. "Can I call him Neddy? I shall anyway," she continued, turning glowingly from Clarence to his friend. "And you, Neddy, must call me Maud." She nodded in satisfaction. "Perhaps you will be my Essex? I have a man's costume, too. It's over there in that box on the chest."

Neddy glanced questioningly at Clarence and then hurried over to the box and took out the red pants and doublet. He stood before the long mirror and held them up in front of him.

"But they fit perfectly!" he exclaimed, and went back again to the box. "Oh, and just look at that sword! Gosh, Mrs. Dash, I mean Maud! Don't you love it, Clarry? Do you think we could go?" He looked anxiously at Clarence.

I didn't have to look at Clarence to know that he would resent Neddy's calling him "Clarry," aping his mother so immediately. He stood there primly, his lips twitching, like a governess who has been overruled by an indulgent parent. Then he turned on Aunt Maud.

"Why must you have an Essex?" he asked sharply. "Would you not do better to search among your own contemporaries for a Leicester? Or even a Burleigh?"

But she simply laughed, this time a high, rather fluty laugh that was just redeemed from silliness by its mockery.

"Because I *want* an Essex!" she said defiantly. "A young attractive Essex." She winked at me. "Clarence is so absurdly conventional," she continued, more maliciously. "He thinks one should only see people one's own age. As if life were a perennial boarding school. But Neddy doesn't have to be Essex, does he, Peter? He could be one of those pretty pages whom the old queen used to favor, tweaking their ears and pinching their thighs." She threw back her head and gave herself up once more to that laugh. "Or even," she added, gasping, "stifling them half to death in her musky old bosom!"

I could see that Clarence was beside himself. I could only hope that he would not interpret her laugh as I did, as a challenge to compare the relative improprieties of Neddy as an escort for her or Neddy as a companion for him. She picked up the ruff collar now and put it almost coyly around her neck.

"Don't you think it's a good idea, Clarence?" Neddy asked hopefully. "You don't really mind, do you?"

"Mind?" Clarence snapped at him. "Why on earth should I mind? You don't expect me to decide every time you go to a party, do you?"

He got up and walked across the room to the little balcony and, going out, stood by the railing and stared down into the canal. Neddy was at first abashed by his sudden exit, but after I, at Aunt Maud's bidding, had mixed a shaker of martinis from the ample ingredients with which she always traveled, he cheered up again. In a very short time he and Aunt Maud had discovered a series of mutual acquaintances and become positively noisy. I had to leave early and went out on the balcony to say goodbye to Clarence. He was still standing there, gloomily watching the line of gondolas arriving at the hotel bringing more and more guests to the hated ball. He hardly turned when I spoke to him, but simply pointed to the scene below.

"I warned Neddy about this, but he wouldn't believe me," he said. "All hell is breaking loose here."

The very next morning he came alone to see me at my hotel. He looked tired and worn.

"I want to ask a favor of you, Peter," he said gravely.

"A favor, Clarence? How unlike you. But go ahead, I'm delighted."

"It is unlike me," he agreed, frowning. "I am not in the habit of asking favors. I am sure you will be sympathetic when I tell you that I do not find it an easy experience."

I hastened to cut short his embarrassment.

"What can I do for you, Clarence?"

"You know my mother," he began rapidly. "You understand her.

She'll listen to you. You can tell her that she mustn't take Neddy to this ball."

"But why mustn't she?"

"Why?" he exclaimed in a suddenly shrill tone. "Good heavens, man, you can't have known Neddy all your life and not see what this will do to him! Just now, of all times, when he's really painting, when for once he's got parties and girls and drinking out of his mind —"

"But one ball, Clarence," I protested.

"One ball!" he almost shouted. "One marihuana! One pipe of opium!"

"But what am I going to tell your mother?"

"Tell her —" He paused and then appeared to give it up. A bitter look came over his face. "Oh, tell her," he went on harshly, "that as long as she's taken everything she could from me all my life, she may as well take Neddy too. But why she has to have her gin-soaked body hurtled in a plane three thousand miles through the ether just to interfere with the only friendship I've ever had —"

"Clarence!"

But he was completely out of control now.

"Why do I ask you, anyway?" he cried. "You like people like her, you even write about them! You think she's admirable, the old tart!"

"All right, Clarence, all right," I said firmly, putting my hands up to stop him. "I'll speak to her, I promise. But calm down, will you?"

He seized my hand in sudden embarrassed gratitude and hurried away without trusting himself to say another word. I shook my head sadly, amazed to have discovered such depths of feeling in him. I had always known that he had disliked his mother; I had not realized that he hated her. She must have seemed, in the isolation that even as a child he had preferred, the very essence of the vulgarity of living and loving as the world lived and loved, the symbol of the Indian giver, because for all her vitality he may have instinctively suspected that she wanted back the one pale spark she had emitted in bearing him. And even now, when she came to his beloved Italy, wasn't it the same thing all over again, didn't she participate more in the carnival life of the country by attending one crazy ball than he with all his monographs? That, she must have known, was his vulnerable point; that was why she struck at it year after year. It was as if she resented the very existence of what he called the gemlike flame within him and had determined to blow it out.

I telephoned Aunt Maud and invited her to have cocktails with me at Harry's Bar that afternoon. She arrived in high spirits, in a red dress and an enormous red hat, and, as I had known she would, flatly refused my request about Neddy.

"What's wrong, infant?" she asked suggestively. "Do you want to take him to the ball yourself?"

"I'm only thinking of Clarence," I retorted. "This whole thing is bothering him terribly."

"And why should it bother Clarence?"

I noted the glitter in her eyes. It was as if she had been playing bridge with children and had suddenly picked up a slam hand, a waste, to be sure, but a hand that she could still enjoy bidding.

"You know perfectly well why, Aunt Maud," I said wearily.

"My dear Peter," she said firmly. "I know a great many things, including what stones do not bear turning over. I have no idea of asking Clarence to explain to me, his mother, what his involvement with this young man is. But I cannot see that borrowing his precious Neddy for a single evening is interfering very much. Must he have Neddy with him every second? Why doesn't he keep him in a harem?"

"You don't understand, Aunt Maud," I tried to explain. "Clarence thinks that Neddy has finally settled down to be a painter and —"

"Nonsense," she interrupted firmly. "It's selfishness, pure and simple, and you know it, Peter. Clarence is simply scared to death that Neddy will find the big world more fun than his cell. Which I should hope he would!"

"Aunt Maud," I said desperately. "*I'll* take you to the ball."

"Thank you very much, Peter, but I haven't asked you. It's all very well for Clarence to go on about my interrupting Neddy's work, but I'll bet he doesn't begrudge him the hours they waste sipping chocolate on the Piazza San Marco while he rants about his poor old mother's wicked life. Oh, I know Clarence, Peter!"

This was a home thrust that I could not honestly deny. And what could I do, in any case, for Clarence, with a mother who felt this way about him? When I wrote him that night, for I couldn't bear to face him, I made as light of it as I could. Aunt Maud, I told him, had refused to give up her "hostage."

I saw neither Clarence nor Neddy for several days, but one morning as I was picking up my mail I encountered Neddy again at the American Express. He had evidently been waiting for me for he came right over and asked if he could talk to me.

"Why not?" I said, glancing through my envelopes.

"I wonder," he began in a rather embarrassed way, "if you're not doing anything tonight, whether you wouldn't have dinner with Clarence and me. Quite frankly, I think we need a change."

"Why? Are you bored with each other?"

"It's not that exactly. But I'm worried about Clarence. He's got this fetish about my not going to that damn ball."

"Why do you go then?" I asked coldly.

"Why shouldn't I?" he protested. "Who do you think I am, I'd like to know, that Clarence can boss me around?"

"It's not a question of bossing. It's simply a question of doing a very small favor in return for the considerable number you have received."

Neddy smiled uneasily, probably the way he used to smile at his poor wife when she reproached him for spending his evenings in bars. He had almost a genius for evading any unpleasantness in the facts that surrounded him. When I failed to return his smile, however, he rather drew himself up.

"Any small financial aid that I have received from Clarence," he told me with dignity, "will be paid in full when I'm on my feet. It will not be difficult, I assure you. You probably know your cousin well enough to be aware that he doesn't play fast and loose with his money."

The impudence of this quite took me aback.

"Why do you stick around him, then?" I demanded.

"You think it's all one-sided, don't you?" he retorted. "Well, you don't know the half of it. You don't have to listen to his ravings day in and day out. And when I say ravings, I mean ravings!"

"What sort of ravings?"

Neddy proceeded to tell me. I leaned against the counter and puffed gloomily at a cigarette while he unfolded, with the relish of one unjustly accused, the whole sorry picture. For the past five days, apparently, the ball had been the sole subject of their conversation. Whether in the studio while Neddy was trying to paint or during their long dinners in little restaurants, and even on Sunday when they had been lying on the sand at the Lido, Clarence had held forth on the iniquities of Olympia

Lorisan's friends and their destructive effect upon all who had any serious purpose in life. Neddy, thoroughly bored, had answered less and less, but Clarence, straining after his attention, had only become more vehement in tone and more fantastic in argument, hoping apparently by the very hyperbole in his speech to instill into his threadbare subject some dash of interest to make him listen. He had exhausted the epithets of his rather chaste vocabulary in withering descriptions of the aging guests and how they would look in their monstrous costumes. He had even tried to shame Neddy by telling him how contemptuously people spoke of impecunious young men who acted as escorts for rich old women and to alarm him by insinuating what attentions his mother, aroused by champagne and late hours, might take it into her head to expect from so junior a companion. He had cut reports out of the paper of the magnificent preparations for the party, insisting on reading them aloud with prefaces such as: "Neddy, listen to this! This really *is* the limit!" And when all else had failed, when he was desperate, he had actually resorted to the argument that the ball was a Communist plot designed to bring discredit on the idle rich of the Western world.

I listened to it with a sick feeling. I could hardly deny that the whole account, even exaggerated, had an unmistakable ring of truth. But in my sudden confrontation with the full extent of Clarence's obsession, I found myself losing my temper at its fatuously smiling cause. Neddy stood before me smugly relishing each detail of his sorry story, pleased at my obvious dismay, satisfied that I would have to concede to him now that anything Clarence might have done for him was only a token compensation for what he, the long-suffering, had had to put up with.

"You're nothing but a goddamn sponge, Neddy Bane!" I exclaimed angrily. "You don't deserve to be considered anything but what you are considered!"

He turned pale.

"And what is that?"

"As Clarence's kept boyfriend!"

He stretched out an arm to me in shocked protest, he opened his mouth to remonstrate, but I turned quickly on my heel and strode away.

I was quite unable to do any writing that morning. I thought how abominably Neddy had treated his wife and children, how shamelessly he had used his old mother, and even went farther back to our school days, when he had always been careful to curry favor with the strongest clique in the class. I conjured up other and more stinging things that I could have said to him and reminded myself that I had only done my duty. But at heart, all the time, I knew perfectly well that I was only repressing my own uneasiness at what I might have done to Clarence.

Retribution did not wait long. When I walked through the hotel lobby at noon, on my way out for lunch, I saw Clarence standing at the desk talking to the clerk and then I saw the clerk nod his head and point to me. He turned around as I started over to him, and I saw that he looked pale, almost stunned. His eyes met mine and wandered off in a way that was not like him.

"He's gone," he said as I came up to him. "He's gone to Padua to paint. He said he couldn't paint with me nagging him. He said awful things to me."

"Let's go out, Clarence. Let's take a walk or have lunch or something."

He followed me obediently into the little square on which I lived.

"He said you said terrible things to him," he continued in the same dazed tone. "Terrible things, Peter."

I said nothing.

"Do you think if we both went to Padua," he asked desperately, "and if you apologized and I promised not to nag him anymore, he'd come back?"

I shrugged my shoulders.

"You don't think he really might?" he insisted.

"Clarence," I said firmly, turning to him, "for God's sake, let him go. You ought to be congratulating yourself that you're rid of him. You don't know that guy, Clarence. You don't know what he's like. I'm sorry I ever brought you together."

"Sorry!" he exclaimed, coming suddenly to life again. "Sorry! When it's the one thing you've ever done for me! The one thing *anyone's* ever done for me! Don't you know what Neddy is to me, Peter?"

I looked down, embarrassed.

"Perhaps!" I muttered.

"Perhaps!" he repeated scornfully. We had stopped walking and were facing each other, Clarence again the dominant older cousin of my childhood, simply angrier, that was all. "Why, you couldn't even guess! For all your reading, Peter, and for all your parade of tolerance, you're as bad as Mother. You don't want anyone to be happy unless they find their happiness in some noisy ordinary way. You tremble at the least deviation from your own mean little code or even the appearance of one. That's why you and Mother leer and sneer and pretend I do things with Neddy that Italian boys do with middle-aged male tourists for a few lira!"

"But, Clarence, I never —"

"You pretend to be on the side of the angels," he continued excitedly, "but I wonder if you're not really the worst of all bigots. It's amazing to me, Peter, that someone who even pretends to write should be so entirely incapable of visualizing the kind of pure love I feel for Neddy, a love that I've looked for all my life — ah, but what's the use?"

He broke off and left me, and I stood there thinking of the hopelessness in his face, the hopelessness of ever explaining to me that even if there *was* something on which to base his mother's leer, even if her leer was inevitably and forever tied up with every emotional state on his part, still there was a quality in his feeling that was over and above what is called sublimation, a quality that made of it something higher than — but what, I asked myself with a sudden shrug of the shoulders, echoing his thought, was the use? I hurried after him, determined that while he was desperate I would not leave him alone.

On the night of the ball Clarence and I went for a walk through the crowded streets of Venice. Olympia Lorisan had come through with an invitation at the last moment, but I did not feel I could leave him. Besides, I had no costume. In the neighborhood of the Palazzo Lorisan wine was being served to the public from huge vats, and in the little squares boys shinnied up and down the greased poles. There was dancing in the streets near the palace, both for the public and for those guests who found it more fun there; ladies in sixteenth-century costumes whirled about in the arms of Venetian boys to the hectic music of strolling players. Standing on a bridge in the area we had a view of the great baroque façade of the palace, lit up by rows of lights attached at the floor levels. In front was a wide platform, covered in red, where the guests were disembarking from gondolas freshly painted in gold or green or yellow and covered with wide silk canopies. Other gondolas glided under the bridge where we were standing, and the laughter of their masked occupants floated up to us. From one in particular we heard a loud and familiar laugh; it came to our ears while the gondola was still under the bridge, and Clarence drew back quickly as it emerged, but not so quickly that he didn't see his mother in her enormous ruff, a small jeweled coronet perched on top of her pink hair, gesticulating with a paste scepter to friends in other gondolas. At her feet in red tights and smiling up at her — well, we did not need to look more closely to see who that was. Clarence turned away from the palace, and I followed him. Obviously he did not wish to be observed, lonely and ridiculous, watching their gaiety from the shadows. We did not talk but as I walked behind him, observing the straightness of his back, the erectness of his carriage, I had a feeling that there was a process of exorcism going on inside him, a process that was symbolized in his very act of walking away. If his mother liked a circus, the stiff back of his neck seemed to be saying, if Neddy liked it, if the Venetians liked it, if *that* was all they cared about, poor creatures, to be distracted in a distracting world, were they really to be blamed? Was it even reasonable of him, he seemed to ask himself, to assume that Neddy had the patience and devotion to tend the hard gemlike flame that burned within? Should not the true flame-tenders, the people like himself, enjoy in solitude the special compensations of their devotion? I realized suddenly that I had become accessory, irrelevant, and I stopped, calling after him that I was going back for another look at the ball. He barely turned his head to bid me goodnight as he continued his resolute stride away from the lighted palace and the gondolas that swarmed about it like carp.

The Money Juggler

1966

W E H A D , the four of us, two things in common: we were all members of the Columbia class of 1940, and we had bought or rented summer cottages in the Hamptons on Long Island's southern shore.

Townie Drayton, as befitted a Wall Street broker and a Drayton, lived in Southampton; Hilary Knowles, as a popular columnist of manners, good and bad, who had to thread his precarious way between the artistic and the ultrafashionable, rented in East Hampton; and John Grau, a hard-working corporation lawyer who came to the Island only to relax, exercise, and see his family, preferred the comparative simplicity of Westhampton. I, vice president of an auction gallery in the city which collected its treasure hoard from the estates of decedents in all the Hamptons, owned a small, weather-beaten shingle cottage in neutral Amagansett which did not boast a single object that could remind me of those that poured through the doors of Philip Hone & Sons during the eleven other months of the year.

We had been closer friends at college than we were now; indeed, the past was the only real reason for our annual summer reunion at the Dune Club, where, after a Saturday morning's eighteen holes, we would sit on the veranda overlooking the ocean and the slapping breakers and drink many rounds of gin. We must have enjoyed ourselves, for we rarely lunched before three, talking with the easy familiarity and bluntness that had characterized our younger days. I believe that the charm of these sessions lay in the very fact that we were no longer intimate, so that our stories evoked a past that had not been blurred by constant familiarity. It was an added advantage that, living so near to each other, our gatherings had none of the forced hilarity of a college reunion.

The great event that had occurred between the summer of 1965 and its predecessor was the failure and flight from justice of our classmate Lester Gordon, the "boy wonder" (if one could still be that at forty-seven) who had made fortunes in one enterprise after another — real estate, magazines, the stock market — only, at what had seemed the apex of a career of miracles, to plummet, a cherub (which he always a bit resembled) from a golden heaven to a most bankrupt hell. Needless to say, such a fall aroused the most complacent feelings in the hearts of those who had envied him, and there were four such hearts around the table at the Dune Club that day.

Hilary Knowles now regretted his friendship with Lester. "How can I write a really candid column about a friend in trouble?" he asked with a moan. "And yet it's the perfect story of our time, tailor-made for my space, a bright, jingling morality tale. Think of it! Everything about Lester was what we were told as children to distrust: he was too glib, too smiling, too quick. He was all glitter and no substance, all hands and fingers and no soul. Do you remember how he was at college: round and ruddy-faced with that thick curly hair and those ghastly shirts and ties, pushing, giggling, unsnubbable? You couldn't get rid of Lester; he stuck like glue. Until he had what he wanted. And then, when he used you as a ladder, he moved so lightly you hardly felt the foot on your face. Aren't we all the better for his fall? The church bells can ring out bravely again, and we can stroll down Main Street in our Sunday best. God *is* in His heaven, and all's right downtown!"

I don't think any of the rest of us would have placed much money on the proposition that Hilary was *not* going to write that column. It seemed to me that it was half done already. Hilary was as thin and sleek and dark as he had been at college, but he was more hirsute; black bushes rustled under his red silk sport shirt, and his sharp, feral countenance was a closely shaven blue. His language was precise, his accent affected, his gestures on the verge of the effeminate. Yet he considered himself irresistible to women, and according to what I heard about him, fatuity must have been half the battle with the fair sex in East Hampton. He had had three famously beautiful wives.

"Lester Gordon was a kind of one-man inflation," Townie Drayton observed. "Almost a one-man revolution. By driving up prices and destroying old values he could make the wealth of a whole community change hands. And in the turnover, of course, Lester would come out on top. Before we knew it, there he was in every club, on every board of trustees, in control of the old institutions, making one welcome in one's own backyard —"

"Even marrying a Drayton," Hilary interrupted, and we all laughed, for Lester Gordon had married a cousin of Townie's.

"Well, exactly," Townie agreed in all seriousness. "I don't mean to sound overly snobbish, but when I first met Lester at Columbia, I certainly never expected to see *that* in my family."

Townie had only joined us in Columbia after he had been fired from Yale for taking all the radiator caps off the cars parked outside Wolsey Hall on a concert night. He had been one of the handsomest members of our class, but those fine youthful looks had long been buried in the heavy flesh of his middle years. His glassy gray eyes, thick lips and broad aquiline nose would have seemed as coarse as his bulky figure, had it not been for a certain decadent imperial air, the flash of a Caesar, a Nero. Townie, after the Yale escapade, had tried to alter his ways and had tended to pooh-pooh his old Manhattan lineage and land, but as life had developed neither his brains nor his imagination, and had swelled only his girth and the value of his earth, he had come to lean more frankly on these once nominally discredited assets.

"I think that what we all really resent in Lester," John Grau suggested, "is that he understood the heart of our world so much better than we did. Don't you remember his total indifference to the causes that interested us before the war: communism, socialism, pacifism? It wasn't really even indifference; those things actually had no existence for him. What he saw and all he saw was the innate toughness of the capitalist system."

"Oh, come now, John," Townie protested. "There were plenty of us who believed in capitalism, even back in the blackest days of the Depression."

"No, Townie, you don't see what I mean," John insisted, in his clear lawyer's voice. "You believed in it, but you didn't believe it would endure. I remember distinctly, when you were first kind enough to ask me to visit your family on Long Island, and we went to some of those fabulous debutante parties, your friends would always say the same thing. As soon as they caught sight of the marquee, the lanterns, the two orchestras, they would exclaim: 'End of an era!' That was the cry to everything, half laughingly, half seriously: 'End of an era!' If I had predicted, in 1938, that in twenty years' time the two gubernatorial candidates in New York would be a Rockefeller and a Harriman, each richer than ever before, I would have been laughed out of court. By everyone but Lester."

John Grau seemed at first blush older than the rest of us because his hair was gray. But except for this, which suited his sobriety, his gravity and the legend of his constant toil, he was in the best physical shape and the best-looking of the group. His wide brow, square firm face and broad shoulders gave a formidable backing to his vigorous language, and yet his intent gray-green eyes preserved an enthusiasm that was almost youthful. It was as if the idealist of college days had been better preserved in John's cell of hard labor than in the more dissipated existences which the rest of us had led.

"Lester perfectly understood," John continued, now with a touch of bitterness, "the modern alliance between capital and labor to load the costs of private wealth and public welfare on the backs of the professional classes. He wasn't fool enough to become a lawyer like me."

"Oh, come, John, you do pretty well," Hilary pointed out. "If I were to tell you that your income would be under seventy-five grand this year, I bet you'd shriek bloody poverty."

"But look at the tax bracket I'm in!" John exclaimed indignantly. "What do you guys know about taxes? Townie here lives off capital gains and tax-exempts, while you, Hilary, swim in a sea of phony deductions."

"Boo hoo!" Hilary cried. "Let's weep for the destitute Wall Street lawyer!"

"Gentlemen, gentlemen," I remonstrated, "to hell with your taxes. Let's get back to Lester Gordon. I want to know much more about him. I want to know *why* this thing happened. What were his origins? So far as I'm concerned, he was born freshman year at Columbia. Do any of us know who his family were or even where he came from?"

"I do," replied Hilary, our always documented columnist. "I got it from his first wife, Huldah. Lester was born Felix Kinsky, the son of a Lithuanian haberdasher in Hamburg. His parents brought him here to escape the Nazis, and both died early. He lived in Queens with a cousin of his mother's, one David Gordon, originally Ginsberg, a minor building contractor. Lester took his guardian's name, or at least his new name, and later married his daughter. You can readily see from that much that he grew up without any of the usual commitments: religious, national or even family. His parents were Orthodox Jews, but the Gordons were not, and Lester became a Gordon. He had no ties with Lithuania or Germany, and he took people literally when they described America as the land of opportunity. We four were inclined to be snotty to him at first, when he cultivated us at college. We considered ourselves the big shots of the class, and we didn't want to be cultivated for our big-shottiness. What fatuous asses we were! As if a man starting from scratch should not aim as high as he could!"

"Particularly when our usefulness only *began* at college," Townie added. "Lester made a very good thing out of every man at this table."

"Well, I don't know about me," I demurred. "He bought the usual 'chic' collection of impressionists at Hone's, but that was more our making a good thing out of *him*. You were the one, Townie, who gave him his real start. Tell us about it. Weren't you and Lester together in the war?"

"Just at the beginning," Townie replied, pausing to suck deeply on his cigar. "We were both in the Army Signal Corps and had adjoining desks in Washington. After Pearl Harbor everybody screamed for overseas duty, including Lester. But there are ways and ways of screaming, and it did not surprise me much, when I was shipped off, that he remained, as 'indispensable' to General Miles. Years later, in the Normandy invasion, I saw him again, a smart, blustering little lieutenant colonel, attached to some big brass well behind the lines. Oh, hell, I can't blame him for that." Townie seemed bored, as I think we all felt, at the prospect of reviving the tired old hatred for the desk soldier. "Anyway, he kept things cheerful in the dull Washington days, and he always wrote me afterwards. When the war was over he called one night on Ella and me, and we sat up late drinking and reminiscing. He had a lot of good stories and knew what had happened to everybody in our class. But he seemed particularly interested in where we lived. Father and Mother had moved out to the old family homestead in Queens and had turned over to us the pretty Georgian house in Eighty-seventh Street that Mott Schmitt had built for them in the late twenties. I must say, Ella and I rather rattled around in it, and when Lester suggested a price that was well over the current market, we were interested."

"Where did he get the money?" I asked.

"Oh, he had made use of army connections. He had friends in banks. Besides, he had married that builder's daughter. And there was a big mortgage, of course. But after Ella and I moved out, we never could walk through that street again. It was what afterwards became known as a standard Gordon operation. A cheap front was put on the two lower floors to make it as ugly as the restaurateur who had leased it could wish, and the rest of the building was cut up into small apartments with papery walls. There were plenty of violations, but before they were discovered Lester had sold out and was off to bigger deals."

"Is that the way he did it?" I asked. "From house to house?"

"And from corner to corner, from block to block. He and his father-in-law formed a company called Atlas that did a lot of buying in Queens and Brooklyn. They had a reputation for block-busting, probably well deserved. But the most amazing thing to me about Lester was the way he could do the same thing to you twice. He was a bit of a magician: he could show you his hand and then play it. The Eighty-seventh Street house was only a warm-up. What he really wanted was the old Drayton homestead in Queens. You remember it, John. You came out for a weekend once, didn't you? There were sixteen acres and a beautiful white eighteenth-century farmhouse, a landmark if ever there was one. But taxes were high, and my parents were getting older and found it hard to get the maids to run the place. When Lester turned up in my office, with a face as round and bright as a newly minted fifty-cent piece, and offered me a quarter of a million in cash for the property, I didn't see how I could turn it down. Indeed, despite what I knew about him, I thought he was doing me a favor, as there were several other sites that he could have purchased for his veterans' housing development. I wanted to save the family home if I could, and he said it might be used as a clubhouse for the center of the development."

"And you *believed* him?" Hilary demanded.

"I wanted to believe him," Townie replied with another shrug. "It was a good deal. You know how those things are. Of course, once the deed was signed, the old house was wrecked before you could say 'Jack Robinson.' Obviously, Lester had planned it that way, and obviously I should have seen it. Then he leased the land for twenty-five years to one of his corporations, which borrowed the money from the FHA to construct an oval of twelve highrise apartment houses. The company then leased the apartments to veterans at a rental that covered taxes, interest and amortization, plus a tidy additional sum for the landlord. Thus at the end of twenty-five years, a point of time rapidly approaching, Lester will own — or would have owned — his apartments free and clear, the whole tab being picked up by the FHA. I figure conservatively that an original investment of two hundred and fifty grand will net him a cool twenty-five million."

"But if he was ever to get his buildings back," I asked, "wouldn't he regret having made them so bare and cheap?"

"No. Because the likes of Lester would have built all the other buildings in the area, and there is nothing else for people to live in. And the irony is that he christened the project Drayton Gardens."

"Well, after all," Hilary remonstrated, "the Draytons got a quarter of a million for it. You may sneer at that sum, Townie, but it can still feed and clothe a good many little Draytons. Even if they eat at the Colony and dress at Bergdorf's."

"You can't compare it to twenty-five million!"

"That's the price you pay for being too grand to go into the real estate business," Hilary pointed out scornfully. "But it still took two to wreck the Drayton homestead. And you were one!"

"All right, goddamnit, Hilary," Townie rejoined roughly, reddening to the color of real anger, "suppose *you* tell us the story of when you became Lester's hired hand?"

"I shall be glad to," Hilary said coolly, crossing his knees. "Presumably, you are speaking of the time when Lester acquired *Blackwell's Bi-Weekly*, using, no doubt, some of the profits from his coup with the Draytons' 'cherry orchard.' I was then drama editor on that esteemed but impecunious periodical. When the news leaked out that Lester had bought it, the other editors, knowing I was his classmate, scurried to my office to find out what their fates might be under the new management. I could offer them little comfort. What would a realtor of that stripe care for a bleating herd of intellectuals like us? I was surprised, therefore, when our new owner, instead of summoning me to *his* office, came to mine. You should have seen him! Short as ever but stouter, red-faced, with that eternal smile and boyishly curled hair, a painted tie dotted with gold balls, a ring with a big diamond, mammoth cufflinks with sapphires and a pair of yellow gloves that he kept slapping against his noisily tweeded arm. The King of Philistia astride the throne of Athens!

" 'I suppose you think your money can buy the muses,' I told him. 'I'm afraid you'll find they're not for sale.' 'There you go,' he retorted; 'like all the rest, you're telling me what my money *can't* buy. I know I can't buy the muses. But can't I purchase a little seat from which to see them at work? Is that asking too much?' As he paused for an answer, I had to agree that this might not be asking too much. 'Very well!' he exclaimed, leaning back with folded arms. 'Then here I am watching.' 'And what are you watching?' I demanded. 'Why, my new editor-in-chief, of course!'

"Well, gentlemen, I guess we all have to admit that Lester has charm. It may be a vulgar, repulsive sort of charm, but it's still charm. If anyone had told me the day before that I was going to give up my career as a drama critic to become the amanuensis of Lester Gordon, I'd have called up Bellevue and told the little men in white coats to come and take me away. Yet that is precisely what happened. Of course, he promised me a *carte blanche* and a salary double what I was getting. The picture that he drew of the future of *Blackwell's* was an editor's dream. Everything was to be increased: the circulation, the quality, the illustrations, the text, the advertisements, the staff. Even if one *knew* it was a pipe dream, it was still impossible not to try to believe it."

"But did you succeed in believing it?" Townie interrupted, remembering, no doubt, Hilary's question to him.

"Not really — never really," Hilary admitted. "But I thought I might be able to have things my way with the new *Blackwell's* for a year, and a year's a long time in journalism. The first step I took was to house myself and my staff in súmptuous new offices. Lester was perfectly affable about this, as he was about all the people I wished to hire. He did not bat an eye when I added a music editor, an art editor and an architecture editor to our roster. *Blackwell's* was to be the review of reviews; it was to point the way forward to the best in all the arts everywhere in America."

"But, as I remember it, Hilary, *Blackwell's* did in a way become that," I objected. "For a while, anyway. Wasn't it *after* Lester sold it that it went to the dogs?"

"Perfectly true," Hilary agreed readily. "But that leaves out of the picture *why* Lester sold it. You see, Lester knew from the beginning that a magazine genuinely dedicated to the arts could never be supported by the greater public. He also knew that the town was full of fat cats who were dying to own just such a magazine, but who were terrified of losing their shirts. For this reason he calculated that by souping up *Blackwell's* to look both intellectual and successful, he could make a quick killing. So *Blackwell's* got a large shiny new format, some dazzling photography, a galaxy of brilliant names for one-shot contributions, interviews with such unlikely persons as the Pope, Stalin and Lady Macbeth and a big promotion campaign. By its third issue Brian Longford, a third-generation soft-drinks heir, who was tired of boozing and marrying and wanted to 'contribute' to mankind, was trailing Lester all over town, begging and bawling to buy his magazine. Lester at last, out of the kindness of his heart, agreed to swap *Blackwell's* for a little bottle cap company that Brian happened to own. It also just happened that this little company had a portfolio of vital contracts with Brian's family corporation. By the time the latter had awakened to the necessity of getting the bottle cap factory back, Lester's price was five million!"

"And *Blackwell's?*" I asked. "At least poor Brian Longford had *you*, Hilary."

"Yes, he had me, and a lot of good it did him. I was as much taken in as he was. I had no idea, as Lester had, that four issues of brilliant ideas could not be repeated indefinitely and that the new *Blackwell's* was 'too much, too soon.' I was astonished when subscriptions began to fall off and suggested to Brian, as disaster followed disaster, that we go back to the old format. But the old *Blackwell* subscribers had been alienated by our flashy changes and could not be coaxed back to the fold. Brian kept the magazine going as long as his tax lawyer allowed him and then closed shop and threw his staff into the street."

"Some of them evidently managed to scramble out of that street," John Grau observed dryly.

"And it's interesting, isn't it," Townie suggested, for we were nothing if not critical that day, "that when Lester wanted an editor to give *Blackwell's* the meretricious gleam that would attract the greater multitude, he knew just where to find him."

"And even more interesting," I pointed out, to add my own small bit, "that that same editor went directly from the obsequies of *Blackwell's* to his own greatest triumph as a columnist in *The Knickerbocker Gazette*. Would you have got that job, Hilary, without the fame you acquired in the brief but giddy heyday of Lester's magazine?"

Hilary was not in the least put out. He lit a new cigarette and waved the match slowly back and forth, as if he did not really care to extinguish it. I suppose my word "triumph" made up for everything. "We should be grateful, I suppose," he said with a wink, "that anything at all was saved from so disastrous a wreck."

"Tell us about Lester during the *Blackwell* era," I suggested. "Did he take an active interest in it?"

"Not really. He left the running of it to me. But we were all surprised at how much he was there. I don't think a day went by that he didn't come to my office to chat, to listen in at editorial conferences, to look over galleys. At last it began to dawn on me that Lester had had a subsidiary interest in acquiring the magazine. He wanted to educate himself."

"In art?" Townie demanded in surprise.

"In everything. Or rather in everything fashionable. This was the period in Lester's life when he began to be interested in society, and he took me for his guide and mentor. I considered it a case of symbiosis, or living together for mutual advantage. He would let me run his magazine, and I would try to make him presentable. We started with clothes. I made Lester jettison all his wardrobe and jewelry; I stripped him, so to speak, to his checkbook. Then we took a trip to Europe: to London for suits, to Paris for shirts and ties, to Rome for boots and accessories. But it was a dismal case of *plus ça change*. Lester remained stubbornly Lester. Dressed by a duke's tailor, he was still the realtor from Queens. Fortunately, that doesn't matter in the fluctuating society of modern New York, particularly in the world of fashion magazines and charity balls."

"Hairdresser society," Townie sneered.

"Society is always society," Hilary retorted coldly, "and as Oscar Wilde so wisely put it, only those who can't get in abuse it. The Draytons and Livingstons and Stuyvesants have had their day. Nobody who really counts gives a hoot about family anymore. But I will admit that I could never persuade Lester of this. He was as loyal to the old Knickerbocker families as Townie himself. At least he was *then*. The very ease with which he was accepted by the international set made him suspicious. When he found himself sitting at the Duchess of Dino's table at the Heart Ball, his triumph was clouded by the sad reflection that only a *déclassée* duchess could be the friend of such a meatball as Lester Gordon!"

We all laughed, and I asked: "But where was Huldah in all of this? Did she, too, make the grade with duchesses?"

"Ah, no, even *that* world has its limits. Poor Huldah was left to sulk at home. Lester, with his customary tact, suggested that she take lessons in voice and deportment and learn to be a lady, and she threw a vase at him. Yet he was fond of her in his own way, and when he begged me to intercede and persuade her to grant him a divorce, he wept at the cruelty of a world that made him be so cruel. Napoleon had to cast off Josephine for an Austrian archduchess. Lester Gordon had to have a Drayton!"

"How did he ever pull that off?" John Grau asked, turning to Townie.

"Ask Hilary," Townie replied with a shrug. "He's telling the story."

"Can I speak frankly, then?" Hilary asked Townie.

"Oh, Lord, yes. Gabrielle's only my second cousin. I told her she was a goose to marry him, and she sent me smartly about my own business. That was the last time we spoke until he absconded, and then she came around humbly for my advice. Go ahead, Hilary. I'd like to know myself how she ever talked her father into it. Cousin Bronson once told me he'd rather see his daughter in her coffin than married to a Jew!"

"Gabrielle's father wasn't talked into it," Hilary explained. "He was told. She and her mother, like most women, could be very practical on occasion. Gabrielle, unlike Townie, was a poor Drayton, over thirty and, despite a regal nose and sandy hair, something less than a beauty. She and her mother sneered at Lester when he started calling after meeting them at Townie's, but all sneers ceased together when he made the offer of his hand — even before it was out of Huldah's grasp — and a settlement of a million bucks!"

John whistled. "That's what I call taking a place by storm!"

"Gabrielle and her mother promptly reversed course, and the Drayton aunts were given the family line to spread over town. Lester a Jew? Hadn't people heard of integration? Lester married? Well, was he the first man who had to buy off an adventuress who had trapped him into matrimony in college days? Lester sharp in business practices? Wasn't that what people always said of the successful? Lester not a gentleman? My dear, who *was* these days? By the time Lester and Gabrielle were united, there was even talk that one of her uncles might propose him for the Union Club!"

"And did he?" I asked when Hilary paused to sip his drink.

"He might have, had Lester not lost interest. The same inner principle that made him devalue a charity-ball world as soon as it accepted him depreciated an old New York that no longer sneered. Lester was oppressed by the stuffiness of Gabrielle's world — as who would not be? — and soon set his sights on higher goals. He was looking now toward big business, the management world, the politicians, control of the human destiny. He chafed at the mild, softly chatting dinner parties at Gabrielle's mother's. He found that his wife had used all her energy to fit him into *her* world and didn't have an ounce left over to cultivate the people *he* cared to cultivate. Gabrielle was always deploring the low standards of the Social Register, yet to be in it was at least a *sine qua non.* It was only a matter of months before she became an actual liability to Lester."

"Oh, come off it, Hilary," Townie interrupted, irritated at last. "I know things have changed, and the parents of half the people Ella and I see socially today would have been sent to the servants' entrance by our parents —"

"Thanks!" Hilary interrupted with a sneer. "I guess that takes care of John and myself."

"Don't get huffy," Townie retorted. "I'm only trying to point out that an item can drop in value without becoming worthless. I cannot allow that Gabrielle was ever a hindrance to Lester's social career."

"Ah, but you see, Townie, you *don't* really know how drastically things have changed!" Hilary exclaimed, rising to the climax of his argument. "The social scene has become so diffuse that it's not at all unusual, for example, for a woman like Mrs. Knossos, whose face by Elizabeth Arden and jewels by Schlumberger are known to every reader of the evening papers, never to have heard of the Draytons. I insist that Gabrielle's habit of snubbing people who thought they were simply being kind to Lester's awkward wife did him more damage than all of Huldah's boners. Really, from a purely practical point of view, and leaving aside the moral question, I don't see that Lester had any alternative but to shed Gabrielle. The churning waves of high finance bobbed before him. But that is the tragic denouement, and John's part of the story."

John Grau had been listening carefully as he drank. He was a weekend drinker, for he worked too hard at other times, but when he did drink, he did it thoroughly, like everything else. His capacity seemed unlimited, yet he never showed the effects, except that he very slightly softened. The hard, handsome, regular squarish face relaxed, and the usually pursed, almost censorious lips spread in a half-smile. One was no longer so aware of the gray hair, the humped, about-to-spring quality of that craggy, muscular body. When John smiled and gave one of his intense gray-green stares, he had charm. It may have been the charm of the totality of his temporary commitment.

"When Lester threw his derby hat down on my desk and said airily that he wanted a 'Wall Street lawyer,' I practically told him to go to hell," John began. "I don't think I'd seen him more than half a dozen times since college, and I didn't like anything I'd heard. I informed him that we had only a very small, accommodation real estate department, at which he roared with laughter and said that we weren't nearly tough enough to handle his housing matters. No, he was coming to us, he explained, only for his securities work! Well, I got so mad at the idea of our being too soft for one thing and not for the other that I told him that if we weren't good enough to advise him generally, I wasn't interested. And then, of course, he had me, for he offered me the works: housing, building, finance, and told me to name my own retainer. The upshot of it all was that he took me to lunch, and I had a new client."

"So you *did* do the real estate," Townie interpolated.

"There wasn't much of it left," John replied. "Lester had pretty well sold out of it by then, except for Drayton Gardens. As Hilary implies, he was ashamed of it. He wanted something with more 'tone.' No doubt, he considered that he wouldn't be in 'trade' if he dealt with intangibles, if he sat in a great gleaming office downtown and pushed buttons and talked on the telephone while he bought control of vast enterprises. We always keep coming back, don't we, to the child in Lester, the dreaming, scheming child? I'll never forget the first deal I handled for him. He had figured out that S. & T. Manley's, the old jewelry store on Fifth Avenue, was a ripe fruit to be plucked. Under a gentle family mismanagement the stock had declined in value to a point where it was worth considerably less than the inventory. Swoop! Lester pounced from the sky in the fastest proxy raid I have ever witnessed, closed down an ancient and distinguished firm and sold out the inventory for a spanking profit."

"All handled by you, John," Hilary pointed out.

"Oh, yes, all handled by me, I admit it," John rejoined with a rueful, impatient shake of his head. "What is one to do? I practice law in Arnold & Degener at One Chase Manhattan Plaza. Who am I to turn down high-paying clients with legally honest deals? What would my partners say if I did? For Lester pays well — make no mistake. I've never seen him haggle over a bill. He even once sent me a check for double the amount charged with a note that read: 'I want the best securities lawyer in town, and this is what the best securities lawyer should get.' How many clients do you find who give you that kind of appreciation? Is it *my* job to look out for old mismanaged stores?"

"Of course not," Townie agreed firmly. "You've got to live in the present. We all do."

"Not I," I protested. "I'm an auctioneer. I live in the past and off the past."

"And as a commentator," Hilary insisted, "I live off the immediate future."

John's expression became harder. "I'm not apologizing for myself," he said, "but neither am I praising myself. I knew what I wanted to be when I was in law school, and I'm only sorry that I can't be it more often. I wanted — and want — to be the kind of lawyer who builds, and Lester's genius was always for destruction. If he pieced together a little railroad empire, it was to close it down in favor of his noisy buses. If he laid his hands on a picturesque country inn, it was to replace it with a cheap motel. And his favorite game was the simple taking over and looting of companies, passing on the empty, glittering shell to the unwary public that thought it was protected by a benevolent government. Sometimes I tried to excuse Lester as a frustrated would-be pioneer who had been born too late. What would Vanderbilt or Rockefeller have done with their energy in our century with the frontiers gone? Might they have not torn each other to bits, like so many Lester Gordons?"

"Is that why Lester turned ultimately on himself?" I asked. "Wasn't there an element of financial suicide in the last debacle?"

"I think there was," John agreed, nodding. "Lester was tired of having everything give way before him. He may have experienced an odd kind of relief when he batted his head at last against the hard wall of crime and knew that detection was a minute-to-minute possibility. But first I must tell you about Luella. Let the cold Wall Street lawyer tell you boys about love. True love!"

"Oh, come, John," Hilary protested, "you're not going to try to convince us that Lester was in love with that little tramp."

"Ah, but I am!" John exclaimed. "Lester was very much in love with that little tramp. Or thought he was, and what's the difference?"

"Lester in love," Hilary sneered. "It's a contradiction in terms!"

"But Lester is always in love," John insisted. "And he always was. Lester from the beginning was in love with the whole beautiful world that he wanted to possess. You remember how he was at college: so intense, so interested, always listening, bubbling with curiosity, affectionate, gay? Well, he's still that way, damn him! Lester studied the world because he had to *have* the world. And he had to have it because he loved it."

"Even when he was block-busting for Huldah's father?"

"Even then. Lester doesn't see things the way other people do. He is so totally devoid of any kind of racial prejudice that it strikes him, when it's stuck in front of his nose, as simply another aspect of the human equation to make money out of. People like mountain scenery, so one buys up mountains. Other people don't want Negro neighbors, so one brings in Negroes to induce them to sell cheap. It's market, pure and simple, the supreme law of the market! Lester, you might even argue, was the last of the pure capitalists. He wants to believe that the best of all possible worlds will materialize if the Lesters are only left free to make their profit."

"He couldn't!" I exclaimed incredulously.

"I said he *wants* to," John emphasized. "Of course, he doesn't believe it. Like the rest of us, he sees clearly enough that the world which Lester conquers is an inferior place to the one which Lester assaults. He sees his shoddy houses, his tinsel motels, his soulless stores. He understands that he has made his fortune by swimming in a sea of junk. But hope keeps bubbling. What else keeps him alive? Somewhere, somehow, he has to believe that the brightness and smartness of a good boy like Lester is going to produce something admirable, something permanent, some bit of merchandise that will not fall to pieces before one has got it from the shop down into one's car."

"And that was Luella?" Hilary exclaimed with a snort.

"That was Luella. Exactly. Luella was beauty and sex and love and ideals, like the advertisement of a new car. Huldah, after all, was a bit of a dog, and Gabrielle, saving your reverence, Townie, was no rose, but every man at this table will have to admit that Luella was a dish."

"But a dish for the multitude," Hilary added. "Who has not partaken?"

"Luella was a typically American phenomenon," John continued, again in his lawyer's voice. "Blond, curved, with pouting lip and bad temper. She was the personification of the *appearance* of sex, the symbol, if you like, of fleshly passion. You might say she was a sort of female Lester, a capitalist in love, who gave the least for the most, who wanted a man's soul in return for a wriggle of her fanny. It's elementary psychology to speculate that she was probably no good in bed."

"You needn't speculate," Hilary put in flatly. "I can assure you she was not."

The rest of us were careful not to give Hilary the satisfaction of so much as a cocked eyebrow. As Townie used to say, given enough rope Hilary would prove every hour on the hour that he was no gentleman.

"Very well, then," John went on coldly, "we need not speculate. We know. The importance of Luella in American commercial society is not what she gives her possessor, but what people may be induced to believe that she gives. She is as much a status symbol as a Gauguin or a Rolls-Royce. Everyone seeing Mrs. Lester Gordon can be counted on to envy Mr. Gordon his nights. If this is so, does it very much matter if they sleep in separate bedrooms?"

"But you said he was in love with Luella," I protested. "Surely that implies something beyond impressing his neighbors!"

"No, with Lester I honestly believe it does not. Indeed, I suggest that this is of the essence of Lester. He *doesn't* see the difference between the outward and visible sign and the inward and invisible truth. If Luella is sex to the multitude, then Luella is sex to him. When he came to my office to tell me that he wanted to marry Luella, he was so excited that he could not keep still. He kept jumping up and running about the room, playing with the window shade cord, rustling papers, lighting and putting out cigarettes. Luella was a goddess; Luella was Cleopatra; Luella should be a movie star! Huldah, Gabrielle, all the other women in his life, had been mere shadows. With Luella, at last, he was living!"

"Why was he telling *you?*" I inquired, for John seemed an odd confidant in such matters.

"Because I was his lawyer. And he certainly needed one. One doesn't divorce a Drayton with impunity, does one, Townie? Also, Luella had a rather sticky spouse of her own to shed. I tried to sober Lester down by pointing out that of the eight lawyers who would necessarily be involved — four for each party in New York and four more in Reno — he would have to pay at least six, and if Luella's husband was angry enough, all eight. But nothing bothered him. He was in euphoria! 'I don't care what it costs,' he told me. 'I've got to have my Luella!' "

"How did Luella feel about him?" Townie asked. "Or was it simply a question of dough?"

"Oh, Luella liked him well enough. To marry him for a few years, anyway. I don't suppose even Lester expected that she would be capable of the smallest sacrifice in this respect. I know he was not surprised when she threw him over at the first hint of trouble. But he was a big spender who loved late hours and nightclubs: Luella's ideal of a man. And he was willing to take on the trouble and expense of her own divorce — oh, he was worth it. So Arnold & Degener went to work to clear away the legal underbrush that stood between the union of these two passionate lovers."

"I hope you're not referring to my poor little innocent cousin Gabrielle as legal underbrush," Townie intervened with a chuckle.

John flung up his hands. "When it comes to settlements, I'd rather fight a blond gold-digger from the Follies than a brownstone miss from old New York," he emphasized. "When your poor little innocent cousin was through with us, she had clear title to the whole Drayton Gardens project!"

"And I'm happy to tell you that the first thing she did was to re-christen it Queen's Gardens," Townie informed us in all earnestness. "I'm glad to say that the family name is no longer associated with that dump."

"Only the family income," Hilary retorted.

"What a pity," I added, "that Gabrielle's delicacy in nomenclature could not restore the family landmark."

Townie merely grunted as John continued: "Negotiations went on for months. Luella's husband had to be squared as well, for it turned out that he was shattered at the idea of losing *his* status symbol, or at least of losing her to Lester. When the agreements were all signed, Gabrielle insisted that Lester and not she have the bother of going to Reno, although she knew that he was in the midst of the biggest proxy fight in his life and from which she stood to profit: the battle for Atlantic Enterprises." John paused and looked around the table. "But you all know about Atlantic Enterprises?"

"No, John," I answered, "we don't. Or at least I don't. Please remember that we're not all lawyers."

"Atlantic," he continued, "is a holding corporation that controls a string of department stores, a bus line, a theater chain and some three dozen parking lots, all just outside the city limits. Lester was already president of the company, but he wanted control. He had a Napoleonic scheme of uniting Atlantic to his other interests, and to some further ones that he had in mind to acquire, in order to spread a belt around the city. He saw that New York was sliding into poverty and despair and that the middle and upper classes, together with most of the businesses, were fleeing to the suburbs. Out of this hegira Lester would make himself lord of the future. He would put himself in a position where all the insoluble growing problems of our time — overpopulation, racial strife and the growing indigence in the city — would operate to fill his pocketbook. How could he lose? As he once told me: 'Only an ass can be poor these days.' And I really believe that he might have achieved his goal had he been able to be in New York continuously during the battle. His particular kind of genius required him to be always on the scene. But in the hottest part of the fight he was stuck in Reno, having to check in at court every other day to establish his residence. He had a jet plane in which he tore back and forth through the ether. Never shall I forget the picture of that desperate little man, living on benzedrine, a telephone constantly cradled to his ear, talking, shouting, laughing. For that was the thing about Lester: he was actually enjoying the whole thing. And when I think what he was *doing* all the time, the risks that he was taking, when I think that he knew all along what was hanging over his head, I cannot decide whether he is the bravest man I ever knew or a simple lunatic!"

"But *what* was he doing?" I demanded.

"Man, didn't you read the papers? The market had broken, money was tight, and Lester was always a borrower up to the hilt. I could not imagine where he was getting the money to buy Atlantic stock. I did not find out until Lester's house of cards fell in that he had been using Atlantic's treasury to buy Atlantic stock."

"And that was wrong?" I asked. "Wasn't he president of Atlantic?"

"Small wonder that morals are on the slide," John answered with a snicker, "when the public no longer knows what's right or wrong. Perhaps it's not the public's fault. Perhaps our laws are too complicated. But in this case it would be simple enough even for you, Roger, to understand. The officers of a corporation are not supposed to use its assets for their personal market speculations. Even when they claim, as Lester did, that they are supporting the price of the company stock. But Lester's luck had run out at last. It was no fault of his that he encountered the worst stock market slide since 1929. It was a brief one, but it did for Lester. He ran short of money before he had completed his control of Atlantic, and that was the end. In a single day everyone turned on him. He lost his companies, he lost his reputation, and, needless to say, he lost Luella. In fact, on the rainy morning when he donned dark glasses and boarded the plane for Lisbon, he was not even divorced from Gabrielle."

"So he's still your cousin, Townie," Hilary observed dryly.

"No, Gabrielle went out to Reno after he absconded and got the decree herself," Townie hastened to inform us. "I advised her to do it. How much of what Lester settled on her she will be able to keep is a moot question, but you'll be glad to know she's got a crack lawyer."

Hilary and John and I burst out laughing at the idea of our being "glad" to know this, and Townie's cheeks reddened.

"Speaking of lawyers," I said, turning back to John, "do you still represent Lester?"

"No, I had to give him up. You see, Arnold & Degener are general counsel to Atlantic, and there was an obvious conflict."

"You mean," Hilary put in quickly, "that having to choose between two clients, you kept the best?"

"Not at all," John retorted indignantly. "You don't understand these things, Hilary, and you shouldn't be so smart about them. We dropped Lester because he had deceived us. That was not true of Atlantic."

"But didn't Lester *bring* you Atlantic?" Hilary demanded, and seeing that John was now becoming as angry as Townie, I intervened.

"But I thought you had seen Lester in Lisbon?" I asked him.

"I did see him. I stopped there on my way back from a business trip to Madrid. But I went to see him as a friend, not as a lawyer."

"And what happened when you saw him?"

"We went to a bar and spent a couple of hours together. Lester was nicer than I've ever seen him. Subdued, but far from crushed, and utterly devoid of self-pity. He blamed no one but himself for the debacle and showed no bitterness toward his former business associates who had shrilly reviled him to reporters. As to Luella, he simply said that she had acted as he had told her to act, and even claimed that he had composed her savage press release. Townie and Hilary may sneer at him for being a parvenu, but he was a true gentleman that day. It was an odd background for him: that beautiful, quiet, decadent capital. Possibly some of its ancient style had crept into him through holes battered by disaster."

"You're breaking my heart," Hilary drawled. "Pray tell us, John, before you've sunk to the bathos of a column by our late lamented Elsa Maxwell, what Lester is going to do now. Will he be extradited?"

"It won't be necessary," John snapped. "He's coming back. He's going to give himself up."

"And will he go to jail?" I asked.

John shrugged. "Very possibly. Though he may get a suspended sentence. In any event, it would be a short term."

"And then?"

"Oh, and then he'll go back to business. Lester is far from downed. As I said before, he may even be glad to find that he can't get away with everything. He's like a schoolboy — there I go again! — who has almost taken over the school with his tricks and wiles. Finally, just as he is about to light a fire in the wastepaper basket under the headmaster's desk, he is caught and has his ears roundly boxed. For the first time he respects the institution!"

"And will he make another fortune?" I asked.

"Who knows? He may. But I doubt it." John frowned and shook his head. "I believe there's just so much energy and just so much luck in any man. Lester has drawn heavily on his capital."

Silence enveloped our table now for a minute as we drank and smoked reflectively. Glancing from John to Townie to Hilary, I was suddenly struck by the size of their common denominator. It was in their eyes, in the opaque glitter of their distrustful eyes. They were all prosperous, all expensively and similarly clad. I would have defied John O'Hara himself to have told, in that assemblage of colored shirts, which was the descendant of a colonial governor, which the popular columnist and which the Wall Street lawyer. Over their apparel, which was as beautiful as a *New Yorker* advertisement, glowed the snakes' eyes that saw the world at a snake's level: one inch above the ground. Oh, yes, they saw it whole and they saw it clear — one inch above the ground.

"What a society we live in," I exclaimed, "that such men as you three should all have worked for such a man as Lester Gordon! And you all made a good thing out of him, too. Oh, granted, he made a thousand times more out of each of you, but you've had the last laugh, for you've still got it, while he is bankrupt. What impresses me — or rather *depresses* me — is the fact that you were his agents, that *he* was always the principal. You, Townie, with all your lineage and traditions; you, Hilary, with all your cultivation and sophistication; you, John, the brightest boy in Columbia law, were glad to be the servants of an adventurer whose god was the dollar and whose law was to get it for nothing. Is that capitalism? That the aristocrat, the intellectual and the professional are bound to the chariot of the money juggler? It seems to me that by contrast the Middle Ages, where the priest and soldier ruled, was a time of enlightenment!"

"You talk like a goddamn red," Townie growled.

"More like a John Birchite, I would say!" cried Hilary.

"It's easy enough to be detached if you're tucked away in an auction gallery, selling old lamps and pictures," John pointed out. "If you'd been born in your precious Middle Ages, Roger, you'd have scrambled to the nearest monastery and told your beads."

"Not at all," I retorted. "I'd have copied out the *Iliad* and saved it for future generations!"

"Gentlemen, gentlemen," Hilary exclaimed, waving for silence with both hands, "don't you realize that we have in our presence the most gigantic hypocrite of all? When poor Lester Gordon's art collection was placed on the block by his creditors, who do you think sold it, item by item, but our friend Roger here, the same Roger from whom Lester had bought it. And didn't the whole works make a record-breaking price for ultra-fashionable impressionists? And didn't Hone's take its twenty percent pound of flesh? We three may have been the midwives of Lester's fortune, but Roger was the undertaker!"

In the explosion of laughter that followed this revelation, which, of course, I had known was coming — and would have volunteered myself had I not wished Hilary to have the pleasure of it — the irritation engendered by the afternoon's discussion trickled off, and we were once again our congenial golf foursome. Why should we not, after all, have been the best of friends? What were we but four junior Gordons?

The Wagnerians

1966

Dᴇᴀʀ Mʀ. Sᴛʏʟᴇs:

When I told you that I would not "write up" Uncle Ed for your history of opera in the Americas, you implied that I was being stuffy. Privately I have no doubt that you used a harsher word. "What bad luck," you must have said to your fellow editors, "that the only person living who remembers Edmund Stillman should be a prudish niece who is determined to take her sixty-year secrets with her virginity to the grave!" Oh, yes, I can imagine how you young writers talk. I have not always led the cloistered existence of the New York old maid, bounded on the south by Carnegie Hall and on the north by the Colony Club. No, Mr. Styles, you will be surprised to hear that I had an operatic career of my own! I sang in public — on one occasion.

And that is precisely why I have now revised (not changed) my position. I have decided that my reluctance to write about Uncle Ed must spring from my identification of his failure as manager of the opera house with my own failure as an opera singer. What egotism! To compare his magnificent and catastrophic experiment with ten years of voice lessons ending in a single appearance as Ortrud in a road company *Lohengrin!* And so I have resolved that I will do what you ask and record here my memories of my uncle. But, there is one very stiff condition. You may not publish it in my lifetime. For even though these memories are so ancient that they have ceased to hurt, there are still some that I do not care to see set forth in the impertinence of print: the quizzical, puzzled stare in Uncle Ed's eyes after too many brandies, my father's embarrassment before the devoted ushers at the opera house, who he feared were his brother's unpaid creditors, my grandmother's bewilderment at finding herself choosing to side with her own world against her favorite son. But when I am gone (and I am past eighty), you may do as you like with these pages. They will be in nobody's memory then.

I shall start, being old-fashioned, in the time-honored way of Balzac (the only novelist I still read), by saying a word about the position of the Stillmans in the New York of 1890. We were one of those unremarkable families, indigenous to the "best" society of any large city, who seemed to have no particular claim to our position other than the fact that we had always had it. By a claim I mean such an obvious thing as a fortune or a distinguished lineage or simply a relationship to some great man. There are New York families that have their colonial governor as Roman families have their Pope. But each generation of our Stillmans had managed to move gracefully across the social scene without particularly distinguishing itself or particularly disgracing itself and always without leaving more than a modest competence to the succeeding one. They were great believers in the "here and now." So long as their dinners were good and their clothes in style, they did not much care what sort of old brownstone (provided, of course, it was in the right neighborhood) housed them. They found the world as it was a pretty good place. Of course, they didn't go around turning over stones or poking behind curtains. They did not conceive that to be their function. But if a curtain happened to fall and a skeleton was revealed, if a moral issue developed and people started to raise their voices and take sides, if, in other words, the chips were down, the Stillmans, God bless them, were apt to be on the side of the angels.

Uncle Ed, my father's bachelor brother, was the Stillman who came closest to breaking the family rule of "Nothing in Excess," but his excess was of a Stillman sort. In personal adornment he was a bit of a peacock, even in that gaudy age. Look at the photograph of him in Gustav Kobbé's *Complete Opera Book*. The long slim body in the perfectly tailored Prince Albert with the velvet collar seems to flow gracefully upward to the grave bearded face, the reflective eyes and the glistening, narrow-brimmed stovepipe hat. The beard is neatly trimmed to follow the contours of the squarish chin and also those of the gently drooping mustache. It would be altogether the portrait of a dandy of the period, with a bit of the hardness of one of Whistler's *boulevardiers*, a touch of the cruelty of a Paul Bourget hero, were it not for the eyes, large and brown and almost brooding. Oh, yes, the eyes gave Uncle Ed away as they gave my father away. They were eyes that could see the main chance, but beyond the main chance they saw perfectly the price that one paid for it.

A more serious excess in Uncle Ed was his drinking, but this, too, was done with Stillman style. There was never (at least before his final European chapter) anything so vulgar as intoxication. Uncle Ed, as Father used to put it, was like a noble greensward that needed a constant, gentle sprinkling. Each drink had its consecrated hour: the mid-morning sherry flip, the noon gin fizz, the afternoon cognac, the evening "cocktail" at the men's bar, the midnight whiskey, without mentioning the diverse flow of mealtime wines that constituted the central river to which the other drinks were tributary. The family used to ascribe Uncle Ed's drinking to his lack of steady employment, and from my earliest years I remember table discussion of how to lure him from his bibulous idleness. Uncle Ed, apparently, was always willing to try anything once, but his jobs had a way of terminating after a few months, always with the remarkable circumstance of his remaining a fast friend of his former employer.

It was my father who first conceived the idea of finding him a job at the opera house. Father was always the most imaginative member of the family. Physically, he resembled his brother, but it was as a guinea fowl resembles a pheasant. Father was much less elegant and, by like token, much more responsible. But he had the kindness of the Stillman men, and when he put his mind on his brother, he thought of his brother and not of himself thinking of his brother.

"Everybody wants Ed to do what *they* happen to like doing," he told my grandmother, above whose sober widow's establishment Uncle Ed maintained a bachelor's top floor. "Uncle Harry wants him to go into the iron business. My boss keeps urging him to become a banker. And Marion Crawford tells him to write novels. We ought to be trying to make a life for Ed out of the things that *Ed* likes doing. Now what are they? Well, first off, he likes the opera. Couldn't Uncle Harry get him something to do there?"

It was the ace of trumps on the first draw! Granny Stillman's older sister, my Great-Aunt Rosalie, was married to Uncle Harry Belknap, a rich ironmaster from Troy and a director of the opera. Nothing was easier for him than to secure for his wife's nephew, whom most of the boxholders knew and liked, the position of secretary to the company, and for the next two years (an unprecedented tenure for him) Uncle Ed attended the board meetings faithfully and ornamentally, kept the minutes neatly and concisely and busied himself about the office, at least until the early afternoon. He even took to dropping in on rehearsals, and with his knack for friendship he soon became intimate with the leading singers and musicians. The opera house developed for him into a combination of hobby and club, and my family breathed in relief at Father's brilliant solution of the problem.

Promotion followed swiftly. In those days the gulf between the owners of the opera house, all New York businessmen, and the artists, already dominated by Germans and Wagnerites, was almost unbridgeable. Neither side could even listen to the other, and opera was produced in an atmosphere of what we would call a "cold war." But Uncle Ed could talk to Mr. Morgan and to Mr. Damrosch and make each feel that he was on his side. When the general managership fell vacant in 1890, the board, after several long, wrangling sessions, was suddenly united by the prospect of this dark but very glossy horse.

There was an outburst of enthusiasm. What did it matter that Ed Stillman was not a musician? Was there not too much expertise already? Were the directors not sick of managers who swore guttural oaths and regarded "opera" and "Wagner" as synonyms? The only trouble seemed to be with Uncle Ed himself, who resisted the appointment with a stubbornness that surprised everybody, and, when at last prevailed upon, accepted it with a gravity of manner that seemed almost Teutonic. Had the directors paused, however, to remember how the miter had changed Thomas à Becket (which, needless to say, they did not), they might have consoled themselves with the thought that they were twelve King Henrys to his single archbishop.

One person who had no reservations over Uncle Ed's promotion was his sixteen-year-old niece. I was already a devoted opera fan, with a picture by my bedside of Melba, whose London debut as Lucia had been the great moment of my life. I attended the Brearley School, but books, and even, in holiday parties, boys, hardly existed for me. I lived for the afternoons and my singing teacher, Miss Angela Frith. Uncle Ed, whose courteous demeanor to the young raised them briefly to the paradise of adults, was already my favorite relative. Now he became a god.

Mother, who considered herself vastly more liberal than the Stillmans, was as one with them when it came to any serious extension of the arts beyond the parlor. She laughed at my musical pretensions, when she was not irritated by them.

"Why don't you take Amy to one of your rehearsals, Ed?" she asked my uncle one night. "I wonder if seeing the opera house in its shirtsleeves wouldn't cure some of her fancies?"

Poor Mother! If she only had known what oil she was pouring on my fire! I waited breathless for Uncle Ed's answer, afraid to ruin my chances by showing my enthusiasm, but his smile recognized my palpitations. He knew that waiting was torture to the young.

"Why, certainly, any rehearsal she wants. We're running through the second act of *Tristan* tomorrow afternoon. How will that do?"

And so, after a sleepless night and a morning at school in which I took in nothing, my dream came true. There was I, Amy Stillman, seated with my uncle in the center of the second row of the orchestra pit in the great dark, empty opera house before a stage covered with cartons and dirty canvases, watching two stout middle-aged persons, a man and a woman in modern dress, sitting side by side on a small wicker divan. And when the conductor raised his baton, and we started right off in the middle of the love duet, I thought it the most romantic setting that I had ever seen. So much for Mother's precautions!

I was familiar with *Lohengrin* and *Die Walküre*, but I had never heard a note of *Tristan*. Its effect on me was ambivalent. I was intrigued and excited by the violence and surge of the music, but at the same time it made me restless, apprehensive, almost afraid. Of what? Of love, of physical love? I have often asked myself since. But I do not think so. It was difficult for a girl in my time to associate love with the portly middle age represented by the two performers. No, there was something else in that churning, seething music, something like being caught in the backwash of a big breaker when surf bathing in Southampton on a visit to Granny, tossed and pulled by the hissing water and borne out ineluctably to sea, to be smothered, perhaps to be drowned in a terrible peace beneath that tormented surface. I had no idea that this was a common reaction to *Tristan*, and I became at length so agitated that I was relieved when the music director called to the conductor through a little megaphone to stop the music.

The woman who was singing Brangäne had been delivering the offstage warning in a voice that was almost inaudible. She complained that the strain on her vocal cords was so great that she could not sing in full voice until the performance. It could be then or now, she concluded defiantly. The *Herr Direktor* could choose. The latter turned to Uncle Ed.

"Which shall it be, Mr. Stillman?"

"Tell her to sing today," Uncle Ed snapped, and the rehearsal went on. Inexperienced as I was, I could sense that he had already taken hold of his company.

In a break, after the duet, Uncle Ed suggested a turn around the block. I was very proud to be on the arm of my handsome and distinguished uncle, and I admired the easy courtesy with which he raised his hat to any members of the company whom we passed, without interrupting the flow of our discussion. He asked me which I preferred, *Tristan* or *Lucia*, already knowing that *Lucia* was my favorite opera.

"Oh, *Lucia*," I said promptly. "But *Tristan* is more interesting," I added politely, suspecting his own preference.

"Interesting," he repeated thoughtfully. "Perhaps that's just what it is. Look down Broadway, Amy." We paused at the corner and gazed south at the great thoroughfare. "Look at all that gray dirtiness and listen to all that strident clamor and tell me if you really think our modern life corresponds to the tinkling tunefulness of Donizetti."

"You believe it should?"

"Well, don't you think there should be *some* relation between daily life and music? Or do we go to the opera just to dress up and see our friends?"

"But Uncle Ed," I protested earnestly, "shouldn't opera help us to forget all that dirt and clamor?"

"Spoken like a true boxholder! You'll be like the other dreamers in Number Seven, Amy. Your grandmother sighs for Edgar of Ravenswood, and even your Great-Aunt Rosalie wants to immolate herself with Rhadames in a living tomb!"

"And I can be Carmen!" I exclaimed, feeling very adult to be joking about such things (particularly Granny!) with the older generation.

"I'm sure a very proper Carmen," Uncle Ed added with a chuckle. "Maybe even a rather severe one, like dear Lili Lehmann. She sings the 'Habañera' as if it had been written by Haydn. I suppose, Amy, I sometimes feel that our life is such a continual fancy dress ball that I want — just for a minute, mind you, just every now and then — to slip into plain old clothes and be myself."

As I took in with a quick glance my uncle's rich brown tweeds, the maroon polish of his shoes gleaming beneath his spats, the red carnation in his buttonhole, the walking stick with the silver knob, I could not but wonder if *these* were his plain old clothes. "Does your *Tristan* 'correspond' to modern life?" I asked timidly.

Uncle Ed became immediately serious at this, more so than I could ever remember having seen him. "That's a good question, Amy. No, Wagner's operas don't correspond to modern life because Wagner didn't believe in modern life. Not in ours, anyway. He thought that it didn't exist, or if it did, that it was too trivial, too unheroic, too sordid, to be worth commenting on in musical terms. If a man was to write opera, it should be about valiant mythological figures, gods and goddesses, and if there weren't any gods and goddesses, he ought to create them. Think of it, Amy!" Here Uncle Ed's eyes really sparkled. We stopped walking, and he spread one arm in a broad gesture. "Ever since Shakespeare we have taken for granted that the artist must deal with mortal men, that his province must lie in love and compassion. You remember what Pope said: the proper study of mankind is man. But Wagner did what nobody has done in the whole history of art, except perhaps the ancients. If he was compelled to comment, he would create a world worthy to comment upon. He despised mankind, but did that stop him? He saw that the only beautiful thing in the world was death, and he made love to it in *Tristan*. Oh, Amy, when once you *feel* Wagner, there is nobody else. There is nothing else."

How vivid that moment is to me this day, more than sixty years after! For I saw things then that were beyond the comprehension of my years in a terrible flash of divination. It was not that I agreed with Uncle Ed. I didn't then, and, thank God, I do not now. But I *saw*, and the vision scared me. I saw into the awful emptiness of his soul, and I felt the well of pity bubbling up in my own. Because, you see, Mr. Styles, I felt that I had seen into something essential in the nature of my family, or at least of the Stillman side of it, something that Granny had all along suspected and that she fought blindly, without understanding. And this was it: Uncle Ed's elegance, his smartness, his whole air of exquisite maintenance, was the same gallant but essentially futile effort to decorate the void of God's or non-God's neglect that he fancied he could detect in the tumultuous creations of Wagner. It all had to end, as it ended in *Tristan*, in a death that one could only pretend was a love death.

My shudder was barely perceptible, but Uncle Ed perceived it. He shook his head, apologized for his theorizing (always, in his opinion, "bad form") and led me back to the opera house. "If Granny Stillman hears I've been trying to convert you to Wagner, there'll be the devil to pay," he said with a wink, as we took our seats. "If she asks you what was being rehearsed today, tell her it was *Les Huguenots.*"

Granny, of course, had not been born a Stillman, and she had none of their characteristics. She was a good deal tougher and less imaginative, and she was much more innately conservative. Where Father and Uncle Ed were by temperament aristocratic, she was bourgeois to the marrow of her bones. She had been widowed early in life and had managed her small inheritance so well that she was now able to maintain a house on Sixty-fifth Street and a shingle cottage in Southampton and to keep a butler and four maids. But always frugal, she depended on her richer sister for the luxuries of a carriage and opera box.

I look at Granny's photograph as I write, with the pale oval face, the high-piled, elaborately waved gray hair and the large, watery, apprehensive eyes, and I think how she would stare at the liberties I am taking with her! Yet I have started this thing, and I have to make her understandable. Granny believed in the present, the present instant, the concrete thing before her eyes. Having said she was bourgeois, I will now say that she had a bit of the peasant in her. She accepted the mores of her New York as if established by divine decree. When her favorite niece lay dying, we were all surprised that she seemed wholly concerned with whether or not to call off a dinner party. But this was not from lack of feeling. It was from a deep-seated belief that doing the "right thing" was paramount to personal grief, and it gave an oddly impersonal quality to her snobbishness. She never scorned outcasts, any more than, conventionally anti-Semitic and anti-Roman, she in the least disliked or disapproved of Jews and Catholics. She simply would not pick her friends among them.

I believe that Granny loved Uncle Ed more than she had ever loved another human being (unless it was the rather shadowy figure of my long-dead grandfather), but when rumors began to circulate that he had "gone over to the Germans" and even that he had "betrayed his trust," she found herself in an acutely painful position. She and her sister, Aunt

Rosalie Belknap, were close with the peculiar closeness of their generation of siblings: they lived on the same street in Manhattan and on the
same sand dune in Southampton and saw each other every day of the
year. Aunt Rosalie, being older and cleverer and a great deal richer,
dominated Granny, while Uncle Harry, who took care of her business
interests, represented "men" in her respectful widow's heart. If the
Belknaps were against the "new music," how could a Stillman be for it?
How much less could a Stillman be for it who owed his very job to Uncle
Harry?

Matters came to a head on the Sunday after that rehearsal, at Granny's family lunch. As in other brownstones of that period, the dining
room was the one handsome chamber, always on the first floor back,
shrouded in kindly darkness, high-ceilinged, with perfectly polished
silver gleaming in crowded density on the sideboard and with high,
carved Jacobean chairs looking like antiques under the crystal chande-
lier. When I inherited Granny's and put them in a good light, they
showed up as bad fakes.

Aunt Rosalie, as was to be expected, led off the discussion. To tell the
truth, I always found Aunt Rosalie, who dyed her hair a jet black and
wore too many rings and bracelets, the least bit common, whereas
Granny, even at her most worldly, was always totally a lady. Money
sometimes had that effect on old New York. Granny may have owed her
relative refinement to her relative poverty.

"They tell me young Damrosch is twisting you around his little finger, Ed," Aunt Rosalie began. "They say we're going to have nothing
but darkened stages with earth goddesses moaning about time and fate."

"Oh, I think I can promise you a Rhine maiden here and there, Aunt
Rosalie," Uncle Ed drawled in his easiest tone. "And we've installed
some very curious machinery to make them appear to be swimming
about under water. I think it might interest you to see it. Would you
care to come down to the house one morning next week and let me show
you?"

Uncle Ed could have his way with most women, even with Aunt
Rosalie, but not when she was on the track of something. "It'll have to
wait, I'm afraid, for I'm tied up all next week. But Harry and I would
like very much to know what you're planning to tell your board when
they find that all their lovely Traviatas and Aïdas have been traded in
for a parcel of shrieking Valkyries. Wouldn't we, Harry?"

"Very much, my dear."

"Ah, but I'm all ready for the board, Uncle Harry, I assure you," Uncle Ed exclaimed, turning deferentially to the old white-whiskered gentleman. "I have ordered a new dragon for *Siegfried*, and you can't even object to the expense, as I've raised the money myself. It is guaranteed to send shivers down the hardiest spine. Fire and smoke come out of its jaws, and its eyes goggle hideously. I predict that even you, Uncle Harry, won't sleep through that scene!"

Uncle Harry grunted, and I giggled and Mother smiled, but there was a distinct feeling at the table that Uncle Ed was going rather far. Granny did not attempt to conceal her apprehension.

"I don't think that's very polite to your uncle, Edmund," she intervened, as if he were five and not forty-five. "After all, it was he who suggested your name originally to the board. He is going to bear the responsibility for what you do. *He* is going to be the one to face the boxholders!"

"I know that, Ma! I couldn't be more aware of it. But the day is also coming when Uncle Harry will be proud to have made me the manager. He will be known in musical history as the man responsible for the first all-star Wagner performances in this country!"

Uncle Harry looked so uncomfortable at this that even Aunt Rosalie saw that the conversation had better be changed, and we turned to the happier topic of who could be dropped that year from her ever-expanding Christmas party.

The struggle between Uncle Ed and the boxholders came to its crisis during a Monday night performance of *Tristan und Isolde* with the same cast that I had seen rehearsing it. I sat as usual on family parties in the front row of the Belknap box between Aunt Rosalie, who always occupied her special armchair on the left, and Granny. It was a trying seat, for I had to sit up as straight as they did. Aunt Rosalie even had a little cushion, as hard as a board, which hung down over the back rest to keep her from tilting. But what was far worse than the strain of the posture, at least to a music lover like myself, was the way, with a license as broad as their physical freedom was narrow, they exchanged comments about the opera across me in perfectly normal speaking tones.

In the second row were my parents and Miss Behn, one of those soft, chattering, semi-indigent old maids, always smiling, always looking to the "bright side" of their faintly illuminated existences, who attached themselves to the Aunt Rosalies of that era as pilot fish to sharks. And alone in a corner at the back of the box, a nodding Jupiter, Uncle Harry slept the sleep of the just fiduciary.

Why did they go to the opera? What took them, *every* Monday night, year in and year out? Could it have been only snobbery, as people believe today? I would be the last to deny that snobbery played its part, but it seems to me that there had to be something else, something deeper in the folkways of human communities. Monday night at the opera was like a village fair or a saint's festival. Society was still small enough so that one knew, if not everybody, at least who everybody was, and who were their guests and why. Many young people today do not know what this pleasure is. The impersonality of the modern city has destroyed it. But in New York you can still see a strange atavistic yearning for something not unlike it in the Easter Parade. What used to be a leisurely stroll of familiar figures in new finery down Fifth Avenue after church has become a turgid human river, overflowing the sidewalks and filling the thoroughfare to the elimination of all vehicles, a dense, slowly moving mass without origin or destination, drawn from the desolate suburbs, thousands upon thousands of women in silly hats, staring and being stared at, recognizing nobody and ignorant of why they are there, zombies seeking a lost ritual of community living that they will never find. Thank God my life has been largely lived in another day.

We arrived very late that night, to my distress but hardly to my surprise. Tristan and Isolde were already drinking the potion, and Granny and Aunt Rosalie were sufficiently diverted by the shouts of the sailor chorus so that no real ennui had settled in before the long entr'acte. In the second act, the love duet held everyone's attention, but trouble came, after the interruption of the lovers, with King Mark's long aria. The ripple of conversation through the boxes swelled to a gurgling stream.

I had done my homework on *Tristan* since the rehearsal, and I remember thinking that it was ironical that Granny and Aunt Rosalie's world should be most bored when Wagner was speaking most directly to them. For Mark sings of the day, which in *Tristan* is always compared unfavorably to the night. The day is reality: it is harsh and bright and garish. It is full of things that boxholders like to talk about: honor, loyalty, ties of blood. But the night, which to the lovers has become the only truth, is dark and lush and sleep-inducing. The night is death and love.

The chatter in the boxes reached a pitch that I had not heard before. It was actually difficult to catch some of Mark's notes. Suddenly, appallingly, silence fell with the unexpected downward swoop of the great curtains, the music stopped, and the lights went up. A tall bearded gentleman in white tie and tail coat strode quickly across the proscenium and faced the audience across the prompter's box. It was Uncle Ed. His high tense voice rang out in the auditorium.

"When the boxholders have concluded their conversations, the performance will be resumed. That is all. Thank you."

And he walked offstage as rapidly as he had come on. There was a moment of shocked silence, then a buzz of startled whispers, then some whistles and finally the roar of resumed conversation and a stamping of feet. The boxholders consulted each other indignantly; there were shrill complaints and some laughs. From the galleries came catcalls that might have expressed anger at the interruption or approval of the management. One could not be sure of anything in the general confusion.

In the midst of it all Uncle Ed appeared again, but this time in the back of our box where he took a seat beside Uncle Harry, for once thoroughly awake. Uncle Ed tilted his chair back and crossed his arms over his chest in the gesture of one who was prepared to wait all night. In a minute the entire diamond horseshoe was aware of his presence there. The issue was joined.

I am sure that that was the most terrible moment of Granny's long life. I had heard of her near insanity at the early death of my apparently charming grandfather, and I was later to minister to her in her desolation at the death of each of her two sons. But there is a compensation in the very fullness of the tide of love that creates the agony of bereavement; there is the luxury of memory always open to us. No such leavening existed that night for Granny. She could not even console herself that her most beloved child was showing an admirable courage in his isolation. It is always difficult for the conventional to recognize courage in what they deem ridiculous causes. Here was Granny, surrounded by the only world that she knew and admired, in the very heart of it and at its dressiest moment, and having to behold it united in an anger and contempt, which to her, alas, was a *justifiable* anger and contempt, by the perverse, misguided son who sat behind her with folded arms and icy countenance, identifying her and her family and her sister with his foolish fads. It was as if a respectable Roman matron, on a holiday matinee at the Colosseum, should have had the shock of seeing a son leap into the arena to shield some dirty Christian from a hungry and deserving lion. Granny's discipline was of the tautest, but I could see her jaw tremble as it only did in moments of the very gravest tension. Then, without turning to me, she touched my elbow.

"Ask your uncle to have the performance resumed," she murmured, as I leaned over to her. "Tell him I say: 'please.' "

It was in our family a lady's SOS, the ultimate appeal. I stepped to the back of the box, terrified to think that the eyes of the multitude were upon me, and whispered the message hastily in his ear. He nodded gravely, and in the second that I caught his eyes I read in them all of his gallantry and all of his defeat. He rose and left the box, and in five more minutes the curtain rose again, before a still chattering house, on the garden by King Mark's castle. It was then that I grew up — in a single minute — and felt at last the full tragedy of what had happened.

Only two days later Father gave us the news at breakfast of Uncle Ed's resignation.

"I'm afraid it's a case of 'I quit,' 'You're fired,' " he said with a sad headshake. "He's going abroad almost at once. Your grandmother is terribly upset, Amy, and she finds it easier on her nerves not to be left alone with him. I think you'd better take the day off from school and spend it with her."

"But why is it hard for her to be alone with Uncle Ed?"

Father and Mother exchanged glances, and then he abandoned the subterfuge. "Well, I guess you're old enough to hear about it. Your uncle has run up some very serious debts, and he will find it cheaper and more convenient to live in Germany while arrangements are being made about them. Your grandmother can't afford to dig any deeper into her capital than she's already done, and she's afraid that he will try to persuade her."

I do not know if it was the restraint of my presence, but Uncle Ed certainly made no remark during lunch at Granny's that could even remotely be construed as referring to his financial exigency. Indeed, anyone watching the three of us in that dusky, silent dining room would have assumed that Granny was the one harassed by creditors. For all the reputed discipline of her generation, she made not the slightest effort at conversation, but simply sat there staring with tear-filled eyes at the errant son who was holding forth gracefully to me about the reasons for the popular failure of German opera.

"Haven't we heard enough about that sorry business?"

"Very well, Ma."

"I don't see how you can be so cold, so casual."

"I don't see how you can be so flurried, so emotional!"

"Edmund!" Granny cried. "I can't bear it! You know, my dear, that I would give you what you ask if it was fair to the others . . ."

"I know, Ma. Of course. Please! Remember Amy."

After lunch, when Granny had gone to her room for a nap (nothing ever interrupted that), Uncle Ed followed me down to the hall and helped me into my coat. It was a long red coat with some twenty buttons down the front, and in my nervousness and distress, I buttoned one in the wrong hole. Uncle Ed turned me around to face him and carefully unbuttoned it to button it again properly.

"It doesn't matter," I murmured. "I'm only going home, just a block."

Uncle Ed raised a reproachful finger. "It always matters, Amy. Remember that. It *always* matters. Those are the only words of wisdom — the only assets, in fact — that your departing uncle leaves behind."

And then, like Granny, I too broke down. I threw my arms around his neck and sobbed.

"Poor Amy," he said, stroking my hair, "life is going to be hard on you, too. Just remember what I told you about the buttons. It doesn't sound like much, and it's *not* much, but it may be better than nothing. If it's all you've got."

I ran out the door and down the stoop, and I never saw him again.

Three years later, when I was in Paris with Father and Mother, they went to see him at his hotel, but they would not let me go with them. By then he was intoxicated most of the time, and in a few more months his liver mercifully gave out.

My own story is only a sad postscript to Uncle Ed's. Without his example I might have faced the fact earlier that I did not have a voice for Wagnerian opera and reconciled myself to marriage and children. But the idea of a Stillman carrying on where he had failed became a fixation. I even believed that I owed it to him to sing the great roles as gloriously as he had dreamed of hearing them. Had Mother and Father ever divined this madness, they might have helped me, but it was part of my crazy integrity to tell them nothing.

After graduating from Brearley School, I refused adamantly to "come out," and I opposed my mother and grandmother so violently in every other plan which they proposed for me, that Father, always the peace-maker, at last had to take charge of the situation. He decreed that I should be allowed to study the voice under professional auspices. Of course, it went without saying that I should continue to live at home, but I was permitted to spend my mornings in the studio of Madame Grisi-Helsinka, to be ostensibly trained to appear in benefit performances on the concert stage. Of course, *I* was determined that I would make my debut as Sieglinde, but there was no need to throw it in my family's face until the time arrived.

My teacher scoffed at my Wagnerian pretensions and tried to turn me to operetta. My voice, such as it was, turned out to be nearer contralto than soprano. But there was still Fricka, Erda, Ortrud to be sung. I persisted in my lessons. For ten years I studied German opera, the same decade that witnessed the great popular triumph of Wagner in New York that Uncle Ed had predicted. The irony of my situation and the endless queries of my family drove me at last abroad, where, at the age of thirty, I sang Ortrud for a road company in Rouen, my debut and my finale.

For a cable came, not of congratulation but of recall. Granny was ill. She had had a stroke, which I was made to feel was not unrelated to the absurdity of my operatic career. Father had at the same time come down with a kidney disease that was to kill him, and as Mother had to spend all her time with him, she insisted that my place was with Granny. I debated my reply for a desperate week, and in the end I decided that Mother was right. I sailed home from Le Havre and spent seven dreary years with Granny until her death at the age of ninety-one. By then I was thirty-seven, and there was no further question of an appearance in opera. The family had won — or thought they had.

But I must insist on one point. Everybody has always taken for granted that I was talked into looking after first Granny and later

Mother. They say: "Poor old Amy. She wanted to have her little fling, you know, but old Mrs. Stillman put a stop to all that. They preferred to have her a useful 'companion' to an indifferent opera singer." Everybody assumes that I was simply another of those weak-minded spinsters of the late Victorian era who bowed their heads submissively as they were cheated of their birthrights by selfish mothers and grandmothers. But it wasn't so. It cannot have been so! What I did, I did under nobody's persuasion but my own. I took a long clear look at my opera career and weighed it against what I could do for Granny. Had I had the voice for Isolde I hope I would have had the divine egotism and the courage to let Granny die alone. As it was, I could not sacrifice the small consolation that I was able to bring her for the chance to sing second-string roles in third-rate opera companies.

But we had our moments, Uncle Ed and I. Who knows, as Robert Browning might have put it, when all is finally added up, if we will not have had as much as the others? It is more graceful, anyway, to think so. It is like keeping that twentieth button properly buttoned on one's coat. And so I am going to be glad for what I have had. I am going to be glad for my little night in Rouen, and I wonder if Uncle Ed, even in those sorry last years, was not occasionally glad that he had had the thrill of producing *Tristan*, if only to a golden horseshoe of chattering friends and relations.

Sincerely yours,
AMY STILLMAN

The Prince
and the Pauper

1970

1

BROOKS CLARKSON knew at once when his wife had gone too far. For years he had waited for the moment, knowing that he would recognize his doom when it fell. And, what was more, he was convinced that the other guests at that little Saturday night party in Glenville, all contemporaries, all weekday commuters like himself, had recognized it at the same time. That might have seemed curious to some. Was it so unusual for one of his crowd, on Long Island's not notedly puritan north shore, to get roaring drunk on Saturday night? If Fanny Clarkson, so gay, so fée, such a bewitching little wisp of a blond doll, kicked off her slippers, stripped to the waist and sang an obscene song, wasn't it the natural release of any poor female after a week of suburban coping? Doomed? Brooks Clarkson doomed? Doomed at thirty-nine, when one was as handsome as he, a partner, like his father before him, in the Broad Street firm of Emmons, Taylor & Clarkson, with a beautiful house in Glenville, a beautiful wife and three beautiful daughters? Yes! Certainly!

Fanny, like Eve, had first tasted of the apple, but he, like Adam, had readily followed. For years now they had been going to bed half sozzled. It was such a simple way to cloud over the beady eyes of the world: the eyes of his law partners, who suspected that his smooth talk and high connections covered a deficiency in aptitude, the eyes of his fellow trustees of the Glenville Library, the Glenville Museum, the Glenville Art Society, who suspected that he used his civic positions as a cover for his spiritual emptiness, the eyes of Fanny herself, who suspected that he was only half a man. Oh, blessed sin, blessed whiskey! But, of course, he and she were bound to drink more and more, and people were bound to get sicker and sicker of them. And that, in the long run, would provide a kind of dim solution.

Brooks had a theory of what was wrong with him. He had never divulged it to a living soul, not even to Fanny, and he never would, but he hugged it to his heart. It was a conceited, odious little theory, but it did not have to be either conceited or odious if no one knew. It was simply that he was different from other people. He was different from his clients, his partners, his Glenville friends, his cousins, even his brothers and sisters. He was different because he was an aristocrat, the last of his breed.

It was not, obviously, considering those who were *not* aristocrats, a mere question of birth or money or position. These things were only the outward and dispensable signs. It was a question of soul, and questions of soul could never be hidden. Somehow he stank of it, somehow it exuded from him, and, inevitably, like some bleeding creature in the ocean, he was bound to attract the notice of carnivorous neighbors. For his fellow Americans might worship wealth and admire arrogance; they might be dazzled by power and taken in by strutting, but they would never pardon an aristocrat. They could never forgive a man who conceived it his duty and privilege to serve his social inferiors. They would never forgive *noblesse oblige*.

And now the farce was almost over. Now the last invitations in Glenville would cease. Now his partners would meet secretly without him to discuss steps to be taken. Now he had been summoned, so to speak, before the Committee of Public Safety, and everyone knew how *that* had to end. There would be a brief incarceration; there would be the travesty of a trial; there would be the ride in the rumbling cart through narrow, jeering streets and finally the relief of turning into the big sun-bathed square and seeing ahead, soaring over the upturned faces of the vulgar and curious, the tall narrow instrument that guaranteed his swift release.

Fanny could not suspect all this, but she suspected something. She gazed at him darkly over the rim of her cocktail glass the next day, a Sunday, when they were alone before lunch. Brooks stood with his back to her at the bar table, slowly mixing his own, feeling the intensity of her gaze.

"Why do you give me this drink, darling?" she asked in her high, bright tone. "Shouldn't I be punished?"

"Punished? For what?"

"For disgracing you. For behaving in a way that would have convinced your late sainted grandmother that I was the Whore of Babylon.

Don't minimize it, Brooks. Be angry. Don't you see, I want to be punished?"

"You were a bit gay. Why not? Is that a crime? Remember what Sylvia Fales did last week."

"Ah, but she's not a Clarkson."

"She's married to my cousin, isn't she?"

"Somehow it's different. Anyone can do anything but a Clarkson. As a matter of fact, any Clarkson can do anything but a *Brooks* Clarkson. Tell me the secret, honey. Why do you bear the sins of the world alone? I pine to know."

"There's no secret, Fanny." He turned and brought the shaker over to fill the empty glass that she held out to him. "You're imagining things. All I want is to have you enjoy yourself. All I want is to have you be happy."

"Even if I'm a happy lush?" She took a deep sip from her refilled glass. "Even if I made an ass of myself again next Saturday night?" Her luminous, faintly feverish eyes followed him about the room. "Sometimes I think you'd be glad if I went to pieces. To get it over with, once and for all."

"Fanny!" he cried. "How can you say anything so horrible? Don't you know I want the world for you?"

"Oh, your world!" She laughed desperately. "What do I want with your world, Brooks? What could I possibly do with it? Does it even exist?"

Brooks never had anything to say to this kind of comment, and when he had finished his drink, he quickly poured himself another. Not until the third, however, did he begin to sense the tingle in the ears, the prickle in the chest, the glow about the heart, that accompanied the gradual cessation of pain. With gin they would get through until the guillotine.

2
—
✸

Brooks had no real friends, but, as appropriate for an aristocrat, he had a protégé. Patronage was a function of his class, and he took it seriously. He made himself responsible for Benny Galenti, whose position in life he saw as the inverse of his own. If this were so, the ultimate outcome had to be as happy for Benny as it should be sad for himself.

Benny had started in Emmons, Taylor & Clarkson as an office boy. He was the son of Italian immigrants on the Lower East Side, and his original ambition had been to be a lawyer. He had a slight, tight physical build, thick shiny black hair and blue, staring eyes, slightly misted, as if the sunny Sicilian sky of his family's origin had been diluted with the smog of a new world. Like many second-generation Italians, he had lost the color and excitability of the first. He was careful, methodical, almost Nordic. He had gone to night college and completed one year at law school when the disaster of his fiancée's pregnancy had necessitated their marriage and the permanent abandonment of law.

Brooks had been attracted to him from the day when Benny, intuitively sensing the junior partner's need to befriend an inferior, had walked into his office and asked for a loan. His wife, it seemed, was having a second child, who would be an "Irish twin" of the first. Brooks at once advanced the money, which was promptly repaid, and later made many other loans, which enjoyed the same happy fate. Benny, eased of his burdens, shot ahead in the firm. He seemed pushed by a demoniac energy that might have been designed to prove that he was as good as any lawyer. When he finally achieved the post of office manager, petted by the partners and feared by the clerks, Brooks was especially gratified. If he was the soft old past, Benny was the ruthless future.

But there was one thing on which he had not counted: Benny's gratitude. Brooks was considerably disconcerted to find that his protégé was determined not to let him go to the devil with impunity. Benny would come to his office, close the door and subject his benefactor to endless sermons.

"You've got to kick the booze, Brooks, and you've got to watch your office hours. Do you think your partners don't know just how many Fridays you've taken off this past year? And just how many days you've wandered in at noon? Do you think they don't know about that bottle of bourbon in your desk? Quit kidding yourself! They know all those things and many more. They're planning right now to cut your percentage by a full half! Mr. Emmons is claiming our biggest estate, Carey, as his client. He says you've let him do all the work too long."

"But Gus Carey was my own great-uncle," Brooks exclaimed, raising his hands in mock dismay. "What are we old families coming to?"

"A fat lot they care about that! Old family connections, old school ties, those things are great, so long as they're kept current. But you're slipping behind, Brooks. Catch up!"

"I wonder if these trends are reversible," Brooks speculated with a yawn, jabbing his blotter with a paper cutter. "The social scene, like the human body, seems to have to change its cells. We Clarksons used to have a fleet of clipper ships in the China trade. White sails speeding across the broad Pacific! Where were the Galentis then, I wonder. One family declines, another rises. It's rather beautiful, really."

"Who's rising?"

"You are, Benny. You've only just started."

"Brooks, you're getting to be a bore on that subject. Maybe I could have had a future once. If I hadn't married so young. Or been a member of a church that didn't ban birth control. But as it is, my friend, Benny Galenti has gone quite as far as Benny Galenti's ever going. Why, I can't even afford to move to a decent neighborhood! You talk to Teresa and see what a big success *she* thinks I am!"

"Can't you get a mortgage?" Brooks always seized any chance to get the subject away from his own drinking. "Or would you rather finance it privately? I'm perfectly willing to stake you to a move to the suburbs. Why haven't you asked me?"

Benny seemed suddenly embarrassed. Was it, Brooks wondered, because he had planned the conversation this way? If he had, it would be only natural. What was the good of a Brooks Clarkson except to help a Benny Galenti?

"No, no, Brooks. You've done too much for me anyway, and, besides, you're going to need all your money if you keep on this way. How do you expect to live when . . . ?"

"Why don't you move to Glenville?" Brooks interrupted in a sudden inspiration. "You could have the old superintendent's cottage on our place. It's a shingle horror, but it's got plenty of room. We could fix it over for you. I was going to have to do that, anyway."

Benny's stare might even have meant that he had considered this, too. "What about my kids? Where would they go to school? We can't afford your private academies."

"Do you think everyone in Glenville is rich?" Oh, he had shut him up now! The terrible sermon was over. "We have one of the best high schools on Long Island. It would solve your vacation problem. You wouldn't have to take your family to the beach."

Benny's expression of embarrassment and gratitude was moving on a face that was usually so noncommittal. "I couldn't accept it, Brooks. You know that. Why, you could rent that cottage for a fortune these days!"

"Ah, but I won't!" Brooks cried, elated at the realization that his inspiration was actually going to work! Teresa, he suddenly saw, would make Benny accept, even if he balked now. "I can't have anyone that close to me who isn't absolutely congenial. And I'm very fussy! If you don't take it, it stays vacant. So there!"

3

Fanny was upset when Brooks told her that night of his offer of the cottage. She had always been jealous of his admiration of Benny.

"You mean we'll have those Galenti children all over the place! How many are there now? Six? Why, Brooks, we won't be able to call our home our own!"

"You'll find that Teresa has total control of her children. You'll never even know they're there. Besides, this will help me at the office."

"Are you crazy? Is Benny Galenti anything more than a glorified office boy? How can he help *you* at the office?"

"Benny is a very good friend to have," he said stubbornly.

"Why not give him *our* house then? And we can move into the cottage!"

"Don't be difficult, Fan. I know what I'm doing. It will all work out for the best."

"Will it? Best for whom? For us? Will we absorb by osmosis some of the vigor of the proletariats who squat at our doorstep? Is that the idea?" Fanny was inclined to be dramatic after her second drink. After the third she became playful, after the fourth self-pitying, after the fifth despondent. Now she was still in high, if rapidly souring, spirits. "Perhaps the virtue of this brave new world will inoculate our old stock so that we *shall* relish of it! Perhaps Fanny Clarkson will learn to be a model of sobriety, and Brooks, at last, will be at ease with the lower orders! Perhaps our daughters will be saved from dissolute Prince Charmings by sturdy bricklayers!"

"Please, Fan. You know I can't bear that kind of talk."

"Well, don't despair. I shall learn my good manners from Mrs. Galenti!"

Brooks feared that she would not even *show* good manners to Teresa Galenti, but even he was not prepared for the terrible scene that took place, six months later, when Benny and his wife, after settling themselves and their children in the now spotless and repainted cottage, paid their first call at the big house. Benny was in a blue suit, and Teresa, a small, firm, hard-eyed woman with the blackest hair anyone had ever seen, was wearing a red dress with a red hat that was too big. Fanny, despite all Brooks's advance warnings of the call, was dressed in a negligee that had two coffee spots on the front.

Brooks saw his house, his wife, himself, through the dark, darting eyes of Teresa Galenti. He noted the faded curtains, the cigarette holes on the sofa, the children's schoolbooks piled on the floor. He heard his daughter Anne's violent stamping on the stairway and winced as she slammed through the living room without pausing to greet the guests. Fanny, reclining languidly on a chaise longue, was in her "literary" stage of inebriation, where most of her references were to books.

"What must you think of the state of things in this house, Mrs. Galenti? Oh, you must be shocked, don't deny it! Those curtains should have been changed a year ago. How you stare! Or how you *would* stare if your manners weren't so good. I haven't intruded on you yet in the cottage, but I confess I've walked by and peeked in the living room window. How neat and trim and freshly painted it all is! Oh, it puts us quite to shame up here in our Cherry Orchard!"

"I think of you as very fortunate indeed in having such a charming home," Teresa Galenti replied firmly.

"Do you? How charming of you. Isn't it charming of Mrs. Galenti to say that about our 'charming home,' Brooks? But perhaps I may be allowed to console myself with another comparison. Your cottage, Mrs. Galenti, is orderly, serene, peaceful. But up here on the hill we're Wuthering Heights! Uncomfortable, if you like, unpainted, if you will, unadorned. Yet we still clutch to our remnant of soul. Or do you think I flatter myself, Mrs. Galenti?"

"It must be nice to have read so many books." Teresa's tone was perfect. She knew that she was being insulted and that she could not strike back. But she did not whine; she did not crawl; she did not scratch.

Her contempt was as high and cold as the wind on Wuthering Heights.

Brooks was suddenly furious. He could have forgiven Fanny anything but an attack on Benny's wife. Now the cruelty of his revenge was in proportion to her long immunity. "I don't know why Fanny has to delve so deeply into the literary past for comparisons to our house," he said bitterly to the Galentis. "I should think modern writers had examples enough. What about *Tobacco Road?*"

Fanny turned on her husband, her eyes vibrant with the shock received. "Oh, Brooks, how *could* you!" she cried, and, clapping her hand to her mouth, she jumped up and ran sobbing from the room.

Benny rose and walked over to his wife. "Come on, Tessie. It looks like we've picked the wrong day to call."

Brooks followed them to the door, muttering apologies, but Benny was very short with him. Brooks understood. It was not so much Fanny's scene that Benny minded. It was the scene he would have to face from Teresa when they got home.

That night Brooks got very drunk, and the next day he did not go to the office. The following night he got drunk again, but on the morning after Benny called at the house and insisted on driving him to town. All the way in he lectured him.

"You've got to pull yourself together, Brooks. I won't mince words. The gossip is all over the office that you're going to resign. Mr. Emmons is spreading it. Teresa thinks your case is hopeless. She says I'm wasting my time."

Brooks, holding his head still to diminish the throb of his hangover, thought how much easier it would be for them both if Benny would only conform to the role that destiny had assigned to him. If he would only concentrate on moving forward and upward, without looking back at those who slipped! Life might be almost endurable if people would stick to their parts and not keep ad-libbing sentimental clichés into a script that was beautifully hard and true. What was intolerable was this constant stopping of a show and turning on the lights, this endless inquiring of "Where are we *now?*" But how could he stop Benny?

"A man has just so much energy," he said at last. "Keep yours for those six young Galentis, will you?"

"I can do my job and still look after you, Brooks. How much energy do you think it takes to be an office manager?"

"You should save it for the future, then."

"Whose future, for God's sake? Where do you get this crazy idea that I'm going places? A man doesn't go places from my job. In a capitalist world he's got to have capital. You know that. You're just trying to get me off the subject. I've got a plan that you're not going to like, but it can't be helped. I want to put you in the sanatorium at Brunswick and get you dried out. I . . ."

"Benny, listen to me!" Brooks interrupted excitedly. Oh, he saw his way now! "About this capitalist world. What about the new duplicating machine you talked us into putting in the back office? Didn't you say it was some kind of miracle?"

"The Xerox? Of course, it is."

"What's Xerox stock selling at now?"

"Around a hundred."

"Well, go buy it, man! Isn't that your fortune? Buy Xerox!"

"I have bought Xerox. I've got a hundred shares. But even at that I had to borrow at the bank and dip into the children's college fund. If Teresa knew how much, she'd clip my ears back!"

"Buy a thousand! Go ahead. I'll stake you to it!"

"Jesus, Brooks, do you mean it?"

As Benny gripped the wheel on top, both hands together, and stared tensely ahead down the parkway, Brooks had a sudden suspicion, despite all Benny's kindness and his conscience, that he had foreseen from the beginning of their drive, not only that this offer would be made, but that it would be accepted. What of it? There would be no further talk now of "drying out."

4

In the four years that followed the date of this conversation the face of Glenville was lifted — or dropped — depending on one's point of view. The last line of the old estates was broken, and housing developments proliferated in their debris. Destruction was not confined to the works of man. Hills were leveled, ponds drained, streams deflected from their course. A person who had been away for six months could hardly find his way about; he would discover a supermarket where there had been a meadow, a golf course where there had been a thick wood. The Glenville Country Club, lying across the route of the new parkway, was condemned, and the members were obliged to buy a new site and to plan a new clubhouse. To meet the great expenses of this project the governors decided to enlarge their membership, and it was to induce Benny Galenti to join that Byron Fales, the club president, called on him and Teresa one weekday night after dinner.

"You've got a fine place here, Benny," Fales told him when Teresa had brought him his whiskey. "Such a relief after all the modern junk you see. I like a window to be a window and a door a door. And, goddamnit, I still like a bathroom to be a bathroom."

Benny watched his guest taking in, piece by piece, the furniture which Teresa had bought at Sloane's in Manhasset. But Fales was not sarcastic like his cousin Brooks Clarkson. His expression of admiration was perfectly genuine.

"What did the whole thing cost you?" he continued, in his blunt manner. "No, don't tell me, let me guess. Do you ever watch 'The Price Is Right' on TV? I bet the whole works cost you — with the furniture — a hundred and seventy-five g's."

Benny laughed. "It's a good guess."

"You could have afforded more, of course. I've noticed the guys with new fortunes these days are usually conservative spenders."

"We have everything we need, Mr. Fales," Teresa said in a slightly sharp tone. It amused Benny that for all her passion to get in with the Fales and their group, she could never wholly control her hot temper. "We have our home and two cars and all the children in private schools. What more do we need to be happy? A Renoir?"

Byron Fales laughed easily. His self-confidence was sublime. He was a Fales, and he had made as much money as Benny in Xerox. His cousin Brooks had told him, late one Saturday night at the club, four years before, in 1962, of his loan to Benny for the thousand shares, and he had been much struck. The following Monday he had purchased a thousand shares for his own account. Did he care that he was stout of girth and coarse of manner, that neither his conversation nor his demeanor suggested the expensive private education, lavished upon him in childhood, that people like the Galentis now sought for their own offspring? Why should he? He knew that all they wanted was the opportunity to bring up their sons to be like Byron Fales.

"A Renoir? I don't know if you're talking about a car or a picture, as the Texas oil tycoon is supposed to have said. But is that right? Are all the kids in the Horton School now? I thought Giulia was still in Glenville High."

"No, she's in Horton, too," Teresa said with satisfaction. "Fortunately, there was a vacancy last month."

"Fortunately, Tessie?" Benny asked dryly.

"Well, fortunately for Giulia, I mean."

Fales looked shrewdly from Benny to his wife. "What was the vacancy? Oh, yes, that was the Clarkson kid, wasn't it? Anne. Jesus, can you beat that! Fifteen and taking pot! But what can you expect with parents like hers? Brooks is my cousin and all that, but they've certainly let themselves go. Have you been by their house recently? It looks as if they were hanging washing out the window! The new people on that road have complained they're depreciating the neighborhood."

"Brooks Clarkson depreciating the neighborhood!" Benny exclaimed with a scornful laugh.

"Well, why not, Benny?" Teresa demanded indignantly. "Mr. Fales is quite right, and they're his cousins! You've got a fixation on Brooks Clarkson, that's your trouble. A drunk's a drunk, no matter how blue his blood. Isn't that so, Mr. Fales? Why, do you know he shoots holes in his ceiling at night, lying on the floor? He's going to kill somebody one of these days. And his girls are nothing but tramps. People won't even have them as baby-sitters!"

"Shut up, Tessie!"

"She's right, Benny," Fales intervened authoritatively. "She's absolutely right. Ever since he got kicked out of his law firm, he's been going downhill like a crazy wagon. If it weren't for that last little trust my uncle set up, he'd be on relief."

"What's that to me?" Benny cried. "I owe him everything!"

"That's ridiculous. But I didn't come here tonight to talk about my disreputable relatives. I came to talk about the new clubhouse. We want you to join, Benny."

Benny caught the instantly earnest look in Teresa's eye, her quick small gesture of appeal, and he turned away to hide his mortification. "You must need the money awfully bad," he muttered. "What's the tariff?"

"Now that's no attitude to take," Fales reproached him. "I'd expect you to take ten thousand of the new club bonds. Sure. That's what I'm expecting of *all* the new members. I'm taking twenty myself, in case you're interested. But that's not the point. I can get any number of new members for that price. People are lining up around here to get into the Glenville Country Club. The point is that we want people like you."

"Why? Because my parents were first-generation Italian immigrants? Because I'm a graduate of CCNY? Because Teresa and I are Roman Catholics? Or mackerel snatchers, as you probably call us!"

"Benny!"

"Don't worry, Mrs. Galenti," Fales reassured her. "He's not going to get my goat, no matter how hard he tries. I'll tell you why we want you, Benny. We want you because you and your family are decent people, and that's a breed that's getting kind of rare in Nassau County. We want you because you believe in things. Because you believe in your own marriage, for example. Because you believe in bringing up your children properly. I'll bet none of *your* kids go in for dope. We want you because you're the kind of people who still take pride in the American flag and aren't ashamed to admit it. So there! Call me a Fourth of July windbag. Go ahead!"

"You're a Fourth of July windbag!"

"Oh, Benny," his wife cried. "Must you throw away every favor that comes our way? Why do you do it? To spite me?"

"What have I thrown away? Have I thrown away this house or your clothes or our private schools or any of my fabulous Xerox stock?" Benny got up and paced the room angrily. "What have I done since I made my lucky strike but look down in my stupid lap as it filled with treasures?"

"Lucky?" Fales broke in. "You call it luck to take the calculated risk that *you* took? To sell everything you had, to borrow every cent you could and put it all in one stock? That took guts, man!"

"It took despair," Benny retorted sullenly. "Oh, all right, so it took a bit of nerve, yes. But why should a bit of nerve be rewarded so extravagantly? Why should it make me a fat cat, a sleek citizen, a gentleman of clubs, a friend of Byron Fales, a pillar of the community! A man ought to work his way up the ladder, rung by rung. He ought to have to save, pinch and scrape. Then there'd be some kind of substance to him when he got to the top!"

"But we *did* all those things, Benny," Teresa pleaded. "Didn't we learn everything the hard way? The only thing that ever came fast was the Xerox!"

"But all that pinching and scraping didn't *contribute!*" Benny protested, beginning to feel that he was making a fool of himself, but unwilling to yield on what he deeply felt must be a matter of some kind of principle. "I was nobody till I had my lucky day. I might as well have made it in Las Vegas!"

"We stockbrokers don't care for that kind of comparison," Fales retorted, with a wink at Teresa. "But let us agree to disagree. With me Xerox was sheer financial acumen; with Benny it was dumb luck. But do please, Mrs. Galenti, bring your lucky husband to the club dance on Saturday night. Dine with us first at eight. I'll have a nice little party, and I think we'll persuade Benny that we want you both for your *beaux yeux* and not your market portfolios."

"Oh, Mr. Fales, I promise you!" Teresa exclaimed, with clasped hands. She might have been a schoolgirl whose head had just been patted by the principal.

"Benny," she began imploringly, after Fales had left, "tell me you're not going to spoil this for me and the kids!"

"I can't talk about it till I've seen Brooks."

"That rotten rum pot, that . . ."

"Oh, shut up, Tessie!"

Ten minutes later he drove alone to the Clarksons'. In the moonlight he could make out the ragged countenance of the old place: the choked, unweeded garden plots by the gravel drive, the broken windowpanes in the garage, the peeling paint, as he approached it, on the front door. Brooks opened it, drink in hand, and bowed sardonically.

"If it's not the Caesar of Xerox! The duke of duplication! Come in, Caesar. Come in, Duke. Fanny has gone to bed, and I was just yearning for someone to drink a nightcap with. Of course, I had not aspired so high as yourself, but if you will only 'condescend,' as the immortal Mr. Collins would have put it, we may still salvage a bit of the moonlight."

Benny sat in the chair and drank silently as Brooks went on in this mocking strain. There was no interrupting him, no shifting of his mind to serious topics. Brooks was reaching the final stage of his decline: a maudlin monologism. To Benny it was more terrible than it had been at any of the worst moments of the past four years. What Brooks had been destroying up until that night had been his career, his family, himself. Now he was destroying his romance.

"I came to ask your opinion," Benny interrupted at last. "I came to ask if you think I'd be doing a cruel thing to Tessie and the kids if I turned down your cousin's invitation to join the Glenville Club."

Brooks stared at him for a moment and then rose. He looked almost handsome again as he reached down to throw some kindling wood on the dying fire. "You'd be doing a cruel thing to *me*," he said with surprising lucidity. "What else do you think I've lived for but to see you in that club? Isn't it the last delicious twist of a crazy world? Please, Benny, you can't deny an old friend a laugh like that! Did you know they threw me and Fanny out?"

"What else could they do? You wouldn't resign and you wouldn't pay your dues!"

"Ah, but that was just the excuse. There have been plenty of examples of the board's looking the other way when *desirable* members defaulted on their dues. But one Saturday night, at the weekend dance, a rather grotesque little incident occurred. Fanny and I had made a wager that I could use the ladies' room and she the men's, on the stroke of midnight, without anyone's noticing, and . . ."

Benny could hear no more. He needed all his concentration to arrest his tears. He was rarely emotional, but when it happened, it could be very bad. He was apt not only to weep but to sob. For a moment he closed his eyes and saw before him the old portrait — or self-portrait — of Brooks Clarkson, of the ancient Clarksons, with his fine triangle of long wavy hair retreating from a noble forehead, a figure that would have dignified the bridge of a clipper ship in fine old days of China trade or the pulpit of Grace Church, robed in shimmering white, or the back of a sweating pony on the polo field at Meadowbrook. But the decline of the dream and the decline of Brooks Clarkson had now fused into the shabby sight that confronted Benny's reopened eyes. Brooks was not passing from the scene as a beautiful memento of a day that could not coexist with the Xerox machines that duplicated to infinity the jargon of a world of irretrievable vulgarity. He was perishing as something too vulgar himself to be duplicated.

"I *shall* join the club," Benny announced, as he rose to leave. "And you shall have your long awaited giggle. I can only hope that the irony of the situation will be all that you have so eagerly anticipated."

The last Saturday night party at the old clubhouse was an affair of almost frenzied nostalgia, but Byron Fales, after the orchestra drums had rumbled for silence, struck the note of the future by toasting a model of the new clubhouse, an ingenious combination of modern and Georgian styles designed to conciliate all tastes, as it was borne in by four waiters, in a blaze of candles, and placed on a table in the middle of the dance floor. The tumultuous applause that followed allowed the members to fold their regrets, like wet umbrellas, on the advent of sunny skies. It was widely agreed that Byron Fales had been, as always, perfect.

At his table, Teresa Galenti seemed perfectly happy. Benny noticed that she did not have much to say to either of her neighbors, or they to her, but obviously this did not matter. She was a seraph in heaven, and as long as seraphs were destined to sing everlastingly, it could hardly matter if they took an occasional night off. But he could not join her because Byron Fales, the star of the evening, chose to monopolize him. Perhaps Fales was sufficiently arrogant to enjoy the anomaly, at the old clubhouse's final party, of devoting his time to a new member.

When Benny had drunk double his normal quota of Scotches, he dared at last to bring up the topic that had been on his mind all evening. He asked if it might be possible to restore the Clarksons to membership if he paid up their delinquent dues.

"The offer does you credit," Fales replied, knitting his brow, "but I'm afraid there's not a chance. Brooks has made his bed, or rather unmade it, and I'm afraid he'll have to toss on the bare mattress. After that last trick that he and Fanny pulled, the board wouldn't want them back, even if they were on the wagon."

"Is there no way to help them, then? Must we just let them go?"

"They've gone, fella. Ask any newcomer what 'Clarkson' stands for in Glenville today, and he'll tell you: booze. Brooks and Fanny are suffering from an incurable disease: decadence."

"But how can you say that?" Benny cried in astonishment. "You, of all people! Isn't he your own cousin?"

"My mother was a Clarkson, it's true. She was Brooks's aunt. But there's never been anything wrong with the Clarksons. Brooks's mother was a Fortescue, and we know about *them*." Fales rolled his eyes and tapped his temple with his forefinger. "Still, I can't believe it's only a matter of genetics. The individual may degenerate, even though the family's sound. You find the same kind of rot in poor whites in the South. You find it among the red Indians. Once it starts, no surgery can stop it. All you can do is make the patient as comfortable as possible."

"By pushing another drink his way?"

"Allow me to push one yours."

Benny watched grimly as those thick, facile hands busied themselves with the bottles and glasses massed in the center of the table. "Make me comfortable, by all means. But there's still something I don't see. How can Brooks be decadent and creative at the same time?"

"What do you suggest he has created?"

"Me!"

"Oh, come off it, Benny. Just because he loaned you some dough in a tight spot doesn't mean . . ."

"Now listen to me, Byron. It was Brooks who singled me out of the office boys in his firm and pushed me ahead. It was Brooks who sold me to his partners as office manager. It was Brooks who got me to move to Glenville and loaned me the money to buy Xerox. It was Brooks . . ."

"Well, if he's so damn creative, why didn't he buy Xerox himself?"

"Because that isn't his way."

"He could have, couldn't he?"

"I suppose."

"But he'd rather watch, is that it? He'd rather sit back and gaze into his man-making machine? Do you know that you've just proved the very point you were trying to rebut? You've described the most decadent creature that ever drew a fetid breath!"

Benny broke off the conversation and went to look for Teresa, who was dancing. Whether Fales was right or Fales was wrong, all that he, Benny, could do now was to put on, as gracefully as possible, the emerald snake's skin that Brooks had shed for him. It might be instructive, at the least, and perhaps of some future utility, to contemplate the affluent festivity of the evening where Xerox was the bridge between the new riches of the Galentis and the renewed riches of the Faleses, and to consider that the switch of rungs between the Clarksons and the Galentis on the Glenville social ladder had taken just four years. But then Brooks had always known the quickest way to do things.

The Prison Window

1970

"YOU ALWAYS FORGET, Aileen, that we're not an art institute. Perhaps it would be more fun if we were, but we're not. The Museum of Colonial America, as its name implies, exists for a very specific purpose. We're a history museum. That doesn't mean, of course, that there aren't a great many ways of accomplishing that purpose, such as awakening the young to a proper sense of their heritage and revitalizing the old forms of communication . . ."

"I know, I know," Aileen Post interrupted. It was not the thing to do for a curator to interrupt the director, but when the curator was middle-aged and female and the director male and very young, exceptions had to be admitted. "I know all the jargon. I realize that we have to be 'relevant' and 'swinging' and 'up to the minute.' I understand very clearly that we have to be everything on God's earth but simply beautiful!"

"History is not always beautiful, Aileen."

"Oh, Tony! Don't be sententious. Save it for the trustees. You know what I mean. The *illustrations* of history should be beautiful! We can read about the horrors. We don't have to look at them. Why should there be any but lovely things in my gallery? Why should I have to put *that* in the same room with the Bogardus tankard and the Copley portrait of Lillian van Rensselaer?"

Here she pointed a scornful finger at an ancient rusted piece of iron grillework that might have fitted into a small window space, two feet by two, which lay on a pillow of yellow velvet on the table by Tony Side's desk.

"Because it's a sacred relic," Tony replied, with the half-mocking smile that, as a modern director, he was careful to assume in discussing serious topics. "Because tradition has it that it covered a window on the ground floor of the Ludlow House in Barclay Street. During the Revolution it was the sole outlet to a large, dark storage room in which Yankee prisoners were miserably and sometimes fatally confined."

If the distressed virgin curator of beautiful things suggested too much the past, her superior was almost too redolent of the present and future. He had long chestnut locks — as long as his trustees would tolerate, perhaps half an inch longer — that fell oddly about a pale, hawklike face and greenish eyes that fixed his interlocutor with the expression of being able to take in any enormity. Tony twisted his long arms in a curious ravel and nodded his head repeatedly as if to say, "Ah, yes, keep on, keep going. I'm way ahead of you, *way* ahead!" It might have been the point of his act to be both emperor and clown.

"It's not that I haven't any feeling for those poor wretches," Aileen protested, her face clouding as it always did at the thought of pain. "God knows, it isn't that. But must their agony be commemorated in *my* gallery? It isn't as if there weren't memorials enough everywhere to dead patriots."

Aileen herself might have been an academic painting of a martyr. One could imagine viewing the long, gray, osseous face and those large, gray, desperately staring eyes raised heavenward, through the smoke of a heretic's pyre. It seemed a wasteful fate that had cast her, tall and bony, with neatly set hair and black dresses, in the role of priestess of antiques.

"Your concept of history is too limited, too snobbish," Tony warned her. "It's odd, for you're completely unsnobbish yourself. But be objective for once and take a new look at your eighteenth century. Aileen Post's eighteenth century. Isn't it all tankards and silverware and splendid portraits and mahogany furniture? Doesn't it boil down to the interior decoration of the rich? Where are your butchers and grocers? Where are your beggars? Where are your slaves?"

"But you shouldn't judge beautiful artifacts by their owners!" Aileen exclaimed with passion. "They represent the aspirations of the age! The way the spire of a Gothic cathedral represents the thrust of man's soul toward heaven! What is history but the story of his reaching? Do you want a museum to show the whips and manacles, the starvation, the failure? Leave that to Madame Tussaud and the printed record. I want the person who comes into my gallery to breathe in the inspiration of the past!"

"Tut, tut, Aileen," Tony warned her, wagging a finger. "You're playing with nemesis. In your books the rich and mighty enjoy not only the delights of this world but the respect of posterity. What is left for the wretched but that pie in the sky they no longer believe in? Watch out! Those wretched can be very determined. They want their bit of the here and now."

"Who? The dead? The dead poor?"

"Why not?" Tony smiled broadly. "Aren't I helping them right now? By setting up the prison window in the very center of your gallery?" He got up and made her a little bow. "Those are orders, my dear."

Aileen left the room without another word. She knew that, mock bow or no, his orders were to be obeyed. Tony Side, under his perpetual smile, was a very serious young man who had no idea of staying in the Colonial Museum for more than a few years. It was too obvious that he was headed for greater things. He would keep his name before the eyes of other institutes — and particularly before the eyes of their trustees — by arranging shows that need have only slender ties to the colonial era. Already he had achieved a considerable success with a gaudy display of eighteenth-century balloons and primitive flying machines against a background of blown-up photographs of Cape Canaveral. It had even been written up in *Life*.

Traversing the Ludlow Gallery of decorative arts on her way back to her office, Aileen noted bitterly that there were only two people in it. Two visitors on a Saturday morning in the middle of the biggest city of the nation! It spoke little for the much touted "cultural revival." Aileen scorned the huge, mute, unthinking crowds that pushed by the high-priced masterpieces of the Metropolitan and the shaggy youths and pert-eyed, trousered girls who gawked at abstracts in the Whitney and the Modern. She told her friends at the Cosmopolitan Club that beauty was obsolete and fashion despot. She nodded grimly when they laughed at her. They would live to see their idols perish as hers was perishing.

When she had first come to the Colonial Museum, twenty-five years before, it had seemed a symbol of permanence in an ever-changing city. The great memorial plaques in the front hall, the names of benefactors carved in stone, the portraits of former presidents and directors had heralded one into the glittering collection as a released soul might be heralded into perpetual bliss. The institution had seemed to rise above its paucity of visitors; its dignity had waxed with its noble and solemn emptiness. The solitary wanderer was rewarded by the rich sustaining silence in which he found himself embraced. It was as if the museum, with its high task of preserving beauty for eternity, could afford the luxury of being capriciously choosy as its votaries.

But now all that was over. Modern New York had repudiated the concept of permanence. No grave, no shrine, no cache of riches was any longer safe. No quantity of carved names on marble, no number of "irrevocable" trust instruments drawn up by long dead legal luminaries, no assemblage of conditions, prayers, engraved stipulations or printed supplications could arrest the erosion of endowments or the increase of costs. The "dead hand" of the past became as light as dust when the money it once represented had slipped away. Aileen found herself faced with the probability that she might survive her own selected tomb.

It was unthinkable. The treasures of the Ludlow Gallery were like so many members of her family. At least a third of them had come to the museum as a direct result of her own detective work and solicitations. The great Beekman breakfront she had discovered in a storage house; the tea service of Governor Winthrop had been redeemed at a sheriff's sale; the Benjamin Wests of the Jarvis family had come as one man's tribute to the "ardor and faith" of Aileen Post. She could smell out eighteenth-century artifacts through stone walls; she could track them down in the dreariest and most massive accumulations of Victorians. How she pitied people who spoke of her misguided adoration of the inanimate! As if a Copley portrait could be dead! As if a coffee urn from Westover could be without life! Only ugliness was dead, and it was Aileen's passionate faith that it should never be resurrected.

⁜

Certainly nothing seemed deader than the iron window. Tony, who for all his vulgarisms was a gentleman at heart, had allowed her to choose its site in the gallery, but she knew that he would correct her if she tried to hide it. She had placed it finally, framed in dark polished mahogany, upright, in a glass case, in front of the Wollaston portrait of Valerian Ludlow, the owner of the house from which it had come. Certainly it was conspicuous enough there, in the very center of the gallery. Peering through it, on his first inspection, Tony was pleased.

"It makes it look as if old Ludlow were behind bars," he pointed out with a chuckle. "Very likely he deserved to be."

Aileen at first tried not to see the window when she passed through the gallery. She would keep her eyes averted and quicken her pace as she approached the hated object. But she found that this made it worse. What good was it to banish it from her vision if she only succeeded in summoning it to fill her mind? Somehow she would have to make her peace with it, before it became an obsession.

She then adopted the practice, each time that she had to pass it, of making herself pause to look at it, or really to look through it, for there was nothing to see but its rusted blackness. She observed that one side was slightly more rugged than the other and had probably been the external side, facing on Barclay Street. Gazing through it, as if from inside the Ludlow house, she tried to imagine that thoroughfare as it must have appeared to an incarcerated patriot. Then she would walk around the grille and peer in, as if from the street, to visualize, with a shudder, the dark, fetid hole where the prisoners might have been penned. Sometimes visitors in the gallery would stop to watch her, and, when she had finished, take her place to stare through the window to see what she had been noting. Aileen, amused, became almost reconciled to her new "artifact."

One morning, however, when she was alone in the gallery and looking through the grille from the "prison cell" side, she had a curious and rather frightening experience. Ordinarily, she had not looked through the bars *at* anything in particular, but rather at her imagined reconstruction of an eighteenth-century street. That day when she happened to glance at the portrait of Valerian Ludlow, it struck her that he would have often passed that barred cellar window, in his own house, on the way to his own front door, and she attempted to picture him as he might have appeared striding by, viewed at knee height. The portrait helped her by showing him full length, standing by an open window, looking out to a sea on which floated two little vessels, presumably his own, with wind-puffed sails. The expression on his round face (the cheeks seemed to repeat the puffed sails) was one of mercantile complacency. Mr. Ludlow had obviously been one of the blessed of earth.

But now Aileen seemed to see something in his countenance that she had not noticed before. The eyes, instead of being merely opaque, either because of the artist's inadequacy or the subject's lack of expression, had a hard, black glitter. They changed the whole aspect of the portrait from one of seemingly harmless self-satisfaction to one of almost sinister acquisitiveness. At the same time the quality of the paint seemed to have lost its richness and glow. Mr. Ludlow's red velvet coat now had a shabby look, and the sea on which his vessels bobbed was brown rather than a lustrous green. Yet these changes, instead of making the whole picture more trenchant, more interesting, as they might have, seemed instead to push it back into an earlier era of clumsy primitives. Ludlow was now not only disagreeable; he was badly painted. Was his new degradation of character simply the artist's error? Had he come out mean, in the way of a clown drawn by a child? Or was Aileen seeing the real Ludlow for the first time?

Walking now quickly around the grilled window, with a conscious effort of will — for she was distinctly frightened — she turned suddenly and looked through it from the other side. She gave a little cry and then stopped her own mouth, for the sensation that had abruptly appalled her had as abruptly ceased. She had, for two seconds, stared into an absolute blackness, and at the same time her nostrils had been filled with a suffocating stench. Now she smelled nothing, and she was looking once more through the window toward the great glass case that housed the tankard collection.

Badly shaken, she returned to her office to go back to work on her article for the museum magazine on Dutch silver. But she was clear now that she would have to deal strongly with this preoccupation. In future she would walk by the window, not with consciously averted eye, not with undue attention, but simply taking it in casually, as she might take in any other exhibit. She would not flatter it with her fear or with her disdain. She would treat it, if its emanations compelled her to pause, with an icy disapproval, as she might treat a snoopy guard, set there by a jealous director to catch her out in something wrong.

By staying away from the window, she avoided any repetition of the shock of the sinister Ludlow and the black pit (figments, she assured herself, of her overcharged imagination), but she was not sure that she had eliminated all of the window's influence. She still had a sense, whenever she passed it, of some small, crouching, indistinguishable creature, some huge insect or tiny rodent, humped there by its base. And whenever she had to work near it, in the center of the gallery, she was conscious of something in the air, an aroma or maybe just a thickening of the atmosphere, that at once depressed her. If she looked about at the treasures of the gallery from any spot in the immediate circumference of the window, they appeared unaccountably drab. The silver seemed to thicken and tarnish and to lose the special elegance of its century. Bowls, plates, urns suddenly resembled the kind of ugly testimonials given to railroad presidents in the era following the Civil War. The beautiful carved wooden lady of victory that had once adorned the prow of a clipper ship might have been a widening, middle-aging nursemaid in Central Park. And the portraits, *all* the portraits, not only Valerian Ludlow's, seemed to have hardened into so many dusty merchants and merchants' wives as might have choked the wall of the Chamber of Commerce.

Sometimes she would watch visitors furtively from the door of her office to see, when they were standing near the prison window, if they noticed what she had noticed, but if they did, they showed no sign of it. Yet how could she be sure, if the things actually had changed, that they would notice it? Perhaps what she saw, under the malign influence of whatever the squatting creature was, was simply *their* vision of beautiful things. Perhaps that was the mystic significance of the window: that, peering through it, one saw art as it appeared to the Philistine! Aileen's mind had become a sea of hateful speculations.

One afternoon, at her desk, she looked up and gave a start to see an old lady standing before her. She had not heard anyone come in. It took her two or three seconds before she realized that she knew who it was. It was Mrs. Ada Ludlow Sherry, one of those "old New Yorkers" who made life for the curators both difficult and possible. She gave money and she gave things, but her gifts were hardly a *quid pro quo* for her almost daily interference. She was small and bent but very strong, and her skin, enamel-like, and her hair, falsely red, gave the impression of having been preserved by a dipping in some hardening unguent. Her agate eyes snapped at Aileen.

"Are you aware, Miss Post, that an atrocious act of vandalism has been committed in your gallery?"

"Oh, no!"

"Some villain has poked a hole in my great-great-grandfather! Don't you ever check up on your portraits? There's a ghastly, gaping rip where his left eye was!"

"In Valerian Ludlow!" Aileen jumped up and ran into the gallery to the Wollaston painting. Sure enough, old Ludlow blinked at her with one black eye and one blue, the latter being the color of the wall on which he was hung. Aileen gave a little scream of panic.

"This was done within the hour!" she cried. "He had both eyes when I last went by!"

Tony Side was summoned, the alarm was rung and all guards were questioned. Nothing was discovered, and after an hour of futile excitement Aileen was back again at her desk, depleted and scared, with the irate Mrs. Sherry, who refused now to depart. Aileen felt nothing but antipathy as she listened to the old lady's animadversions. Obviously, Mrs. Sherry cared far more for the grudge than for the grievance. She had none of Aileen's nausea at the damage to a beautiful object or her despair for the soul of the perpetrator.

"Some black boy, of course," Mrs. Sherry was grumbling. "Unless it was a Puerto Rican. They're always prating about the hard times they've had, always griping about how they've been deprived of education and opportunities. Is *this* what they want opportunities for? I'd like to see the cat-o'-nine-tails brought back. I'd like to see these boys lashed before the public in Times Square! What do they exist for but to tear our world apart? They don't care that they have nothing to put in its place! It's revenge, pure and simple."

"Revenge," Aileen murmured thoughtfully, glancing apprehensively through the doorway toward the iron grille. Could it be the revenge of a Yankee prisoner of war? But why? Revenge against whom?

"Everybody's too soft and sentimental with them," Mrs. Sherry continued. "If it *is* softness. If it isn't just cowardice, as I suspect it is. Where have our guts gone to, Miss Post? Where are our men, that we are exposed to all this? I tell you one thing, young lady. Nobody would have poked an eye out of Valerian Ludlow's portrait in his day!"

"What would he have done?"

"Don't you know what he would have done? Haven't you read his journal? *He* knew how to handle insubordinates!"

As Aileen watched the terrible old woman, she had just for a second the same eerie sense of blackness that she had experienced in peering through the iron grille. Then, as it passed, she felt a sudden, odd detachment from the immediate scene. She found herself observing Mrs. Sherry as if the latter had been a monologist performing at a private party. She noted the protuberance of the front molars and the drops of saliva at the corners of the thin lips. She marked how the almost transparent, onion-skin eyelids snapped up and down and how hatefully dark were the merciless eyes. Except for the teeth, Mrs. Sherry might have been a bird, a big, dark bird of rich, subdued colors whose feathers only made more horrible its dark face and beak, a condor tearing at a carcass. Both of Aileen's hands went to her lips in horror as she saw her world in a sudden new light. The feathers, the feathers alone, were art. The head, the beak, the glazed eyes, the talons were — man!

"Oh, be quiet! Be quiet, please!"

Mrs. Sherry stared down at Aileen incredulously. "I beg your pardon?"

When Aileen, stunned, gathered that she must have actually uttered her reproach aloud, she desperately summoned up the courage to go on. "You're saying the most dreadful things, and you have no business to. You don't know who damaged that portrait. You have no idea. It might have been a guard. It might have been me. It might have been you, yourself!" Aileen rose as if propelled by two strong hands clutching her elbows, and she spoke with a passionate urgency, a wondering, bemused prisoner of her own new flow of eloquence. "How do I know that you're not just trying to get someone in trouble? Or a whole race of people in trouble? How do I know what mad, twisted motives you may have? Look at your umbrella. You might have done it with *that!* But, my God, there's something sticking to it!" She seized the umbrella and rushed out into the gallery crying, "Guard! Guard!" When the bewildered man hurried up to her she shouted, "I've got her! The vandal! She did it with this! Look!"

Here she held the umbrella up to the portrait, the tip toward the hole. Then she lowered it slowly, dumbly, apologetically, looking shamefaced at the shamefaced guard. For the round tip of the umbrella had a thick rubber cover. Mrs. Sherry must have made it do double duty as a walking stick. Pushed into a canvas, it would have made a much bigger hole than the one in Valerian Ludlow's left eye.

"And now, Miss Post, will you be so good as to return my property? And let me ask this gentleman to conduct me to the director of this institution that I may complain of your insane behavior."

Mrs. Sherry was so carried away that, turning from the stricken Aileen after she had snatched back her umbrella, she made the mistake of taking the guard's arm. Her exit was comic rather than magnificent. But nothing could console Aileen.

Tony, when he came, was very kind. He said that the vandalism had obviously unnerved her. He regretted that so important a member of the museum as Mrs. Sherry should have been insulted, but he hoped that she could be placated. He suggested that Aileen would do well to take a few days off and get a good rest.

"No, I'm all right, I really am," she insisted in a stony voice. "I promise, you won't have to worry about me."

When Tony had left, obviously much concerned about her, Aileen sat for ten minutes, absolutely still. Then she rose and strode with a new resolution to the middle of the gallery. As she leaned slowly down and stared into the hated window, she whispered hoarsely:

"Who are you, in there? Why have you come back to haunt us? Are you the spirit of some poor boy who died in that black chamber?" As she listened, she felt her first impulse of sympathy for whatever might be behind those bars. She had a vision of a thin, undernourished face, that of some nineteen-year-old Yankee boy, with long light hair and eyes liquid with homesickness, pressed up against the bars. "Were you left behind in General Washington's retreat? Was that how the British caught you? But why do you hate the Ludlows? Wasn't their house requisitioned by the governor? Was that their fault?" In the silence, as she listened intently, she had again that eerie sense of a close malevolence. "Or do you know something about them that we don't know? Was Valerian Ludlow a secret Tory? Was he a traitor?"

The blackness that she imagined behind the bars seemed now to lift, and her eyes fell upon the great portrait in the corner of the gallery of General Cornwallis, his hand on a globe on which the eastern shoreline of the thirteen colonies was clearly visible. Aileen straightened up and returned to her office. There would be no further revelations that day.

The following morning she was greeted by the doorman with the news: "There's been another of them vandals in your gallery, Miss Post." When she arrived at her floor, breathless, after running up two flights, she found Tony and three guards standing before the glass case of the silver tankards. He silently pointed to something as she hurried to his side. On the top tray one of the tankards lay toppled over. Its cover had been wrenched off the hinges and had fallen to the bottom of the case. The coat of arms had been gashed several times by a heavy instrument, possibly a stone. She did not have to look twice to recognize the Ludlow crest.

"Nobody's to touch it until the detective from the police department comes," Tony explained. "This is a weird one. The glass, you see, has not been removed." He put his arm around Aileen's shoulders and led her out of earshot of the guards. "It had to be an inside job," he told her.

"Whoever did it must have got the key to the case from your office. But we've checked, and your key case is locked. He may have slipped into your office one day when it was open, taken the key, had it duplicated and put it back. It might have been the same guy who used your umbrella to poke the hole in the Ludlow portrait while you were out to lunch."

"*My* umbrella!"

"Well, I didn't want to upset you, but we found a smitch of canvas by the rack in your office where you keep your pink umbrella. It has to be some nut, of course, with some fantastic grudge against the Ludlow family."

"Oh, you've put that together, have you?" she murmured. "You've recognized the Ludlow tankard?"

"My dear Aileen. Even though I'm a museum director, I'm not a complete nincompoop."

Aileen was seized with a fit of violent trembling. She felt the same fierce prosecuting excitement that she had experienced when she had denounced Mrs. Sherry to the guard. Pulling Tony further away down the gallery, she whispered desperately, "Maybe *I* did it! Maybe I poked the hole in the portrait and then tried to throw the blame on Mrs. Sherry! Maybe I came here last night and let myself into the gallery and scraped the tankard!"

Tony's little smile never failed him, but she could tell by the way it seemed just to flicker that he did not wholly dismiss the theory. "But assuming all this, my dear, what on earth would be your motive?"

"I had no motive."

"Then why would you do it?"

"Because I'm the instrument of a fiend! The fiend that you brought in when you made me take *that!*"

Tony took in the little barred window, and at last even his smile ceased. "I said before that you needed rest," he replied in his kindest tone. "This time I insist upon it. I want you to take three weeks off, and I want you to see a doctor."

꩜

Aileen was surprised and heartened by her own reaction to this disaster. Instead of crumpling before circumstance, she discovered that her spirit was strong and her emotional state serene. When Tony told her that the police detective had said that the force used in rubbing the stone or other substance against the crest of the Ludlow tankard had been greater than that of a woman, she had merely nodded and taken her dignified leave of him. She had recovered faith in her own sanity and did not need the confirmation of a cop. She had promised that she would consult a psychiatrist, but she was already resolved that she would not. There was no use in a confrontation between the world of medicine and the occult. It could result only in her commitment to a lunatic asylum.

She was grateful for the solitude of her enforced vacation and of the time that it afforded her to deal with her ghostly opponent. For she knew now that she had one. No human being could help her. It was her grim and lonely task to track down and outwit the sinister spirit that was seeking to destroy her gallery.

She spent her days in the library of the New-York Historical Society, reading everything that there was to be read on the history of the Ludlow family. The material was rich. She found considerable evidence of a curious effeminate streak in the Ludlow males of the eighteenth century. The first Ludlow in New York, a royal governor, had insisted on wearing women's robes while presiding at the council, on the theory that he thus more appropriately represented his sovereign, Queen Anne. A generation later, his son had been criticized for making his more muscular African slaves wait on table half-naked, and this son's son, in turn, incurred the resentment of society by keeping exotic birds, expensively imported from Rio, loose in the house where they pecked his guests. The wives of all these gentlemen, on the other hand, had been big, blocky, plainly dressed women, such as one might expect in a community that was still, after all, almost the frontier.

Aileen, like many old-maid scholars, was as sophisticated about the past as she was timid about the present, and she perfectly understood that there might have been a streak of cruelty, or even sadism, in such eccentrics as the male Ludlows. But nowhere could she find the slightest evidence that any of them had been guilty of any public or private injustice, and the record of Valerian Ludlow in the Revolution seemed to repudiate the least imputation of Toryism. She had come almost to the end of her documents when a librarian asked her if she would like to see the microfilm of the manuscript of Valerian Ludlow's journal.

"I should like to look at it, of course," she replied. "I've read it so often in print, I know it almost by heart."

"You mean the DeLancey Tyler edition."

"Well, yes. Isn't that the only one? It's supposed to be complete."

"*Supposed* to be."

Aileen looked more closely at the young man. "You mean it isn't?"
He shrugged. "Tyler was a great-grandson of the journalist. He published his book in 1900. You know how prudish people were in those days."

Aileen knew by the bound of her heart that her search was over. She spent the next two days tensely reading the diary of Valerian Ludlow on the microfilm machine. The librarian had been quite right. There were substantial sections omitted in the Tyler edition. Ludlow had been a vain and easily offended gentleman of exquisite tastes and domineering manner. He had entered in the journal every slight that he had imagined himself to have received, and he had carefully recorded every punishment meted out to a servant. His descendant and editor had left in all his purchases of artifacts, all his recorded dealings with architects and decorators, all his conversations with the great, but he had carefully suppressed the invidious details of the correction of his staff and family. Aileen read breathlessly as she cranked the machine, turning the pages of the neat, flowing, somehow merciless handwriting. The realization that she was on the threshold of her revelation was actually painful.

She found at last this entry, dated July 30, 1747:

I have neglected my journal for a week because of a disturbing episode which, through God's grace, has now ended happily for most but not all. A group of slaves last Tuesday seized a farm on Lydecker Street and held it against the bailiff and his men for twenty-four hours. What the purpose of these ignorant fellows was we do not know, and they all fled. One constable, however, was killed when his own rifle blew up in his face. Public feeling has been very passionate, and on Thursday morning a large mob called here to demand my Rolfe. I met the leaders at the doorstep, and, I must say, they were very civil. They explained their reasons for believing that Rolfe had been the leading insurrectionist. I found these reasons convincing, the more so as I had had to confine Rolfe to the storeroom only that morning for insubordination. I delivered him up for what I understood was to be a trial, but I doubt that he had one. What is sure is that the mob burnt him alive in Bowling Green. It was a slow fire, and they say the poor fellow's bellows could be heard for six hours. I have discussed this unfortunate matter with Attorney Reynolds, and he advises me that if no trial occurred, I may be able to demand the price of Rolfe from the City Council, as he was taken under a show of authority.

Aileen turned from the machine with a gasp and rocked to and fro in her agony. For minutes she writhed as if she had been that wretched creature on the fire. How could flesh endure it? Six *hours?* The tears came at last to her eyes as she gave herself up to the relief of hating mankind. Mankind? Could she hate Rolfe, too, bellowing hour after hour, bound over a small flame like a sausage? Could she hate the man who must have listened, agonized, at that storeroom window while his master negotiated with the mob? Oh, God, God! But there was no God. There was only beauty, and whatever commiseration she felt for Rolfe, she had to prevent him from destroying that. She jumped up as she came out of her daze. If she were only in time!

When her taxi arrived at the museum she fled up the steps and jammed her way through the revolving door.

"Is everything all right, Tom?" she asked the doorman.

"Never a dull moment these days, Miss Post. What had quite a scare an hour ago in your gallery. There was some defective wiring in the broom closet that started a small fire. We've had the chief and hook and ladder and all. Some excitement! But it's all out now."

She bounded up the two flights to her office and fumbled crazily among her keys until she found the one for the prison window's case. Then she sped down the gallery and opened it. She paused for just a moment as she faced the hated bars, and murmuring, "Forgive me, Rolfe," she picked them up and bore them to the window over the courtyard. Looking down to be sure there was no one beneath, she shoved them out, closing her eyes as she heard the clangor of the smashing to a hundred pieces.

For a moment she felt as if someone were pulling her over the sill, dragging her after it. With a violent effort she bounded back and stared about her. She was alone, perfectly alone, although below she could hear the shouts of the alarmed guards. In a moment they would come up, and all would be over. She would lose the job that was simply her whole life. As the inky depression began to surge and bubble about her, like rising water in a filthy tub, she saw at last what it was that the squatting spirit had been after.

"Why me?" she could only groan. "Why, in God's name, me? Was it such a crime to think that even their possessions were beautiful?"

The Novelist of Manners

1973

ONLY A YEAR after he had been made a partner in Shepard, Putney & Cox, Leslie Carter, at thirty-one, was sent abroad to take charge of the Paris office. In the 1950s this post had been regarded as a sinecure, to be held by a semiretired partner with a taste for Gallic life and a secretary who could get theater tickets for traveling clients. But with the boom of American investment in Europe all this had changed, and by 1972 the position required an expert in international corporation law. Leslie Carter not only fulfilled this requirement; he had always believed, with Oscar Wilde, that when good Americans die, they go to Paris.

He had originally wanted to be a writer. As a Yale undergraduate he had majored in English, specializing in the "lost generation." The Paris of Hemingway and Fitzgerald had seemed to him a paradise in Technicolor. Like so many of his contemporaries, he had interpreted the postwar malaise of these expatriate novelists, their disillusionment and mordant cynicism, their haunting doubts as to their masculinity, as mere romantic poses adding the final titillation to a world that seemed as colorful as modern America was dull. Leslie wrote his own *Gatsby* in his senior year, and it was the shock of finding his typescript-baby born dead that had precipitated his decision to go to law school. And for all his success there and afterward, for all his editorship of the *Yale Law Journal* and early partnership in Shepard, Putney & Cox, he had continued to nurse a secret dream that one day he would awaken with an idea for a novel as perfect as *Madame Bovary* or *The Ambassadors* and would shut himself away in the proverbial garret to write it out, in a sacred rage, from the first page to the last. It was only a dream, but it was serious enough to keep him from marrying.

Paris did not give Leslie the idea for a novel, but it gave him another. The explosion upon his senses of the City of Light was dazing. He had so long crossed off his physical surroundings in New York as useless to the imagination that he now found aesthetic adventures in every street corner. Was it his destiny, after all, not to write about life but to live it? He occupied the firm's beautiful apartment in the seventeenth-century Hôtel de Lucigny in the rue Monsieur, where he was ministered to by a discreet valet and a perfect cook. After only a few months he began to lose that look of cellar whiteness that half a dozen years of overwork in New York had produced. The image in his shaving mirror still had black circles under dark eyes, but it struck him now that his thick, inky hair was more lustrous, his pallor almost romantic. As he crossed the courtyard in the evening on his way out to one of the dinner parties that were now a regular part of his duties, he would liken himself to an elegant young man in an Ingres drawing, a Balzac hero, a Lucien de Rubempré or a Eugène de Rastignac, ready for the conquest of Paris.

Nor was this fantasy wholly absurd. If the representative of Shepard, Putney & Cox enjoyed no great position in the French capital, he still had easy access to many worlds. This would have been of small benefit to a dull legal specialist with a frumpy wife, but when the word got about that Mr. Carter was young, single, personable and that he spoke quite passable French, he became the favorite *jeune américain* of many hostesses.

Hubert Cox called him one late afternoon at his office.

"We hear you're a *succès fou,*" came the sarcastic voice from across the Atlantic. "I hope you still have time to mind the shop."

"I was here at eight this morning. And I stayed last night till seven. What do you want? Blood?"

"You're doing fine, kid. Just fine. But I've got a little job for you. You've heard of Dana Clyde?"

"The novelist? Of course I've heard of him. He was the only thing I read in three years of law school besides cases. He lives here in Paris."

"Yes. His publishers have retained us to defend a libel suit brought by Giles Stannix. The Washington lawyer-lobbyist."

"Oh, I know Stannix. Robin Hood in reverse. He robs the poor to give to the rich. And saves his soul by defending an occasional Red in the Supreme Court."

"You're worse than Dana Clyde. Anyway, Stannix claims that Clyde libeled him in his last novel, *Mary Bell*. With a character called Ebenezer Kline. Look it up. Talk to Clyde. We think Stannix will settle for an apology."

Leslie was thrilled. Dana Clyde was his favorite contemporary author. If he did not number him among the great, he put him in a more beloved category: those who wrote fiction as Leslie Carter might have written it — if Leslie Carter could have written fiction. When he put through a call to Clyde's apartment in Neuilly, he had the good luck to find himself talking to the great man himself. Clyde's voice was bland, aristocratic, bored.

"Look, my dear fellow, it's absolutely preposterous. This fellow Stannix is a notorious shyster. It can't be anything but a nuisance suit."

"Very possibly, sir. I still think it would be helpful if you could come to the office to see me."

"But you know, Mr. Carter, I'm a very busy man. As you are too, I'm sure. Couldn't we just chat on the phone?"

"I'm afraid that won't be enough."

"Oh, very well. If I must, I must."

In the weekend that had to elapse between this call and their appointment, Leslie reread not only *Mary Bell* but several earlier Dana Clyde novels. If they now seemed a bit dated, they were still wonderful fun. In an era when the term had not been pejorative, they had been called novels of manners. The opening chapters were usually set in some great Connecticut or Long Island estate, at a brilliant house party presided over by a witty and charming hostess with a mind wide open to all points of view. Her guests would consist of a radical daughter, her surly Red lover, a Joe McCarthy senator, an evangelist aunt, a Pentagon general and so forth. Everybody would be very much aware of who everybody else was, what clothes they wore, what income they enjoyed, what ancestry they boasted of or concealed. There would be passionate arguments and passionate resentments, usually based on each character's anticipation of a snub by another. But the talk was the great thing, the wonderful, frothy, scintillating talk that splashed and sparkled and finally piled up into waves and breakers that overwhelmed the last chapters in such a riot of fantasy that the end would seem to come in a vapor of bubbles. Dana Clyde was a literary magician, pure and simple.

At their first meeting, in Leslie's office on the boulevard Haussmann,

Clyde sprawled in the armchair before the desk, smoking an English cigarette. He was one of those men who seem to bloom in their late fifties. There was an odd boyishness in his high clear brow, in his furtive eyes, in the ease of his motions, in the surprising raucousness of his laugh. He made Leslie think of a slim, gray, aging Pan.

"This whole business shows how utterly people misconceive the true nature of fiction. My character, Ebenezer Kline, is a universal type. As a matter of fact, I'm a bit ashamed of him. He's one-dimensional. He lacks flesh and blood. In Restoration comedy he'd have been called Miles Malpractice or Sam Simony. It shows what a guilty conscience Stannix must have if he sees himself under that label. All I can say is — if the shoe fits, let him wear it."

"Unfortunately, you saw fit to endow Ebenezer Kline with some nonuniversal characteristics. Was it necessary to your plot that Kline should be twice divorced and married to a girl half his age? And that he should live in a yellow colonial house in Georgetown?"

"I had no idea what color Stannix's house was. On my honor!"

"And did Kline have to have the habit of twisting his hair in back into a tiny ball?"

"Pray tell me, Mr. Carter, whose side are you on?"

"I'm preparing your defense, Mr. Clyde. Sometimes we lawyers have to be novelists, too."

Clyde chuckled. He was obviously a man who hated to lose his temper. "But there's still no basic similarity. My character is a bigger man altogether. He has wit and charm, whereas Stannix is only a cheap wisecracker. To tell the truth, Mr. Carter, if Kline is Stannix, it's the greatest compliment Stannix has ever had."

"He doesn't seem to appreciate it. He alleges in his petition that your branding him a shyster has cost him one of his most important clients."

"But everyone *knows* he's a shyster!"

"So it *is* Stannix."

"Oh, of course, it's Stannix," Clyde retorted impatiently. "I have to get my characters somewhere, don't I? The point is, it's Stannix bigger than life."

"I'm afraid that won't help us. There is, however, one possible out. We've had a veiled hint from plaintiff's counsel that he might consider a public apology in lieu of damages."

"Never!"

"Think it over, anyway."

"Never!"

Leslie had learned to let time rather than argument take care of clients' questions of principle. Their meeting ended on a pleasant note.

Leslie next met his client at a dinner party given by Mrs. Kenyon, part of whose dividends as a large stockholder in Clyde's publisher was the supply of authors as guests of honor. She took it as much for granted that her shares in a literary venture should make her literary as she did that her residence in Paris should endow her with its luminous qualities. Leslie, obviously, was there on duty as a lawyer, but he wondered why Dana Clyde should have bothered to accept. Surely he was too successful to have to please Mrs. Kenyon. With all Paris to choose from, what did he see in that handsome, banal, Louis XVI apartment with its handsome, banal view of Parc Monceau and its handsome, banal, expatriate guests of long-practiced sociability? The food and wine were good, to be sure, but no better than Dana Clyde could get elsewhere.

Yet he was obviously enjoying himself. The whole table listened and laughed as he described the ridiculous scenario that he was writing for a historical movie called *Nero and Poppaea*.

"My inspired director, Mr. Millstein, has moments of pure genius, particularly when editing my script. Take, for example, his contribution for last week. The heroine's mother, a patrician Roman but a secret Christian, is giving a select soiree for others of the unavowed persuasion. At an imperial party in Golden House she murmurs in the ear of a prospective guest: 'Do come in tomorrow after dinner. Just a few of us. Quite informal. Peter and Paul are coming.' "

Leslie, even at the risk of being conspicuous, declined to join in the roar of general laughter. Later, in the library, where the men had assembled for brandy and coffee, he was surprised when Clyde took him by the shoulder and propelled him to an empty corner.

"Let us have a little private moment. I detest the American postprandial habit of knocking their President."

Leslie swallowed half his brandy. He was ready now. "I have to tell you, sir, how upset I am that you should throw away your genius on the kind of hokum that Millstein churns out."

"My dear fellow, you're very flattering. But I assure you there's no better place for my poor old 'genius' today. Nobody wants to read my kind of novel anymore. It's passé. I've said goodby to fiction."

"But it's only five years since *The Lifeline* was a national bestseller."

"And only one since *Mary Bell* was a flop. With the critics, anyway. Oh, I have a following yet, I grant. There are plenty of old girls and boys who still take me to the hospital for their hysterectomies and prostates. But the trend is against me. The young don't read me. The literary establishment scorns me. It's better to quit before one is kicked out. Society is intent on becoming classless, and the novel of manners must deal with classes."

"There still are classes! All over the world. Most of all at home."

"Well, maybe there are. But not my kind. Oh, you know what I'm talking about, dear boy. Don't pretend you don't. I have always dealt with the great world. The top of the heap. How people climbed up and what they found when they got there. That was perfectly valid when the bright young people were ambitious for money and social position. But now they don't care about those things. They care about stopping wars and saving the environment and cleaning up ghettos. And they're right, too. When the world's going to pieces, who has time to talk about good form and good taste? What are such things but pretty little blinds to shut out starvation and mass murder? Do you know what I call the young people today? I call them the moral generation. They're the first that have ever showed a genuine social conscience."

Leslie wondered if those bland gray eyes were laughing at him. "Even conceding all that, does it mean there's no more room for beautiful things? Must literature be confined to the politics of survival while Dana Clyde writes *Nero and Poppaea?*"

"Oh, that's just a game I play. I do it for the money, of course. I confess to an incorrigible sweet tooth. I like all this." Clyde waved an arm to take in the paneled library with its gleaming shelves of sets, the big table of glinting decanters, the softly talking, black-garbed men. "The *douceur de vivre*. I'm damned if I'll starve for a muse — or even go hungry for one. I like driving my Silver Cloud Rolls and seeing my little Boudin over the mantel in my den. I want my wife to be smartly dressed. When my children were young, I had to have them at the best schools. You don't do those things on a pittance, you know."

"You could still write a great novel."

Clyde's smile was glorious. "Still?"

But to Leslie the occasion was too rare and the issue of too high a seriousness for ordinary compliments. "Oh, you've written beautiful things, wonderful things — there's nobody like you. But you still haven't written your *Madame Bovary*. I may be just a lawyer, but all my life I've wanted to write novels. I can't. That's my tragedy — or my pathos, or bathos, if you will. But you can and must! And *now* is the time. Now is always the time!"

The other men had risen to join the ladies, and Clyde got up, too. In the intensity of his emotion Leslie remained seated, staring up at his client and new friend.

"It's not the time, it's far too late," Clyde protested mildly. "And now we really must go into the other room." Yet when Leslie rose, Clyde put out his hand to catch him and hold him back for one more moment. "I'll tell you one thing, my friend. I *could* have done it once. I could have been as good a writer as any in the world. So you see, I'm not modest. On the contrary, I'm vain indeed!" He still paused, hesitant. "All right. Tell me something, my brash young man. What would I write this great novel about?"

"Paris, of course!" Leslie stretched an arm toward the window. "Look about you. Where else do the individualists congregate: the artists, the movie stars, the maharajas, the ex-kings, the Greek shippers, the Texas tycoons, the supercrooks, the last saints? All over the globe equality in mediocrity triumphs. Even the East has succumbed to highways and supermarkets. What used to be called American vulgarity is a universal virus. America was the first victim, that's all. Paris, of course, is doomed, too. But Paris will be the last to go. There's your subject!"

"My God, it might be. It just might be."

Leslie noted an odd gleam in his eyes, but only for a second, and then Clyde released him, after a friendly squeeze of his fingers, and sauntered across the parlor to their hostess.

After that night it was tacitly taken for granted that Leslie Carter should become an intimate of Dana and Xenia Clyde, or at least of the former. Xenia was a dark, small, silent, rather formidable woman to whom Clyde was ostensibly very devoted, but out of whose presence he seemed sometimes to skip with the bound of a schoolboy leaving his classroom. On the excuse of the lawsuit he lunched frequently with Leslie and took him afterward to private viewings of art shows or to galleries of museums not generally open to the public. He seemed determined to impress the younger man with the full range of his sympathy and wit, and indeed it was a rare performance. Even after the settlement of the lawsuit, premised, as Leslie had known all along it would be, upon Clyde's apology and retraction, the relationship continued.

Leslie was flattered by the great man's attentions without being overwhelmed. He understood perfectly that what Dana Clyde really wanted was a disciple. All Clyde's professed resignation at his own diminished role in the modern world was an arrant pose. Underneath he yearned, he panted, for the tributes of the young. And Leslie was perfectly willing to represent his own generation and to give Dana Clyde all the laudations that he could swallow. But on one condition: that Clyde should write the great work that Leslie could never write. For Leslie was perfectly clear now on the nature of the mission that had awaited his arrival in Paris. It was *not*, after all, to live. It was not even to write. It was to save Dana Clyde and make him compose his masterpiece.

Xenia Clyde regarded her husband's new friend with unconcealed suspicion. She had black bangs and thin, tight lips, and tiny hands that were always on the move — but her agate eyes seemed to indicate an intelligence quite the equal of Clyde's. One night at Mrs. Kenyon's she and Leslie had what was almost a row.

"I want to know what you're up to," she began crisply.

"Do I make any mystery of it? I want your husband to go back to his real work."

She appeared to consider this carefully. "He tells me that I should like you. That you help him."

"Dana has charming manners."

"He has to make up for mine. Somebody said that Dana always approaches a new acquaintance placatingly — on the presumption that he had probably, at one time or another, been insulted by his wife."

"Do you always insult people?"

"Only when they have pretensions. What do you want Dana to do that he hasn't already done?"

"I want him to write a great novel. An immortal masterpiece."

"You don't consider *The Lifeline* that?"

Leslie shrugged. "Then I want him to write another."

"Why are you so sure he won't? Without your prodding?"

He glanced impatiently about the room. "Because he says he won't. And because he spends so much of his time at parties like this."

"What about you? Don't you feed in the same trough?"

"But I'm not an artist!"

Xenia seemed mollified by this. Her countenance relaxed, and she resumed the needlework that she was never without. "Of course, you must think Dana and I are fearful snobs."

"Not at all. I only wonder if you see the danger in the life you're leading."

"I see what you see." She paused to study her work with a judicious eye. "But I also see something you don't. This kind of party is not a bad compromise for Dana. Literary people drink too much and argue too much and never go to bed. He requires good food and regular hours. Social life like Mrs. Kenyon's is a kind of cordon sanitaire. It protects his genius."

They were suddenly both aware of Dana Clyde standing behind their chairs. "It protects my genius to have a good night's sleep," he said with an easy laugh. "Come, Xenia, it's time you took me home. I shall need all my energy for the great task that Leslie has set for me."

"Does that mean you plan to embark on it?" she asked sharply.

"Shall I tell you both something? I just might. I really just might." He put his long fingers on his wife's shoulders. "What would you say, my dear, if I asked you to hole up for a year in Vichy or Aix while I composed what Leslie likes to describe as the last great novel of manners of the western world?"

Leslie looked from Clyde to his silent wife. "You're making fun of me."

"On the contrary," Clyde retorted. "I have never been more serious. I shall retire, like Proust, into a cork-lined chamber to write my masterpiece. No more jokes, please! Do you remember, Leslie, what that delectable priest Talleyrand whispered to that fatuous ass Lafayette as he stepped forward to celebrate the revolutionary mass before the mob in the Champ de Mars?"

"What?"

" 'Ne me faites pas rire.' "

⁂

Dana Clyde was good to his word. He and Xenia went to Málaga, where they leased a little white house on the summit of a high hill overlooking the Mediterranean and for a year saw none but a few intimates. Leslie was not included in the latter group, although an early postcard had led him to expect an invitation. None came. There were two more cards, and then silence. He had the mortification of hearing only from others about the Clydes. Even a direct appeal remained unanswered.

Leslie at first assumed that the novel must be going badly, and that Xenia, holding him responsible for her husband's useless sacrifice and disappointment, had shut off communication with him. But then reports began to filter in that, on the contrary, the novel was going well. Xenia, apparently, was writing everyone that it would be his masterpiece. Leslie could now think of no other reason for his disgrace than that the Clydes did not care to be indebted to him for Dana's finest hour. He hated so to judge them, but no other theory seemed to fit. Disillusioned but resigned, he tried to dismiss the matter from his mind. Fortunately, a case involving the French government and the mining rights of an American company in Nouméa came into the office and occupied all his time. For six months he was unable to dine out. Paris was like New York again. But at least he was distracted.

One morning, some eighteen months after the departure of the Clydes, Leslie found on his desk the galleys of *The Twilight of the Goddess* by Dana Clyde, sent air mail from New York by his publishers to be checked for libel. Leslie at once told his secretary that he would see and talk to nobody and locked his door while he read the novel at a sitting.

It was certainly Dana Clyde at his best. It was the story of the many husbands of a great American heiress: the handsome boy from next door in the early days before the fortune is made, the designing lawyer who handles the first divorce, the mortgaged Italian count, the stony-hearted French communist. With the communist the heroine moves to Paris, where she buys a vast hotel in the avenue Marigny and assembles at her international parties the world that Leslie had suggested that the author delineate. And there she meets her fifth husband, Gregory Blake, toward the end of the book.

Leslie's feelings, as he recognized the model for Gregory Blake, were not bitter. It was a relief, after all, to have solved the riddle of Clyde's silence. His involvement with the latter's "genius" needed at least the dignity of a third-act curtain. It was better to know that Clyde would not face him because he *could* not face him than to speculate that Clyde was ungrateful. It was better to have the novelist wicked than petty.

And wicked he had certainly been. He had torn his poor disciple to ribbons. The character Blake was an American lawyer in Paris, pathetically if absurdly in love with the glamour of the city's past. The old Duchesse de Foix, the heroine's social mentor, says of him: "I'm gonna wash that Proust right out of his hair." But she can't. Gregory sees the other characters cleansed of all their tawdriness, arrayed in a glory appropriate to their wealth or titles or talents. For this reason he enjoys a passing popularity in the social world. He is a kind of panacea against revolution and taxes, against death and decay, against the gray future of a mechanized, socialized universe. It is as if by touching him they may save themselves, redeem their silly souls. The heiress, vicious but still beautiful, woos him and marries him. But Gregory is impotent. After his wedding night, he commits suicide.

Leslie finished the book by lunchtime and then reread the publisher's letter. Mr. Clyde, it informed him, was staying at the Crillon.

In the lobby of that hotel he ran into Clyde himself, but the latter hurried by him with averted eye. Leslie was not even sure that Clyde had seen him. The boy at the desk, however, informed him that Mrs. Clyde would receive him in her suite. He found her engaged, as usual, with her needlework.

"Why did he do it, Xenia? Why did he want to hurt me like that?"

"He always takes his characters from real life. You *knew* that, Leslie. Why didn't you stay away from him?"

"Oh, it's not being in the book I mind. It's not even being made such a fatuous ass. That was fair enough. But the impotence and the suicide! They seem to show actual malevolence, as if he was out to get me. Why?"

Xenia's brief silence indicated some inner debate. "If ever I saw a man put his head in the noose, it was you. I tried to warn you off, but you stuck like a leech. Still, I admit, he treated your abominably. Even for him. Tell me something. What did you think of the novel? Other than the character of Gregory Blake?"

"I thought it first-class. First-class Dana Clyde, that is."

"But is it a great novel? Is it that last great novel of manners of the western world?"

"It is not."

"You say that very positively. Didn't you assure him it would be?"

"I was a fatuous ass. I was Gregory Blake."

"I'm afraid you were worse than that, Leslie. You badgered Dana into writing that book. You never stopped to think it might hurt him. Well, it did. It hurt him terribly. That's what he can't forgive you."

"But I never meant it to hurt him!"

"Of course, you didn't. You're not a sadist. But it still did. You see, Dana had a secret fantasy. He liked to think of himself as a genius, but a genius manqué. He liked to tell himself that if it hadn't been for his love of the good life — the *douceur de vivre*, as he always called it — he might have been another Flaubert. 'Ah, if I could only work as he worked,' he used to say. Well, he worked at Málaga. He really did. And you see what he produced. He sees it, too. He can no longer kid himself that he could ever have written *Madame Bovary*. So he took his revenge."

Leslie stared. "But can't he persuade himself that he simply started too late? That if he *had* worked hard enough, early enough, long enough, he *would* have been a Flaubert?"

"No." Xenia laughed her dry little laugh. "Because a genius, even a genius manqué, could never have written anything as magnificently second-rate as *The Twilight of the Goddess*. But don't worry about Dana. He always gets through. It's you I'm worried about. I hope that my husband's silly book isn't going to ruin your young life."

Leslie, looking at the tough little woman before him, felt the surge in his heart of liberation. For a moment he could not even articulate an answer to her suspicion that his life might be affected by so shallow a creature as Dana Clyde. He turned away from her and went to the window to look down on the Place de la Concorde and its eddies of darting traffic.

"No, I'm grateful to Dana. He was wrong about the novel of manners. It *does* still have a function. If only to prove to a poor thing like Leslie Carter that he doesn't want to write one anymore."

In the Beauty of the Lilies
Christ Was Born Across the Sea

1976

🙟

1

W INTHROP WARD LIKED to have his wife come downstairs for breakfast. He did not like to ask her to do so — that was not his way. He preferred to feel that she herself recognized the propriety of the mistress of the household and the mother of three sons joining with the latter in the initiation of a busy and useful day rather than — like so many women in Manhattan's "better" society of the eighteen-fifties — reclining in her bed till noon with a coffee cup and the fashion column. Rosalie and he had never brought the matter to specific debate, but he nonetheless feared that the billowing pink dressing gown in which she had recently chosen to appear, so suggestive of upper stories and closed doors, was somehow an indication of silent dissent, an "exception," as he would have put it in court. It was fortunate that none of the laxity of the gown was transmuted into its wearer's face. Rosalie's features were as bland and flat as if she had worn more formal attire, and her small lips were pinched into her usual mien of reservation. Reservation of what? Reservation, Winthrop could only infer, of any general approval of himself.

No, breakfast was never quite what he yearned it should be: the friendly, even humorous conveyance by father to sons of useful precepts for a day that would be only too full of particular problems: the confirmation of family solidarity; the pleasant reminder, before the taking up of diurnal tasks, of such manifold blessings as the comfortable house on Union Square, the cozy dining room with its bay window opening onto a tree-filled yard, the smell of sizzling sausages and bacon passed by the smiling Irish girl in her yet unspotted uniform. Alas, no. Instead, the boys were disputatious, and Rosalie seemed always to be against him.

James, sixteen and earnest, began. "Andy Thayer says he has an uncle who helps runaway slaves to get to Canada. He runs a station in the Underground Railroad. Isn't that brave?" A small pause followed. "Well, *I* think it's brave!"

"His uncle's a fool to talk about it," said Fred, fourteen and law-abiding. "He could go to prison, where he belongs."

"I agree with Fred," Alexander, the youngest, observed. "Slaves are private property. Father says so, and Father's a lawyer."

"Oh, Winthrop, have you been telling the boys that?" Rosalie wailed.

"My dear, they are private property. You can't deny it. I never said they *should* be. That's another issue altogether. But I happen to believe in obeying the law of the land. At least until the Congress sees fit to change it."

"You haven't lived in the South as I have, Winthrop!" she cried. "And that is why I must beg leave to differ with you, even before the children. You know, boys, I spent a winter in New Orleans with my Aunt Estelle . . ."

"We know it, Mum," came the weary chorus.

"Well, know it again. And know that no matter what the law says, God's law says that no man can own another. It is because the Southerners have tried to make that a Christian principle that their society is rotten."

"Do you mean," demanded Fred, "that if they admitted slavery was wrong, they'd be all right?"

"They'd be better off. At least their creed would be pure. This way, slavery is in everything they think and do."

Winthrop was impressed, in spite of himself. Rosalie undeniably had a strong mind. It was a pity that she made so little use of it. Or was it? He coughed loudly now, as was his habit before making a family pronouncement.

"In times as emotional as these I find that I must constantly reiterate my central position. Otherwise I am regarded as a Simon Legree in my own house. So, boys, pay attention. When we created our Union, we had to compromise with our Southern friends. Their price was the acceptance of slavery — at least in their states. We agreed to pay that price. We wrote it into our Constitution. How can we renege on our word now?"

"It's not reneging on our word to refuse to return their slaves!" James exclaimed hotly. "The slaves should be free the moment they set foot on free soil!"

"The Supreme Court has ruled against you, James."

"The Supreme Court is packed by slaveholders!"

"If we are going to maintain the Union," Winthrop argued, trying to hold on to his temper, "we must learn to recognize the other man's point of view. Do you claim, James, that the South is not entitled to be represented on the Court?"

"What do they know of justice? You've said yourself, Father, that they're blinded by arrogance. I've heard you!"

Winthrop found himself considering the surprising little fact that — for that moment at least — he actually disliked James. "God help us to preserve our nation if the young all feel as you do," he said piously.

Rosalie sniffed. "There you go again, Winthrop, with your sacred Union. Why must we stay together? Why should we be shackled to people who beat women and children and separate families? Why not let them go? Why not let them stand up alone before the civilized world as the only nation where white men have slaves? They won't last long."

"My dear, I must ask you to be silent!" Winthrop rose solemnly to his feet. "I cannot admit the advocation of dissolution of the Union. Even from my wife. That is one heresy I will not tolerate in this house. My great-grandfather fought and died for the Union. When I hear the call, I am ready to do the same. I only pray that civil war, if it must come, may come soon enough to spare you boys. And now, having finished my breakfast, I shall proceed to my office. A good day to all of you."

There was a muffled, embarrassed murmur around the table of something that Winthrop decided to take for a general apology, but in which Rosalie obviously did not join. On the whole, however, he did not think badly of his exit. In the black, paneled hallway where Molly, the waitress, helped him into his fur coat, he listened to his heart and decided that his overexcitement was already ebbing. He chose a cane from the rack. Had he been absurdly dramatic in referring to a call to arms? Would anyone ever ask *him* to serve in the army? A lawyer, a family man, forty-three years old, with a heart murmur?

"Take the scarf, Mr. Ward. It's cold out."

"Very seasonable, Molly. It's always mild between Christmas and New Year's. May the eighteen-sixties prove as mild!"

As the door closed behind him, and he gazed down from his brownstone stoop at Union Square, fresh and glittering in the diamond morning air, he adjusted the onyx pin in his cravat. Taking a deep cold breath, he went briskly down the steps and headed south for his daily hike to Wall Street. He counted on those thirty minutes, not only for his exercise — the only kind he took — but for the opportunity to review and settle the disturbing thoughts and emotions of the early morning so that he might arrive at his desk serene and ready for the day's work.

As he headed down Broadway, however, towards the happy Gothic conception of Grace Church, he was uncomfortably aware of continued tension in his chest. Damn the South for all the trouble they caused with their slaves! Triple damn them! He paused, as he habitually did, to admire the façade of the church and to speculate on what America might have been without the slave trade. What but a paradise, what but a simple Garden of Eden! He stamped his foot. Why had the first blithering idiot to bring a black man in irons to the New World not been hanged for his pains? He recalled now the condescending words of his neighbor in Newport, Colonel Pryor of Charleston:

"My dear Ward, what in the last analysis are we talking about? An issue that could only be settled by a war in which the Northern states couldn't possibly afford to engage. For where's your military tradition? Who would be your officers? Let us face the fact, my friend, that only a few families in New York, Boston, and Philadelphia, such as your own, were reared in the aristocratic tradition. The rest are good burghers who are quite sensibly concerned with filling their pockets. All very well, my dear fellow, but you don't put burghers in a battlefield against Southern gentlemen. At least I should never advise it! Leave us our peculiar institution, and we'll leave you all of yours. It's a better way to live, I promise you."

Burghers! Winthrop snorted as he marched on downtown. It was all very well for Pryor to make a polite exception for the Wards, but Winthrop knew that it was only politeness. Pryor, of course, was sneering inwardly and lumping him with the other shysters and shopkeepers: Yankee trash, nigger lovers. Well, those slaveholders would see! They would see — that is, if they ever tried to break up the Union — how little a society of sportsmen dependent on surly blacks could prevail against millions of free men! They would be lucky if they did not live to behold their plantations burned and their sacred womenfolk raped by lusty niggers . . .

Winthrop paused, and rapped with his cane on the pavement. Really, he must control himself. What would all that adrenalin do to his heart? And, quite aside from his health, what about his eternal soul? Were those *Christian* visions? Even if the South should secede and God should then order the freeing of the slaves, would that be any reason for His holy army to indulge in scenes of rapine and murder? Never! They should go into battle like crusaders in white tunics with red crosses, singing hymns.

"Well, if it ain't Mr. Astor himself, in all his fur and feathers! Good day to ye, Mr. Astor. Have ye foreclosed any mortgages? Should I pray for a bit of snow to turn the widows and the bairns out into?"

Winthrop paused in utter astonishment before the tattered, bearded inebriate who was sitting on the curbstone squinting up at him. In the shock of the onslaught he forgot his rule of ignoring such creatures.

"I shall instruct the next policeman I meet of your insolence and whereabouts! You had better get packing!"

Accelerating his pace as the brown square tower of Trinity Church came into view, he was now a senator, addressing a gravely attentive Senate:

"It is my painful duty to bring to the attention of this august chamber the dire consequences of our rash policy of unlimited immigration. It is rank folly, merely in order to boast that we are the refuge and haven of the poor and oppressed of old Europe, to fill our land with the refuse of a cynical continent delighted to slough off its human responsibilities. How long can America be strong, how long can America be pure, how long can America be free, if we continue to dilute the blood of our Anglo-Saxon and Dutch and German settlers with that of an Irish peasantry, stupefied by ignorance and superstition, the slaves of whiskey and Rome, whose only demonstrated skill is for worming into and corrupting our municipal governments?"

He slowed his pace to slap his clenched fist against his open hand and to stare defiantly at an old woman who hurried by, afraid that he might accost her. She probably deemed him a street preacher or similar harmless lunatic. Perhaps she was right! Smiling now at his own absurdity, refreshed by his eloquence, he proceeded in silence to Chambers Street, where he paused to consider the better view of Trinity Tower. A fit of dismay seized him. Was its sooty face reproaching him? He closed his eyes and prayed in a whisper:

"Dear God, only God, beloved father of us all, forgive thy servant, Winthrop Ward, for traducing thy other children. Help him to realize that the Irish, however misguided, are as dear to thee as he is, dearer perhaps, for they are not so puffed up. Help him to comprehend that it is no such great thing to descend from John Winthrop or to be a Ward, that his bit of money is a rag and his social position an illusion. Teach him humility, dear Lord, dear Christ, that he may come to thee and lose himself in thee."

Winthrop now shut his eyelids so tight that his eyeballs hurt and then opened them suddenly to a sky full of white stars. When his vision was adjusted, he walked on, reminding himself solemnly that every cart-pusher, every smutched-faced little boy, every black-gowned, musta-chioed old Italian woman was as good as he in the eyes of God.

Passing City Hall, he frowned at the sight of the tall, slim figure of Daniel Allen in striped pants and a black frock coat ascending the steps. Old Vanderbilt's broker on his way to see the mayor, no doubt! Winthrop burst into an impassioned appeal to the membership committee of the Patroons' Club:

"Of course, gentlemen, I recognize the principle that society must continually be opening its ranks to admit new members. We are a commercial community, and new money must always have its claim. But I hope we may never lose sight of the rule that new money must be *clean* money. To an old pirate like Vanderbilt, who boasts in public that he has bought our legislature, the doors of gentlemen must be forever closed!"

This peroration took him to Sixty Wall Street, a handsome white four-story building with freshly painted green shutters, the first two floors of which were occupied by the law chambers of Ward and Ward. Winthrop, who believed in hearty morning greetings, spoke and smiled to each of the firm clerks, to the old bookkeeper and to the office boy, before mounting the stairs to his own office in the rear and closing the door behind him. The room was clean and bare, with cream-painted walls and no accessories beyond the portrait engravings of Lords Mansfield and Cole, a bookcase of law reporters and a Sheraton table-desk on which were stacked neat piles of papers.

Ah, how quickly now his heart resumed its normal beat, how keenly his mind began to function! What a blessing was law. What were books and deeds and documents but receptacles — like pans set out in a drought — to catch the divine drops from the sky? *Here* was what distinguished men from apes. The big Celtic toughs looking to their fists to terrify the timid, the crooked financiers filling the pockets of politicians, the fire-eating Southerners with their contempt for the free world — let them look to the law books — let them beware! Let them writhe like Laocoön and his sons caught in the coils of the beneficent serpent which God had sent down to guard the meek! Winthrop jumped nervously at the sudden knock on his door.

"Mr. Charley wants to see you, sir."

"Very well," Winthrop snapped. "Tell him to come in."

"Beg pardon, sir, he asked if you could come to him. I think he's not feeling quite himself."

Winthrop at this got up and went down the corridor to the office of his partner and cousin. The moment he saw the latter's face he knew why the day had started badly. He must have had an intuition of trouble. Charley Ward looked haggard and sleepless. He might, that morning, have been forty-three, like his cousin, and not a decade younger. Winthrop had a sudden picture now of how Charley would look in a few more years, when middle age should have eroded the fragile beauty of his blond, pale type, when the still abundant smooth hair should have thinned, the round cheeks swollen to give the face a pear shape, the small blue eyes receded into dark cisterns in the skull. Winthrop loved Charley and loved his looks, and his heart was stirred even by the prospect of their evanescence. For he felt that Charley's need of him as a mentor and his own need of Charley as someone to protect might be actually intensified when Charley's appearance, puffed and etiolated, should correspond more nearly to Charley's mind and character. It was part of Charley's strange charm that weakness and mildness should so lurk behind the bright bravery of his exterior.

"This note came for my wife last night from Jane King. Or purportedly from Jane King." Charley threw down a piece of pink notepaper on the desk before Winthrop. "The sender did not know that Annie had gone to Yonkers to spend the night with her uncle. I opened it, thinking it might be something that I could take care of for her. I was wrong."

Winthrop looked at the paper without touching it. "Does your wife know you have opened it?"

"Not yet. But she shall."

"Does anyone else know?"

"What a lawyer you are, Winthrop! Read it."

Winthrop read the following message in a large, jagged masculine hand: "Beloved — can what Jane tells me be true? Are you really reconsidering? Can you deny your own soul and mine? Send me word that you are true. Save your Jules from black despair." He looked up at Charley.

"Bleecher," Charley replied to the silent question. "Jules Bleecher."

Winthrop shuddered. He saw the florid face, the French goatee, the big wet doglike eyes, the large, fleshy nose, the heavy, tumbling hair, the great overdressed body, the effeminacy that was worse for being affected — a parvenu's idea of a cultivated manner — a brown bear with a monocle and top hat. Good God, could Annie Ward fall for *that?* A poetaster, a scribbler of sentimental drivel, a society journalist, a social climber who pranced around the ladies in every evening party, an "ooer" and "aaher" at concerts, a gossiper in the back of opera boxes, probably a Jew . . . what else?

"He's been coming to the house for a couple of months now," Charley explained. "Annie met him through Jane King. I saw no harm in it. Somebody told me he was a philanderer, but I thought he was too obvious a one to worry about. He was the kind who would lean over when some fat old dowager was tucking her lorgnette into her bosom and murmur: 'Happy lorgnette!' The man seemed a farce to me. He and Jane King were always giggling and snickering in corners."

"I never met him in your house," Winthrop observed.

"That was because I knew you didn't like him. Oh, you can be sure, Winthrop, that Annie and I are always very careful whom we ask when you and Rosalie are coming."

Winthrop sighed. "But do you deduce from this letter that your wife has . . . has, er . . ."

"Fallen?" Charley's laugh was a jeer. "Not necessarily. She's a cool little minx under all that gush. But what I *do* deduce from that florid epistle is that she gave Bleecher an assignation and then got cold feet. She may have even agreed to go off with him."

"And desert Miss Kate?" Winthrop cried in horror. The sole, six-year-old child of the Charley Wards was so designated because of her little-lady airs.

"It's so like you, Winthrop, to put the child before the father. But yes,

I think that Annie would be capable of deserting Miss Kate. She has no real heart. Once she decides that life with me is not what she wants, nothing is going to hold her. You can talk of oaths and sacraments and family ties until the cows come home. You won't reach her."

"What does she want?"

Charley strode up and down the chamber now, clapping his hands together as he brought out his argument in sharp, jerky phrases. "What do you think she wants? What do any of them want? She wants a man who will live up to her dreams of sexual performance. I tell you, Winthrop, we men are the losers in this system of keeping girls in ignorance until they marry. It's damnably hard on the poor groom. He suddenly finds he's got to be all the impossible things that an uneducated, feverishly sentimental mind has concocted out of fantasy and dirty talk with other ignorant girls. Give me a prostitute from Mercer Street any night in the week. At least she knows what a man is! But these innocent debutantes! They smile and simper behind their fans; they blush crimson at the tiniest impropriety, and then, suddenly, after a big society wedding that hasn't tired them one bit — behind closed doors, alone at last — they turn into fiends. 'All right, big man. This is life, isn't it? Show me life!' "

Winthrop actually shivered, so violent was his disgust. If his interlocutor had been anyone but Charley he would have walked out. But he was responsible for too many things: for the partnership, for Charley's dependence on him, for the very marriage to Annie Andros that he had so fatally sponsored. He could not help glancing back to his own wedding night. Not that Rosalie had been the tigress that Charley depicted. On the contrary, she had been silent, compliant, perhaps the least bit passive. But hadn't there been an implication of something like disappointment in the determined way in which, early the following morning, she had sat down at their hotel drawing room table to write thank-you notes for her wedding presents?

"So what do you propose?" he asked Charley.

"Immediate and final separation."

"And Miss Kate?"

"She can live with us alternately. Provided, of course, that Annie does not set up house with her paramour."

"You are determined then to advertise your shame to the world?"

Winthrop stood up to give posture to the high stand that he had elected to take. "Do you want people to say that you couldn't hold your bride?" Seeing Charley bite his lip, he followed up in words from Charley's customary vocabulary. "Do you want even the debutantes, in their kittenish sessions between the dances, upstairs in their hostess's bedroom, to whisper with high giggles that you have no balls?"

"Oh, shut up, Winty! Don't be such a bastard. What else can a man do in my situation?"

"Well, he doesn't have to throw up his marriage and ruin three lives — yours and Annie's and Miss Kate's — for what may turn out to be only a flirtation. I'm sorry, Charley. I can't believe that Annie really cares for a man like Bleecher. I'm sure she has simply lost her head for the moment. Perhaps she is actually ill. If we can only get rid of this oily cad, who knows? Maybe you and Annie will find a new life. You may even discover a deeper congeniality."

Charley's impatient toss of his head showed what he thought of this. Winthrop perfectly understood what his cousin was looking forward to: a return to bachelor freedom, a liberation from Annie's cloyingly female, looped and tasseled interior. Cousin Winthrop must have seemed like a stiff, prissy teacher holding him after class on a summer afternoon when all the other boys had gone fishing. But Winthrop knew that he could still rely on a teacher's authority.

"Your position as a lawyer, as a father, as a member of society obliges you to do everything you can to avoid a scandal," he continued sententiously. "You can't shirk this one, Charley."

"What do I do then?" Charley asked sulkily.

"Leave the next step to me. Go home and get some sleep. I'll go to Annie's uncle and ask him to keep her at Yonkers for a week. And not to allow Bleecher in the house."

"How can he do that? He can't use force, can he?"

"I don't have to tell Lewis Andros how to do anything. My confidence in him is complete. If all New York were as he, there would be no Bleechers invading the sanctity of our homes. Will you be guided by me, Charley?" There was a pause, as Winthrop stared impassively at his cousin. "Don't you think I am entitled to ask that of you?"

Charley turned away, his face puckered as if he were going to weep. "Have it your way, Winthrop. You always do. I'm going out for a drink. For several drinks."

Fifteen minutes later Winthrop entered the central hall of the Bank of Commerce and walked briskly down the aisle of yellow marble, past standing clerks at counters making entries, to the rear, where the president sat at a vast roll-top desk under a gas light in a green bowl suspended directly over his head. But Lewis Andros's apparent availability to the public was an illusion. There was an unseen wall that protected the desk and its occupant, and if a stranger dared to intrude, or even to address the silent magnate without authority, he would receive for all his answer a slow raising of the great head and a vision of the whites of eyeballs before which he could only beat a stuttering retreat. Very different, however, was Winthrop's reception.

"Ah, my dear boy, we see too little of you these days, far too little. I was asking Carrie only yesterday: when shall we have the Winthrop Wards for dinner? We cannot afford to neglect the parents of three strapping boys, can we? Certainly *I* cannot, with granddaughters their age, as well as daughters."

As the great man rose and gripped his shoulder, Winthrop reflected that Lewis Andros managed to give a sexual flavor to every topic. It was always perfectly proper, if rather heavily connubial, but there it was. The great tan eyes may have been limpid, the splendid nose arched, the lips thin and intellectual, the gray curly hair venerable, the voice rich and cultivated, but all of these aspects seemed to merge in the likeness of a velvet cloak flung over an old bull. Mr. Andros had children in their thirties and in their teens; twice a widower, he was now, at sixty, the husband of a woman of twenty-five who already looked tired. He was a man, Winthrop conceded with a rueful admiration, who managed to pack the pleasures of the Renaissance into the permissible limits of brownstone New York. Nowhere did one drink finer Madeira or hear wittier talk than at stag dinners in his Fifth Avenue mansion, when his wife and brood were packed off to Yonkers.

"Could I sit down with you for a minute, Mr. Andros? I'm afraid I have a bit of rather nasty news. It concerns your niece Annie and my cousin."

Andros's banker's countenance betrayed nothing during the dreary recital, but at the conclusion he permitted himself a windy sigh and a rueful shake of the great head.

"My dear Winthrop, you and I are men of the world. We know that Annie and Charley were mismated from the start. She is too much of a mouthful for those pearly teeth of his. Would it not be for the best if we arranged a dignified separation? Followed, in due course, by a divorce or even an annulment?"

"An annulment? With a six-year-old child?"

"Such things have been heard of, where there was a basic lack of consent at the outset. But of course I need not point out such things to a lawyer."

"I arranged all the settlements at the time!" Winthrop exclaimed in some heat. "I should regard myself as gravely deficient if the marriage legalities were not entirely in order."

"Oh, I don't mean that, dear fellow. I mean: was Annie's true and free consent given at the altar? I am speaking, mind you, of a woman's psyche. The greatest lawyer in the world need not be ashamed to have failed to plumb *those* murky depths."

Winthrop was shocked that so respected a member of the community should not devote even a passing glance to the moral aspects of what confronted them. "Even assuming that there was a chance for some respectable separation," he countered, "surely it is jeopardized by the presence of such a cad as Bleecher."

"Oh, come now, Bleecher's not as bad as all that. He's not the first man in our society to make up to a flirtatious wife. Carrie and I have found him an agreeable extra man for dinner parties, and even you will admit that he has an eye for a picture. Did you see his *Toilette of the Odalisque* at the Beaux Arts show last winter? Many people preferred it to *The Abbess Detected*, which took first prize."

Winthrop stifled the impulse to parade his opinion of the immorality of last winter's Beaux Arts show. He recollected that Andros's own *Halt of Cavaliers* had been the runner-up. "Bleecher's taste in art is not going to help matters if he runs off with Annie. He has already implicated Jane King in their friendship. If you and Mrs. Andros receive him in Yonkers, he will not hesitate to tell the world you have taken his side."

"His side? How can a man in his position have a side?"

"You will forgive me, sir, if I am totally frank. To me the facts are too grave for parlor manners. It is my conviction that Bleecher is not even the decent simulacrum of a gentleman. He hopes to become your nephew-in-law and to force you to champion him in society."

Andros was suddenly very still. "Force me, you say? How?"

"By implicating you and Mrs. Andros as accomplices in his adultery."

How was it that Andros managed to quicken the air about him? He did not so much as twitch an eyeball or stir a muscle, yet Winthrop felt a throb in the atmosphere, as if, deep within the older man, some heavy cylinder had started to revolve.

"Mr. Bleecher will find that he has mistaken his party," Andros said dryly. "What steps do you propose?"

"I propose that you keep Annie at Yonkers this week and see that Bleecher is not allowed on the grounds."

Andros's shaggy head went up and down several times. "The latter is simple enough. But my niece is a grown woman and married. I can't force her, Winthrop."

"We all know how Annie looks up to you. You've been a father and mother to her, as well as an uncle. She'll do as you say."

"You have more confidence in my power over young ladies than I do."

"I have utter confidence in your powers!" Winthrop exclaimed, feeling that it was the opportune time for a show of emotion that was only half feigned. "And the day we New Yorkers lose faith in Lewis Andros, we'll have faith in nobody!"

This was a bit strong, and Winthrop feared that he might have gone too far. But no. Andros rose, and Winthrop rose with him. Once again the big hand gripped his shoulder.

"Winthrop, my friend, you may count on me. I shall lie before Annie's door like an Indian servant and guard her with my life. As for Mr. Bleecher, I shall not soil my hands with the likes of him. But I have some strong young men on the place — not to speak of two Russian wolfhounds — who may be less fastidious. You had better warn him to stay in the city!"

"I knew I could count on you. With your permission I shall drive out to see Annie in the morning. And in the meantime I guarantee Charley's good conduct. The matter may yet be contained."

2
—
⁂

At breakfast the next day in Union Square, Rosalie lingered at the table after the boys had gone off to school.

"Don't you think it might be better if I went to see Annie with you? Or even if I went in your place?"

"I'd rather not have you mixed up in this, my dear."

"Oh, Winthrop, I know all your theories about sparing the gentler sex. But you and I must occasionally deal with particulars and not always with generalities. I know as much about this situation as you do. That is, if you've told me the whole story."

"I've told you all I know. A man, of course, may have his own insights."

"And a woman hers. In such a case a couple would be better than one."

"Listen to me, Rosalie. I am not claiming any masculine superiority. I recognize that you might handle Annie quite as competently as I. It is not you, Rosalie Ward, whom I wish to keep clear of this sordid affair. It is you, Mrs. Winthrop Ward, the mother of my sons."

Rosalie raised her hands in mock surprise. "Men make such interesting distinctions. A woman would never have thought of that!"

Winthrop looked down at his newspaper and tried to read about President Buchanan's diplomatic reception. It proved impossible. Would Rosalie never give up? His tense fingers crumpled the journal.

"If you only didn't enjoy it so much," Rosalie continued, "I think I might mind the whole thing less."

"Enjoy it! Charley's humiliation?" As Winthrop stared across the table at his impassive tormentor, he felt his eyelids suddenly smart with angry tears.

"I didn't mean to imply that you enjoy Charley's humiliation. I meant that you enjoy the prospect of correcting Annie."

"I have always been devoted to Annie!"

"Oh, I know *that*." Rosalie's face hardened as she moved to a more direct offensive. "Where do you think I've been for the last seven years not to know that? You're obviously jealous of Jules Bleecher."

Winthrop felt the sudden drop of anger in his heart. So that was it. So like a woman. So rather touching, really. He should have anticipated that Rosalie, like any good, loving wife — and who was a better, a more loving one? — was quite incapable of the smallest objectivity with respect to any member of his family. She was jealous, quite naturally, of anything that presented a potential wedge between her and him. She had always resented his love of Charley, always despised Annie . . .

wasn't it really better that way? How else could he be sure that she loved him?

"I am certainly not going to try to rebut your last statement," he said with what he intended to be an air of amiable dignity. "At the risk of appearing stuffy and self-complacent — if that be not giving myself the benefit of *your* doubt — I should say it would be beneath my dignity. I confine my defense to this: if I get any pleasure, as you aver, out of this whole sorry affair, it is the pleasure — and a very mild one, I assure you — that every man is entitled to derive from the sense that he is doing his duty."

"Oh, go to see Annie, for heaven's sakes," his wife retorted brusquely. "I don't even want to come with you after *that.*"

Winthrop had been looking forward to the drive up to Yonkers, well muffled, on that cold but pleasant December day in his new runabout with two fast trotters. There might have been in it some of the excitement of an unexpected holiday. But now all was made as bleak as the winter sky by Rosalie's relentless denigrations. Why was it so necessary to her contentment — or to at least the lessening of her perennial discontent — to pull him down so? She was always quick to flare the egotistical motive under the seemingly generous actions in *him.* But when it came to some ranting, bushy-bearded abolitionist who wanted to blow up the world to cover his own failures — did she flare any ego? Oh, no! Then Mr. Bushy-beard was a saint, a prophet!

The sight of "Oaklawn," one of the last summer residences in Yonkers, always made him sit up. To Winthrop it was a thing of peerless beauty, Richard Upjohn's masterpiece, and he would have liked nothing better than to recreate it in Newport. The approach was down a long straight avenue, soft even in winter, under two brown Gothic archways, at the end of which was the glazed brown multi-turreted, castellated structure with tiny windows in the turrets and painted tin awnings over the larger windows of the main floor. A groom waiting at the front door took his carriage, and Winthrop was ushered at once into a small study with wicker furniture, lamps with beaded shades and several small dark examples of the seventeenth-century Italian school.

"Mrs. Ward will be with you in a moment, sir."

And indeed Winthrop already heard the rustle of her skirts. Annie came hurrying in and threw her arms around his neck.

"Oh, Winthrop, sweety, at last! I've been dying to see you!"

She was dressed in black, as if in mourning. It perfectly suited the pallor of her complexion and served as a sepulchral setting for her long raven hair and thick eyebrows, her thin long figure, her flat chest. Yet for all of this Annie was the antithesis — and herein, as Winthrop well knew, lay the secret of her immense charm — of the death look in her garb and complexion. For she was all movement, all life, all gaiety. Even now, as she took in his effort to assemble his features into a becoming sternness, she burst into a peal of high laughter, too infectious to be as mocking as she may have meant it to be.

"Oh, Winthrop, that *look*. Please, not that look. You're going to make me die of giggles when I want to be so serious. When, really, I've got to be serious. This is no time to play the Puritan ancestor. We have things to discuss. Things to decide."

"I don't know what we can have to discuss but your promise never again to see or communicate with Mr. Bleecher."

"Not to see Jules!" Annie stepped back and stared at him as if he had said something ridiculous. "But, of course, I can't give up Jules. He's the only man who's made life tolerable for me in the past year. Jules *amuses* me, Winthrop!"

"Will he amuse you enough to make it up to you if Charley repudiates you?"

Annie uttered another high peal of laughter. "Oh, quite enough! Would Charley really do that? Repudiate me. What a beautiful word!"

"I doubt that you'd find it so beautiful if it happened. What would become of you, Annie?"

"I suppose I'd have to go to Paris. Isn't that what fallen women do?"

"And what would you live on?"

"What would I live on? Why, what do I live on now? My own income, thank you very much. Or would the law — *your* law — give that to Charley?"

"No, that would not go to Charley. But may I remind you that your money's all in trust, and that your trustees have a certain discretion about the payment of income. If you were living in Paris with a man not your husband . . ."

"With a paramour!"

"With a paramour, then. Your trustees might see fit to accumulate the income until you came to your senses."

Again that laugh! Winthrop reflected that his ancestor, Wait Winthrop, would probably have hanged this girl in Salem.

"Confess you're bluffing!" Annie challenged him. "Trustees may be afraid of sin, but they're much more afraid of lawsuits. And I'd sue them. Believe me, I'd sue!"

"Well, even *with* your income," Winthrop retorted, with a touch of impatience, "what sort of future would you have in Paris? No respectable people would receive you."

"How terrible!"

"And Bleecher, cad that he is, would desert you the moment he felt like it."

"Ah, that he wouldn't." Annie did not laugh now, and her eyes had a sudden gleam. "I might leave Jules, for *I* am a bit of a cad, but he would not leave me. You underestimate my charms."

"I have never underestimated your charms. But what I think you have underestimated is the difference it would make to Bleecher if he found you a social liability instead of a social asset."

Annie paced the length of the little room. She stood for a moment, her back to him, before turning. "You're playing a role, the family friend, the family lawyer, the guardian of morals. I wish you'd stop. I want to talk to you seriously."

"What about?"

"Well, in the first place, Jules is not what you think him at all. He loves me dearly, faithfully. I should trust him implicitly, even in Paris. I know when a man is not to be trusted. Charley is not to be trusted. Besides, he hates me."

"He's your husband. He's the father of your child."

"Oh, Winthrop, be reasonable. Are you trying to tell me that Charley gives a hoot about me?"

"Deep down, yes."

Annie laughed again. "Angels save us from that 'deep down'!"

"But you can't give up your marriage just because you and Charley have a misunderstanding!"

"A misunderstanding or an understanding?"

"Either." Winthrop tried to look his most earnest. "A marriage must be worked on. Even if you don't believe it's a sacrament, you should recognize that our society is based on it. And your child — how can you abandon her? A court, you know, would give her to Charley."

"Then I'd hardly be abandoning her."

"Tell her that when she's grown up!"

Annie at this looked grave. "Ah, yes, I can imagine what you Wards would have done to her. Even you, Winthrop." She sat down on a plush stool and folded her hands soberly in her lap. Winthrop remained standing. "Yet you were my best friend after my marriage," she continued wistfully. "You were all kindness and sympathy and understanding. At first I thought you were too stiff, too moral, too much older, and, of course, I knew that Rosalie disliked me. She hates feminine women. But then, gradually, I came to recognize that you loved Charley and, through him, me. I loved Charley, too, in those days, but as I began to understand his weaker side, I became frightened. And then I saw that you understood it, too, and were trying to help me. I accepted your help, perhaps too greedily. It was naughty of me, but Rosalie's anger made it such fun."

Winthrop had turned away, pained by what she had said about Rosalie hating feminine women. It was true, of course. "Go on," he muttered. "But leave Rosalie out of it, please."

"She was never really in it. What kind of idiot says there can't be a friendship between a man and woman? *We* had such a friendship. Now don't say I'm being unladylike!" Again her laugh pealed out. "You know it was true — on both sides. And you helped me, that's the point. But all those books we discussed together, all those poems and plays — what were they really about? *Jane Eyre* and *The Scarlet Letter* and *Madame Bovary*? They were about passion! Do you remember when we went to see Rachel in *Phèdre*?"

"What are you getting at?" Winthrop asked abruptly.

"Simply that those books taught me that passion is the whole thing in this world. That if you miss it, you miss everything!"

Winthrop was able to turn back to her now, sobered by the enormity of her misconstruction. "But those books and plays all point out the pitfalls of illicit love. Look what happens to Madame Bovary and to Phèdre and to Hester Prynne. *Jane Eyre* ends happily, it is true, but only because she keeps away from Mr. Rochester until his wife dies."

"And until he goes blind," Annie added with a giggle. "But it doesn't matter what happens to the heroine *afterwards*. The point is that the great experience is passion. Maybe it's punished — *tant pis*. But it's still worth it. For without it, what are you? Phèdre doesn't give a hoot about going to hell. The only thing that keeps her from Hippolyte is that he won't have her! But Jules, dear Winthrop, is no Hippolyte."

"Do you love him?"

"How you bite the word!" Annie shrugged. "Perhaps I do. More than I do Charley, anyway."

"Annie!"

"Oh, go home, Winthrop, if you can't talk. What did you come out here for? Jules is willing to give up everything — his job, his career, his position in New York — to go off with me. How many men would do that?"

"Many. Who had as little to give up as he."

"You're not fair. Uncle Lewis tells me his prospects are excellent. He's the rising journalist on the *Daily Post*. Everyone's talking about him."

"If they're not, they will be. When *this* thing breaks."

"Well, what do you offer me instead? A dull, loveless brownstone life, paying and receiving calls and learning to look the other way when Charley exercises the right of his sex to seek his pleasures elsewhere. Oh, Winthrop! A woman needs a faith greater than mine to make her stick to such a course. What do you offer for my pleasure? Or don't women count at all?"

"There's your child."

"Nothing else?"

"Well, isn't there literature? Art? As you've just said?"

"So life is made up of bad people who live and good people who read about them?" Annie gave herself over to the longest and most exuberant of her laughs. "And Uncle Lewis who does both!"

For the first time Winthrop joined in her laughter. She came over and fixed her dark eyes with a smiling intensity on his. "Let me ask you something," she said. "If you will promise me an honest answer, an absolutely honest answer, I will promise to consider taking your advice."

"Only to consider it?"

"Oh, that's a great concession for a naughty lady who's contemplating an illicit trip to Paris."

"If she really *is* contemplating it."

"Well, if she isn't, what do you have to worry about?"

"All right. I promise to give you an honest answer."

Annie nodded and removed her hands from his shoulders. "I want to know if art, if the life of the imagination, makes up to *you* for the dullness of your life with Rosalie."

Winthrop stepped back. For a moment he considered leaving the house without a word. Then he remembered his mission.

"Suppose I reply that my life with Rosalie is not dull?"

"Then I shan't believe you. I know there has to be something outside of your marriage that keeps you going. And I doubt that it's the law. I do you the honor of supposing that when you recommend to me the consolation of the life of the imagination, you are recommending a consolation in which you have a strong personal belief."

Was it his growing belief that she was *not*, after all, in love with Bleecher that brought the sudden exhilaration to his heart? Not that she was in love with Winthrop Ward, or ever had been — that was manifest. He was too middle-aged, too spare and lean, too ascetic, too darkly garbed, for such as she. She liked him, played with him, understood him — in part. Was he really and truly in love with her? Did it matter if he never voiced it? He would have to remember to pray all the way home and to give thanks to the Almighty that Annie had never guessed!

"I am waiting for your answer, Winthrop. Does the life of the imagination make up?"

"Make up?"

"You know for what!"

"Yes," he said at last. "It does."

The wonderful girl knew when not to laugh. She became even paler. "Thank you," she half whispered. "I know what that cost you. Go to Jules. Talk to him. I'm in your hands. Goodbye."

When Winthrop went to the door to the hall, she had already disappeared up the staircase. Her young aunt, Carrie Andros, was on the landing. She came hurriedly down to speak to Winthrop. Her big soft worried eyes seemed to pop out of her heart-shaped face. She was a child, a child who had already borne four children to the old bull.

"Is it all right, Winthrop?" she asked tensely. "Can things be arranged?"

"I trust so."

"It'll be all right between her and Charley?"

"Let us pray."

"Ah, yes. Let us pray, by all means." But Carrie Andros's anxiety seemed now to give way to a sterner mood. "And let us pray, while we are at it, that Charley will appreciate the sacrifice that she is making."

Winthrop stared. "The sacrifice, ma'am?"

"The sacrifice of love, Winthrop! The sacrifice of everything her heart has dreamed of."

Winthrop was too stupefied to reply. Was it possible that adultery could be thus publicly denominated in the front hall of a mansion built for Lewis Andros by the architect of Trinity Church? Was *this* what the world had come to? Had Annie and her aunt been confiding in each other, whispering of plans for escape and love? Of course they had! Had Carrie not used that same vulgar word?

Winthrop disposed of his embarrassment as best he could, aided by a quick bow, and took his immediate leave. But on the way back to town, amid a lightly falling snow, he allowed himself to speculate if there was any essential difference between the ladies of the highest Manhattan society and the commercial dames of Mercer Street! He did not remember the prayers he was to make until he was on the barge over the Harlem River, and he then recited them with chattering teeth. Happily, it was never too late.

Back in town he drove directly to the Patroons' Club, where he wrote a note to Bleecher, requesting him to call that night at Union Square on a matter of the utmost importance. He sent the note to the *Daily Post* by messenger, together with one for Rosalie, instructing her to leave word with the servants that Bleecher should be ushered into the library if he called but not received upstairs. Then he went to the bar, where he was sure of finding Charley.

"Bleecher will come to my house tonight," he told his now rather shaky cousin. "I plan to give him this one chance. If he will agree never to address your wife again, in conversation or by letter, I shall advise him that the Wards will take no further action against him. It will simply be understood that he will abstain from all further social relations with our family."

Charley seemed to have some difficulty taking this in. "And if he refuses?"

"Then we destroy him."

"In a duel? Thanks for the 'we.' Do you know that Bleecher's a first-class shot? He fires one bullet between the wife's legs and the next between the husband's eyes. Don't you give a damn about me, Winthrop?"

Winthrop contemplated Charley's sagging pale cheeks and moist, rolling eyes. Why, he wondered, was panic so contemptible? It was sickening to consider what the wretched Bleecher was costing them, but the worst casualty of all might be his own love for Charley. Could nothing in their family survive the raid of this big, buzzing, gilded bee, this coprophagous poetaster?

"No, of course there will be no duel. Why should you submit your life to Bleecher? Gentlemen don't duel in New York, and if they did, they wouldn't duel with the likes of him. No, I mean destroy him financially and socially. I'll close every pocketbook and front door in New York to him!"

"How?"

"You'll see, my boy. Just leave it to me. And in the meanwhile I want you to purge your mind of all those filthy thoughts about your wife. I know you've been under a great strain. Otherwise I should not tolerate your language. But you must get this through your head. Annie has *not* been unfaithful to you. I'll go to the stake for that. She has been indiscreet, yes; she has been foolish, yes; she has been naughty, yes. But she has not been wicked. She has not submitted to the lewd embracements of that fiend."

"What makes you so sure?"

"Because I know Annie. And because I know she loves you." Winthrop stared Charley coolly in the eye until the latter had to look away. "You and she have had your difficulties, I know. Annie is a very emotional creature and inclined to hysterics. She leaps to conclusions. She probably decided that you didn't love her anymore and that her marriage was over. So she turned in desperation to flirt with the first man available, who happened to be Bleecher. She needs help, Charley, not abuse. You and she are going to be all right, I promise you!"

Charley was again the surly schoolboy, but this time the schoolboy who has misread the calendar and finds that his vacation is almost over. Winthrop decided that he had better stay and dine with him. In the course of their meal and a bottle of wine Charley was finally induced to give his sullen word that he would welcome Annie back from Yonkers if she would promise never to see Bleecher again.

This accomplished, Winthrop returned to Union Square, where he found Molly waiting in the front hall to tell him that a Mr. Bleecher was in the library. He could see through the half-open door the stocky back and curly black hair of his detested visitor. Bleecher was studying his little Kensett, a Newport seascape.

"Ah, there you are, Ward," he exclaimed, turning to flash his dark, impudently friendly eyes on Winthrop. "I'm admiring your Kensett. Such a subtlety of coloring. It's hard to tell where the sea stops and the horizon begins. I can see why people speak of your taste as advanced. While the rest of us are buying Italian peasant scenes and Turkish marketplaces, you're putting up your money for something as good as this. Congratulations!"

This appeal was to Winthrop's most vulnerable side, for he fancied his own eye as a collector. But that night he was unassailable.

"Never mind the compliments, Bleecher. May we get right down to business?"

Bleecher stared at him for a moment, then smiled and nodded briskly, as if he, for one, could never have been responsible for such a breach of good fellowship. "I'm at your service, Ward. I assume from your tone that you prefer to remain standing?"

"Much."

"Very well. Excuse me." Bleecher went over to a table and crushed out his cigar in a bowl. "Let us eliminate the last traces of conviviality."

Winthrop declined to notice the sarcasm. "Your correspondence with Mrs. Charles Ward has been discovered."

Bleecher's bushy eyebrows rose. "Do you imply that it was concealed?"

"I most certainly do. It was delivered clandestinely, through Miss Jane King."

"It was delivered through Miss King. Let me ask you something, Ward. Whom do you represent in this matter?"

"The family, of course. The outraged family."

"I see. But do you represent Annie?"

"Do you refer to Mrs. Charles Ward? I do indeed. *And* her husband."

"You mean you are speaking to me tonight with Mrs. Ward's authority?"

Winthrop could not resist a little snarl of satisfaction at the note of surprise in his antagonist's tone. "That's a bit of a shock to you, isn't it, Bleecher? Yes, I am speaking to you tonight with her authority. I received it today at Yonkers."

"Where she is residing, I gather, as the virtual prisoner of her uncle. Mr. Andros had better remember that there is such a thing as habeas corpus in this country."

"Can it be invoked by the would-be seducers of married women?"

Bleecher advanced a threatening step towards his host and stopped. He took a heavy breath. "It should be invocable by any man who champions the cause of a poor woman shackled to a swine like your cousin."

Winthrop's heart was beating so hard now that it hurt. He closed his eyes and counted to ten. Then he cleared his throat. "I suppose we had better avoid epithets. Are you prepared to give me some assurance that you will have no further communication with Mrs. Ward?"

"Does *she* ask that?"

"She has placed her case in my hands."

"Then what assurance can you give me that she will be allowed to live a life free from the constant apprehension of violent abuse and drunken threats?"

Winthrop trembled on the verge of incoherence. "Do you presume to treat with me, sir?"

"And why not? Have I not enjoyed Mrs. Ward's confidence? And that of Miss King? Do I not have letters from each? Do you think, Ward, that you are living in Turkey, where women are kept in harems and put in sacks and thrown in the river if they are disobedient? Let me disillusion you. The days are past when a married woman can be incarcerated by an old bulldog of an uncle while the family lawyer lays down ridiculous terms to her friends!"

"There is no more to be said, Mr. Bleecher! Kindly leave my house."

When Winthrop heard the reverberation of the slammed front door, he stirred himself from his reverie and strode to the table where Bleecher had deposited his ashes. Picking up the small crystal bowl which contained them, he dashed it to pieces in the grate. He heard a short laugh from the hall.

"How you must have enjoyed that!" Of course, it was Rosalie.

3

On New Year's Day the principal families of Manhattan maintained open house, but it was the custom of the hosts to desert their wives and to join the call-paying throng. Winthrop, when weather permitted, would start in his carriage as low as Canal Street, where a few old relatives still held out, and, proceeding north up Broadway, would make as many as a dozen calls — including one to his own house — ending at his Aunt Joanna Lispenard's on Forty-fifth Street. But on January 1, 1860, he set about these calls with anything but a New Year's spirit. Though careful to keep a holiday look in his eye, he was concentrating on grimmer matters, and his sips of eggnog were mere tokens. Still, there had to be an element of excitement in the execution of a clever plan, and Winthrop was not despondent as he made his way quickly through the crowded drawing rooms and clicked his glass against those of friends.

By the time he had arrived at Lewis Andros's square brownstone house on the corner of Great Jones Street and Broadway, he had accomplished the minor part of his mission. He had placed suggestions in half a dozen important ears. But the big job was still before him. When he spied old George King, the white-haired, tight-lipped, soft-voiced "landlord of the Bowery," at the end of Andros's crowded picture gallery, where Christian slaves and lions, Western sunsets and hunting Indians looked like canceled postage stamps amid the waving arms and nodding heads, he put down his glass, made his way towards him and led him apart from the others. Mr. King listened, nodding sagely, as Winthrop rapidly and succinctly delivered his message.

"Bleecher's name will come up at the next meeting of the Admissions Committee," King responded.

"Then I am just in time. I am sure you agree, sir, that we do not wish such a scoundrel in the Patroons'."

The King eyebrows formed a brief, black triangle, an odd patch under a cloud of white. "If we were to lose every member who had ever lusted after his neighbor's wife, you might be surprised at the gaps in our midst. To tell you the truth, Winthrop, there is a certain solidarity among men in these matters. I am not even sure that the scoundrel, as you call him, would be blackballed on your facts."

"A neighbor's wife! How about a fellow member's wife?"

Again the triangle appeared, higher, isosceles. "You didn't mention that to be the case."

"I had hoped it would not be necessary."

"Ah, but I'm afraid it is. And what is worse, I shall need to know which member."

Winthrop hesitated. "It's a very delicate matter."

"But you are asking me to perform a very delicate task."

"That is true, sir. It is my cousin Charley."

"Charley Ward! Dear me." King shook his head to indicate that Winthrop had not improved his case. "Charley Ward is not in very good odor at the club. He imbibes too much, and two years ago there was some trouble about a bill . . ."

"I paid that, Mr. King."

"Yes, no doubt, my dear fellow, and everyone at the Patroons' admires and respects you — I shouldn't be at all surprised to see you in my chair there one day — but don't you think that these things are better patched up or hushed up? Surely, Charley has nothing to gain by letting this sorry tale get about. Mightn't it make matters even worse for him?"

"Do you imply, sir, that the board might *still* elect Bleecher?"

"Well, it's hard to predict these things." King's shrug was a bit impatient now. "Mightn't it be better not to risk it? You would lose so much more in defeat than you would ever gain in victory."

"I am sorry, then, Mr. King, that I cannot spare you my further information. Bleecher used your daughter Jane as his intermediary. She carried his letters to Annie so that Charley would not know." Winthrop did not quail before the old man's acidulous stare. "You cannot think that I would say such a thing if I were not sure of my facts."

Both men now looked across the gallery to where Annie Ward, precariously reunited with her husband, and Jane King were giggling together. Jane was small and dark and sounded very silly. Charley Ward, standing beside them, seemed absorbed in his dark glass.

"I shall take care of the matter you speak of, Ward," the old man said gratingly. "But God help you if your facts aren't right!"

"Happy New Year, Mr. King," Winthrop rejoined coolly, with a departing bow. "I hope it will be happier for all of us — but one."

As Winthrop walked up to Annie, she threw back her head to emit the famous laugh.

"Hello, King Arthur," she greeted him in her deep voice. "Here are all your court! There may be a few dents in the Round Table, but nothing that can't be hammered out. If one has a good hammer. And you always *do* have one, don't you, dear?"

"I try to please." Nothing could dampen Winthrop's sudden exhilaration. Here were Annie and Charley together, and his plans for Bleecher were working!

"What have you been saying to my father, Winthrop?" Jane King asked with a little grimace. "I never saw such a scowl."

"Oh, I'm sure he'll tell you about it," Winthrop responded cheerfully. "Don't you and he have little father-daughter chats from time to time?"

"Angels protect me!" Jane turned to Annie. "What do you suppose Winthrop's telling him?"

"I hope he's told him what you've been up to," Charley said to Jane with a sneer. "I daresay the old man won't fancy the kind of service you apply to Annie's journalist friends . . . oh, dear!" Seeing Winthrop's frown, Charley clapped his hand over his mouth with mock dismay. "I promised not to mention a certain name, didn't I? I promised to leave *him* to Cousin Winthrop!"

"And you had better keep that promise, too," Annie retorted with heat. "Or our so-called reconciliation will be of brief duration."

Winthrop, seeing Lewis Andros in the doorway, escaped to his side. "Have you a word for me, sir?"

"Yes. Are you calling on the Cranberry Hardys today?"

A wrinkle of scorn slid over Winthrop's face. "I wouldn't normally."

"Well, I suggest you do. His store takes a full-page advertisement in the *Daily Post* twice a week. A word from him to the editor, and Bleecher's out of a job. I've sent my son-in-law to broach the matter with Hardy. It's up to you to close it."

Winthrop's nod was military in its abruptness. "I'm on my way, sir."

Cranberry Hardy had built the largest mansion in Manhattan, larger even than Mr. Astor's. Its four tall stories were encased in white marble, covered by a high mansard roof and studded with clusters of Corinthian columns. Hardy was the greatest merchant of New York and the proprietor of the largest department store, but the money was new and the family plain, and the Ward ladies had never called. Winthrop, however, had met Hardy in Trinity Church business matters and had received his New Year's bid. It was the perfect chance; he was not expected to bring Rosalie.

He donned his friendliest smile as he passed through the crowded reception rooms of the marble mansion. He was careful to betray none of the condescension that he felt for the over-opulent interior, filled with marble statues from American studios in Rome: a Cleopatra, an Augustus, a Miles Standish, two fighting gladiators. Winthrop recognized none of the guests; he wondered if Hardy recruited them from the store's personnel.

He found his host puffing at a large cigar and talking to a small, respectfully listening group of younger men. Hardy was a bald, heavy-jawed man with tiny, glistening eyes. He broke away without a word of apology to his audience when he saw Winthrop. Taking him firmly by the elbow, he propelled him to a corner.

"So you'll call, Winthrop Ward, when you want a favor from the merchant. Is that about the size of it?"

"So it might appear. But it also so happens that I was planning to give myself the pleasure of calling today in any event."

"Without the Mrs.?"

"My wife is receiving today."

"How would I know? She didn't ask me."

"She will next year."

Hardy snorted. "Well, enough of that. I shouldn't be too rough with a man who comes to bid me a happy New Year. But this business of Jules Bleecher sticks in my craw. What's it to me that the man's a bounder? Why should I care if he hankers after one of your society matrons? Can't you take care of your own? Must I get the poor lecher fired for you?"

"We hoped that you might regard our cause as yours," Winthrop answered smoothly. "And that you might agree that such a wrong inflicted on a gentleman like my cousin affected all the leaders of the city."

"I ain't in your crowd, Ward."

"Isn't that your choice, sir?"

Hardy stared. "Are you telling me that I could get into the Patroons'?"

Never had Winthrop's mind worked so fast. "I am not telling you that you could get in. That would be a question for the Admissions Committee. But I can certainly tell you that I should be glad to write you a letter of endorsement."

Hardy snickered. "I know that dodge. 'Dear Board of Admissions: I promised Mr. Cranberry Hardy that I would write a letter for him. This is the letter. Very truly yours, Winthrop Ward.'"

Winthrop breathed in relief. Now he had him! "Mr. Hardy," he said in a higher tone, "I cannot conceive what there may be in our past relations to justify your impugning my honor. If I were to write for you, it would be to heartily endorse your candidacy. And I should stand by my letter. After what you've just said, of course, there can be no further question of that."

He turned to go, just slowly enough to give Hardy the time to catch him by the arm. "Don't take offense, Ward. I was too hasty."

"I'm afraid you were."

"Maybe one day I'll ask you for that letter. But not yet a bit. In the meantime, thank you. Tell me, what's old Andros going to do if I don't bring him Bleecher's head on a platter? Have the Bank of Commerce call all the store's demand loans?"

"Not at all. Mr. Andros is simply asking a favor from one business leader to another. He may be in a position to return it one day."

Hardy put his thumbs in the pockets of his red waistcoat and balanced to and fro, his lips pursed as if to whistle but emitting no sound. "Well, I confess that I wouldn't mind having a few more friends in your crowd. God knows, Jules Bleecher doesn't mean a damn thing to me, and he's probably a horse's ass anyhow. But I don't much care for the idea of old Lewis Andros sending first his son-in-law and then you. Damn it all, Ward, if Andros wants Bleecher's head, let him come here and ask for it!"

"Today?"

"Well, there's no time like the present, is there?"

"I can't guarantee it, but I'm on my way back to Great Jones Street!"

4

Ten days later, at nine o'clock in the evening, Winthrop again received Jules Bleecher in the library at Union Square. This time Winthrop sat at his desk, touching his fingertips together, his face impassive, grave. Once again his heart was beating uncomfortably, but this time the discomfort was punctuated with the tickling of a fierce jubilation. Bleecher, with darkened countenance, was walking up and down the Persian carpet.

"My first impulse was to call you out," he was saying, "but I knew that would do no good. You burghers don't fight. Then I thought of going to your office with a horsewhip. But that would have been playing into your hands. Your friends on the bench would have put me in jail for a year or more. And then, thinking it over, I began to cool off. I began to be even interested in what had happened to me. What sort of a man are you, Winthrop Ward? Or are you a man at all?"

"What I am need not concern us, Bleecher."

"Oh, but it concerns *me*. I find myself without a job and without a friend in a city of brownstone fronts with locked front doors. How the hell did you do it? And why? You're not her husband. You're not even a very close relation." Bleecher paused to stare at his silent host. "It couldn't be that you're in love with Annie yourself?" He shook his head slowly as Winthrop failed to move a muscle. "No, that would be impossible for a snowman like you. But I still must ask of someone, as Othello asked of Lodovico:

'Will you, I pray, demand that demi-devil
Why he has thus ensnared my soul and body?' "

Winthrop's lips tightened in contempt. How typical of the poetaster to turn to Shakespeare in his ranting! "You and I, Bleecher, will be bound to disagree on which is the demi-devil. You have lived much abroad and cannot be expected to understand the customs of simple American gentlemen who still believe that a marriage vow is sacred and that homes should be protected."

"But from whom, in the name of God? Your cousin is the one who has threatened his own home from the beginning. Have you any idea, Ward, what his wife has had to put up with?"

"I think I have an idea."

Something in Winthrop's tone made Bleecher stare at him again. "Maybe you're not a snowman, after all. Be frank, Ward. If you did what you did out of jealousy, I'll forgive you all. I'll even shake your hand!"

Winthrop rose. The exhilaration had departed from his chest. "We could talk all night and never understand each other. Let me put my last proposition before you. You have in your possession certain letters from Mrs. Ward and Miss King. Is that not so?"

"Why should I tell you?"

"Because I want them and because I'm in a position to barter for them. If you will deliver them to me, I will ask the *Daily Post* to reemploy you as a foreign correspondent. You will be able to live in London or

Paris. I have no doubt that you will find life in one of those cities, particularly the second, preferable to our quiet existence on this side of the Atlantic."

Bleecher looked at him now with something like fascination. "And will the *Daily Post* do as you tell them?"

"I think so. If my proposition be endorsed — as I trust it will be — by certain gentlemen of prominence in this town."

"Like Messrs. Hardy and Andros. I see. And now the bounder is supposed to crumble. Or, like Shylock before Portia, be sent to renounce his faith. Only you have the wrong script, Ward. In *my* script, the villain turns upon you with a splendid defiance. You may take your proposition and cram it up the aperture — if indeed there be one in a snowman — in the nether part of your frozen body."

Ward averted his eyes from his foul-mouthed visitor. "I suppose I should expect such talk from you."

"You will be relieved to hear that I am removing myself from your 'quiet existence.' I have a standing invitation to come to Richmond and write a column for the *Enquirer*. It will be pleasant to be among gentlemen again. Perhaps I can help to warn them in the South what they are up against. They think, because they know how to fight bravely, that they are bound to prevail in a struggle with men of straw and men of ice, such as I have met up here. But they may well be wrong. If your millions of labor-slaves are ever harnessed into an army and sent into bloody battle by such remorseless bigots as you and Andros and Hardy, who can tell the outcome?"

"Then you keep the letters?"

"What I may do with the letters must remain the one little cloud of uncertainty on your cerulean sky of fatuity. Keep your eye ever peeled on it, Ward! Keep your umbrella in constant readiness!"

"Even if you want revenge of me," Winthrop protested earnestly, "must you take it out on Annie, too? Must she live in the daily fear of seeing her letters printed somewhere?"

Bleecher's gasp was incredulous. Then he burst suddenly into a harsh, raucous laugh. "Annie! That teasing, tantalizing little bitch? Do you honestly think she'd give one holy goddamn if I told the world she copulated with sailors every Saturday night on a public pier?"

"Get out of my house!"

"You don't know her, Ward."

"Get out of my house!"

"I can't go fast enough."

Winthrop drank two whiskies before he went upstairs. Rosalie was at her dressing table, already in her nightgown. As she removed her earrings, she studied his face in her mirror.

"You didn't get the letters."

"No," he replied with a sigh, sitting down on the bedside.

"I didn't think you would. But it doesn't matter. He'll never do anything with them."

"Now what makes you say that?"

"Because he's a gentleman."

"Oh, Rosalie! Are you trying to annoy me?"

"No, dear. But I think you should face a fact every now and then. Even a disagreeable one."

"He's going to Richmond. He loves the Southern aristocracy. Slaveholders! How does *that* go down with your abolitionist principles?"

"Very badly." Rosalie's smile was obscure. "I never said I liked him, Winthrop. Or that I approved of him. I merely said he was a gentleman. To me that is a technical term. But one can deduce certain things from it. And one is that he'll never use those letters."

"And what about me? Am I a gentleman?"

"No, I don't really think you are."

"Rosalie!"

"I don't really think any man in New York society is. It's not what we go in for here."

"I'm tired. I'm going to bed."

"Good, dear. Do."

But later, in the dark, she put another question to him. "Tell me something, Winthrop. Do you really think you have done a good turn for Annie and Charles in salvaging their marriage?"

"I did what I had to do."

"What *you* had to do? Why you? Nobody else felt that way. Certainly none of our friends or family. You were the designer of the whole plot. Has it ever occurred to you that you've been playing God, Winthrop?"

"Maybe that's what I meant by doing what I had to do. Maybe there are times when one has to play God — when everyone else seems to forget He exists."

But Rosalie seemed unimpressed by his religious turn. "Do you suppose that's how history's written?" she mused. "Like a play being put together for the dress rehearsal? With one little man rushing about, shouting directions and trying to get people into the right costumes? Not necessarily a powerful man — simply a man with an *idée fixe*. A man with a sense of how things should at least *look*. Even a fussy man, a . . ."

"Rosalie, I want to go to sleep."

When a silence of several minutes followed by gentle snoring indicated that he had no further interruption to fear, Winthrop moved his lips in silent prayer:

"Dear God, if I have ever thought of Annie carnally, please forgive me. Remember that I have never given her or anyone else the right to say so. My conduct has been correct, even if my heart has been sinful. And let me face the facts of my motive in doing what I have done to Bleecher. Did I destroy him because I was jealous? Perhaps. But would I not have done so even if I had not been wickedly attracted to Annie? *Yes!* Yes, I would have! So is it a sin to enjoy performing a task essentially done for thee, O God? Is it wrong if jealousy gives a fillip to doing one's duty? Make me humble, dear God. Crush me, overwhelm me. I am nothing, nothing, nothing . . ."

Winthrop felt calmer now and hoped that he would doze off before his excitement returned. Two drinks! He should never have had two drinks. Oh, why had he remembered them? He was wide awake again, watching the curtains gently blowing in the moonlight. The *Enquirer?* The Richmond *Enquirer?* Bleecher would be writing for *that?* Was that not the rag which had urged secession that very morning, suggesting that the Southern states place themselves under the protection of Louis Napoleon? What traitors! How could one govern a nation with such firebrands trying to pull it apart?

"Dear God, of course I know that we must allow our Southern states to live in peace. But if in thy great wisdom thou seeest fit to permit them to strike the first blow, if thou turnest thine eyes away and allowest them to secede, *then* will it be wrong if we leap to arms with joy and jubilation in our hearts and if we bring the devastation of thine anger to their fair land, burning their plantations with a cleansing fire and chastising their rebel people with the sword? Or even with worse? Wilt thou blame us if their women are raped by the very slaves whom we have freed, if . . ."

He started as he heard Rosalie's voice. "What's wrong, Winthrop? Are you having a nightmare? You're rocking the bed!"

The Fabbri Tape

1980

I HAVE BEEN FRETTING for some days now over an article in the *Manhattan Law Review:* "Hubris and the American Lawyer," which contains, in addition to essays on Alger Hiss, Dean Landis and John Dean, a piece on myself entitled "Mario Fabbri, Merchant of Justice." Ordinarily, in the now considerable literature dealing with the bribery trial of Gridley Forrest, it is the judge who occupies center stage, and indeed it is hard to imagine a greater exemplar of the arrogance so fatal to the Greek tragic hero than my late, unhappy friend. But this particular author has chosen to see *me* as the principal villain, the mastermind behind the tragedy. And he has taken the trouble to carry his research down to this year of our Lord 1975, for he ends on this note: "Fabbri, hale and hearty at eighty-four, sole survivor of a scandal that four decades ago shook our bar from coast to coast, cheerfully persists in his ancient error. 'Believing what I then believed to be the facts,' he told a reporter recently, 'I'd do the same thing again!' "

It is perfectly true. I would. But it behooves me, I suppose, in an era of general review of moral values, to make some effort to set down my reasons for the benefit of any posterity that cares to hear them. We live in an age of records, where history is transcribed on a minute-to-minute basis. So long as I am still in possession of my faculties, I may as well add my tape to a heap already so high that future scholars will be tempted to make a bonfire of it. Why not? Doesn't each generation want to rewrite history according to its particular lights?

Young people today, including my grandchildren, are very busy re-evaluating the morals of the past. They tend to see American history as a study in hypocrisy. To them crime is largely a technical matter. If you are caught, you go to jail, and that is that. You are no longer made an outcast as I was. Unless, of course, you have been guilty of discriminating against an ethnic or religious minority, and then you *are* wicked. Sometimes I think that is the only moral value we have left.

But that is all right. I can live with that. I grew up as a youngster in Manhattan when to be poor, Italian and Catholic was hardly a ticket to fame and riches, and although I always regarded social prejudices as simply hurdles that I had to get over, I can agree that in a decent society they should be eliminated. And as to the concept of other crimes being technically rather than morally reprehensible, I can only point out that that was precisely my own gospel and the reason I did what I did. In an era that valued appearances I strove to save the appearance of the bar, the appearance of the judiciary, indeed the appearance of our whole legal system. I still believe it would have been better for everybody had Gridley Forrest never been found out.

My late wife, I should admit, never agreed with me. She believed that I had been profoundly evil and left me for a time because I would not repent. She would have loved me as a sinner, but only as a repentant sinner. And in the end it was her duty that made her return, not my persuasiveness. She decided that a wife never has the right to give a husband up.

Let me fill in, as briefly as I can, the minimum of background that the person listening to this tape should know. My parents emigrated from Genoa in the late eighteen-eighties and started an Italian restaurant in Twelfth Street. I was one of eight children, but because I was bright my father lavished his particular attention on me. His small means required him to pick and choose among his offspring. It was through him that I got a job as an office boy with Mr. Findlay of the great Wall Street law firm that bore his name. Mr. Findlay was a bachelor who lived on Washington Square and frequently dined at my father's place. After my employment he kept a sharp eye on me, and finding me quick, responsive and able, he decided to put me through college and law school and then to hire me as a clerk. Once I had a hand on the bottom rung of that ladder I never loosened my hold. I stayed in the firm until I became a member and, after Mr. Findlay's death in 1930, I succeeded him as managing partner. That is the story, in its very briefest form, of my rise.

Let me say just a word about Thomas Findlay. He was the most impersonal man I have ever known, a close-mouthed, hard-hitting, utterly industrious Yankee. He lived, so far as I could make out, for the love of the law alone. He never spent much money on himself, and he bequeathed the substantial fortune that he made to a hospital in which he had shown only a perfunctory interest in his lifetime. Our relationship was one of symbiosis. As he grew older, he leaned increasingly on me, but he always recognized that I needed him quite as much as he did me. He never praised or dispraised my work. He knew that I knew just how good it was. And somehow, without ever expressing his affection for me, he managed to make me feel it. I was the nearest thing that he had to a son, perhaps the nearest thing to a friend.

The gulf between us, as I look back, seems limitless. He was small and dry and lived to work. I was large and, in my young days, rather floridly handsome, and I craved pleasure as much as work. I loved music and art and food and wine and women. He did not so much object to these tastes as to seem to find them irrelevant to what life, to him anyway, was all about. The nearest thing we ever had to an intimate conversation was when I told him that I had fallen in love with Pussy Fish, the daughter of one of his partners.

"I suppose it's a social step up for you," he observed, with his usual candor. "But not very far up. And you're quite capable of making it on your own."

"But, Mr. Findlay," I protested, "you don't understand. I love the girl!"

"Of course you do, my boy. I didn't mean to imply the contrary. But girls like that . . . well, they either believe in the things their parents pretend to believe in, or they don't. And I don't know which is worse."

I didn't know what Mr. Findlay meant by that, but it didn't worry me. I was too much in love. I see it now, however. He wondered what would happen to me if I were absorbed into what we now call a WASP culture. Mr. and Mrs. Fish, unlike Mr. Findlay, who had been a poor parson's son from Fitchburg, Massachusetts, were "old New York." Mr. Fish was an elegant, rather wizened, very thin and very brown-faced gentleman who owed his position in the firm to a long-deceased father. He had lost his lawyer's nerve (if he had ever had it) and tried to make up for this deficiency by charming manners. He and his rather mousy wife made no objection to my suit for their only daughter; indeed, they seemed to encourage it. After Pussy and I were married, I discovered that they had almost no means besides the slender percentage of the firm's profits that Mr. Findlay allowed my father-in-law in deference to *his* father's memory. They had regarded *me* all the while as a catch! And indeed, from their point of view, I suppose I was one.

I should say at once that Pussy belonged to the first category of Mr. Findlay's "girls like that." She believed in what her parents professed, not in what they did. There was not a worldly bone in her body.

It is common today for young people to speak scathingly of the former domination of American culture by WASPs, but, for all their violence, they have little conception of just how dominating it was. In my youth American society and government were almost entirely in the hands of big business and the legal profession, and both of these were very white and very Protestant. What we now call ethnic groups, Jews, Irish, and Italians, had managed to get hold of political organizations in the larger cities, but even there the financial districts — the real centers of power — remained predominantly WASP. I do not mean that there was not plenty of opportunity in New York City for a young lawyer of Italian-American origin, but if he wanted to join the Union Club or the Piping Rock, if he wanted to send his sons to Groton or Andover, if he hoped ever to be president of the American Bar Association or achieve high federal office, it was going to be a lot easier for him if he became an Episcopalian and treated his homeland as an exotic memory rather than a present-day inspiration.

Yet it would be totally to misinterpret Mario Fabbri to assume that I adopted a religion and a social philosophy — indeed, a whole new code of life — for self-advancement only. As a boy I associated the Catholic Church and my family's Italian traditions with the rigors of an ancient class system of which we had been the victims. I *believed* in the American way: in its deity, its ideals, its good manners, its restraints, its orderliness and its cleanliness. I still do. Of course, I perceive its faults — what child of Italian parentage would not? — its priggishness, its prejudices, its materialism, its hypocrisy. But it still seems a lot better to me than what my parents ran away from. The tragedy of American civilization is that it has swept away WASP morality and put nothing in its place. Franklin Roosevelt was not a traitor to his class, as his old college classmates maintained: he was its last great representative.

When Pussy and I were married in 1915 I was not yet a partner in the firm, but I was headed for it. Mr. Findlay accorded me the signal honor of attending my bachelors' dinner and even had several more than his usually moderate quota of drinks. When I asked him confidentially if he did not recant of his proffered warning, he simply shrugged and said: "Well, you picked a fine girl. Pussy has none of her father's weakness. We can be frank, my boy, you and I. But what she will never appreciate is your success, or why you care about it. I told you how it was, Mario. They go either one way or the other. And I don't know which is worse."

It was not long before I discovered what the old man meant. Pussy was the dearest little thing you can imagine, with brown eyes and chestnut hair and a kind of breathless enthusiasm, and she had seemed to find it terribly exciting that I was Italian and Catholic. I had been aware that she had a deep puritan streak and an exaggerated sense of civic duty — she spent half her evenings at a settlement house teaching poetry to telephone operators — but I had never doubted, despite my boss's warning, that I would be able to change all that. Once married to me, would not Pussy be glad to shed her girlish fads and share my tastes and enthusiasms? Should I not open up to her a larger life?

Never was fatuous man more deluded. What I had not gleaned — what man of Mediterranean background could have? — was that once married to me, Pussy should have conceived that I had become incorporated into the tight box of her own gray puritan fate. Oh, she loved me, yes, but she loved me now as a fellow prisoner, as one who had volunteered to leave his privileged seat in the arena and leap down to join her amid the hungry lions. The sacrifice was touching, no doubt, even overwhelming, but for better or worse I was now subject to *her* god.

By which I do not mean an Episcopalian god. Far from it. Pussy, like many religiously inclined Protestant agnostics of her generation, cared nothing for sect or dogma. Her god refused to be tied down; he was too busy tormenting consciences. Pussy was even shocked at my giving up Catholicism. She said it might look as if I were doing it for social reasons.

"Do you mean I can't give up something I don't believe in because someone might call me a toady?"

"I don't know," she murmured doubtfully. "Is that what I mean? Perhaps it is."

Let me hasten to add that, for all our differences, Pussy and I were basically happy. Not that she ever changed. Oh, no! The big income that I ultimately earned, the ostentatious way of life that I adopted (a Georgian town house in the East Sixties and a country estate on the north shore of Long Island), the private schools to which I sent our son and daughter, even my art collection of Post-Impressionists and Fauves — all of these she accepted without in any way altering the basic pattern of a daily existence largely devoted to school and hospital work. She never sneered at my enthusiasms; she rarely even criticized them, but she sometimes looked askance. She lived like an unimpressed poor relative in the midst of my glory. She was always perfectly amiable, if slightly *distraite*, as my hostess at dinner parties where the guests, wines and menus were chosen by me. I think that without my considerable contributions to her charities, she might have absented herself from some of these. But her puritan conscience would not allow her to accept something for nothing. Oh, yes, she was always just.

And she was the stronger of us two. That showed in the children. Both Alma and Tomaso were essentially hers. They were obedient and respectful to me, at least until they went to college and became tinged with radicalism, and I think they cared for me, in their own way, but Pussy was always the "real" parent. Her murky god got his long fingers into their consciences, too, and made them view me somewhat in the light of a genial Philistine. Alma, fortunately, majored in the history of art and gave me substantial help with my art collection. It was thanks to her advice that I bought the Pissarro from the sale of which Pussy and I have largely subsisted since my disbarment.

Which ugly term brings me at last to Gridley Forrest. I had known him slightly ever since my marriage, for Mathilde, his wife, had been a classmate and cousin of Pussy's, but the two girls were too different to be congenial, and we had seen little of the Forrests until the late nineteen-thirties, when he became a judge at the federal circuit court of appeals. It was he who then sought my company, he who initiated the friendship, if that is the proper word for the relationship that developed between us.

But a word first about his wife, Mathilde, which name she pronounced in the French way. She had been brought up in the same fashion as Pussy, but if ever there was an argument in favor of heredity over environment, it was the contrast supplied by these two. Mathilde, presumably, was the other type of New York girl to whom Mr. Findlay had so darkly referred. She was no more like my Pussy than if she had been born and raised in the Antipodes. To begin with, she was beautiful and blond and had a bewitching charm of manner. And then, instead of suffering from Pussy's deep sense of personal unworthiness, Mathilde took for granted that every gift life tossed in her lap was not one jot more than her due. Indeed, as a girl she had considered that fortune had rather scanted her. Why had her family had to make do with a shabby brownstone house off Gramercy Park when the Vanderbilts had marble palaces?

Her marriage to Gridley Forrest, a young man of no particular means or social position at the time, had come as something of a surprise to her friends, but when they learned that he was not only brilliant but forceful, they decided that she knew what she was doing. His legal future seemed assured, and Mathilde certainly did not care whether money was old or new so long as she had it. When it later became apparent that Gridley had political and judicial ambitions, these were perfectly acceptable to her, so long as he had put aside enough to make up for any diminution in income.

Mathilde would never, beyond the merest civility, have much to do with any of her husband's legal or political associates who were not of her own social set. In this she actually regarded herself as morally justified. Once, when I ventured to suggest to her that it might help Gridley if she would broaden herself a bit, she retorted that, thank you very much, she was not going to turn herself into a hypocrite for the sake of money or high office! But I must admit that she was a delightful woman — when things were going her way. She was bright and observant and could be very funny. And she certainly played a marvelous game of bridge.

Much later I learned another of her characteristics. She was a tribal creature, and when society condemned her husband, she accepted the verdict without question. Yet I do not believe that she had the smallest sense of personal outrage at what Gridley had done. That was all some kind of senseless men's business. But when she heard the chief medicine man, so to speak, proclaim the outlawing of her husband, what could she do but join the others in the ritual dance? She was decent enough to Gridley when he came out of prison, for she had a basically kind nature, but she continued to dine out and to play bridge in houses where he could not accompany her. Perhaps it was just as well. Cooped up alone they might have come to loathe each other.

Gridley Forrest, I sometimes think, was put on this earth to destroy me, the one being equipped by a malign creator with the apparatus fatal to my defenses, as the mongoose is to the cobra or the desert wasp to the tarantula. That word *wasp* again! He had an uncanny way of seeming to enter inside of one, to rummage around in one's basement or attic, turning up this or that, pulling soiled clothes out of baskets, and all with an air of total matter-of-factness, as if it were something he had to do, a kind of chore — perhaps, indeed, just such a thing as you would naturally do to him, if you only could.

He was a very large man, portly but square-shouldered and strongly built, with a shiny bald dome and a severe square face, small but pronounced features and gray, cold eyes that glittered with a seeming severity behind his pince-nez. He was always opulently and immaculately dressed, either in dark suits, or, in the country, in rather surprisingly loud tweeds. He was never loved by underlings. Yet he had an astonishing way of achieving rapid intimacy with people, once he had decided that he wished it. It was almost as if he might ask you, on a first acquaintance, if you had slept with your wife before you married her. And yet his manner was so direct, so judicial, that one hardly resented it. There was even something a bit flattering about it. You were raised to his level. You might even begin to wonder if he would not tell you if he had slept with *his*.

The Forrests and the Fabbris exchanged dinner invitations perhaps twice a year, but Gridley and I did not become personal friends until my election to the Greenvale Country Club in 1934. I should admit here that election to this club was the social triumph of my life. I never could see why Pussy and the children found it stuffy. I enjoyed it just as much as, during my two years on the waiting list, I had thought I should. I loved the big white shiny clubhouse, always so freshly painted, with its porticos overlooking the green stretch of the golf course merging in the distance with the green or golden woods; the huge sapphire swimming pool; the grass courts; the smart women in tennis clothes with well-set golden hair and golden jewelry. My son, Tom, said that I liked it because it looked like a Packard advertisement. But wasn't a Packard advertisement meant to convey the idea of a luxurious and agreeable existence?

Forrest played golf every weekend at the club, and soon after my election he started asking me to join him. In the course of a year this became an established thing. We met every Saturday to play eighteen holes and have a couple of drinks afterwards in the bar that looked over the riding ring. Forrest never asked anyone to join us, and he was not a man whom one approached without a bidding, even in that club. I don't think he was ever much interested in people. An audience of one was all that he needed to discuss his two favorite topics: the craft of judging and the state of the real estate market, in which he had invested Mathilde's money and his own savings. Of course, I was more interested in the former, but with a couple of large construction companies among my clients, I cared a good deal about the latter as well. Forrest would always indulge my curiosity with fascinating tidbits about his cases and fellow judges before pumping me about housing developments. I was perfectly aware that I was being pumped, but I had no objection. Was I not, in my own way, pumping him? It was useful, in my practice, to know all I could about his court.

He knew that I admired him as a judge, and he took my admiration, like everything else, for granted. He had a just rather than a conceited view of his own distinction, and he fitted himself appropriately, I thought, into the history of the American judiciary. Only he was less sanguine about his future than I. He shook his head with sudden, sharp irritation when I once predicted his ultimate elevation to the Supreme Court.

"Not a prayer!" he retorted. "I'd have as much chance as John W. Davis."

"But Davis is an arch-conservative. Even if he is a Democrat. You haven't opposed the New Deal."

"But a man's got to be more than neutral these days. He's got to be committed, dedicated. From now on every justice appointed to that Court is going to have to be a man who will make old MacReynolds and Butler vomit all over their black robes!"

The image seemed unduly violent. "Roosevelt isn't going to be in office forever."

"Don't bet on that! We're living in a revolution. It's going to be a long time before moderate men are listened to."

"I hate to think that."

"Then think *this*," Forrest said grimly. "In any other period of American history I could have looked forward with some confidence to ending my career as one of those nine men. Not now. And yet some deluded folk think I've had a successful life. Why, I've been the unluckiest man of my era!"

It was rare that our talks struck so emotional a note. Gridley Forrest was not often given to dramatics. Even when the day came that he offered me a front-row seat to the greatest of dramas, you'd never have guessed it from his tone.

It was on a Saturday at noon, after our usual round of golf, over our usual whiskey. As I think back, perhaps he *was* a bit graver than usual. I had been talking about my score, a record for me, when he suddenly interrupted.

"I assume, because you are involved in patent law, that you have read the decision in McFarley against Baker Thermos?"

"Oh, yes. A surprisingly good opinion. For Judge Freer."

"You agreed with it?"

"I did. Although the question was certainly a close one. It must have been a happy day for the thermos company."

"Very happy. An adverse decision would have bankrupted them."

"I didn't know old Freer was so expert in patent law. Did you assign him to the case?"

Forrest's stare now became almost hypnotizing. "I did," he replied in a rather gravelly tone. "And I even gave him some assistance in the opinion."

What was I supposed to say to *that?*

"That surprises you?" he continued.

"Until you have explained it."

"Preston Saunders is president of Baker Thermos. He paid me — shall we call it a retainer? — to assure the decision. I gave Freer twenty percent of it."

What do you feel when you are face to face with history? A curious numbness. I saw a picture with Forrest in it, and with myself in it. I was a person quite apart from myself. I heard a voice droning somewhere behind me. The voice seemed to be telling me that this was the greatest judicial crime in the history of the United States. But it wasn't real, or if it was real, it was something flat and ordinary. There was not, it seemed to me, so much difference between fact and fiction, or even, for that matter, between crime and innocence. There was simply the judge and I, and our golf game, and now his sale of justice. His simple, matter-of-fact sale of justice.

"You are speechless. It isn't surprising. You see a desperate man before you, Mario. Everything I have is tied up in real estate. I had to do what I did to avoid foreclosure on the key parcel. I saved myself in

the nick of time." As I simply continued to stare at his impassive countenance, he went on in a brisker tone: "You wonder why I am telling
you. Because the case is on appeal. To *my* court, of course. And Saunders couldn't keep his mouth shut. What corporate executive can? He
blabbed to one of his VPs. And now that VP has sent me word that if
they lose the appeal, he will expose me. So there you are, Mario. If the
decision in the district court is not affirmed, you will see me prosecuted,
convicted, imprisoned and forever disgraced. My name will become a
symbol of infamy in the history of American law."

How could a man take it that way? How could he sit there,
surrounded by all the showiest trappings of an American success
story, and so resolutely face his own annihilation? For a moment the
little girl on her pony preparing to take a jump in the ring beneath us
was blurred. Then I saw her again. She was on the other side of the
jump. She had cleared it nicely. I recalled somebody's theory that no
moment of time is ever lost, that they are all recorded somewhere, in
an infinite library of tapes. Surely this moment would endure as long
as any.

"You are still speechless. Do you think I am pulling your leg? Or do
you think I have taken leave of my senses?"

"No, no. I believe you. You couldn't joke about such a thing."

"Good. Then, to the point. Will you help me? If not for my own sake,
for the reputation of the bench?"

I gazed at him in surprise. Then I nodded. "For *your* sake, Gridley."

His answering look betrayed nothing. He might or might not have
been touched by my personal concern and affection. But I suspected
that he took these things, like everything else, for granted. Which did
not mean that he did not value them. "Very well. I accept your
kindness. Indeed, I must. I have discussed the case with Judge Tobey.
He is adamant for reversal. He considers himself an expert on patents.
That leaves Judge Isaacson. I think he might be persuaded. But I shall
need to show him a draft of my proposed opinion affirming the
decision of the lower court. It must be very persuasive. It can be
written only by you."

※

I went to work immediately to write a legal memorandum, or what
really amounted to a brief, that Forrest could offer Judge Isaacson,

presumably as his own work or that of his law clerk, to persuade him to sustain the opinion of the lower court. I knew that the argument would have to be short and to the point; it would have to be in the form of a note, or series of notes, that Forrest might have dictated to his secretary in order to set down on paper the ideas that had occurred to him in reading the briefs of opposing counsel. In preparing my paper I was resolved to use no assistants, neither a junior partner nor an associate nor even my secretary. I would not so much as ask the librarian to bring me a reporter: I was determined to get all the books for myself.

"No, Mrs. Millis, I want to see if I know where everything in the library is," I told that loyal but bewildered lady. "The trouble with us older partners is that we get too dependent on helping hands. And I'm going to work right here at this table, if you don't mind."

"But can't I get Miss Stairs to take down your notes, sir?"

"And bother everyone in the library with my dictation? Certainly not. I shall write out my own notes like anyone else."

Some of the younger partners, alerted to the senior's "mysterious research," came in to offer to help me, and I had to try my darnedest not to betray my irritation.

"We have really come to a pretty pass," I could not help retorting testily to one of these, "when the presence of an older partner in the library, reading a Supreme Court opinion, is news that rings from one end of the office to the other!"

What I was doing was attempting to encapsulate my crime, so that nobody else would be in the smallest degree contaminated. I take no great credit for this; it seems to me that it was only elementary decency. But I never believed that I was doing a thing that was morally wrong; indeed, I believed that it was morally right. Which does not mean that I was under any illusion as to how my conduct would appear against the canons of legal ethics. I knew that I was engaged in assisting a bought judge to persuade an innocent fellow judge to sustain a bought decision. I did not even try to persuade myself that it made any difference that the brief I was writing might have been submitted with perfect propriety by counsel for the litigant for whom I was indirectly working, or that I was not being paid for my efforts. I knew that, even had I been the innocent counsel of the bribing appellee, my clear duty on learning of the hanky-panky in the tribunal below would have been to alert the appellate court.

Disbarment would be the inevitable and deserved result of my being caught.

Yet I was actually exhilarated! I was strangely clear in my mind and heart that I was not only justified but praiseworthy in my act of judicial subornation. I say "strangely," not because I have changed my opinion today, but because, in view of all the horror that ensued, it does seem curious that I should not have had more doubts. I think I may have felt some still unsettled debt to the great nation that had rescued my family from the sad poverty of its origin. I had believed in the American system, in hard work, in getting ahead, in a society that at least tried to be fair to the individual if that individual had only some respect for it. I had prospered in that society, and now there was something I could do to show my gratitude.

A coverup, the listener will shriek. How could anyone feel that way about a coverup? But remember that the term has been given a particularly foul name by Watergate. Who knows how many of the heroes and inspiring events of our history do not owe some of their luster to coverups? Are we absolutely sure that secret tapes in the White House would not have told us some very disturbing things about Thomas Jefferson and Abraham Lincoln? And be frank now, you who hear this tape. Supposing — just supposing — it had been possible to cover up the Watergate break-in and spare the world a knowledge that has disillusioned millions with the very concept of democratic government. Would you not have done so?

The basic moral question is whether or not he who covers up believes, with any basis of reason, that the criminal will not repeat his crime. I believed, certainly, that Forrest had taken only one bribe and that he would never take another. And I accepted — and still accept — the principle that the concealer of a crime must be condemned, legally and perhaps even morally (though the latter may seem illogical), if his attempt fails. His is a lonely decision. He has taken the law into his own hands. He must not complain if he is caught. He has elected to be his own judge and jury. He has sentenced himself.

But I refuse to hang my head; that's the point. Even today.

Pussy, who always seemed indifferent to my enthusiasms, was extremely sensitive to my anxiety.

"You're worried about something," she said, when I was having a double whiskey before dinner on the day that I had delivered my handwritten memorandum to Forrest. "Has it anything to do with Gridley Forrest?"

I could not help staring at her as if she were a witch. "Now what on earth gave you that idea?"

"I had lunch with Mathilde today."

"You did? I thought you never lunched with her."

"Well, she joined me at the club. She wanted to talk to me. She's afraid that Gridley's having some kind of a nervous breakdown. Very moody and can't sleep at night. Drinks more than usual." Here Pussy glanced at my dark glass. "She thought he might have told you something about it."

"When?"

"In one of your golf games."

"We haven't played in two months. Perhaps he's worried about his work. It can be a heavy burden to be a judge."

"It would be for me, I'm sure. But for Gridley? I should have thought he was the perfect Solomon. Utterly cold and detached."

"Perhaps he's worried about Mathilde's bills. She lives very grandly for the wife of a federal judge."

"Well, that's his fault. He should put her on a budget."

"I didn't say it wasn't his fault," I retorted testily. "I was attempting to explain his anxiety."

Pussy considered this for a moment. "Yes. It would be hateful to be married to Mathilde if you couldn't give her everything she wanted."

"You've never really liked Mathilde, have you?"

"Oh, 'liked,' " Pussy shrugged. "Does one really like or dislike childhood friends? It's a special relationship."

It was not long after this that rumors began to circulate in the downtown bar that Judge Forrest was on the take. The first one that I heard was from one of my partners at lunch. It was Tom Tray, a younger man, very serious, a dedicated lawyer for whose rise in the firm I had been directly responsible.

"I know you're a friend of Judge Forrest's," he told me gravely. "That's why I wanted to be sure you know what people are saying. No matter how unfounded it may be."

"They're saying he sells his decisions?"

"They are."

"How can people be so irresponsible?"

But Tom did not even shake his head. "They say his wife's a reckless spender. Isn't it the oldest story in the world?"

"But a circuit judge, Tom!"

Tom gave me what I thought was a rather queer look. "I guess they're not all angels."

A week later the story broke. Gridley Forrest was indicted for bribery. The news ran in mammoth headlines. In that less sophisticated era when, to quote the disillusioned Macbeth, we were "but young in deed," the public outrage reached a pitch almost inconceivable today. We had not seen both a President and a Vice President resign from office under fire. But my personal dismay may be imagined when I read in the newspapers that the United States attorney had selected as the basis for his prosecution *only two* cases of Forrest's alleged sale of decisions. And these, according to general rumor, were but the tip of the iceberg! Forrest had apparently been seeking money wherever he could find it. To shore up his collapsing little empire of stores and warehouses in Queens and Brooklyn he had been desperately bartering justice to the first comer, receiving every kind of shady middleman in his very chambers, talking unguardedly on a tapped telephone, even committing himself to signed memoranda!

But my dismay was equaled only by my consternation on the morning when I faced the indicted judge himself seated before my desk. Gridley Forrest was actually asking me to represent him! He was as grave and impassive as if he were having a drink at the Greenvale Club after one of our golf games. None of the tenseness of which Pussy had spoken was visible now.

"Of course you're pleading guilty," I managed to articulate.

"Guilty? Certainly not. I deny the whole ridiculous business."

"But, Gridley! You *know* what I know!"

"Never mind what you know or don't know. It will be your job to see that the U.S. attorney proves his case. *If* he can. There is no end of hurdles that can be set up. Hearsay, privilege, malicious intent to defame a judge, even entrapment."

"You mean you're really going to fight this?"

"To the end!"

For several moments I sought words in the angry red tumult of my mind. Then I gave up. "Not with me, Judge."

"You mean you decline to represent me?"

"Absolutely."

Oh, that gray metallic stare of his! It was the last time I ever saw it. Or him.

"You'll let down a friend in need? Take care, Fabbri. The friend in need may let *you* down."

I rose. "Good day, Judge."

卐

Unlike my former friend, I did not fight my accusers. When the Bar Association, acting on the evidence introduced in the trial by Forrest's attorney of my participation in the patent case, instituted disbarment proceedings against me, I was permitted to resign as an attorney in the state of New York upon admission of the charges. Although I was not technically disbarred, my disgrace was complete. I have been able to make only a small living since as a real estate broker. But for the sale of my art collection I should at times have suffered actual need.

The hardest part of the whole business was my family. Pussy greeted my misfortune as an early Christian might have greeted the chance to detach a centurion from a Roman legion and lead him with her to the glory of martyrdom. Her nobility in disaster was almost unendurable. The only thing that kept me from leaving her was that she left me. She was so horrified when I told her that I felt no repentance that she moved for a time to her old mother's. But when she came back, it was to accept me, brazen and unrepentant as I was. We managed to remain on civil terms until her death two years ago.

Tom took the drastic step of changing his name. I believe that he did this to show that he was not afraid of incurring the odium of deserting a parent in trouble. It takes guts for a gentleman to look like a cad, but Tom had those guts. He detested my crime and deplored my intransigence; he saw no alternative but to cut himself off from me forever. I simply hope that he has not regretted it. If he has, he has shown no signs of it. He is a successful physician and has a large family that I have never seen. God bless him.

Alma accepted me and my crime. It was happy for me that in marrying she was able to shed my name without a moral problem. Her children are almost cozy with me; they think I was a "victim of my time," whatever that means. Alma has a comfortable theory that I was confused between an Italian Catholic upbringing and something she calls "the Protestant ethic." Between them, anyway, I am considered virtually without blame, a dear old wop grandpa who is not to be taken quite seriously.

There is a young man today, however, who is writing a Ph.D. thesis for Columbia on the implications of the Forrest case. He has been to see me several times, and I have come to like him. He has a theory that Gridley Forrest was subconsciously trying to destroy the judicial system of the United States in revenge for not having been appointed a justice of the Supreme Court. He was delighted when I supplied him with the confirming evidence of Gridley's hatred of FDR. I do not know if I believe in his theory, but it certainly gives a dignity to my saga which is preferable to Mathilde's shopping bills.

Portrait of the Artist
by Another

1987

THE REPUTATION of Eric Stair, who was little known at the time of his death in the Normandy invasion of 1944, has grown steadily in the last four decades, and the retrospective show this year at the Guggenheim has given him a sure place among the abstract expressionists, although that term was not used in his lifetime. Walking down the circular ramp past those large imperial bursts of color, those zigzagging triangles of angry red piercing areas of cerulean blue which seem to threaten, in retaliation, to encompass and smother the triangles, those green submarine regions occupied by polyp-like figures, those strangely luminous squares of inky black, I wondered that there could ever have been a time when Eric Stair had not struck me as a wonderful painter. And yet I could well remember myself as a fifteen-year-old schoolboy at St. Lawrence's in 1934 staring with bewilderment at the daubs of the new history teacher from Toronto, who had turned his dormitory study into a studio. Nothing could have seemed stranger or more out of place on that New England campus than an abstract painter who was rumored not even to believe in God.

My bewilderment, at any rate, had not lasted long; I had soon become an admirer of the man without whose example I might never have become a professional painter at all. Not that I have become an abstract expressionist. Far from it. What, I wonder, would Eric have thought of my portraits? Would he have simply raised those rounded shoulders and grinned his square-faced grin at the sight of all those presidents of clubs and corporations, those eminent doctors and judges who make up the portfolio of the man sometimes known as a "boardroom portraitist"? "Jamie Abercrombie," I seem to hear him saying, "may have made it into the world of art, but he has certainly carted all his lares and penates along with him!"

What I suppose I shall never fathom, no matter how deeply I dive into the subaqueous caverns of the past, is the exact balance between benefit and detriment that I derived as a painter from my juvenile acquaintance with Eric Stair. If it be true that his example deflected me from the paths of banking or law, it may also be the case that, discerning early how much he could accomplish in the field of the abstract, I became too fearful of competing with him there. Maybe I slammed that door prematurely. Maybe I was too anxious, in confining my art to portraiture, to hide away in a world where Eric would never seek to follow or humiliate me.

And there is another thing. I can face it now I am growing old. Without what happened at that school might I not have painted the nude? When I cast my inner eye over the long gallery of my portraits, it strikes me how covered up the figures are, how draped and buttoned and tucked in, how expensively and colorfully added to, how bolstered and propped! Even my ladies in evening dress seem to reveal to me, in their alabaster arms and necks, in the exposed portions of their breasts and shoulders, how much more they are hiding from intrusive eyes. It has been said of Philippe de Champaigne that, being obliged as a strict Jansenist to eschew the flesh, he limited himself to ecclesiastical or judiciary subjects where all but the face and hands could be enveloped in voluminous robes, white or black or scarlet red. The peak of his great art was in the portrait of Cardinal Richelieu, where the sweeping cassock expresses the power and energy of the ruthless statesman. I have sometimes in preliminary sketches attempted to convey the character of my sitter in the suit or dress alone, as a kind of reverse nude. But that is as near as I ever come to it.

At any rate, all I can do is write down the facts, at least as they appear to me, and see if some kind of answer can be deduced from them.

⁂

I grew up with a feeling of "not belonging." Some people claim that this has become so common a social phenomenon that the rare state is that of the child who feels himself a square peg in a square hole, but in my case the psychosis may have been intensified by my being the youngest, smallest and most subdued of a clan of Abercrombies who were generally large and noisy, and by my own uneasy suspicion that even if by some trick of fate I should become a true Abercrombie, I'd still be a fraud. For I cannot recall a time when my family did not seem to be trying to look brighter and funnier and richer and more fashionable than they were. Or was that true of everybody in the years of the Great Depression?

Mother dominated us all, as a famous old actress will dominate the stage. She was plump and rackety and full of high spirits, and she adored company. Her rich auburn hair, which surprisingly was not dyed, rose in a high curly pile over a round powdered face with small features and popping black eyes. Mother was thoroughly unintellectual and unartistic; she read nothing but detective fiction, and she never tired of cards or gossip. What saved her from being banal was the quality of her affections; she loved people, and she loved to laugh with them and at them. She was the presiding spirit of the summer colony in Southampton; a watering place was her natural milieu. She would amble down the sand to the Beach Club, close to our shapeless, weatherbeaten shingle pile on the dunes, and then back; these two sites made up her summer universe, except, of course, for the houses in which she habitually dined. Poor Mother! When the Depression obliged us to give up the brownstone in Manhattan, and she had to spend the winter months gazing out on the tumbling gray Atlantic, it was a hardship indeed. But her spirits never flagged. She always found just enough "natives" for her daily game of bridge.

It sometimes seemed to me, because my siblings so strongly favored Mother, that I should have inherited some of Father's traits, but I could never really believe this to be the case. Father did not seem to have many traits to bequeath; his function must have been completed when the queen bee had been fertilized. Yet he was not subservient to Mother. He acted more like an old and familiar employee, a kind of trusted but peppery superintendent whose management of the household was never challenged. Father was bald and stooping; he would gaze at us with watery eyes that seemed to anticipate nothing but irrational conduct that it would be his tedious task to clean up after. His other children took him entirely for granted; only I made an effort to establish a relationship with him, and here I failed utterly. When I would ask him questions about his boyhood and the problems of growing up, he would look at me as if I had inquired as to the whereabouts of the washroom. Human intimacy must have struck him as a total irrelevance.

I realize now, looking back, that some of my sense of our being on the fringe of society may have been justified. We were as "old" as many other families, but we were a good deal poorer than the average in the world to which we clung. Father, so far as I could make out, had nothing and did nothing, other than to sell an occasional insurance policy, and Mother's trust fund was woefully inadequate to pay the bills with which she was constantly dunned. Of course, our state was a common one in the Depression, but when club dues and school tuitions were left unpaid while Mother continued to entertain and gamble, she and Father came in for some harsh criticism. And I was early assailed by the uncomfortable feeling that, because I was plain and unathletic, I could not claim the partial exemption from social contempt that my exuberant, party-loving older siblings, no doubt unfairly, achieved. I deemed myself hopelessly encased in the parental tackiness.

There seemed, at any rate, just enough cash (plus a partial scholarship) to send me to St. Lawrence's, and I entered that school with a sense of profound relief. Here, I hoped, I would not stand out as the child of my parents; I would be on my own. The whole tightly organized academy, with its ringing bells and hurrying boys, with everything happening at exactly the time it was supposed to happen, struck me from the start as a welcome proof that a world existed outside the papier-maché one of the Abercrombies, a "real" world, properly possessed of order and neatness, of heaven and hell. I found absolution in its regularity and blessing in its very sternness, and I became an overnight convert to the conservative social values that it enshrined. Even today, when I visit the school and behold the tall dark Gothic tower of the school chapel rise over the trees as I approach it from the railway station, I feel that actuality, even if it be a rather grim one, is taking the place of illusion.

St. Lawrence's was considered architecturally a handsome school. Some four hundred boys slept and worked and exercised in long Tudor buildings of purple brick picturesquely situated along a creek that wound its snakelike way through the landscaped grounds. Sometimes, particularly in spring, the place seemed to exude a rich, throat-filling emotion, but in winter, under rapidly dirtying snow and a hard pale sky, it took on a somber gloom, and the narrow mullioned windows put me in mind of Tudor prisons, of Tudor discipline, of pale, tight-lipped Holbein victims and torturers, of the ax and stake. Emotion was never light at St. Lawrence's; life was always earnest. I thought of Christ, as the near-mystic headmaster evoked him, the Christ of the passion, whose nails and thorns were far more than symbols, an elongated tortured gray body hideously twisted on the cross and illuminated by streaks of lightning against a weird, flickering El Greco background.

There was some hazing in the first year, but being small and inconspicuous and having learned early the art of protective coloration, I passed largely unnoticed and was able to make my early peace with the school. I became fascinated with the figure of the headmaster, Mr. Widdell, a tall, bony, balding, emaciated man, himself a bit of an El Greco, who preached sermons with such intense zeal that he alarmed some of the parents. It began to seem to me, listening to him, awestruck, on Sunday mornings, that he was the nearest thing to God I should ever experience, that for me it would be enough if he *were* God. And I rightly inferred that in his capacity of deity, as opposed to that of a busy and overtaxed headmaster, he would have as much interest in the one as in the many, that his love (yes, his love!) could include me as well as the faculty, the student body, the harassed Irish maidservants and the grave, slow-moving old men who took care of the grounds and were known to the boys as the "sons of rest." I had the nerve, or the inspiration, to take my doubts to Mr. Widdell himself.

"Yes, Jamie, of course, you can ask me any question you like. That is what I am here for."

I sat, a huddled little bundle of nothing, across the great square desk from the aquiline nose, those huge, glassy eyes. Between us was the white stainless blotter of his total attention.

"It is the commandment about honoring my father and mother, sir. I wonder if I can honestly say that what I feel for them is honor."

Mr. Widdell's gravity did not seem to deepen at this, and my confidence grew with this further assurance of omniscience. "Let me ask you just one thing, Jamie. Do you love your father and mother?"

"I love my mother, sir. My father doesn't seem to have much to do with love."

"But you have no aversion to him?"

"Oh, none, sir."

"Well, then, your case may not be as bad as you fear. Love of one parent is a good start. Can you tell me why it is that you feel you cannot honor them?"

"It does not seem to me, sir, that they lead lives that I can honor. My father is occupied with very small things, like winding clocks and seeing the oil is changed in the car. And my mother plays cards and gossips. I mean, sir, that is *all* she does."

"But the commandment is not to honor their conduct, Jamie. It is to honor *them.*"

"No matter what they do?"

"No matter what they do."

"Even if they're thieves and murderers?"

There was a gleam of something like a smile in those glistening eyes. "Hadn't we better wait till we get to it before crossing that bridge?" The total gravity, however, soon reestablished itself. "Seriously, my boy, you must consider that God expects of his children only what they can give and only in the way they can give it. Your father, in his daily maintenance of the household, and your mother, in the cheer that she imparts to others, may be doing more for God than you suspect. In any event, it is not for you to judge them. And not judging them, you will find that you can and indeed will honor them."

I left the presence on wings of elation. How easily did he dispose of my nagging problems! And, on his side, feeling that he had done something for me, the great man warmed to me. He always greeted me now, when we passed on campus, and I was on several occasions honored with the much coveted invitation to breakfast at the headmaster's house. I worshiped Mr. Widdell. It was as if I had died and gone to a paradise where everything fell into its proper place. God ruled us with an awesome benevolence, and under his sway all was for the best. Resentments and harsh criticisms of one's family were as unnecessary as they were presumptuous. How did one know that they, too, were not serving to the best of their capacity? Beyond the walls of the school lay a nation throttled in depression, but what did these few minutes of misery matter in the blaze of eternity? I learned from the headmaster that although it is our bounden duty to alleviate the sufferings of the human body, our first concern must always be with the soul. Perhaps too hastily I found myself willing to render unto Caesar just about anything Caesar claimed was his. I did not then understand that Mr. Widdell was different from me in that he had something of the saint in him and that to those who were less than saints his doctrine had pitfalls.

I had drawn pictures since I was a child, and now I took to sketching in earnest. I drew the chapel, the altar, the reredos; I made copies of the stained glass windows and illustrated biblical stories. Some of my things were reproduced in the school magazine, and I felt very holy indeed. I must have been quite unbearable.

It was in the fall of my fifth form and next-to-last year that Eric Stair, then aged twenty-five, joined the faculty of St. Lawrence's. He was a Canadian, from Toronto, an artist who had come down to New York to work on a mural in a bank, the contract for which had been canceled for lack of funds. Jobless and penniless, he had been recommended by the bank president, a St. Lawrence graduate, to fill a vacancy in the school's history department. He certainly did not seem the type for a New England prep school; he was short, heavyset and muscular, with a craggy face, small, suspicious, staring eyes and thick, messy red hair. There was a rumor that Mr. Widdell had asked him if he was willing to attend all chapel services and received the answer that he was willing — if he didn't have to pray. He was reserved and minimally polite, and seemed to look about him at the boys and the school with a faint bemusement, as if not quite believing they could be true. But his personality was strong; he had no difficulty keeping discipline. The boys knew a man when they saw one.

I had a double connection with the new master, for I was in his dormitory as well as in his class of European history. As I was very much of a "mark hound," seeking to make up for my small stature and athletic nullity with high grades, and as history had been my best subject, I was inclined to show off in class discussions. Mr. Stair watched me with a sardonic eye. He was not impressed.

"But Germany started the war, sir," I protested, when he questioned the wisdom of the sanctions imposed at Versailles. "She was greedy and cruel. The Kaiser wanted to take over the whole British empire."

"And hadn't the British wanted to take it over?"

"But the British had it, sir!"

"Hadn't they wanted it before they had it? If coveting empires be a crime, shouldn't we start our sanctions in London?"

"Well, even if there were some wrong things about acquiring their empire, haven't the British made up for it by using it as a force for civilization and world peace?"

"How wonderful that I, a colonial, should learn the glories of empire from a Yankee lad with a Scottish tag!"

The class chuckled; I was deeply humiliated.

"But whether or not the Kaiser wanted to rule the world," Mr. Stair continued, "I think we might find him easier to deal with today than this new chap, Hitler."

I could not avoid the temptation to reinstate myself in favor by impressing him with my special knowledge. "Quite so, sir. After all, the Kaiser was a grandson of Queen Victoria."

But the old queen's name did not have the magic with a "colonial" that I had anticipated.

"Is that so, Abercrombie? Well, let me ask you something. Do you know how many individuals were in domestic service in the United Kingdom when Victoria the Good breathed her last in 1901?"

"No, sir."

"More than two million. Does that tell you anything about the reign of the good queen?"

"Only that the stately homes must have been kept spick-and-span."

"Not a bad answer, Abercrombie. I can think of others."

When he gave me only a B on my paper on the influence of Colonel House on Wilson, an essay that I had entitled rather flamboyantly "Gray Eminence," and I protested to him, he replied:

"You see history too dramatically, Abercrombie. Your mind is full of kings and cardinals and royal mistresses. You must learn that it's also full of little people. Slaves. Serfs. Abercrombies. Stairs."

Stair did not advocate any political policies, domestic or international, in his classroom. Like Socrates, he simply questioned everything. But because a certain antiestablishmentarianism emanated from his very failure to enunciate or endorse any of the usual school values, he became popular with the more sophisticated members of my form, who saw in cultivating him a way of developing their own independence of home and academic rule, an independence that largely boiled down to the desire to indulge in activities neither permitted nor even possible on the campus: smoking, drinking and necking. Talking more freely than they could to other masters in Stair's study before "lights," they could at least pretend they were doing those things.

My own position with Stair was different. Because I was determined to make him give me better marks, I studied ways to please him, and I soon discovered that, for all his craggy integrity, he was not entirely immune to flattery. My genuine fascination at his utter freedom from all my hang-ups may have tempered the unctuosity of my approach and made me less objectionable. He was also amused by my drawings and in helping me to improve them. Although I could at first make nothing of the dots and squiggles of his own abstract designs, subjects of considerable mirth in our dormitory when he was not present, I was already enough of an artist to perceive that the few strong lines he would introduce into one of my sketches had radically improved it.

I was very much surprised and pleased when he asked me to sit for a charcoal sketch, although I could not help asking why an artist of his school needed a model.

"I do not limit myself to abstracts, Abercrombie," he retorted. "Every now and then I feel inclined to do a likeness."

"Why me, in particular?"

"Let's put it that I want to catch the spirit of this remarkable academy in which I find myself. As the headmaster is not an available sitter, I must seek the next closest. I think you may do very nicely."

I knew him too well now to take this as a compliment, but I was nonetheless flattered to be considered the "spirit" of anything. Something, however, a bit more serious than his gibing came out on the second and final sitting.

Stair had a bad cold and was in a foul mood, something rather rare with him. I made the mistake of asking him why he thought me representative of the school.

"You're not," he snapped. "You're representative of what they're trying to turn the boys into."

"And what is that?"

"A man who believes in the whole bloody mess." He worked vigorously for a silent minute on his sketch, as if he were cutting me into slices. "For God, for country and for a small New England church school named for a minor saint roasted on the gridiron by Romans who, perhaps because of their very lack of imagination, may have had some small glimmer of reality."

"And the other boys don't believe in that?"

"They take it for granted, which is different. I suppose one can't really blame them. They're cooped up here nine months out of the year. Hardly a whiff of the Great Depression outside gets through. Their families are basically unaffected. Oh, true, they've had to give up a butler or an extra cook, or close down the cottage in Maine or the fishing camp, and a few, perhaps, have actually gone to smash, but they're mostly still rich — stinking rich in contrast to ninety-nine percent of the other ants in the heap. And I suppose it's only human not to give a damn about other humans. If their parents and teachers don't, why the hell should they? But you, my lad, are a different breed. You have some kind of pygmy sense of the misery outside the gates, but you resent it. You fear it. You're like my old granny in Toronto. You think the poor are poor because they drink."

"Aren't you being a bit stiff with me, sir?"

"I don't think so. And you don't have to 'sir' me when we're alone. Well, all right, you may not be as bad as my granny, but you believe in the upper classes. You believe the Royal Navy is keeping the peace, and the British tommy is preventing his little black and yellow brothers from killing each other, and that over here, in God's country, Mr. J. P. Morgan is fighting to keep the madman in the White House from wrecking the economy. Isn't that about how you see it?"

"Well, I certainly don't think everything's so fine in the Soviet Union."

"That's right. Win the argument by calling me a commie." He made a vigorous stroke now, as if he were slashing a line through my countenance. But he wasn't. A model was a model, however much of a fascist.

"Well, *aren't* you a socialist?"

"Never you mind what I am, sonny. I told the headmaster when I came here that I wasn't going to be political, and I shan't be. But that doesn't mean I can't prick an occasional bubble of self-satisfaction."

I was thoroughly angry now. If he wasn't to be "sirred," he could take potluck in the dialogue. "If anyone pricked yours, it might blow up the campus!"

Stair threw back his head at this and emitted a roar of laughter. "So you can bite back. Good. There may be hope for you yet." He paused, his head to one side as he contemplated his work. "Well, I guess that's it," he said in a milder tone. "Want to have a look at it?"

That look may have changed my life. For what I saw in that dark, brooding, huddled figure, drawn with amazing power in so scant a number of strokes, was something more than the fear and the resentment in the features. These emotions I had known about. What I saw for the first time was the intensity of concern in the eyes fastened on the painter. The boy was alive! Alive as the painter was alive! It had never occurred to me that I was alive. And it had certainly never occurred to me that a painter obsessed with geometrical figures that were never completed, lines that went nowhere and dots that floated in limbo, could be the one to prove my existence. "I am in a Stair drawing," I could murmur after Descartes, "therefore I am!" I knew then and there that I was in the presence of a great artist.

From now on I attached myself, as much as the school schedule permitted, to Eric Stair. Perhaps because he regretted the harshness of his strictures on one so young, perhaps because every man has a corner in his heart for a worshiping slave, a devoted spaniel, he tolerated me. He even allowed himself at times to be amused by me. And he gave me serious instruction now in my art.

The headmaster, the angels, the glory of God, disappeared in a clap of thunder like Kundry's castle in *Parsifal*. I made desperate plans in my mind — not daring to tell my family — of skipping college and going straight to art school. And then there came a chance of actually introducing my new hero to my family.

Mother and Father never came up to school, but in the Easter vacation of that year they had received the loan of a large apartment in New York from a cousin of Mother's, and all the Abercrombies moved joyfully into town. I had a room with two beds, so I could have a guest, and when I heard that Mr. Stair had no place to go over Easter and was planning to stay at the school, I made bold to invite him to come to us. He accepted, with evident surprise, but with alacrity. I did not know at the time that he had a girlfriend in New York.

He and Mother hit it off immediately. I was rather disgusted to note that she seemed to be actually flirting with him! They both showed me sides of themselves I had not seen before: Eric lost his sardonic, superior, detached school air and was full of chuckles and slightly off-color jokes, while Mother showed a concern about modern art and letters that I had not previously suspected.

"Your ma likes a man around," Eric told me one morning when we were alone at breakfast. "She hasn't totally forgotten she's a woman."

I was a bit shocked. "Why should she? She has Father."

"What is it they say? Thirty years is a long time with the same piece of meat?"

"If you're implying, Mr. Stair, that my mother —"

"Isn't dead below the waist? Yes, I am, my friend. Of course, no son can abide the idea that his mother is subject to sexual urges. But that doesn't mean she's neuter."

I was startled by this idea of Mother, so stout and matronly. But my respect for Eric was all-encompassing. What I minded far more than the impertinence of his suggestions was the ease with which Mother had taken him away from me.

He was not, however, as it turned out, discussing sex — or even the fantasy of it — between himself and Mother. He was discussing sex between himself and somebody else. What Mother was doing, incurable romantic (like so many gossips) that she was, was persuading him to marry his girlfriend then and there and present the headmaster, at the beginning of the spring semester, with a fait accompli. And she succeeded. One morning at breakfast, as she beamed at him down the table, Stair announced to my bewildered and disapproving self that he and I and Mother would be going at noon to the Municipal Building, where he was to be joined in wedlock to a Miss Janice Hart.

Mother had not met Miss Hart, and even she was a bit disillusioned when we encountered this handsome, marble-faced, raven-haired, and only too evidently efficient and officious young woman in the little lavender room where the godless marry without benefit of clergy. Miss Hart would have given the back of her hand or worse to a priest. She greeted Mother and me in a clipped, perfunctory manner and proceeded to take over Eric and instruct him on what had to be done as if he were a tousled schoolboy and she a matron who could spare little time with recalcitrant pupils. When we repaired to our apartment afterwards to drink a bottle of champagne, she offered a mock toast to the school whose faculty family she was about to join.

"To St. Lawrence's Academy for conspicuous consumers!" she announced in a loud clear tone. "May we help to move it into the twentieth century!" Then she turned to Eric. "Or must we get it into the nineteenth first?"

What did he see in her? Or she in him? I suppose he saw a splendid figure possessed by a woman able and willing to dedicate it to his sexual delight. And I suppose she may have divined in him the artistic genius that she hoped she would one day to able to harness to the Communist cause. For that she was a Communist I had little doubt, even if she did not carry an actual card. She was committed, I felt sure, not only to the overthrow of the government by force but to the overthrow of just about everything else. Certainly she was willing to overthrow Mother and me, bidding farewell to the former with a casual: "Thanks, old dear; you made an admirable Cupid," while pulling me aside and whispering in my ear an anatomical precaution against the presumed sexual aggression of other boys at St. Lawrence's.

Mr. Widdell was startled, no doubt, when Eric arrived at school with a wife, but he declined Mrs. Stair's offer to stay at a local inn while her husband continued to manage his dormitory, and provided them with a tiny vacant apartment in the house for visiting parents, filling Stair's dormitory position with a bachelor master. The faculty and wives were no doubt astonished by Janice's personality, but she behaved herself better than might have been expected, was decently civil to all and spent most of her time in her apartment working on what we much later found out was a tract against the crimes of private education in New England.

The Stairs, of an occasional Saturday evening, would ask some of his old dormitory boys to drop in for cider and cookies, and on these occasions Janice showed herself more relaxed. She enjoyed twitting us about our "plutocratic" backgrounds while Eric puffed at his pipe and sardonically listened. With me, however, she was distinctly less friendly, her woman's intuition having already gleaned that I had the presumption to dispute her absolute ownership of Eric.

One night when she was descanting on the glories of the Russian revolution, I expressed horror at the brutal massacre of the czar and his family.

"Well, you've heard about making omelets and what it does to the eggs," she snapped.

"I don't see how any omelet could be worth gunning down those four lovely daughters and that poor little boy."

"Oh, that bothers Jamie, does it?" she asked sarcastically. "It distresses him that four spoiled brats and a hopeless bleeder should bite the dust? I won't say anything about Papa and Mama, for I guess even you might concede that a couple so bigoted and harebrained as to turn their country over to a crazy monk deserved what they got. Oh, sure, I'd have spared the kids. But what the hell difference does it make, weighed against centuries of injustice, starvation and torture?"

My dislike of my rival helped me to say what would most infuriate her. "You believe, then, that two wrongs make a right?"

"I believe that the undesirable classes do not eliminate themselves!"

"And you, I'm sure, would make a clean sweep of everyone at St. Lawrence's."

"No, I'd pick and choose. But I think I'd start with a snotty kid from Long Guyland."

Now her husband had had enough. "Oh, dry up, Janice. That'll do for Russia for one night. Go home, boys."

On another evening we had an even sharper clash. It was after a forest fire that had come close enough to the school to necessitate the faculty and students joining the local firefighters and members of the recently formed Civilian Construction Corps in combating the blaze.

It had been a startling experience for me. Never before had I been thrown into the company of a large troop of men, most of whom came from what my father called the "lower orders." As the area in which we were stationed was not touched by the fire, which had been brought under control after only a few hours, we had nothing to do but stand about and listen to the men talk. Talk perhaps is not quite the term. What I heard up and down the hillside and across the field where we were scattered was the exchange of obscene words, creating a kind of buzz across the countryside, like a swarming of bees. It seemed to me that all the men about me were talking at once, that nobody was listening, that there was no thought to communicate, that it was rather a litany that was being chanted, even a kind of bead-telling, that their sentences, insofar as they were sentences, were only nouns strung together to give a reason to filthy adjectives. At first I thought they were trying to shock the schoolboys, but at last I realized that I was being initiated into the habitual discourse of young male America.

When I told the Stairs about it, Eric, who had been out with us, was amused.

"Come on in," he grunted. "The water's fine!"

But Janice was odious. She put her arm over my shoulders in mock sympathy.

"Was little Jamie-Wamie shocky-wocky by big bad men? Did they talk too dirty-wirty?"

I shook her off, furious. "It's not a question of being shocked. Although, yes, I was shocked. But what shocked me was how those men

stripped every bit of natural color and beauty out of the whole countryside. They turned it all to a revolting brown."

"If you mean shit, why don't you say shit?"

"Because that's just the point! I *don't* want to say it. It's saying it that
makes it that, don't you see?"

"I guess I don't see, honey."

"You don't see anything!" I cried, released at last by my fury. "And
you couldn't if you tried. What a person to be married to a painter!"

"Go home, Abercrombie," Stair snarled.

"And good riddance!" his wife added.

"Let the kid be," he told her sharply, and it pleased me, as I left the
room, to think they might be going to have a real row.

But if I thought I was going to improve my position with Eric Stair,
I had a lot to learn about marriage, or at least about marriage in its first
year. Eric, I think, had a certain tenderness for the boy who admired
him as I did, but he was not going to allow this to get between him and
the angry, passionate creature he possessed every night. If Jamie Abercrombie had to be sacrificed to her jealousy, he could only shrug his
shoulders and comply. And, after all, Jamie Abercrombie *was* a bit
ridiculous, wasn't he?

Why did she object to me quite so violently? I suppose because she
begrudged the smallest patch of the territory of Eric Stair to anyone
else. Had I paid my court to her, had I pretended to be a convert to her
radical views, she might have allowed me a few square inches of Eric,
provided she could have them back on demand. But she correctly read
the resistance, nay, the hate, in my sullen gaze; she wanted to kick me,
as a cat-hater wants to kick the small black creature, humped up and
staring, that she knows she can neither win over nor fool.

It was now that I developed my theory that Janice Stair was a fatal
presence in her husband's artistic career. If she had originally conceived
the idea that she might convert his brush and palette into tools to
further the proletariat revolution, her jealousy now saw in them mu-
tinous soldiers conspiring to thwart her absolute rule. I had noted her
hostility to abstract art. Of course! How can one arouse the downtrod-
den with dots and lines? I began to indulge in fantasies in which I would
bravely face up to Eric's fury and denounce her machinations to him,
confident that after the raging storm was over, the broken bedraggled
man, a drowned Lear or fool, would seek the humble hut of Jamie's

forgiveness, clasp one of my hands in both of his large ones and murmur: "You've been a good friend, my boy. I see it now. Oh, I see it all!"

And then came the terrible time when a quirk of fate placed it in my power to convert my fantasy into a grotesque reality. God knows how different my life might otherwise have been. Or does he?

Our dormitory, placed in what had originally been intended for a large attic, had a curious zigzag shape, and my cubicle, at the very end, had a window that looked out, as did none of the others, on the visiting parents' house, so that the window of the Stairs' bedroom, on the same level, was only some sixty feet away. One night after lights, just as I was dropping off to sleep, I heard a step on the floor by my bed and sat up quickly to make out a pajama-clad figure standing there. I was about to hiss an angry "I don't play dirty games, thank you," for I was intensely puritanical about certain boarding school practices, when a voice whispered:

"Let's see if we can't see Mrs. Stair's bare ass."

It was Tommy Agnew, our dormitory prefect, a sixth former and captain of the football team. He sat down in the chair by the window to stare into the lit but empty interior across the way, and I sat up politely for a time with him. Any interest in female anatomy was considered sacred, and besides, he was a prefect. At last, however, I grew tired and fell asleep.

The next morning, in the washroom, while brushing our teeth, I asked Tommy if he'd had any success.

"Well, not for hours," he complained, as if he'd suffered an actual injustice. "I thought those people would never go to bed! But when they did, yes, it was worth it." Agnew paused to expectorate into the basin. "That woman doesn't even use a nightgown. Or at least she was bare-assed when she came to pull the shade. Jesus, what tits! And before she pulled the shade down, she gave a sort of sexy twitch of her ass. I think she may have suspected some boy was watching."

"That was generous of her," I observed sourly.

Tommy's information agitated me greatly. All that day I was in a kind of fever. How did that slut dare to intrude her naked loins and breasts and buttocks into the sanctity of a male church school? My mind fulminated with biblical anathemas, and I heaped logs on the crackling fire of my fantasized plans to rescue Stair from his whore of Babylon.

That night I anticipated a flood of visitors to my cubicle to share in

Tommy's discovery, but there were none. The sole sixth former in our dormitory, he must have disdained to share his confidence with juniors, and his own form mates were not allowed in our quarters after lights. Tommy himself, presumably exhausted from his vigil of the night before, did not appear, and I sat by my window in the dark alone.

I think it must have been midnight before she appeared. I had not really thought she would. But she did, and I was choked with hatred and a kind of dizzy lust. When she raised her arms to the shade her fine, large firm breasts jutted at me like two celestial cannons, and, distinctly, before she pulled the curtain she twitched her marble hips. I felt she was looking at me directly, defiantly, imperiously, devastatingly, destroyingly. Then the black shade descended.

That morning I awakened an hour before the rising bell and sketched my memory of that nude figure framed by the window. I worked furiously for the sixty minutes, and I wonder to this day if it wasn't the best thing I've ever done. At the sound of the bell, which almost terrified me with its harsh, jangling, puritanical interruption of my heated and frenetic endeavors, I rose and placed it in my sock drawer. There it was almost sure to be discovered by the snoopy and prudish bachelor, Mr. Morse, who had taken Stair's place as our dormitory master and who was known to investigate both our beds and our bureaus.

Mr. Widdell did not delay in doing what he had to do. He reached into a manila folder, pulled out my drawing and laid it on the desk so that it faced me. "We won't play games with each other, Jamie. Mr. Morse discovered this in your cubicle and thought he had better bring it to my attention. It shows, I believe, a considerable talent. But the subject is not one that I feel is suitable for your artwork. Perhaps later, when you are an adult. I believe there are such things as 'life classes' where you can draw unclad models. But this picture seems to me to have emanated from a fevered imagination. If you have such thoughts, I think you should take more physical exercise. I should like your permission to destroy the drawing, and your promise that you will not reproduce it."

"But it didn't come from my imagination, sir."

"How could it not have? You can't mean that there was a model in the school? And I cannot believe that your parents would have permitted you to attend a life class in vacation."

"No, no, sir, it was something I saw, here at school." I leaned my head over the desk, staring down at its surface, as if struggling with a terrible embarrassment. "I hate to say it, sir, but I don't want you to think that I have a fevered imagination."

In the awful silence that followed I at last looked up. Mr. Widdell's face was stricken with incredulity and dismay.

"You mean, you saw a woman unclothed? *Here* at St. Lawrence's?"

"Yes, sir."

His voice now rose to a bark. "Are you telling me, Abercrombie, that you've been a peeping Tom?"

"No, sir! Please, sir!" I burst into tears. The sudden terror at what I was doing must have had the effect of grief. "I didn't peep. She was right there by the window. For a long time, just like that. She stood there, looking out at the night, and I had plenty of time to study her. I didn't think it was wrong, sir. I thought it was like an art class, as you say, sir."

"She? Who?"

"Mrs. Stair, sir."

"You say you saw Mrs. Stair in that condition? At night?" In the silence, as I waited, I could see that he was mentally correlating the windows of the Stairs' apartment with the windows of my dormitory. "At what time of night?"

"I don't know, sir. It was after lights."

"You shouldn't have been looking out the window. You should have been asleep."

"I know, sir. But I couldn't sleep. It was a warm night, and I got up to sit in my chair by the window."

The headmaster, obviously much agitated, snatched up my drawing and tore it in two. "That will be all, Jamie. We will not speak of this again. You did wrong, but it is understandable. Let us have no more night peerings."

I hesitated as he simply sat there, glaring at me. "Will that be all, sir?"

"That will be all."

"You won't tell Mr. Stair, sir? I mean, he might not understand."

"I shall not mention your name. Now go."

Nobody, including myself, knew just why the Stairs left the school the following week. The headmaster's version — that Mrs. Stair was faced with a serious illness in her family — was believed by no one. It was obviously most unusual for a master and his wife, both apparently in perfect health, to quit before the end of the academic year, with all the trouble to the school of replacing him in his courses, and the enigma was deepened by the fact that the Stairs said goodbye to nobody. They simply disappeared.

Years later I learned that Mr. Widdell had informed Eric that he and his wife were to be moved immediately to a hotel in the village until a new apartment off-campus could be found for them. When Eric had, quite naturally, insisted on a reason, the headmaster had simply replied that Mrs. Stair had been seen by boys in a state of undress at her window. When Eric had demanded indignantly if the headmaster was suggesting that his wife had intentionally exposed herself, and had received no answer, he did the only thing a gentleman could do: he resigned his post after threatening to punch his superior in the nose.

What I did, I suppose, was to suppress, in the psychiatric sense, the whole matter. I simply decided, in the panic that threatened to overwhelm me, that I had to dismiss the subject as far as possible from my mind. I affirmed to myself that there was no necessary connection with what I had wanted to accomplish, that is, the opening up of Eric Stair's eyes to the kind of woman he had married and his sudden detachment from the world in which I lived. I was confident that the headmaster had not disclosed the fact of my artifact; he had, in fact, destroyed it before my eyes. And he never thereafter alluded to the topic. I banished the Stairs from my conversation even at home, responding curtly to Mother's inquiries, and in time I almost came to believe that the episode had not occurred, though I would sometimes wake up in the night with the memory of a nightmare and then, while I was waiting for that soft reassuring feeling that it was all a dream, the horrid notion would steal into my consciousness that it was all too true, and I would jump out of bed and walk briskly to and fro, desperately trying to convince myself that I had blown up the whole matter monstrously out of proportion.

In time I learned to live with myself, and as the years at school and then college passed, it became almost a quaint recollection, like some childish prank that one could tell people about with a smile, even when it was a fairly nasty one. Only I didn't.

Eric had begun to make a name for himself. He had a studio in SoHo, and some of his paintings had been shown at the Whitney and the Museum of Modern Art. I started gradually to allow myself to think about him again, and I would inquire about him, when I was with art enthusiasts who had no reason to suspect that I had known him. I was very excited when I learned that he and Janice had split up and that she had married an active member of the Communist party. Perhaps my now ancient crime had been for the best!

After my graduation from Harvard in the spring of 1939 I came to New York to study at the Art Students League. I determined to call on Eric at his studio, and when I did so, I was cordially received. He occupied a large loft filled with his huge abstracts and seemed contented and cheerful. He acted as if we had parted the day before and did not show the smallest surprise that since our last meeting I had become a man.

After several drinks and much talk of his painting and of mine — he charmingly treated me as an equal — he made a startling suggestion.

"How would you like to take over this studio while I'm gone?"

I looked around me. "But where are you going?"

"I'm going home to sign up. I'll be leaving in a day or so."

I was astonished. Of course he was a Canadian, and of course the war in Europe had started, but somehow I had thought he had joined his destiny with ours.

"You look surprised. I suppose you're recalling that I had it in for the empire." His chuckle seemed quite devoid of partisan feeling. "Well, this war should finish it, anyway, whoever wins. And no matter how I feel about the stately homes and the British Raj, I have to back them against the bad boy in Berlin."

"But your art, Eric!"

"Who gives a blow about art, dear fellow, when the world's on fire? You'll find you'll be coming in yourself. And the beautiful portraits of Jamie Abercrombie will have to wait!"

At that point, a terrible thought struck me. If he and Janice had still been married, they might have had a child or children! He might have had to stay and support them. I leaped to my feet, clapping a hand over my mouth.

"What is it, Jamie? Have you seen a ghost?"

"Yes! Oh, my God!" In that moment I was absolutely convinced that he would be killed. And whose fault would that be? "Eric, I've got to tell you something. I've got to make a confession."

My sorry tale erupted from the mental storage closet where it had been so long and securely kept like a short story read aloud by a proud author, without an "er" or an "ah," in finished sentences. But the author was far from proud. What would Eric do? Would he strangle me? He was strong enough. That craggy face was absolutely expressionless, but I thought there was a glimmer at last of something like amusement in his small blue eyes. When I finished there was a moment's silence. Then he whistled.

"My God, it's like something out of Kraft-Ebing! Those schools should be suppressed."

I stared in disbelief. "Then you don't resent me? You don't think I'm a fiend?"

Eric looked at me with faint surprise. "No, I don't resent you, Jamie. I've made my own life, such as it is, and I've left St. Lawrence's a good way behind me, just as I've left Janice. So none of it matters to me anymore, except that it's amusing. But for you, yes, I guess I can see it's another kettle of fish. Because you have to face the fact that you behaved like a real shit. And there may be some of that shittiness still in you."

How he said that! As pleasantly and with as much detachment as if we'd been discussing a character in fiction. Of course, that made it all the worse. To my own astonishment and shame the tears that I had not shed five years before and that may have been waiting for just this summoning flowed forth, and I found that I was sobbing.

"Jamie, Jamie, my poor fellow," he said, putting an arm around my shoulder, "let it come out — it will do you good. I'll write you from time to time. Just to show you that I'm all right. And that just because you were a shit once doesn't mean that you always have to be one."

I pulled myself together at last, and we went out to dinner and talked of St. Lawrence's until the small hours. He was very funny and mercilessly observant. It seemed there was nothing on that little campus that had escaped his painter's eye. I drank far too much, and he very kindly took me home in a cab. But the next day when I called to thank him he was gone.

He did write me, every few months, during the war, and I received his letters at the Pacific base where I was stationed. Without the mercy of this correspondence I think I might have been emotionally crippled when the news of his death reached me in the summer of 1944. As it is, I have never since been able to draw or paint a nude figure of either sex.

The Reckoning

1987

ROSA KINGSLAND was the same age as the century; she had just passed her sixtieth birthday when she received the final verdict from the Dunstan Sanatorium about her son.

"We are sorry to inform you that not only is there no immediate prospect of Meredith's being able to resume a normal life, but, in the opinion of at least one of our medical staff, it may be years before it will be advisable to release him from the institution. And we are afraid that we cannot advise your further visits while his resentment against his family and home is still so intense."

Rosa stared at the letter, wondering stonily if she were inhuman to see only a bill in its terms. But thirty thousand a year, that was what it added up to, not to mention the other fifteen just to keep her husband in his wheelchair on the floor above. At last slowly, ineluctably, the tears began to bubble up in her resisting eyes. Did tears matter? Did they make her any more absurd than she always had been: a stout Chinese Buddha with a round face and short gray curled hair? But a weeping Buddha — how ridiculous.

Calm again now — as calm and stolid as she usually managed to be — she rose and went to the wall to take down *The Betrothal*, one of Gorky's earlier versions. What should she put in its place? Why, what but what *had* been there, forty-odd years before, in her grandmother's day, and which was still presumably in the attic with the others of the old lady's collection, its face to the wall, the very dearest of dear little Tuscan peasant girls, a pitcher balanced on one shoulder, painted in Florence by Luther Terry in 1876. God.

She turned her reading lamp full on the Gorky and sadly studied it. She knew about the "biomorphic" images drawn from sexual organs, but she had mentally suppressed them. It didn't make any difference what she thought so long as she kept it to herself.

What *she* saw in her Arshile Gorky . . . ah, that was what made the difference. It was simply the most beautiful picture in the world — except for the *Resurrection* of Piero della Francesca that she and Amory had seen at Borgo San Sepolcro and which Aldous Huxley had called the greatest painting ever painted, so that was that. But the Gorky, a symphonic poem of light gray, dark gray and black, with flashes of yellow and red and soothing traces of pale green, evoked for her a fashionable ladies' store on Madison Avenue with round glass-topped tables, lamps on tall steel poles, elegant high-heeled slippers and the suggestion of beautiful women, soft-skinned Circes, worldly-wise, corrupt, stony-hearted. Yet broken up as they were into bits and pieces their menace was muted and their loveliness intensified. It was always so in a world that concealed beauty behind every horror if you could only pull it out. Her imagined ladies made Rosa think of the answer of the Abbé Mugnier to a leering anticleric who had surprised him admiring a painting of nudes bathing: *"C'est un état d'âme, monsieur!"*

She heard the sound of her husband's wheelchair in the corridor and looked up to see the wizened little man squinting at her from the doorway. His eye took in the painting on the floor.

"Poor Rosa," he cackled. "Must that go, too?"

"What else?"

"You could put Merry in a state institution, you know. I would, if I were you."

She noted his "you." Meredith was hers now. This was his way of recognizing that his money had been spent and that they lived on what was left of hers. Oh, yes, it was all hers, for whatever good it might do her, the shabby narrow red brick house with the high Dutch gable on Tenth Street that she had inherited from her grandmother, with the late Victorian horrors for which the old lady had unwisely exchanged her Federal treasures; the dwindling pile of securities at the United States Trust Company; Amory, his wheelchair and senile complaints; and Meredith, dreadful Meredith, at Dunstan. And her pictures. Soon enough, no doubt, to be only a picture. She shuddered at the thought of the Max Ernst downstairs in the tiny gallery that had once been the maids' dining room.

"He'll eat us out of house and home, that's what he'll do," Amory continued petulantly.

"Not so long as I have anything left to sell."

"And how long will that be?"

"A year, maybe."

"I must admit that your crazy things have brought more than any rational man could have guessed. Do you suppose you're selling them too soon?"

"Oh, much too soon! But I didn't buy them to make money."

"And what will you do when the year is out? Though I don't suppose it'll be my problem. I shan't be around much longer." If his pause was to give her the opportunity to contradict his prognostication, it was in vain. "I suppose you can sell this house for a bundle. You won't need more than a couple of rooms then."

"I shall need the house when Meredith comes home."

"And when will that be?"

"When the last picture has been sold."

"Because he'll know there's no more money for his shrinks?"

"No. Because he'll have been cured."

The most shattering discoveries can come very quietly, perhaps because they are not really discoveries. One has suspected them all along. Rosa helped her husband's nurse to push his chair into the tiny elevator, where it just fitted. The nurse closed the door and then descended the narrow stairway to the front hall to meet him and take him for his morning circumnavigation of the block. Rosa, alone in the house, sat on the sofa before the empty grate and allowed the pallid ghosts of her early years to possess her.

She remembered the day when she had told her grandmother about Amory. The old lady had been sitting by the fire in the black silk that she always wore, inattentively nodding that handsome head with the fine Greek profile and high-piled, beautifully set white hair. Her head was like a fine piece of sculpture on a black ball; it moved around on top of a motionless body like an owl's. In her childhood Rosa had used to wonder if she could turn it around entirely and look backwards.

"I'm engaged to Amory Kingsland, Grandma."

"What are you telling me, child? Amory Kingsland? Are you sure you understood him correctly?"

"Quite sure. He was very plain. And anyway, what else could he have meant?"

"What will you live on? I hope he's not counting on me."

"Oh, no, Grandma. He says he can support me. We shan't need a great amount."

Perhaps some memory of her dead son, alcoholic and bankrupt, and of her dead daughter-in-law, victim of an overdose, flickered in the mind of the grandparent. Perhaps even something like remorse. "Well, you'll have what I have when I'm gone, child. It'll be something."

"Oh, Grandma, don't even think of that!"

"I'm sure Amory thinks of it." The old lady snorted. "He must be your senior by twenty years."

"Only fifteen."

"Think of it. Amory Kingsland. Well, I suppose it's better than being the last leaf on the tree."

Rosa thought that it was a good deal better. She knew that tree. It was true that Amory was a fussy, dyspeptic, excitable little man, sputtering with ideas and theories that nobody listened to, and that he had a mincing manner, round soft cheeks and short hair, brushed close to his scalp and parted in the middle, that looked like a wig. And he was always the first on his feet at a banquet to offer a fulsome toast or tribute. But he was harmless and kind, and she fancied that he would not be difficult to live with. He had no job, but he belonged to enough clubs and patriotic societies to ensure his being out of the house a good part of the day.

What was the word for it — symbiosis? If she needed to get away from Granny, he needed a wife to make him look like other men. He was no more attractive to women than she to men. To find a mate, other than each other, they would have had to fish in lower social pools. And she had been right. It had worked.

The only times in the early years that she had found herself impatient with Amory was in their trips to Europe. He fancied himself a connoisseur of the arts and loved to quote John Addington Symonds on the Italian Renaissance. At home Rosa had trained herself not to hear him except for certain phrases that gave her a cue for rejoinders such as: "Really, dear?" or "Amory, you *are* extraordinary," but when they were actually in the presence of a masterpiece she found him tediously distracting. Pictures had always stirred a chord within her that was unlike any other vibration, and she hated to be talked to while viewing one.

On a visit to the Sistine Chapel in the hot summer of 1938 his chatter became suddenly intolerable. He was hopping briskly about, pointing upwards to illustrate the "tactile values."

"But all those terms came later. This was a church, Amory. People came here to worship."

He tittered at her insularity. "Really, Rosa, do you think Michelangelo believed all that rubbish? He only painted religious subjects because the pope made him."

"Exactly. He didn't believe in anything. One doesn't have to believe in anything."

Amory blinked at her. "And just what, pray, do you mean by that extraordinary statement?"

"I don't know what I mean. And I don't care."

"Maybe the heat's too much for you, my dear. We'd better go back to the hotel."

"I'm going to sit right here. Let me be, please, Amory. For half an hour, anyway. Go look at the Raphael portrait of Leo X. That's your favorite, isn't it?"

The next day, in a modern gallery, she bought her first painting. It was a lyrical abstraction called *Hills and Ocean*, a study in pallid, fragile blues and pinks and darker greens, done with thin paint. It made Rosa think of a summer trip that she had taken as a child with her father to Mount Desert Island in Maine.

"Bar Harbor?" Amory inquired with a snort when she showed it to him at the hotel. "It looks more like an old rag the artist used to rub his hands with. May I ask what you paid for it?"

"Two hundred and fifty dollars."

"My God, woman, are you out of your mind?"

But he thought she was even more so the next day when she received a polite note from the artist, a young American, asking her to come to a party at his studio. She informed Amory that she planned to accept.

"But we don't even know him!"

"We will when we get there. He's very pleased at my purchase and would like me to see some of his other things."

"How did he get your name?" Amory demanded suspiciously.

"From the gallery, of course. You don't have to go. I'm perfectly all right by myself."

"In Rome? With a crowd of artists? All Fascists, or maybe even Communists? Of course, I'll have to be with you."

"That's up to you. But in any event I'm going."

The studio was six flights up, on the top of an old house, and Amory protested bitterly at almost every step. They were greeted at the door by the young artist, George, who was small and dark and charming and made Rosa think of Little Billee in *Trilby*. When he handed her a drink and took her to a window to overlook the busy rooftops of the neighborhood, she had a moment of intense pleasure and almost forgot about Amory. In a short time she was actually telling the nice young man what she fancied she could see in his painting. Was it the gin?

"But you must think my approach is hopelessly subjective and sentimental," she exclaimed ruefully.

But he was nice. "Not at all. It's always allowable to see something organic in my work. You should never be ashamed, anyway, of what you see in a picture. It is the creation, after all, of two persons."

"Wouldn't that mean it's not one but several things? Or as many as there are viewers?"

"Well, what's the harm in that? Anyway, I think your eye is a good one. It saw something good in me."

This was delightful, but his friends were bound to spoil it. One of them, a large, unshaven, hirsute man, spoke to her with a rather abrasive assurance.

"Don't believe George, Mrs. Kingsland. He's always trying to appease people he suspects of being antiabstractionists. He thinks, if he allows them their fantasies as to what his lines and squiggles represent, that they will buy his daubs. But some of us are made of sterner stuff. I'd be happy, ma'am, if you'd buy one of mine, but I'm not going to let you think I approve of your finding it 'organic.'"

"Well, I'm sure I shouldn't," Rosa said hastily. "And, of course, I'd love to see your things. What do you try to depict in them?"

"If I could tell you that, ma'am, I wouldn't have to paint them."

"Oh, I see."

The laughter of the little group seemed more mocking than friendly. One of the girls, who had long straight hair, bold eyes and a sacklike dress of dull brown, now asked her in a voice that seemed poised on the impertinent:

"Do many of your class back home still like pictures that tell a story?"

"My class?"

"You know. Society people."

Rosa decided that she had better not be offended. "Well, even if we liked them, where would we find such pictures?"

"She's got you there, Carol," the big man said to the brown dress in a tone that almost made Rosa think he was taking her side. "Those people have been frightened out of their natural tastes. We've browbeaten them into thinking if they dislike something, it must be good."

"Anyway, I don't care for pictures that tell stories," Rosa affirmed.

"Even if you make them up yourself?" the tall man asked with a laugh that was almost a sneer.

Rosa was wondering if she might not find the courage to take him on when she heard her husband's shrill voice across the room addressing another group:

"Well, say what you will, I'd take the Sargent gallery in the Tate for all the modern art on this planet!"

In the silence that followed this she knew that her plight was hopeless. Even if by some miracle of effort she was able to establish a thin line of communication between herself and these young people, Amory would be there to sever it. Never the twain would meet.

In the taxi returning to their hotel Amory rattled on against young "anarchists" and deplored her getting involved with them. She waited for an appropriate pause and then put in firmly:

"It's all right, Amory. You needn't worry. You will never have to go to a party like that again."

"You mean you'll go without me?"

"No, I shan't go either. It's not seemly. We don't belong there."

"Well, I should hope not! And while you're making good resolutions, how about promising me not to buy any more of their crazy pictures?"

"No."

"No?" He glanced at her quickly, surprised at the metallic quality of her tone. "You mean you're going to throw good money after bad? And get more of that junk?"

"Yes, I think I may, Amory."

"And do you expect me to finance this new craze?"

"You needn't. I have my own money now." Grandma had died the year before, having held out till ninety-six and spent most but not all of her principal.

Amory was used to directing even the minor events of their domestic routine, but he knew that on the rare occasions when, for reasons incomprehensible to him, she took a stand, she was unbudgeable. Indeed, she knew how to make him feel at such times that he did not exist as a force in her life. He could then only retreat into sulkiness.

"You'd better hope I don't go mad, too. You'd better pray that our joint exchequers don't founder in lunatic collecting."

"But I should love to see you collect, Amory. You might even find you had an eye for it."

In the decade that followed, Amory never altered his attitude of contemptuous disapproval, but he learned to confine his opposition to that. The years of the Second World War were important ones to Rosa because she made friends with a gaunt and taciturn gallery owner near Washington Square who knew some of the painters who were refugees from France and Germany, and was able to introduce her to the school that became known as abstract expressionism. Silas Levine seemed to understand her intuitively; he never talked technically about pictures, but simply showed them to her. If she liked one, he would nod and show her another. He made her feel that if two people were lucky enough to share a discriminating taste, they had no need to discuss it.

"Come by next week, Mrs. Kingsland. I'll have some drawings of Adolph Gottlieb's that may amuse you."

But if Rosa had reduced her husband to at least a sullen acceptance of her acquisitions, she had no such success with her son. Meredith seemed to have inherited all of the conservative genes of his great-grandmother but little of her ability to cope with the world. When she hung a Miró sketch in his bedroom as a surprise, she found it face down on the floor in the hall the next day.

"At least let me have my own room to myself, Mummy!" he bawled at her. "You've got the whole rest of the house for your garbage!"

Everybody considered Meredith a hopeless problem but Meredith himself. His self-confidence seemed to grow with the hurdles that life put in his way until total failure was crowned with total arrogance. Tall, awkward, with shiny, long black hair, and spindly limbs, his big, staring pop eyes and high, harsh, jeering voice seemed to be calling down the world for its idiotic failure to appreciate Meredith Kingsland. He could never be sent away to camp, boarding school or even an out-of-town college. He was simply too fumbling to take proper care of himself, yet not enough of a freak to win exemption from the physical hostility of his peers. He went for twelve years to a mild, genteel boys' school on the east side of Central Park of which Amory was a trustee, and thereafter took endless courses in literature and history at City College.

Insofar as Meredith seemed able to take in the dismal lacks in his life — lack of a job, lack of a girl, lack of any body of friends — he blamed "Mummy" for them. She had cared too much and too little about him. She had fretted unduly over his health and then criticized him for playing no outdoor games. She had puffed his imagined virtues, making an ass of him in their social circle, and had then been hypercritical of any composition he produced. She embarrassed him by her heaviness and dowdiness and then criticized him for spending so much time and money on his own appearance.

Meredith's greatest ally was whoever happened at the moment to be his psychiatrist.

"Doctor Cranch thinks your real family are your pictures, Mummy. He says that's what's my basic trouble."

"Did he really say that, Meredith? Or did he suggest that one of your troubles might be that *you* thought it?"

"Don't you think I even know what my own doctor says?"

"I think you sometimes edit him for my benefit."

"Why should I want to do that?"

"To get even with me, dear. A son can't lose, can he? He takes full credit for his assets and blames Mummy for his liabilities."

"Really, Rosa," Amory intervened, "aren't you being a bit hard on the boy?"

"Oh, what does she *care?*" Meredith cried angrily. "What does she care for but her silly old art?"

Indeed, Rosa had to admit, after one of these meals, that all she *did* want was to get back to her silly old art. She liked nothing better than sitting alone in a room with her pictures, looking at them and thinking about the things they conjured up in her mind.

She understood that many observers of the art of Franz Kline found in his bold blacks and whites a sense of the violence and power of large, dark, coal-besmirched cities, and in the trajectories of hurtling black across passive white planes an image of encroachment and forcible possession. But what she chose to make out in her Kline was not a twisted mass of steel beams but a giant menacing insect, seen through a magnifying glass, whose only function was to destroy and consume its lesser fellows, and in this horned, multilegged monster she had no difficulty in identifying her late grandmother. Yet this interpretation gave her no pain or unease; on the contrary, it seemed to bind her father's parent into a web of beauty that she could accept and try to love.

Even more factitious was what she read into her Motherwell, one of his *Elegies to the Spanish Republic*. She had heard that Motherwell had not visited Spain until after the civil war, and she had taken this as her excuse to deviate from his title. Besides, were the titles of modern paintings not notoriously misleading? In the old academic days one had known just where one was. *Henry IV Barefoot in the Snow before the Gates of Canossa* meant just that. But did she have to identify the black polelike figure and the two black spheres on either side as the phallus and testicles of a sacrificial bull nailed to a whitewashed wall? No. It was a beautiful evocation of the trunk of the old elm tree in the garden in Newport with the dumpy figures of her two maiden aunts, always in mourning, and the whole concept was death.

Little by little her pictures had begun to fill the house. Amory continued to grumble, but he didn't really care what she hung on the walls, and she put none in the dining room, where the family conversations occurred. Meredith objected more vociferously, but she had given him a whole floor where he could surround himself to his heart's content with his great-grandmother's Turkish bazaars and Tuscan peasant girls. There were moments, however, when she had to remind him that it *was* her house. She dared not go further and suggest that he get his own apartment. Meredith, faced with the smallest threat of what he called "rejection," was likely to become hysterical.

The family friends and cousins, almost without exception, looked upon "Rosa's daubs" as a kind of harmless mania to which it was kinder not to draw too much attention. They could not be unaware of the growing importance of abstract art in the city around them, but they maintained their silent but united front against it, lumping it as one of the not-to-be-escaped evils of a decadent society, along with high taxes, drugs, overstressed civil rights and the bad manners and promiscuity of youth. Yet even in their ranks there was an occasional deserter, and Rosa sometimes found an adventurous individual arriving ahead of the other guests at one of her dinner parties to have a peek at the little gallery off the hall.

Silas Levine decided at last that she had gone far enough to justify him in seeking to penetrate her reserve.

"You know, Rosa, in any other social milieu but yours you'd be considered a remarkable woman. Why do you cling so to your constipated little group of antediluvians?"

"It's my husband's world. He hasn't any other."

"But don't you ever crave the company of people who care for the things you care about?"

"Then I can come to you."

He laughed and gave it up. "All right, Rosa. Maybe you're right. Maybe your pictures are enough."

Sometimes artists wished to see her collection, and she would make arrangements through Levine for them to come to the house at times when neither her husband nor son would be home. This became more difficult after Amory had his stroke and was permanently in the house, but the little hall gallery, discreetly used, still answered her purpose. Only if Meredith happened to be going in or out of the house at the time was the visitor likely to be startled by the shrill voice from the dark hall exclaiming: "Are you in there, Mummy? Who's being polite enough to look at your zany show?"

Meredith, in his late twenties, unoccupied except for his daily hour with his analyst, seemed to have nothing to do now but hound his mother. Family meals had become a torture to her.

"All I really want to find out, Mummy — seriously — is how to tell the difference between a good abstract and a bad one. It can't be by whether or not it resembles something, because it isn't anything, is it? And you can't say that a line or a curve is badly drawn, because the artist can always say that's the way he meant it. So what standard have you left to go by? What do you look for?"

"I guess I just look."

"Oh, Mummy, what kind of an answer is that? You have to look *for* something in a picture."

"Do you, Meredith? But, anyway, I think I *can* tell a bad abstract. There were some at the Junior League show."

"But how did you know?"

"By what they did to me. They gave me a dead feeling. I wanted to turn away. I wonder if that isn't the only way to teach art. Perhaps we make a mistake in dragging classes of children through museums to see masterpieces. It might be more effective to show them the discards in the cellar."

"So that's your only criterion: a kind of gut feeling?"

"I'm afraid so."

Amory, embittered by his stroke, tended to side with his son in these arguments, but not without getting in an occasional thrust at the latter. "Just as I suspected, the whole business is a kind of emotional pudding. But you ought to understand that, Meredith. Doesn't your shrink explain those things to you? Don't you suppose those dots and squiggles are sexual symbols to your poor frustrated mother? Why not? Married to an old man in a wheelchair, she must dream of something better, mustn't she? Now don't get excited, Rosa, I'm blaming myself, not you. What can a poor, impotent creature like me . . ."

But Rosa had already left the table. In the silence of her own chamber she contemplated the serene truth of the parallel lines of her Mondrian and turned her mind firmly from humanity as represented in the dining room below. For once she was not subjective.

⚜

Not long after this conversation Meredith took too many sleeping pills and was revived only with difficulty. It was not clear that he had intended a fatal dose — he might have simply planned a melodrama — but his psychiatrist recommended commitment to the Dunstan Sanatorium, and once there, there seemed little possibility of any early release. Six years elapsed, and Rosa's collection, one by one, ascended the auction block. She thought of them as the pale, proud victims of a reign of terror, silently mounting the steps of the scaffold. She never wished to learn who had bought any of them.

When she went to Silas Levine's gallery to tell him that she would have to sell the Gorky, he threw his hands up in anger and disgust.

"You've said yourself, Rosa, that the whole thing is a kind of mad revenge on Meredith's part. Well, don't give in to it! Tell that monstrous minotaur of a sanatorium that it can no longer have its annual sacrifice. Your son will be no worse off at home than he is there. And you could at least keep the poor remnant of your glorious collection."

"But how can I be sure that Meredith, once out, won't try it again?"

"Well, you have to take some chances. What sort of a life does he have in that loony bin, anyway? Rosa, they're gobbling you up, eating you alive!"

"I see that, Silas. But what you don't see is that I've deserved it."

"Oh, my God, you Puritans! *How*, pray, have you deserved it?"

"Because I've given so little to my husband. And really nothing at all to poor Meredith."

"And what have they given you?"

"Nothing, it is true. But they had nothing to give."

"No love?"

"Some people have no love to give."

"Well, if they gave you nothing, and you gave them nothing — or very little, as you say — why aren't you square?"

"Because, you see, I did have something to give."

"Love?"

"Love."

"And what did you do with your love?"

"You, of all people, should know that, Silas. I'm not complaining. I've had a good life. The time has come to pay for it, that's all."

Levine, staring at her, at last gave up, as he always had to, with Rosa. "Let me do one thing for you, anyway. Let me put together a beautiful album of colored photographs of every picture from your collection!"

She smiled as she shook her head. "Do you really think I need that, Silas?" There was a pause in which he made no answer. "Now tell me. What can I get for the Gorky?"

Àres

1992

1

Castledale, in 1850, was at its zenith, the perfect residence of a Virginia gentleman. Quiet, dignified but at the same time discreetly charming, with none of the swollen pomposity of plantation manors in the deeper South, its comfortable size, its two-story red brick façade, its modest portico of four white columns with Doric capitals, seemed more to evidence a genteel welcome than any need to impress a caller. Indeed, the tobacco planted on its two thousand acres was more for the maintenance of an old tradition than a revenue necessity; Thomas Carstairs was a prosperous attorney in nearby Charlottesville with a practice that his father had had before him and that his son Roger fully expected to carry on. In Castledale the library, with its collection of Jacobean quartos and folios, was quite as important as the manager's office, and the odes of Horace, which Thomas translated for the edification of the students whom he volunteered to teach twice a week at the university founded by Thomas Jefferson, were as needful to his peace of mind as the briefs for which he was more famed.

The house was of two eras. The back part, of gray wood with a mansard roof and narrow gabled windows, dated from the late seventeenth century. The larger and grander frontal section, added in the early 1800s and designed by Mr. Jefferson himself for his friend Oakley Carstairs, was an octagon with six narrow walls and two wide ones, one of the former constituting the façade, which overlooked the green turnaround at the end of the driveway flanked by the towering box, planted according to family legend by a gardener who had once been in service to Queen Anne.

Within, a broad, paneled hallway ran from the front door to the old entrance of the ancient portion, hung with portraits of dead Carstairses, from the stiff primitives of early Colonial days, ladies and gentlemen with severe boardlike faces and unwrinkled raiment, one of the latter shown ensconced by a window through which could be seen the house in which he was presumably sitting, to the finer portraits of the eighteenth century, with the sitters' more splendid attire and more elaborate wigs and hairdos, and culminating with the magnificent likeness of Timothy Carstairs, minister to the court of Louis-Philippe, by Ingres. Roger's favorite room was the neat, still parlor, used only for company, decorated in the frilled and curlicued fashion of the citizen-king's era and dominated by a large conversation piece of the minister's children feeding ducks in a pond in the Jardin des Tuileries.

Roger knew every chapter of the family history and had looked forward, without due apprehension, to playing a role as civic as that of any of his ancestors. The most ingratiating aspect of the tribal tradition was that there had seemed little likelihood of failure for a Carstairs other than easily avoidable vices. If one had not succeeded in becoming governor or a judge or the minister to a European court, one had been equally acceptable to the hierarchy of the past by simply remaining the proprietor of Castledale. How could one lose so long as the world was sane?

So long as it was. Virginia was, but Virginia, alas, had not the sway she had formerly enjoyed. Roger in his last year at the university was vividly aware of the threats to the high civilization of which Mr. Jefferson's serene dome and noble lawn, his graceful pavilions and multitudinous columns, were the fitting symbols. The Greek calm and sense of proportion of the Virginia gentleman were rare qualities in a nation torn over slavery. Did either the arrogant advocates of secession in the deeper South or the hate-mongering Yankee abolitionists properly belong to the ordered and benignant society of which the Sage of Monticello had dreamed?

Roger and his father belonged to the school which regarded slavery as an evil that would in the course of time die out. That time, however, they firmly believed, should not be delayed by Southern fanatics or accelerated by Northern ones. It would be decided for Virginians in Richmond, not in Charleston or Boston. But Roger was unlike his fellows of the Old Dominion in one respect. He had the intense imagination that fitted his romantic looks, his raven hair and alabaster skin. He was able to imagine himself in the position of a slave in Castledale.

How could *he* have endured a life without books, without philosophic discussions, without being able to wander as a student in the shadow of the university dome, without the prospect of one day being master of Castledale? And yet he *owned* human beings who had none of these things!

Roger had one classmate who personified everything he felt to be most dangerous to the peaceful solution of the ugly problem of the Southern states. Philip Drayton, of Charleston, the home of nullification, was a large handsome daredevil of a man, hearty and outgoing, but with a prickly sense of honor and the renown of having fought two duels at home, one with a fatal result, which had earned him the rhyming sobriquet of Satan. It was an apostrophe that he accepted with an easy grace — from his friends.

Drayton had transferred into Roger's graduating class from a college in his home state, perhaps, it was rumored, because of some unpleasantness related to his second duel, but he seemed bent on making his few months in Charlottesville as agreeable as possible. He was affable and charming, shedding the rays of his mildly impertinent wit and rosy puffed compliments on all classmates who came his way. Yet despite this apparent democracy of manners, it was evident that his social goal was to join, perhaps even to dominate, Roger's own clique of Virginia blue bloods. He singled out the heir of Castledale for his particular attention, with something in his air that seemed to imply that they were uniquely qualified, by birth and breeding, for the first position. Yet the strange thing about their relationship, from the very beginning, was that Roger was struck with a morbid little suspicion that in the eyes of the South Carolinian there might be room at the top for only one of them.

What soon enough emerged as their dangerous bone of contention was politics. As he and Satan were riding together on a fine autumnal afternoon over the red clay of the countryside towards a blue forest under a lemon sky, the latter extolled the glories of the old South.

"I am happy to concede that you Virginians got us all going in the first place. You provided the great general of the Revolution and the first president and much of the Constitution, though I'm not so sure the last was such a great boon. But has it ever struck you, my friend, that long years of political success may have infected you with a kind of creeping paralysis? Even here in the university, isn't there a tendency to emphasize words over deeds?"

"But universities have to be concerned with words."

"Only words?"

"No, no, morals too, of course. Ideals, aspirations, all that civilization is about."

"Civilization!" Dayton almost whistled the word. "Can't you imagine a race that has become too civilized? Sometimes I wonder whether we aren't becoming like the ancient Romans."

"And whom do you see as our conquering barbarians?"

"The Yankees, man, the Yankees! Who else in the name of Satan?" Drayton reined up his horse and leaned over to spit vigorously in the clay. "Not that they'd have the guts to strike now. But they're just sitting there, with their beady eyes fixed on us, waiting for the moment when we turn our backs, and then they'll have their daggers ready."

"I think you posit a good deal more unity in our Northern neighbors than I make out. We don't have riots about slavery as they do about abolition."

"Mebbe not yet." Drayton shrugged and rode on. "But we're still being infiltrated. Right here in the university there are men who don't scruple to say out loud that slavery as an institution is doomed."

"And it isn't?"

"No, goddamn it all, of course it isn't! Men have always had slaves. It's right there in the Bible. You see, Carstairs, you've become infected yourself with the disease. Let us pray it's only a mild case. My simple point is that Virginia, as a border state, is peculiarly vulnerable to the Yankee plague. The banner of Southern leadership must pass to the deeper South."

"To Charleston, I take it?"

"Well, what finer metropolis could anyone want? The martial spirit is very much alive and kicking in my home state."

"It's perhaps that which has caused some of its novel interpretations of the Constitution."

"You're thinking of nullification, no doubt? Well, let me tell you at once that the family of Philip Drayton, Esquire, stood to a man behind the immortal John C. Calhoun on that issue!"

Roger paused before asking, "Could the Union exist if federal laws could be voided by the states?"

"And is there any good reason, sir, that the Union *should* exist?"

"But that's treason, Drayton!"

The South Carolinian again reined in his horse. He faced Roger with a bland countenance and the twitch of a smile; his tone was very soft. "I didn't hear you, Carstairs. You didn't say anything, did you?"

Roger shrugged. "I guess not."

"Good."

Roger never doubted that the issue so created was a grave one. He did not try to brush it off as a simple case of tact and common sense intervening to avoid a dangerous and unnecessary quarrel. He knew that in a clash of wills Drayton had prevailed and that Drayton must have attributed his yielding more to fear than to caution. And wasn't he right? What was caution but fear? From now on he had to expect that Drayton would presume on his advantage to create situations, even in the presence of others, where the mask of caution would be stripped off the face of its counterpart. And there was a limit, of course, a very definite limit, to what a Carstairs could accept.

Was he to live then at the mercy of an ass? Here, in the very shadow of Mr. Jefferson's dome, the symbol of high thinking and sober living, with the pavilions and white columns embracing the green Lawn in a clasp of Greek amity, was his mind condemned to exist in the tumult of the ass's braying? Roger groaned aloud at the idea that a whole wonderful life of books and laws and elevated thoughts, of managing the rolling acres of Castledale from the saddle of a noble steed, could be shot away by one bully's bullet. It was not the dread of physical death that agonized him; it was the cause and the folly of it.

Events promptly followed the course he had so grimly predicted. Drayton no longer sought his company alone but in groups of classmates. He would appeal in discussions to Roger for his opinions and advice, lacing his jovial flattery with increasing irony: "I wonder whether our friend Carstairs, whose worship of the Sage of Monticello may even have put him in touch with our founder's spirit, can shed any light on how Mr. Jefferson might have reacted to Mr. Sumner's extraordinary proposed solution to the so-called free soil issue?"

Drayton now revealed himself openly as the advocate of secession and frankly championed the idea of a Southern confederacy. Few of the Virginia students were ready to go so far, but the concept had its romantic appeal. The vision of a brilliant and chivalrous society, based on ancient codes of honor and aristocratic manners, caught many youthful imaginations. To Roger it was simply the essence of everything that was volatile, foolish and extravagantly violent in the Southern temperament, the poison in a society for which Mr. Jefferson's rationalism was the necessary antidote. He waxed calmer now that his growing rift with Drayton was taking on some of the aspects of a national struggle. It would not be folly, after all, to perish for an ideal.

He was first propelled to an open disagreement with his adversary at a reception with dancing given by the rector of the university. Roger found himself in a group of stags at the punch bowl discussing a Boston riot over the recent attempt by the police to seize and return to his owners an escaped slave. Drayton, who had been drinking rather heavily, joined them and, after recognizing the topic, addressed a frankly hostile question to Roger.

"What do you say to all this, Carstairs? Isn't this nullification on the part of Massachusetts?"

"It would be if the state were rioting. But the state isn't rioting. It's trying to enforce the Fugitive Slave Law. In fact, it's the very opposite of nullification."

"Why do you always take the Yankee side? Aren't the rioters trying to nullify the law?"

"Certainly. But they are not officers of the state."

"But don't they represent an attitude widely held in the North?"

"Undoubtedly."

"Well, if so many folk both north and south are nullifiers, wouldn't it be best for the two sections to go their separate ways?"

Roger looked slowly from face to expectant face before enunciating his answer in precisely articulated syllables: "I can only speak for myself as a citizen of the Commonwealth of Virginia. I still owe my allegiance and my life to the Union so long as the rights of my state are not violated."

All eyes turned to Drayton. He seemed hesitant, baffled. Then he shrugged and turned to reach for the ladle of the punch bowl and refill his glass. The right moment had not come.

But now, like the fall of Hamlet's sparrow, it *would* come.

At home in Castledale all one weekend Roger practiced firing at a target. He was a first-class shot — when his head was cool and his pulse steady. He had to train his mind as well as his hand and eye. He had to douse his hatred of Drayton with the waters of will and convert it to an icy remorselessness. For if he had to fight this man, he was determined to kill him. He would be ridding the South of a dangerous firebrand at the firebrand's own invitation.

Matters came to a head at a bachelors' party on the Lawn, at long trestle tables with candles. Drayton got very drunk and proposed a loud toast to John C. Calhoun, "the real hero of the South and the father of what we hope will one day be a new union." Roger, who knew, almost in relief, that he now had no further choice of action, remained seated while the others, even the dissenters, in tipsy good humor, drank to secession, and then rose to direct his cold tight tones to the surly Drayton. He offered a toast to the memory of "a *greater* hero of the South, the founder of our beloved university." Drayton stalked around the table to fling the contents of his glass in the Virginian's face.

※

For the rest of his life Roger was never quite sure exactly how it happened. At dawn, in a field in a forest some dozen miles from Charlottesville, he faced his opponent at fifteen paces before the seconds and a doctor. Drayton, sober now, had actually smiled at him, almost sheepishly, as he had strolled to his position.

"Gentlemen, are you ready? One, two, three . . ."

It has been said that a man's whole life can pass through his mind at the moment of drowning. Roger simply remembered that he heard Drayton's shot. What he was never clear about was whether he saw that Drayton had fired his pistol into the air. But all the witnesses agreed that Drayton had done so and that his basic decency had forbidden him to kill or even wound a man whom he had grossly insulted under the influence of liquor.

But Roger's recollection of what happened next was clear enough. In the three seconds that followed the retort of Drayton's pistol he had recognized with a sharp stab of relief that he was safe and had his opponent at his mercy. With frigid determination, without a nerve twitching, he took careful aim and placed his bullet in Drayton's head.

Death was instantaneous. Roger recalled the grim silence of his companions on the ride back to Charlottesville. No one congratulated him on his survival; he was simply advised to get out of the state until the matter could be settled with the police and the university.

※

When he returned to college after a brief suspension, he found that he was very differently regarded by his classmates. Whereas he had been formerly treated as a man of reserve, whose formal good manners were justified by his lineage and whose romantic concern with the history of his state tinged his sobriety with idealism, he was now seen as a faintly sinister figure, possessed of a cold will power that repelled intimacy. He was respected, however; courage was always admired in Virginia. Some of his old friends insisted that he had been motivated by a high principle, although they did not agree on what that principle was.

Roger himself felt no guilt at what he had done. Drayton had certainly assumed the risk, and the South was the better for the elimination of such a firebrand. But he had to face the fact that the episode had changed him, unless it had simply brought out something that had all along been concealed. He felt that he was now a man with a mission. The nature of the mission he did not yet see, but he was confident that time would bring it out. He did not for a minute believe that he had killed a man for nothing.

Girls were especially awed by his new reputation; his good looks were now described as Byronic. His reticence and solitary habits added to his fascination, and to Kitty Cabell, the prettiest debutante of her Richmond season, he seemed the Corsair himself. Roger had known Kitty since childhood; they were even, like so many of the first families, related, and he had long been perfectly clear that she had the characteristics, both good and bad, of the renowned Southern belle. She was superficial and affected, and she posed as being a good deal sillier and less worldly than she was, but she was also enchanting. She now turned her full lights upon him and soon aroused his lust to the point where he was reluctantly willing to pay society's price to sleep with her. They were married in 1855, shortly after his father's death from a stroke, and settled in Castledale.

Kitty proved one of those rare persons who become perfectly amiable when their ambition is satisfied. As chatelaine of Castledale and mother of a small son, she happily took the lead in the local society and got on splendidly with her docile mother-in-law, who continued to live in the house. That Roger, engaged in his law practice and the supervision of the beloved plantation, should be little concerned with her she accepted as the conventional attitude of a husband. So long as his manners were correct — and they invariably were — she was content with her bargain. But no more children came, and in time he requested his own bedroom. If he ever had an affair, she never learned of it, and that was all she cared about. As for herself, there was never any idea of a lover. She was afraid that Roger might have killed him.

Everything would have been well enough, in Kitty's opinion, had the Yankees only seen fit to leave them alone. She had spent much of her youth in Paris, where her father had represented a syndicate of tobacco planters, and she had viewed with a detachment imbued in her by her older brother Lemuel, a satirical dilettante, the semi-ludicrous efforts of their Francophile parents to be included in the *gratin* of the old faubourg. Lemuel had taken a perverse delight in establishing his dominance over his pretty younger sibling by exposing the silliness of a father who spent an hour every morning practicing his French *r* and of his mother, who thought she would ingratiate herself in legitimist circles by dressing as closely as she could to the Empress Eugénie. He made Kitty understand that Vieille France, however polite, however *amicale,* was never going to clasp to its bosom or allow to marry one of its sons an American girl who wasn't a Catholic and who hadn't a fortune, the plantation at home being morally entailed to the firstborn, a brother older than she and Lemuel. Kitty learned that in a foolish world one had to rely on oneself, and she didn't forget this when the family returned to Richmond. She had no greater loyalty to slaveholding Virginia than she did to the Faubourg St.-Germain. She laughed at the golden calves on both sides of the Atlantic, but she was always careful to laugh to herself.

Roger's attitude to the great issue of the day struck her as just as senseless as everyone else's. He believed that the slaves should be freed, but he was quite willing to kill anyone but himself who proposed to free them. At least that was how it looked to her. He disguised his fierce ego, as she saw it, behind the mask of a Virginia patriot. And after the abortive John Brown raid onto his sacred state's soil, he became as hot a secessionist as the fiery South Carolinian whose brains he had blown out.

In the first years of the fighting, during which she had to manage a crumbling plantation while he was off, all over the state, with Jeb Stuart's cavalry, she sometimes complained to her mother-in-law that the wives and mothers of warriors had the worst of their wars.

"Let us call it our glory," the docile widow would invariably reply.

2
—
※

Hate sustained Roger during the whole of the conflict, hate and, at least in the first two years, his hope that the Confederacy's choice of Richmond as its capital might restore Virginia to the leadership it had enjoyed in the golden days of Mr. Jefferson. No compromise, he always insisted grimly, was possible with the enemy that was ravaging his native state. Although he met some captive Union officers who he had to concede had shown at least the courage of gentlemen, he could only pity them as the tools of an unholy alliance between fanatical abolitionists and avaricious war profiteers. And when, after two years of constant campaigning, he was offered the relief of a staff job in Richmond, accompanied with a promotion, he turned both down to continue in the cavalry. Nothing else seemed to make any sense to him.

The double defeats of Vicksburg and Gettysburg destroyed his last illusion of ultimate victory for secession. No matter how many battles or skirmishes his company won on mangled Virginia soil, no matter how horribly its rich beloved red clay seemed to ooze Yankee blood, there were always new waves of the boys in blue rising out of the very foam of their collapsed predecessors.

He had no wish to survive the inevitable end. He was wounded three times but always slightly; he seemed to be proving the old adage that death avoids those who seek it in battle. The long days in the saddle riding through familiar countrysides, sinister now in their haunting beauty, the nights in the field where he would let his exhausted body drop to the earth after swinging the lead ends of his blanket around his shoulders, began to produce an odd consolation in their very monotony and dreariness. Once when he sat up till dawn couching in his lap the head of a boy whose lifeblood was slowly dripping away, he felt something like peace at his own acceptance of all that the loathed enemy had destroyed. But he could not bear the sight of Castledale; on one of his leaves he put up at a hotel in Richmond rather than go home. And when word reached him that his mother had died, he could only be thankful for what she had been spared.

After Appomattox he had the privilege of a few words with General

Lee, who had stood as godfather to his son seven years before. Like all the army he worshiped Lee, but he was ready to relegate him to the past. "Go home, my friend," the general said. "Now the real task awaits us. God helping, we shall not shirk it."

Roger nodded and went home, but he stayed there only a year. He felt like an atheist who has died only to discover that there *is* an afterlife. It might not be a better one, but at least he would be free of the old.

"I'm going up to New York to see whether I can make a living there practicing law," he informed his younger brother, Ned, a mild and gentle man, a bachelor, who deemed it entirely fitting that he should fall in with all of Roger's schemes. "Look after Castledale and Kitty and the boy. If I don't starve, I'll send for them when I can provide them with a home there. Explain this to Kitty tactfully after I've gone."

A cousin of his mother's had married a well-to-do New York landlord, Basil Tremont, a generous victor, who had answered Roger's letter of inquiry with the assurance that he would help him at least to a modest start.

Roger's cousin had a small office on Canal Street, where he and one old clerk and an even older female secretary handled the Tremont family affairs, largely the collection of tenement rents, and he accorded his Southern relative a narrow cubicle, used for file storage, as his "chambers." But it was free, and although there was no question of Roger's getting his hands on the family law business, he did receive an occasional crumb from that ample table in the form of a small eviction or lease renewal. Furthermore, Basil Tremont was good enough to tout these services to the guests at the Sunday night suppers in Union Square to which Roger was occasionally invited, and he thus picked up some modest retainers, enough, anyway, to pay for his bedroom in Houston Street and his simple meals.

He used his plentiful spare time, both day and night, in studying New York cases and statutes in the library of the Manhattan Law Institute. He had no interest in the social scene or in public amusements. He heartily despised the whole dirty brown noisy city with its Yankee twangs and its Yankee familiarities. He had come north for one purpose only, the recoupment of his fortune, and his eye was rarely averted from that goal. But he perfectly realized that this could not be accomplished by law alone, and he was careful to cultivate the few important men he met at the Tremont Sunday gatherings.

The talk there, however, was dominated by the women, whose importance Roger recognized but did not exaggerate. Mrs. Tremont, a vast cheerful bundle of flesh and red velvet, could get anything she wanted from her pale bald spouse, but she wanted things only for herself and her offspring. She and her fellow matrons had not the smallest interest in business or politics; the power they sought and achieved was purely domestic. They had, of course, the power to ruin a man with their tongues, but any such danger was easily averted by a routine exhibition of Southern gallantry. They were rather titillated at meeting a handsome and impoverished rebel officer; they enjoyed the idea of exercising a beneficent open-mindedness in their affable condescension to a safely defeated enemy. If Roger had been free, he might even, with a skillful play of his few trumps, have secured the hand of one of their well-endowed daughters. As it was, he had to direct his principal attention to the men.

The City Club, a large pink-and-white building on Madison Square with a membership of lawyers, judges and politicians, was more useful to him. The ever-generous Basil had treated him to a year's guest membership, and it was an easy enough matter for a former Confederate officer, dropping into the big bar with the oak-paneled walls and potted palms, to fall into friendly converse with those members who had served in the Union Army and evoke the bond between fighting men that never quite includes even the bravest noncombatant. Roger, in postmortems of battles, was always careful to avoid any criticism of Union strategy. His cool good manners, unaffected by the few drinks he permitted himself, made him popular, and after his year's free membership was up, he found it renewed for another without dues. When he went to the treasurer's office to inquire about this, he was politely shown a minute from a meeting of the board of directors stating that Colonel Carstairs could pay dues "when his ship came in."

Roger decided to accept this. He would not have done so in Richmond, but then Richmond was reality, a quality he was not willing to accord New York.

The president of the club, Charles Van Rensselaer Pratt, turned out to be just the man he had been looking for. He was every inch a gentleman — at least, as Northerners defined that term — tall and grave and dignified, with a short, well-cut beard and dull blue gazing eyes under bushy eyebrows which seemed to be wondering whether you were as much a gentleman as he. His Knickerbocker background would have qualified him more for the presidency of the Union Club than the City, but Roger had heard that his intense patriotism during the war, throughout the whole of which, like Roger, he had fought, had prompted him to resign from an institution some of whose most distinguished members had favored a compromise peace. Pratt at forty looked ten years older, as fitted the senior partner of the Wall Street firm that his late father had founded, and his reputation for honor and high-mindedness was unchallenged. The same, however, could not be said of some of his partners. There were even those who dared to suggest that he was a figurehead of respectability to be displayed in nobly speechifying meetings of bar associations and behind whose broad and stylishly tailored back a good deal of less edifying but profitable business was transacted.

Pratt was intrigued by what he called Roger's decision to "move his career north." He visited the club regularly on Monday nights, when his wife dined with her invalid mother, and made his two whiskies last for two hours. He soon made it a habit to invite Roger to join him at his reserved table in a corner of the barroom. They would talk of problems facing the South and what Pratt called its "future redemption and regeneration." Roger, for whom whiskey had become a controlled solace, found that it increased his tact by temporarily softening his bitterness. He was not even tempted to call the club president an ass.

"Oh, I suppose the South will come back in a way," he conceded as he puffed his pipe, for he smoked now too. "But it will not be in any way that will interest me. I have seen the old days, and there can be no possible revival of *them*."

"But surely in time the great plantations will revive. Will it make such a difference to you that the hands will be paid instead of owned? Mightn't they even be more efficient?"

Roger smiled inwardly at this hint from the counsel to capitalists. "It's not that, sir. I belonged to the civilization that died at Appomattox. I do not care for reconstructions."

"So you will stay here?"

"If I can survive here."

"And bring your family north?"

"In time."

"How do you think they will like it here?"

Roger smiled again, this time outwardly with a touch of grimness. "Kitty will like it, if I can buy the things she wants. The boy, I suppose, will grow up a brave little Yankee."

"And what about your place? It's called Castledale?"

But Roger was not ready to discuss Castledale with even a well-meaning Yankee.

"My brother will take care of it."

"Well, I'm sure that our divisions will heal sooner with men like you in our midst. Men who have fought with courage and conviction for a cause in which they seriously believed."

Roger treated himself to a long sip of whiskey in answer to this. Nothing could be allowed to impede him from finding an opening in Pratt's firm. When he spoke, it was to give the topic a new twist. "Does it ever occur to you that the real winners of the conflict in which you and I battled so long and hard were not the soldiers at all, but the ones who had the wit to stay home?"

Pratt's blue eyes took on something like a spark. "You mean the dastardly profiteers?"

"I mean all those who put business ahead of war. How many of your veterans do you see in the entourage of the new president?"

Pratt's sigh was windy. "Very few indeed, I fear. General Grant seems to have forgotten his old comrades. I cannot see what *he* sees in market speculators of that type."

"If we fighting men would stick together, we might have a chance to run the show."

"Do you know, sir, I *like* that idea! And do you know that of the ten partners in my firm I am the *only* one to have worn the blue uniform?"

Roger raised his glass. "To the blue and the gray!" He just managed to suppress a laugh as Pratt smote the table with his fist in his enthusiasm.

Roger had a project for Pratt on their next meeting. He had been reading in the newspapers about the struggle of the New York and Albany Railway Company to corner the stock of the Ontario line, a client of Pratt's firm. He had obtained copies of all the briefs in the various lawsuits involved and studied them carefully. On a Monday night at the City Club he expounded a plan of defense to Pratt that was so simple as to have escaped the attention of the lawyers on both sides.

"I note that the Albany line has succeeded in obtaining an injunction from Judge Barnard of the Supreme Court of New York County prohibiting Ontario from issuing more stock for any reason. I fail to see the basis for so sweeping an order."

"The basis, I fear, may lie in the venality of His Honor. The Albany line is stronger with the city's judiciary than we seem to be."

"The *city's* judiciary. What about trying a judge farther north? In Sullivan County, say, or Columbia?"

"But what have they to do with us?"

"As much as any of the supreme courts in Manhattan. Doesn't each supreme court have plenary jurisdiction throughout the state?"

"Hmm. That is so, isn't it? But why should upstate judges interfere in matters that don't concern them?"

"You could make it their concern."

"How?"

"How did your opponents do it?"

"You don't mean we should bribe them?"

Roger laughed so that he could retreat into a joke if needed. "Think how much cheaper an upstate country judge would be than one of the gorged jurists of our opulent town!"

"Carstairs, what are you saying?"

"How many of these black gowns were fighting men, Pratt?"

Pratt looked at him gravely and then chuckled. He too would treat it in jest. "Still, the idea of petitioning an upstate judge is interesting. I'll discuss it with my partners. After all, we might find one who would be glad to correct an injustice. Yes, why not? It is certainly a novel idea."

Pratt took the matter up with his firm, and the very next day Roger was summoned to the office of the partner in charge of litigation, Carl Gleason, a ferret-faced little man whose nervous fingers roamed like spiders over the silver objects on his desk while his cold eyes remained fixed on his visitor. Having heard Roger's exposition, he wasted no time in offering him a job as a clerk in Pratt & Stirling. But he was clearly a bit taken aback by how hard Roger bargained over salary; obviously he was dealing more with a fighting colonel than a starving ex-rebel attorney. When they came at last to terms, he issued this parting warning: "I trust it is quite understood that you are working for me and no other partner. And no other partner includes even Mr. Pratt. I am always very particular with that in litigations."

Roger nodded. He quite understood. There were things he might have to do that the senior partner was not to know about. That the senior partner might very well not *want* to know about. And indeed his very first job was to journey north to the township of Ayer in the county of Clinton to consult one Supreme Court Justice Owen, whose initial reluctance to exercise his injunctive powers in favor of Mr. Gleason's client was overcome by an envelope passed silently across his desk.

Thereafter it was always Roger who took care of what Gleason called the "delicate side" of litigation. His salary was increased twice so that after only two years he was able to bring Kitty and young Osgood north and lodge them in a brownstone on Brooklyn Heights. And only two years after that he presented himself one morning before Gleason's desk and coolly demanded to know whether the time had not come for him to be made a junior partner in the firm.

"But you're paid as much as a junior partner now!" Gleason protested. "I thought you were too great a Virginia gentleman to care about our Yankee partnerships."

"Why I care should be obvious to a lawyer as smart as yourself, Mr. Gleason. An associate can always be dumped. I do not wish to be dumpable."

"And if I refuse?"

"And if I go to the Commodore?"

Commodore Vanderbilt was then busily engaged in trying to corner Ontario stock. A former clerk of Ontario's counsel, particularly one who had handled "delicate matters," would find rapid employment with the old pirate.

"Are you trying to blackmail me, Carstairs?"

"The definition is yours. All I ask is fair treatment. We sink or swim together."

"Jeff Davis shouldn't have wasted you in the cavalry. If he'd had you in his cabinet, treason might have prospered."

Roger stiffened. "In the old days I'd have called you out for that. But now may I simply remind you that secession was not treason until established by *force majeure*. And that President Davis, as we referred to our chief executive, would never have stooped to your ways of doing business."

"*My* ways!" Even the hardened Gleason gaped at this. "Well, of all the nerve!" But he was not a man to make an issue out of inevitable things; he even managed a grin. "You'll never believe it, Carstairs, but I was planning all along to make you a partner."

"Of course I don't believe it. But shall we agree that I'm to be a member of the firm as of the first of the month? We can discuss my percentage later."

Gleason threw up his hands. "I agree."

3
—
卐

Roger not only became a partner. Ten years later, when Gleason died of a stroke, he succeeded to his position as chief of the department, with a higher percentage of the firm's profits than the nominal senior partner, Charles Pratt. The older and more distinguished members of the bar may have been disturbed by rumors of his methods of convincing the judiciary, but the tolerant and cynical laymen of the day took for granted that he was probably little worse than his fellow attorneys.

Roger neither made nor sought to make friends in New York. His manners were polite but formal; he asked nothing of his partners or clients beyond completion of the particular business at hand. Kitty, on the other hand, was strikingly successful. She bloomed in Manhattan society and charmed everybody with her revived Southern belle manners. She was as open and witty as he was silent and grave; she dressed and talked well and entertained delightfully in the brownstone mansion of her dreams that Roger had built for her on Murray Hill on condition that he would not have to preside at her parties. For that he summoned north her bachelor brother Lemuel, even more of a dilettante than in his Paris days, and bought a literary gazette for him to edit when he was not escorting Kitty about the town. Society much preferred the genial Lemuel to the austere Roger, and the brother and sister were soon among the most popular couples in Gotham. Much as Roger scorned Kitty's social success, he was too just not to recognize that it ill became a husband who had brought his wife to a strange city to begrudge her her adaptability to its ways.

He gave Kitty what she wanted, but he gave even more to the re-embellishment of Castledale. His brother Ned, too self-effacing to occupy the main house and contenting himself with the old overseer's lodge, lovingly supervised the restorations ordered by his senior: the cleaning and stretching of family portraits, the affixing of new panels to interior walls and new bricks to the outer ones, the installation of plumbing and central heating, the replanting of the gardens and box, and, most important of all, the arrangement, against appropriate settings of new curtains and carpets, of the beautiful Colonial and early Federal furniture and porcelains purchased by Roger at auction sales of the grand old mansions of the South. For if he thus seemed to join the plunderers of the Confederacy, it was only to bring together the finest of its treasures in a museum to be devoted to its memory and to be paid for with Yankee dollars.

This, of course, had to be the justification of everything he had done since Appomattox. His only happy times were the occasional weekends he spent at Castledale, roaming the rooms and corridors and riding over the grounds. Kitty never accompanied him, claiming with undeniable truth that he would rather be alone with his "true love," but in the first years of the restoration he had sometimes taken Osgood. The poor boy, however, was not only plain and stout; he was hopelessly dull. He had at an early age given up trying to curry favor with the stern father of whom he stood in helpless awe; he seemed to divine that it was not within his limited range to gain paternal affection or even approval. Yet Roger sometimes reluctantly suspected that his son would have given anything to be loved a little. Kitty was a demonstrative but easily distracted mother, and the smallest amount of warmth from a taciturn and preoccupied male parent might have made all the difference to the lad. But every time Roger resolved to pay him a little more attention, the boy would irritate him with some odious Yankee expression or demonstration of his ignorance of Southern history and tradition, and at last he resolved to take him south no longer, justifying the decision with the reminder that, after all, he intended to convert Castledale to a museum and sanctuary where Osgood would never have to live.

Ned Carstairs did not approve at all of what he dared to call his brother's demeaning of his nephew, and he stepped out of his usually subservient role to argue roundly that Osgood was the rightful heir to Castledale and should be trained to be a good proprietor. But Roger was not accustomed to taking advice, and least of all from Ned, and he simply shrugged in answer. And so it was that Osgood played little part in his father's life until the night when, aged twenty-four, a bank clerk still living at home, he penetrated the usually forbidden-to-all area of the paternal study to announce that he was engaged to be married. Roger, surprised for once, looked up at the round serious eyes in the round pale face of his only child and felt a pang of remorse that he should not have the least idea of who the young lady might be. In his confusion he took refuge in sarcasm.

"I trust, anyway, not to a Miss Gould or a Miss Fisk."

"Oh, no, Father. To someone you will really approve of."

"Heavens! Do you mean a Virginia girl? I didn't know you knew any."

"Well, no, but perhaps the next best thing. She's the daughter of one of your partners."

Roger was on his feet before he was even aware he had moved. "Good God, not to one of Gleason's girls!"

Osgood looked bewildered by such violence. "Oh, no, sir, I don't even know them. It's Felicia Pratt."

Roger stared. He seemed to recollect a large placid goose of a maiden. "Charles Pratt's daughter?"

"Of course. Isn't that all right?"

"What does *he* say?"

"I don't know. I haven't spoken to him yet. I wanted to get your approval first."

Roger rubbed his brow, wondering how much more there was that he didn't know about this young man he had found so dull. He turned away now from Osgood's anxious expression. He could hardly face the idea of the vexation that a belated regret for his paternal indifference might cost him. It was simply too late, much too late, to establish any real relationship. "Well, if Charles doesn't mind, why should I? You must bring Felicia to the house so that your mother and I may meet her."

"Oh, Mummie knows her and likes her ever so much!"

"Then there you are." Roger contrived a smile. "She must be all right."

4
—
卐

Kitty Carstairs on a dark snowy evening in the winter of 1882 was seated before the dressing table in her pink-and-yellow Louis XV boudoir on Murray Hill, dressed already, as she liked to put it, *en grand gala du soir* and attaching to her lobes the ruby earrings that went with her scarlet crêpe de chine. On a chaise longue by the window lounged her brother Lemuel, languid and splendid in white tie and tails, whom her maid had just summoned up from the parlor.

"Charles and Jane Pratt will be at the Mortimers' tonight. I've asked Clara Mortimer to seat you next to Jane."

Lemuel threw up his arms in disgust. "Just because I couldn't take you to the Sykeses' on Friday? Really, Kitty, how vindictive can a sister be?"

"Bore Insurance should pay you three hundred for her."

Kitty and her brother paid dues to a small private group which listed the biggest bores in Gotham and paid off at so much a head to any member who found himself stuck beside one at a dinner party.

"But it's cheating if you arrange it with the hostess! I'm surprised at you, Kitty."

"*I'll* pay you the three hundred then."

"Happily, I have no prejudice against taking money from a woman."

"It's a comfort that I can always depend on your being devoid of senseless male inhibitions."

"I'm not such an ass, anyway, as to take *that* for a compliment. But tell me what you want me to do with the sublime Jane Pratt. Not make love to her, I trust?"

"Could one? No, I simply want you to convince her that Osgood is in no way like his father. Charles Pratt is actually objecting to the match. He doesn't fancy his beloved Felicia as Roger's daughter-in-law."

Osgood sat up. "His own law partner?"

Kitty shrugged as if the vagaries of the male sex were beyond her. "It seems he objects to Roger's ethics."

"Well, I certainly can't blame him for *that!* But what about his own?"

"That's what Osgood asked. The poor boy is in a terrible state. He had no idea that Roger wasn't like any other lawyer."

"That's the trouble with New York. He is."

"Now, Lem, don't be pompous. I haven't asked you to hold forth on the evils of modern society. Pratt apparently told Osgood that he had stayed with the firm after Roger became a partner only to counteract his 'bad influence.' "

"And to make a very good living as he did so!" Lemuel clapped his hands and hooted. "I'm only sorry the great Dickens is not alive to put

Pratt in a novel. He would excel Mr. Pecksniff as the archetype of hypocrisy. Has Roger heard of this yet?"

"No! And he mustn't or he'll blow us all to Kingdom Come! That's where you come in. I have almost persuaded Jane Pratt to talk her husband out of his silly attitude. I count on you to put in the finishing touches."

"Is it really worth it? I'm not at all sure that Osgood couldn't do better than the Pratts. I was hoping he might catch a real heiress from one of the families that are still climbing. A Vanderbilt, for example."

"No, no, I know where we are socially, my dear. The Pratts are just right for us. It's all very well for you, a bachelor, to talk about our doing better. It's easy enough for you to go anywhere you like. But for a woman it's different. There are plenty of dowagers in this town who are ready to do me in if given half a chance. My success has aroused envy, and don't fool yourself that that war has been forgotten yet. And even if it had been, Roger's snooty attitude about Yankees would revive it. If we had a real showdown with a couple as respected as the Pratts, it might upset my applecart!"

Lemuel appeared to be weighing this. "Well, I suppose there may be something in what you say. Jane Pratt *is* a descendant of Peter Stuyvesant, though I doubt if half the new families even know who he was. How do you want me to approach her?"

"What I really need is to get her to make Charles drop his condition."

"A condition to his consent to the wedding?"

"Yes. It's a very stiff one, I'm afraid."

"What *is* Charles's condition?" came a voice from the doorway, and they both turned to face Roger. Kitty's self-possession rarely deserted her. "Oh, a silly condition," she replied casually, as if relieved that his arrival had saved her the trouble of sending for him. "You know what a stickler Jane is in matters of etiquette. Apparently they're in mourning and don't want to have a wedding reception."

Roger's expression was dangerously impassive as he advanced into the room. "For whom are the Pratts in mourning?"

"Oh, I don't know. Some old cousin three or four times removed. I told Jane that we didn't care about a reception. That we'd give a party for the bride and groom after the honeymoon."

"Just a minute, Kitty. One doesn't forgo a wedding reception for one's only daughter because of the death of a distant cousin. Even for a close relation, one would simply postpone the wedding for a month or so."

"Oh, Roger, you know these old New Yorkers. They mourn for years for the remotest kin!"

"Do they? I saw Charles in the office this morning, and he was certainly not wearing a black tie or even a mourning band. In fact, I particularly noticed his very red cravat." And then his features suddenly hardened. "They're not in mourning at all, are they, Kitty? Not even for a cousin twice removed?"

"Well, maybe they just don't like wedding receptions!" Kitty exclaimed with finely affected exasperation. "*You* should be glad anyway. You hate the damn things and probably wouldn't even go to it. And as for me, the only thing I'd like about it is it would probably bust our Bore Insurance Society!"

But Roger was inexorable. "The reason Charles doesn't want to give a reception is that he doesn't wish to introduce his friends and relations to me. Isn't that it?"

"Oh, Roger, what if it is? What do we care? We don't have to marry *him*, do we?"

"But I care very much. And I shall look forward to having a general clarification with Charles Pratt no later than tomorrow. It will be my pleasure to inform him that if he feels ashamed of this alliance, *I* feel degraded. I shall further inform him that he has been paid by his partners through the years, not for his legal aptitude or his roster of clients, both of which are, to say the least, exiguous, but for his constituting the formal façade of piety which all good Yankee enterprises require."

"Oh, that's just fine!" Kitty rose and faced him with clenched fists. "What fun you're going to have! You'll smash poor Osgood's wedding and maybe even break up your law firm. You'll have all New York society shouting for your head. And best of all, you'll bring me down in the general wreck! That's what you've always wanted, isn't it? Well, go ahead and try! I dissociate myself from you. Osgood and I will make it alone."

"I shall always support you, Kitty."

"I don't want your Yankee money!" she almost shrieked.

But this was too much for Lemuel, who now rose and glanced at his watch. "If you don't mind my interrupting this little scene, Roger, Kitty and I must be off to the Mortimers'. I believe we shall meet the Pratts there."

"Tell Charles I shall come to his office in the morning" was all that his brother-in-law grimly replied.

5

The two years following Roger's rupture with his firm, which resulted from the irate Pratt's demand that their partners choose between the two of them, he spent alone in Castledale. Kitty remained in the New York house, which he supposed she would be able to maintain for a few years on the half of his savings that he had turned over to her. After that he had little interest in what happened. He no longer had any earned income, and the remainder of his capital was destined for the endowment of his museum. It was not a great sum, at least by the standards of the new rich, but costs in Virginia were still low, and, his foundation once legally established, he could move into the old overseer's lodge with Ned. But for the time being he was occupying the big house, a moody hermit amid the splendors of his continued restorations.

He saw almost nobody but his ever-sympathetic brother. The local gentry would have been glad enough to welcome him had he taken the trouble to ingratiate himself, but his aloofness was repelling, and in time the rumors of the bad reputation that he enjoyed even in a city as wicked as New York began to tarnish his image. When, in addition, the respectable neighbors learned that he had deserted a blameless wife and was planning to disinherit a dutiful son, they dug up the old legend of his duel with Drayton and converted it to something more like a cold-blooded murder. It was even claimed that he had known ahead of time that his victim intended to fire into the air.

Roger cared little for their prattle, some of which the more troubled Ned related to him in the vain hope that an ameliorated attitude might appease the countryside.

"But don't you see, Ned, that what they're saying about me is basically fact? Oh, they've added a lot of nasty and false details, it's true. People wouldn't be people if they didn't do that. But I can't quarrel with the main outline of their image of me. I *am* a bit of a monster, you know."

The only criticism that he did mind came from within the walls of

Castledale, not from humans, for nobody lived there at night but himself and only the cook and parlor maid by day. It came from ghosts. The pale wooden faces of the Colonial Carstairses over coats and dresses as unwrinkled as planks looked not at him but past him. The Revolutionary general, whose big nose and alarming sabre dominated the dining room, saw him but did not recognize him. And his mother, looking sad and subdued even as a debutante in the day of Andrew Jackson, seemed to be conveying the timid message that she couldn't talk to him now, before the others, but could she have a word with him later, alone? Yet the note the family appeared to be striking was not one of hostility, or even, really, of disapproval. It was more that he didn't belong there. He had called at a house where he wasn't expected. What did he hope to gain by prolonging the error?

"They want me out of Castledale," he told Ned one day at lunchtime, waving towards the portraits on the wall. "They treat me like a stranger. Even an intruder."

"How ungrateful of them! After all you've done."

"Oh, they don't care about that. They'd rather be shabby. They feel about me the way the Stewarts down the road feel about the rich Yankee who bought High Farm."

"But Castledale is *yours*, Roger!"

"Not in their opinion. I've forfeited my rights."

Ned's finger rested on the base of his wineglass as he pondered something. "There's one way you might bring them around."

"I know. By willing the place to Osgood. You're a stuck whistle on that subject. But he couldn't keep it up, even if he wanted it."

"He could if you left him the money."

"There's not enough. He'd use it for his family, and it'll be needed to maintain the house. Osgood hasn't a penny over his wretched salary. Pratt cut off Felicia when she married without his consent."

"He'll forgive. They always do in the end."

"But he's damn near bust himself! Osgood wrote me about it. Pratt was always the world's worst investor, and he got his ears pinned back in that Montana mine fraud."

"Oh, so Osgood writes you?"

"When he's desperate. Felicia had twins, you know. Oh, I sent him a check, of course. I'm not quite the ogre people say. But the real money has to go to the museum. You know that, Ned."

"*I* don't know it. You may. I have no use for museums, at least in the country. Castledale should be owned by a Carstairs."

One night, after a solitary dinner, Roger had risen and strolled to the fireplace to take his usual leave of the portrait over it of General Carstairs. He would offer his great-grandfather a military salute, but he never went so far as to imagine that it would be returned. But that evening he had a curious feeling that it had been, that the hero of the Battle of Chesnut Hill, in view of some special and perhaps ominous occasion, was offering him a recognition that might never have to be repeated.

And then the blankness returned to those authoritative features, and Roger felt, in a swirling, diving emptiness, that he himself was no longer there.

When he regained consciousness he was in his bed, and Ned, standing by it, was telling him that he had suffered a heart attack.

Roger eyed him curiously. Certainly Ned was very somber.

"What is the prognosis, Ned?" He heard his own voice, but faint and far away. "Facts, please, Ned."

"Not good, I'm afraid."

"How long?"

"There's no time given, Roger."

"But time enough to make a new will, is that it?"

Ned looked pained but still resolute. "I think you'd be more at peace with yourself."

"Good old Ned, you never give up, do you? But you'll be glad to know that I don't have to make a new will. For I haven't got one. I tore up the last one because I had some new ideas about setting up the museum that I wanted to think over. If I died now, Osgood would get everything."

"Except for Kitty's dower rights."

"She waived them when I gave her the New York house."

Ned sat slowly down on the bed. He seemed suddenly very moved. "Roger, my dear brother, it's not just Osgood and the place I'm thinking of. It's you. Believe me. If you could just allow the normal succession of things in Castledale, you might rid yourself of the hate that's been eating away at your heart all these years."

"Hate? What are you talking about? Hatred of what?"

"I've never been sure. All I know is it's there. And that it's always been there. At least ever since I can remember. Of course, I'm seven years younger than you. Did it all start with that duel?"

Roger stared with a new interest at this suddenly penetrating sibling. But he didn't answer the question. "I don't hate you, Ned."

"I don't believe you do. But I'm part of Castledale. And you certainly don't hate Castledale."

"But its ghosts hate me!"

"Maybe you could change that."

Roger considered this. "But if I give up this hate or obsession or whatever it is, won't it be too late? If I've lived with it so long, what will I have in its place? For whatever time I may have left?"

Ned actually shrugged. "Nothing in particular, I guess. What I have. What other people have. Wouldn't that be better?"

"Would Osgood and Felicia live here if the place was theirs? How would they keep it up?"

"They'd have me to help them."

And Roger realized that, of course, Ned had been writing to them. Well, why not? He closed his eyes as he felt the emptiness coming over him again. If it should be another attack, he could surrender to the soothing notion that he now needn't do anything about anything. There was a wonderful ease to Ned's concept of "nothing in particular." The pavilions of the Lawn stretched down the valley of his mind to the great dome with all the grace and tranquillity of Mr. Jefferson's noble scheme. He could forget the fire and the sword and the long sordid aftermath and soothe his tired spirits with the blessed memory of the red dirt and blue hills beyond a serene Castledale.

The Stoic

1993

1

I CAN HARDLY remember a time in my early life, back toward the turn of the century, when I did not worship Lees Dunbar. No doubt many other boys in New York City, or even along the eastern seaboard, felt the same way, for his power as the founder of Dunbar, Leslie & Co., the putter-together of corporate empires, the adviser to presidents, drew daily to his desk the troubled magnates of Wall Street to pour out their problems as he expressionlessly listened, examining rare stamps through a magnifying lens. Detached, Olympian, stern, he was, without a rival, my ideal of a man.

I will admit that he did not look like a great man. He was stout, with a large square face and brow topped by short thick gray hair, one lock of which curved over his forehead like a small breaking wave. His habitual expression was one of barely contained irritation, either at you or the weather, the latter seeming always somehow oppressive, as if prompting him to tear open his collar or throw off his jacket. His voice had an unpleasant rasp, and was never wasted on small talk. He was a man who needed neither friends nor relatives; his wife was a semi-invalided recluse and they had no children. It was assumed that his mind, his stamps and his art collection were all the companions he needed.

He had been a Southerner, a Virginian of gentle birth, who had come north after the Civil War, but who had not fought in it. He had gone to work for a Manhattan banker, his uncle-in-law, whose daughter he had married and whose business he had splendidly multiplied. If he had had sympathies for the Old South, he never betrayed them; it was not his way to manifest the least religious, patriotic or philosophic affiliation. His faith in money as the circulating blood to sustain an otherwise presumably purposeless humanity seemed his only creed.

Socially his life was confined to excursions on his steam yacht, the *Magellan*, and to my mother's salon. Of the latter he was the principal adornment, sitting aside in a corner armchair to which she would bring up those guests, one by one, whom she deemed sufficiently interesting in politics, finance or art to merit a few words with him. If he was in one of his gruffer moods, she would leave him alone to read his book and sip brandy.

On one such occasion I brought myself to his attention by taking a seat opposite him and also immersing myself in a book. The year was 1902; I was fourteen.

"What are you reading, George?" he asked me. "You seem absorbed." I held up *The Story of the Medici*, and he grunted. "Is it for school?"

"No, it's for me. I like to read about men who get ahead with their brains. I've never been much at games and sports."

"That rheumatic fever you had? But you're all over that, aren't you? You look pretty hale to me. A bit skinny, perhaps."

"Oh, I'm all right. But if I'd lived in Italy in those days, I doubt I'd have been much of a warrior."

"You could have gone into the Church. Become a cardinal. They ruled the roost then. Scarlet robes. Marble palaces. Poison. A good enough show. You might even have been Pope."

"But didn't they have to fight, too? Didn't Julius II lead his troops into battle?"

"Only because he wanted to."

"But to be a priest." I wrinkled my nose. "Would you have cared for that, sir?"

"I?" The bushy eyebrows soared. "Not in the least. I've never said a prayer in my life."

"Nor have I. Or one I really meant, anyway."

For a moment he actually looked at me. "You might have been an artist. They were treated as equals by the great Lorenzo himself."

"But I could never draw! Even one of those square houses with a balloon of smoke coming out of the chimney."

I had made him smile. "I suppose you're trying to tell me you'd have been a banker. Well, that's a good thing to be. That book of yours should tell you how the Medici started as pawnbrokers, but succeeded in marrying into every royal house in Europe."

"I know. And it's my one ambition to become a banker. Do you think I could ever get a job with you?"

But this was precipitate. The great man returned to his book. "Work hard at school, my boy. Get to the top of your class. And when the time comes, we'll see."

I was not again guilty of such rashness in the years that followed. I continued to see Mr. Dunbar on his visits to our house and would ask him about any financial matters mentioned in the newspaper in which he had been involved. At times, finding me attentive and instructed, he would answer at some length. He noticed, too, that I never forgot a name, a date or a figure that he mentioned. At last he invited me to work as an office boy for a summer, and I had the tact never to speak to him while on the job. The following summer I was rehired and promoted to the file room. A third summer I was an assistant cashier. By the time I had graduated from my day school (my fever had exempted me from the rough and tumble of boarding institutions), I knew as much about private banking as many adult practitioners.

At Columbia I elected courses entirely in economics and history. I became a work hound with few friends, serious youths like myself who were more concerned with figures and statistics than what some people call life. But I think I had an artist's joy in converting the hash of economic competition into the chaste black and white of a balance sheet.

My relations with Mr. Dunbar had now reached the point where I could confide in him. I don't know even today if he and I ever really "liked" each other in the ordinary sense of that vague term. I needed him, and he came in time to need me. We had the closeness of trust, the word that was the keynote of his existence. He would only do business with men whom he trusted, or purchase works of art in whose authenticity he was convinced, or have social relations with people he knew would not lie to him.

Our important conversation occurred when I was nineteen and had been invited for the first time to lunch with him in the dark tapestried downtown office that he had filled with glinting objects of gold and silver — reliquaries, platters, ewers, ciboria — all paying seeming tribute to the illuminated portrait by Zurbarán of an ecstatically praying monk. It was only on canvas that prayers invaded Mr. Dunbar's ambiance. I put to him my vital question as soon as our brief meal was concluded.

"How much longer, sir, should I go on with college? Is a Columbia degree really worth two more years of courses? I've taken all the ones I want."

"I never took a degree myself. Any man of first-class intellect is going to be his own educator. Good teachers, even great ones, are for the less intelligent. That's their function, though they'd die before admitting it. They like to boast that they 'inspire.' But the men I'm speaking about are already inspired. Did Shakespeare need a professor? Did Napoleon? Did Lincoln?"

"But I could certainly learn from you, sir."

"That would not be school. That would be apprenticeship. A totally different affair."

I turned away so that he might not see that I had closed my eyes. Then glancing at the monk, I *did* offer a silent prayer. "And when can I start that apprenticeship?"

"Tomorrow, if you're ready."

"I'll be here at eight!"

And I was wise enough to depart without another word.

My parents expressed a rare surprise when I informed them of my decision that night. They even exchanged a rather startled glance.

"Mr. Dunbar thinks so little of college degrees?" my father asked.

"He certainly thinks he can teach me more about banking than they can at Columbia."

Another glance was exchanged across the dinner table. It was Mother, as usual, who settled the issue.

"Well, if Mr. Dunbar is really going to look out for George . . ." She clasped her long hands together, the tips of her index fingers touching her lips. "Well, I really don't see how the boy could do much better."

It is time to speak of Dora and Albert Manville.

Mother's "beauty," like everything else in her life, was the product of careful planning, a major part of which was its concealment. One had to live with her to be aware of the rare hum of hidden wheels or to catch the even rarer flicker of exhaustion in the mild stare of her eyes. She knew perfectly how to make a dramatic contrast between rest and motion. The angle at which she held her head as she contemplated her interlocutor with a gently mocking air of surprise would be suddenly broken by a whoop of laughter somehow even more complimentary for being so evidently contrived. Her vivid gestures — clapping her hands or covering her face — her high silvery tones and throaty chuckles offered the continuous pantomime of a dainty romping with accepted values, a mincing two-step with the down-to-earth. Mother's small delicate nose, her rosebud of a mouth, her oval chin and high pale brow seemed almost doll-like until one recognized them as stage properties out of which a good deal of highly visible drama could be made.

Our sober little brownstone on East Sixtieth Street exploded into an elegant Elsie De Wolfe interior of bright chintzes whose chairs and divans seemed always waiting for callers and whose pillows appeared to be plumped up by invisible hands every time they were creased. My sister Eleanor and I were part of the decor, washed and combed and reclad whenever we came in, flushed and rumpled, from school or exercise. Mother treated us with a rather studied affection even when we were alone with her; her "darlings" and "pets" had a faintly theatrical ring, but, though she never lost her temper, there was a quiet ineluctability about her discipline that we knew could never be got around. Mother's children, like her furniture, had to be ready for the maid coming in with a card on a silver tray and her rising to greet a caller with: "How angelic of you to come! I was just hoping that might be your ring!"

Father to the world must have seemed the immaculate club gentleman of the era, with smooth prematurely white hair, pointed gray goatee, long handsome brown face and large aquiline nose. But his light blue eyes were windows that seemed to catch the light and reveal nothing within. Father toiled not, neither did he spin; his days in winter were spent at the card table of his club and in summer on the golf course. His manners were ceremonious even with his children; his temper was fretted only by alterations in his routine. And it was evident even to my boyish eyes that our callers, after greeting him with the false cheer that precedes a quick dismissal, would turn their eyes at once to Mother. Not that he minded. He demanded nothing of any day but that it should be just like its predecessor.

All right, my reader will say. When is he going to come out with it? Does he think we don't *know?*

Of course, all New York knew that Dora Manville was Mr. Dunbar's mistress. The affair had been going on for years, and I'm sure there were those who fancied a resemblance between myself and the great banker, though in most respects we were physical opposites. My parents were regular members of the cruises on the *Magellan* where Mother, in the absence of the always ailing Mrs. Dunbar, acted as unofficial hostess. But the proprieties were at all times strictly observed on each side; no terms of endearment were employed, nor any fond or even affectionate glances exchanged. Father played cards and fished with his host; indeed, the only hint that anything was out of line might have been that Mr. Dunbar, never known for his tolerance of lesser men, treated this guest with a marked respect.

It was not, however, the old French convention that society should ignore what a husband chose to overlook that kept the Manhattan moralists at bay. *They* would never have considered themselves foreclosed by so mean a thing as a *mari complaisant*. No, it was the simple power of Lees Dunbar to make or break a man in Wall Street that induced them to accept his offered bribe of the rigid observance of forms. The more holy could thus pretend they didn't know; the less sanctified had the release of gossip. The affair had the respectability we read about in Saint-Simon of the liaison between the aging Sun King and Madame de Maintenon.

I don't know when I learned of the affair first, but it seems to me I had always known. Had I gone to boarding school, it might well have been flung in my face, but at my academy, where I attended only morning classes, the boys were more tactful or perhaps more ignorant. And then we were always accompanied; in the park and at dancing school there were governesses, and in our military drill at the armory no chatter was allowed. Sex, if not gossip, I learned about in huddles in school corridors and visits upstairs in the homes of other boys. It squeezed itself into our upholstered life, and the usual first question in a boy's mind, "You don't mean Mummie and Daddy do *that?*" framed itself in mine with respect to Mother and Mr. Dunbar.

But he was old, it may be objected, old and stout and ugly. Still, he was dominating, an obvious power. In my fantasies Mother began to play the role of a white slave who had to strip and wave her hips and roll obscenely on a tiger-skin rug before the pale stare of the sultan. As I became more educated in the ways of sex, thanks to the dirtier-minded of my school associates, I pictured her doing all kinds of lewd things to whet the appetites of her jaded lord, her eyes darkening with the dark pleasure of her humiliation. I certainly felt no urge to defend her. She was a whore! A stylish whore who was earning her keep.

Eleanor, two years my senior, was a large, emotional and rather violent girl, obsessed with the snooty little clique of fashionable females who dominated her class at Miss Chapin's School, and she made little effort to conceal what a poor thing she found in me. When she finally discovered Mother's liaison (she was devoid of imagination and had to learn it from a friend), she was appalled.

"I intend to get married as soon as I possibly can," she announced to me in a storm of tears. "Of course, I shan't marry without falling in love, but I'm going to make a point of doing that with the first eligible man that comes along."

"I'd say you got there some time back," I sneered. Eleanor got from me what she usually gave. "Though the eligibility will come as a relief. Last year we thought you were going off with the piano tuner. The one who said you had a touch like Liszt. I hear he's been committed."

She didn't deign to retort. "Seriously, George, I can't stand what's going on. I don't want to live in this house a day longer than I have to."

"If you feel that strongly, why don't you go now?"

"And do what? Beg in the streets? Or worse?"

"Surely one of the aunts will take you in."

"Never. I'd have broken the sacred rule of looking the other way. The holy family commandment of sweeping it under the Aubusson. Every door would be slammed in my face."

"But nobody cares that much."

"Nobody cares at all! That's the trouble."

"Why can't you just let things be? It's not hurting you, is it?"

"That our mother's a kept woman! Does that mean nothing to you? Don't you know who pays for this house? For all the parties she gives? For your and my school bills?"

"Well, so long as they're paid." I shrugged, thoroughly enjoying now my newfound sophistication and her fury at it.

"Well, if that isn't the limit! Splashing about in the dirty puddle of your mother's dishonor! Honestly, George, I never thought even you'd be such a creep."

"Can the big talk. What are you doing but sitting on your backside in that same puddle until some fool of a guy is crazy enough to pick you out of it?"

For a moment I thought she was going to be sick to her stomach. Her face turned dark. "You crummy little bastard!" she almost shrieked.

Then she paused as if hearing her own word. "Oh, my God, I'll bet it's just what you are."

"Doesn't that put you in the same boat?"

"No! He didn't even meet Mother until I was one."

"Well, you can have Father all to yourself, then. You're more than welcome to my share of him."

I guess we were both startled at where we had suddenly come out. Eleanor stared at me in mute amazement for a moment and then hurried from the room. We didn't speak of the subject again. Indeed, she and I made a point of not finding ourselves alone together. We seemed to have tacitly agreed on a kind of armed truce.

But I didn't really believe that I was Mr. Dunbar's son; Mother never seemed to me like a person to whom embarrassing accidents happen. And I shouldn't have minded if I had been. I had matured early in a household where it was evident that a child would have to take care of his own happiness and welfare. If a side had to be taken, it seemed ridiculous not to pick the stronger. Father was all form and outward show; Mr. Dunbar was life and power. If Father chose to accept his degrading position, why the devil should I object? What debt did I owe him, or even Mother for that matter? And as for my honor, how was that concerned? Was *I* sleeping with Mr. Dunbar? Could I have stopped my mother from sleeping with him had I tried? And as for the money, Father *did* have an income sufficient to feed, clothe and school me, which the law anyway required of him. *I*, then, was not legally living off Mr. Dunbar. What did Mother's diamonds (discreetly small, by the way) have to do with me? Did *I* wear them?

2

It was probably significant that when I went to work for Mr. Dunbar, he suggested that I move from home to a small but pleasant bachelor's apartment in one of the brownstones that he owned across the street from his own mansion to protect his sunshine against a possible high-rise. This might have been to make me more available for the nocturnal business conferences frequently held in his library, but I had a notion that he wanted me in a drawer distinctly separate from the one in which he kept my mother. There was to be no overlapping there, and indeed I agreed, for I had already resolved that my relation to my new boss was going to be as important to him as hers had ever been. Her appeal was to his lustful old body, but mine was to his mind, and time as well as his own innate sense of values was bound to be on my side.

From the beginning of my permanent employment with the firm I worked only for the senior partner. In the course of three successive summer jobs I had pretty well mastered the routine of the back rooms, and I was now ready to act as his "snoop," as he liked to call me, in poring through the books of companies in which he had or sought to have an interest. After only two years of this apprenticeship, when I was still a mere twenty-one, he began to send me as his emissary to interview corporate executives. He knew now that he could trust me to be properly modest and to seem as little as possible the "arrogant kid genius" that these gentlemen, however polite to the great Dunbar's emissary, undoubtedly dubbed me once the door had closed behind me.

He was not a patient man, and I saw to it that he never had to tell me anything twice. He preferred silence while he was developing plans, and I never interrupted at such times. He liked my speed and my ruthlessness in cutting out irrelevant detail. He appreciated the fact that I could change the subject from work the very moment I saw he was tired, and although I was not educated in art, I was in history and could talk easily on the historical associations of the pictures in his collection. He would sometimes even seek my advice as to a proposed purchase. After all, his collection formed a substantial portion of his wealth. Yet beyond finance and art and the occasional tales of his great business coups, we had few topics of conversation. But then had he with anyone else? Even here I could be a convenience; when it was time to put the little "genie" back in the bottle, the little genie went home.

My early and even rather dramatic preferment did not arouse as much envy in the office as might have been supposed. I think it was because my case was too special. I had not come up through the ranks; I had suddenly appeared, as Ariel on Prospero's island. It was true that I had worked those summers, but then my status had been so low that only the humblest members of the staff had been aware of me. And then it was in my favor that I had not beaten anyone out for my particular position. Mr. Dunbar had never had a young "favorite" before. Perhaps the firm considered me a first faint harbinger of the boss's senility.

Did we like each other, my old man and I? I still keep asking myself that. Was he a surrogate father? I don't think so, really. It was more that I *was* Lees Dunbar, or a small portion of him, anyway. When I followed him down a corridor to a corporate gathering or sat behind his chair at the long conference table, I felt a tingling pride simply to be coupled with him. Perhaps I was not unlike a mystic identifying himself with his deity. In a curious fashion my ego, at what some might have deemed its grossest period, may have virtually ceased to exist.

I saw my parents very little. Mother seemed perfectly willing to accept my excuses of constant toil at the office, and Father, who surely had guessed by now that I knew all, must have been glad to be free of the embarrassment of my presence. And Eleanor, who had still not found "Mr. Right" to deliver her from a household of shame, had to loathe me for having been the confidant of the plan she had been unable to implement.

But the time was coming when my break with home would be absolute. One night in Mr. Dunbar's library, when we had concluded our discussion of a railroad receivership and I had risen to take my leave, he waved a hand towards the drink tray.

"I want to know what you think of that Van Dyck."

On the easel before the empty grate of the gray stone fireplace reclined the huge portrait that he was presumably thinking of buying. It was his custom, detested by art dealers, so to display for weeks the current candidate for his collection, nor did he hesitate to invite other dealers in to offer their opinions as to merit, authenticity and even asking price. The canvas before me depicted a young Cavalier with a wolfhound. The youth, lace-collared, long-legged, high-heeled, one hand casually on a hip, the other muzzling the affectionate canine, had high cheekbones, long blond hair and blue eyes serenely reflecting the security of his rank and station. One felt that he would have been absolutely charming to inferiors. But they would have certainly been inferiors.

"He was killed by the Roundheads in the civil war." Dunbar slowly lit his cigar. "You can see that, can't you? He has that look of doom. But I doubt he much cared. He wouldn't have regretted a world where a brute like Cromwell could cut off King Charles's handsome head."

"I *do* feel it," I replied with some surprise, examining the picture more closely. "You might even call it 'Portrait of a Lost Cause.'"

He nodded. "And lost causes have their charm. Or don't you agree?"

I studied the canvas for another silent period. What did he want me to say? Could he have supposed that I might derive some instruction from a contrast between the young peer and myself? I too was long and skinny and of a pale complexion, but my eyes were closer together and my brown hair rose in a billow over my high brow. Mother used to say, in her mocking way, that if I hadn't dulled my eyes by squinting at figures, I might have had the air of a poet, a kind of emaciated Yeats, and saved myself the trouble of becoming a banker by courting a newly rich heiress not yet converted to society's love of the athlete. And as I thought of all this, I felt a tug at my heart. Was the Cavalier laughing at me? Or was he sneeringly suggesting that I was a kind of renegade Cavalier who had perversely turned myself into a quill-behind-the-ear Roundhead? But I didn't want to cut off anyone's head, least of all a king's. Was he too much of an aristocrat to see that I hadn't had an alternative to be anything but what I was? I turned back with something like defiance to my boss.

"Lost causes have not been exactly *your* forte, sir."

He sniffed. "Such a preference would hardly have recommended me as a guide to investors. Not that I haven't made a good thing out of *seemingly* lost causes. That's when you pick them up cheap. But the truly lost cause, the hopeless battle doomed from the start, has always had a certain attraction for me. The fact that there's nothing in it for its defenders. Nothing whatsoever. Nothing. So unlike *our* trade, my friend. Yours and mine. Yes, I think I shall acquire the Cavalier."

"Were *you* ever tempted to join a lost cause, sir?"

Ah, that was it; that was what he had wanted me to ask! He sat up. "I *was* tempted. And my whole life has turned on my successful resistance to that temptation. It was the lost cause of the Confederate states."

The pause that followed was so long that I supposed he needed a cue. "You moved north after the war, did you not, sir? From Virginia?"

"No, sir, I moved west. From Paris, after Appomattox. My father had been with the French mission during the war, and I had been his secretary. I was too young to fight in the beginning, but in 1863 I turned eighteen, and there was talk of my going home to join the boys in gray. Father, however, insisted that he needed me to stay on and help him. This was certainly a respectable excuse; it might even have been considered my duty. Henry Adams, on the other side, did the same thing for *his* father in London. I don't think I was ever seriously criticized for not joining the colors. But the important thing to me was that my decision to remain in safe Paris was in no way motivated by a desire to help my father or even the Southern cause. It was purely and simply that I saw that cause as irretrievably lost. I did not choose to lose a finger, much less my life, in fighting for it."

I hesitated, unsure what he wanted. "Surely that was only sensible."

"Ah, but was it *good?* Was it virtuous?"

I gaped. "Virtuous?"

"Yes. You must learn, George, something that I suspect you do not know about your old boss. That what is virtuous and what is not are very important questions to him."

"Well, why was it not virtuous? Your fighting would not have changed anything. Except that you might have been killed or even killed someone else. For no purpose. Wasn't that good?"

He stared at me so keenly that I felt it was I and not he that was being morally tested. "Then I find you're a stoic, like myself. You accept the world and its follies. That is, you seek to redress only those follies you *can* redress. Virtue does not weep over the irremediable woes of man. Virtue does not idly wring her hands."

I had my cue now. Virtue was not what the layman would at once ascribe to a great banker. Very well, we would teach him! Had the Cavalier not been an ass to die for such a fool as King Charles? "Futile virtue is like futile pain. It does nobody any good."

Mr. Dunbar seemed to frown from his great forehead down to his thick eyelashes. And how those pale eyes stared! But it was not a stare that seemed to focus on me; it simply included me in the landscape, solar fashion.

"You would not then involve yourself in a lost cause? Even if it were the lost cause of one of your parents?"

Ah, so *that* was it! "You are not suggesting, I presume, sir, that I should do anything to hurt my mother."

"On the contrary, you would be helping her. Financially, morally, even socially. I am old, George. I wish to dedicate my remaining years to peace and quiet. I even hope to become a better husband to my neglected spouse. But she has exacted that I first make a complete break with a certain part of my past."

That the major decisions of life should come without a struggle! But then was it really a major decision? I had only to be careful to make my face expressionless, my tone neutral. "I understand you, sir. I shall be your legate. There will be no trouble."

Those eyes! There seemed now to be a black spot in the center of each. To express a faint shock, perhaps, that I should be quite so ready, quite so quick? Did it mean that I had a nature too base for larger tasks? Was my willingness to be of service a flaw or a virtue? And then his low grunt of assent seemed to assert his recognition that possibly I *was* the rare bird he had been seeking for his later years, the man of his own genius and philosophy who would carry on what he had started. Anyway, he would try me. That was all I needed. It was all I had ever hoped for.

꿈꾼

"You're not going to reproach me for my life *now*, are you?"

Mother was seated at her dressing table, brushing her hair with sharp strokes, still in her peignoir at ten in the morning. I was standing by the window. And, yes, I was playing with the cord of the shade. For I *was* nervous, despite my apparent containment. She continued now, turning to give me a glare:

"Surely even you wouldn't have the cold gall to do that?"

As I watched her features congeal and her glare harden, I had an odd sense of slipping inside her head and seeing myself through her eyes. Was I an unusually neurotic person, or had the peculiar circumstances of my home environment simply sharpened my perceptions while cooling my temper? For despite the tension of the atmosphere, the reaction of which I was primarily aware was curiosity. Were Mother and I for the first time actually communicating directly, without concern for manners or any of the usual human subterfuges needed to mask the ugliness of the ego? Might we even be able to recognize that our relationship had been reduced to the biological?

But no. Even if it was true in my case, it was not in hers. For she detested me. That was the difference. And now, taking my silence as the sign that I *did* mean to throw her past in her face, she dropped the reins on her temper.

"Who do you think paid for your school and college? For your Brooks Brothers suits and even your economics library? Do you think you'd have lived as you have on your father's skimpy trust?"

"Oh, no. I am perfectly aware of what I owe Mr. Dunbar. And properly grateful. As, no doubt, is Father."

"You'll throw that in his face, too!"

"I'm not throwing anything in anyone's face. We all know the facts. Why not go on from there? It's also a fact that Mr. Dunbar wishes to discontinue his relations with you. Hadn't we better face it?"

"*We?*" Mother was on her feet now, her fists clenched. I had not known that she was capable of such a fit of temper. "Where do you come into it, I'd like to know? What are you but your mother's lover's pimp?"

"I should say my function was just the reverse."

"Ah, how you must loathe me to be so glib!"

I paused to consider this. "That might be what Doctor Freud would call the unconscious. But I'm certainly not aware of any such feeling."

"I hope, anyway, you're not going to tell me you're a loving son. And that what you're doing is for my good!"

"I'm not *doing* anything. I'm simply conveying a message. A message you were bound sooner or later to receive. And I'm certainly not going to claim the status of a loving son. What have you ever done to make me love you?"

Even Mother seemed taken aback by this. "You don't think I've been a good mother? Haven't I brought you up well? What have you ever lacked? Have you no gratitude?"

"Why should I have? To have done any less than you did would have been to expose yourself to criticism as a parent. And appearances you have always been expert in. We *looked* like a happy family. That was the point, wasn't it?"

"No," she cried. "I cared for you as much as any mother. Until I saw you had as much love in you as a lizard. And think of all I did for you and Eleanor and even your father! He accepted my relationship with Mr. Dunbar because he knew he couldn't afford to give his wife and children all the things they needed. He loved me! And in return I made him thoroughly comfortable and never once humiliated him in public *or* in private. But *you!* Your greedy hand was out for Dunbar himself — you couldn't wait to slough me off. Well, let me tell you one thing, you cool young man. If you think you're going to slide into fame and fortune by posing as Croesus' bastard, allow me to assure you that, dislike it as you may, you *are* your father's child. And the great Dunbar is well aware of it!"

But, after all, I had never really believed anything else. And Dunbar would not have been a man to push a natural child, any more than he would have pushed a legitimate one, beyond, that is, a decent provision. No, he was like a Roman emperor, more apt to rely on adoption than generation to obtain the ablest successor. He had no faith in things not under his direct control. And as to what Mother had said about Father, I deemed it the merest twaddle. He had simply, in his own economic interest, known where not to look and what not to hear. But it was interesting that a woman so clear about her goals and how to achieve them should feel the need of crassly sentimentalizing two lives dedicated to simple self-aggrandizement.

It was time anyway to put an end to the discussion.

"I shall tell Mr. Dunbar that we have had this clarifying chat. And you can be sure that the easier you make the implementation of his decision, the more fruitfully will he supervise your account."

Mother's stare had now the quality of near disbelief, almost of awe, as if she were confronted with a creature of nonhuman quality. At last she emitted a hard, jarring laugh. "So I am to find virtue more profitable than vice? Oh, do get out of here before I vomit!"

I left, confident that her innate good sense would dictate a moderate course and that her wrath against me had deflected much of her ire against Dunbar. And so it worked out. We met only a few times after that, but she accepted an income from Dunbar, and after his death from me, as the least an unfaithful lover and ungrateful son could offer.

Now many if not most readers at this point will assume that I have bad character, or perhaps no character at all. I am only too well aware that many men with whom I have done business through the years, and even some of my own partners, have regarded me as a cold fish who cares for nothing but making money. Nor would the fact that I have shown little interest in spending it alter their opinion, as American self-made men are notoriously more concerned with wealth than with what it can buy. Nobody, I am afraid, has ever given me credit for being, in my own way, a consistent idealist. Of course, it is true that I have never advertised the fact.

Let me summarize the aspects of my youth which *might* have turned me into the man so many have deemed me to be. I was raised by parents who did not love me and for whom I had no respect. I had a sole sibling who detested me. An early illness kept me from being sent to a boarding school, where at least I might have escaped the unsavory atmosphere of my home. And finally, I found no one around me to admire and emulate until I went to work for Mr. Dunbar.

What saved me — for I insist that I *was* saved — was my clarity of vision. I *saw* the world I lived in. I saw perfectly that it contained, outside my own family, love and honor and innocence and that it was not my fault that my life was barren of these qualities or that my heart did not beat at the pace that others liked to believe theirs did. Nor did I resent or even much envy persons more richly endowed with the gift of love. The id may be called on to rebut me here, but we cannot deal practically with the unconscious. What I was conscious of was that I had to play the hand of cards I had been dealt and that it would be futile and even ridiculous to waste my life lamenting that it did not contain more honors.

I have always been dedicated to the concepts of order and restraint in the governance of human affairs. Most of the problems of civilization, in my opinion, emanate from messy thinking and sloppy or sentimental feeling. Even Mr. Dunbar allowed his passions to embroil him in a sordid affair from which he was rescued only by the sexual impotence of old age. But he always yoked his ambition to the chariot of virtue. His life goal, he maintained, was to impose a balanced budget on a fevered and reckless world, though only if and where it was feasible. He took no credit for spreading ineffective sentiment over barren soil. Only results counted to him. And to me.

To have or not to have a loving heart is not a matter of choice but of birth. Yet people tend to applaud "warmth" and to condemn "coldness" in a man's nature as if such things were matters of merit. But merit, I insist, should attach only to what a man contributes usefully to the welfare of his fellow beings. Vain efforts, good intentions, mean nothing. That has been my credo, as Mr. Dunbar has been my god.

3

There was a change now, hard to define but nonetheless perceptible, in my relations with Mr. Dunbar. It might have been expected that we should have become more personal in our conversations, but that was not quite it. It was more that we seemed tacitly to acknowledge that we had no further secrets from each other, or at least that he had none from me. I presumably had no secrets at all. The awe, at any rate, that I constantly felt for him when out of his presence I was now able to shed at the door of his office or study. I was at ease with him alone, though this ease, if a sense of it was conveyed to him at all, must have been through some barely visible relaxing of my reserve, never of course through any idle chatter or impertinent lounging. And he, for his part, would utter his thoughts openly in my presence, almost as if I were a recording instrument for possible memoirs.

I was now invited regularly to come across the street to take breakfast with him and Mrs. Dunbar. The morning repast was her one regular appearance of the day; she still spent most of her time in her bedchamber. I was somewhat surprised to find her a dear little old lady, soft, gentle and rosily round-faced, who wore a white cap and a black silk dress in perpetual mourning for a long-dead only child. She would fuss over my not eating enough and warn me, if it was a cold day, to wear a muffler to the office.

But she also worried about my working too hard. She was afraid I was having no fun, no love affairs. And she seemed particularly anxious that I should appreciate the man behind the tycoon in her husband, perhaps suspecting me of being one of those for whom the pedestal obscures the statue.

One morning, anyway, when her husband had abruptly quit the table to take his coffee cup to his library, protesting gruffly that she was spoiling his breakfast with her constant nagging him for her little charities, she offered me this mitigation of his conduct.

"You hear, George, how he grumbles. Yet I never have to wait later than noon before a messenger brings me a check for double what I asked for. I know you young men admire him for his brilliance in business. But what I admire him for is the greatness of his heart. He is basically the kindest and gentlest of men."

I didn't quite like this. I fancied a note of denigration. Mr. Dunbar to me was a man above the world because he was free of the weaknesses that beset mankind: love and hate, pity and cruelty, sentimentality and meanness, religiosity and mendacity, holiness and vice.

"I confess I have not always found him kind and gentle. Nor do I believe that to be his general reputation downtown. No one disputes that he is a great man. But great men are not apt to be gentle."

She regarded me smilingly as if pleased to have kindled the mild impatience of my retort. "Oh, you young men today fancy yourselves such a self-contained lot. What are you afraid of? Wasn't President Lincoln a gentle man?"

"The man who unleashed the slaughter of the wilderness campaign? Hardly!"

"That he could bring himself to do *that* was part of his greater humaneness. It was for an ultimate saving of lives. Yesterday my husband promised me to do something very much against his wishes, and even against one of his old principles, to spare anguish to some persons I love. Never has he shown more tenderly what his deepest feelings have always been for me and mine."

I really sat up now. "Mrs. Dunbar, would you mind telling me what that was?"

But her eyes glistened with sudden tears. "Someday, George. Someday perhaps. Not now."

I left the breakfast table as soon as I decently could and took the subway downtown. In my office I found my throat and tongue so dry I had to drink a glass of water. Then I told my secretary I was to be disturbed by no one (Mr. Dunbar always excepted), closed my door and resumed the inspection of certain papers on my desk that I had left unfinished the night before.

They involved a trust of which Oliver Lovat was the sole trustee for his considerably richer wife. Lovat, a nephew of Mrs. Dunbar, owed his limited and very minor partnership in Dunbar, Leslie & Co. to the fact that he was the grandson of the uncle for whom Lees Dunbar had come to work after the Civil War. Lovat was a handsome if rather beefy gentleman dandy of the period, tweedy, mustachioed, derby-hatted and cigar-smoking, who had a joke for everyone, high and low, and a loud blowy manner that I cordially detested. He did no work for the firm of any significance and lived largely on the income and commissions of the trust for his wife, to whom he was notoriously unfaithful and of which her father had been unwise enough to leave him sole fiduciary.

Now it so happened that the much wronged Mrs. Lovat had at last decided to check on her trustee and had hired an accountant who had asked me, as the clerk in charge of fiduciary accounts, for an appointment at the bank the following week. As a matter of routine I had examined the books myself first, and the securities in our vault as well, and I had been surprised to discover that a number of bonds were missing. Of course, this did not have to mean a misappropriation; Lovat might have removed them for a sale. Yet on the same day, receiving as I did the daily list of Mr. Dunbar's personal market transactions, I noticed that he had acquired the same bonds in the same denominations that were missing in the Lovat trust. And now, after Mrs. Dunbar's mysterious revelation, only one interpretation fitted the facts.

Lovat, a known gambler on the stock market, must have hypothecated trust assets to cover his personal loans and was now unable to replace them. Learning of his wife's proposed investigation, he had thrown himself on his knees before his soft-hearted aunt, and she had prevailed upon her husband to make good the loss.

Now this was certainly a new light on my great man, nor did I welcome the idea of any change in his iron character. He was not simply the major influence in my life; you might say he was the only one. I had liked to think of him as a cold man, but only in the sense that I too was cold: reason ruled our hearts. He was always just and fair in all his business dealings, and his word was his bond. And now was he compromising his standards? The ideal of virtue he had so loftily preached to me?

Surely this would be a relaxation of one of his greatest strengths. He had always stipulated for absolute honesty among his own partners and in his own dealings. Anyone who tried to take crooked advantage of him would never do business again with Dunbar, Leslie & Co. As with the dealers who sold him art, to be once caught in a lie was to be banished forever. He believed that American business could police itself, and he had nothing but contempt for reform politicians.

But now had the bell struck? I am still proud to say that I did not flinch before the challenge. Armed with my list of his recent market purchases, I marched into his office and laid it boldly on his desk.

He picked it up and read it slowly, as if for the first time. I was almost embarrassed for him, which made me even bolder, daring enough to put this reminder to him:

"You once asked me, sir, if your decision not to take a military part in the Civil War had been a virtuous one."

How still he was! But he might have been crouching. "Yes, sir. And, as I recollect, you told me you believed it had been."

"I was deeply impressed at how much you cared that any act of yours should be virtuous."

He nodded. "And now you are wondering how much I still care."

"Precisely."

"You have perceived that I am preparing to make whole my wife's nephew's misappropriations."

"Just so."

"And you are questioning the virtue of what I am considering?"

"No, sir, I am not questioning it. I am condemning it."

Oh, he liked that! He liked to be stood up to by one who knew what he was doing. "Condemning without a trial? Without considering all the facts? I am saving a man's wife from destitution, our firm from disgrace, himself from indictment. And I can police him in the future. I shall require his resignation from his fiduciary position. He will be no further menace to society."

"But you will have concealed a felony. *You* will know that in the future the word of Lees Dunbar will be good only when the circumstances are propitious."

"My word, sir? What word?"

"You will be certifying to an accountant that a trust is in order."

"And will it not be?"

"Only when you have doctored it."

He grunted and now moved for the first time, shifting heavily in his chair. "Let us consider the consequences. Oliver will be a desperate man. He may even do himself in. He's just the type that does. Where will be the benefit to society?"

"Is that our criterion?"

"We? Are 'we' so sure of our own motives? You, for example. Mightn't my nephew offer a possible obstruction to your own advancement in the firm? 'The old boy is getting senile,' my partners may be already saying. 'How many protégés do we have to put up with? First the incompetent Lovat and now this young fellow with whose family the old boy had such a curious intimacy? Isn't one enough?' "

I smiled inwardly. Surely I had achieved the ultimate union with him now. That he should even speak of the "curious intimacy"! "I'm not worried about Lovat, sir. I could lick him in the firm with one hand tied behind my back."

Again that slow nod. "I believe you could. Very well. Let us probe even deeper. Mightn't we — and I do mean both of us — derive an actual satisfaction from the bloody sacrifice we would be making on the altar of our given word?"

"Should the pleasure of doing the right thing disqualify us from doing it?"

A ponderous silence. "Why are you doing this to me, George?"

"Because I believe in you, sir."

"And because you believe in nothing else?"

I must confess, this took me aback. "That could be in it, I suppose."

"That's what I'm afraid of." His sigh, if deep, was final. "Very well. Obviously, I cannot now proceed with my little plan of rescue. But don't worry. I shall not hold it against you. I even sympathize with your point of view. Alas! I must tell the wretched Oliver to look elsewhere for his salvation. What a world! But I had no hand in the making of it."

Oliver Lovat's body was fished out of the East River the next morning. He had joined the army of those despairing souls who elect to solve their insoluble problems by a leap from Brooklyn Bridge. But there was no disgrace for the firm or destitution for the widow, as the real motive for the suicide was never discovered. His debts and disorderly love life provided adequate causes for the journals. And it was I who suggested to Mr. Dunbar that it would now be in order to replace the embezzled securities before the accountant's inspection. There was no longer an embezzler to be prosecuted. But I suspect that Mrs. Dunbar had somehow divined my role. The invitations to breakfast were rescinded on the excuse that she now took that meal in her room.

Her husband made up for the breakfasts by asking me regularly to lunch in his office. There was nothing at this point that he did not discuss with me, from his purchase of a still life to the merger of two railroads. And at the bank I was now universally treated as the established favorite. I did not trouble myself with how much envy and how much dislike might be concealed under the polite exteriors. I knew that none of the juniors would play any part in my rise or fall. I had staked my all on Mr. Dunbar, placing my eggs in a single basket, but having total faith in the reliability of that container. He might die — but a banker must be prepared to take *some* risk.

And indeed it was not long before he advised me that the time had come for me to extend myself socially in the firm.

"We'd better start thinking about a partnership for you. Twenty-seven is young in the eyes of the world, but you have the experience of a much older man. You must become better known to the partners. We'll start with John Leslie. He will ask you for a weekend on Long

Island. He won't, of course, mention that I have suggested the invitation. You will be your discreet self about that."

"Of course, sir."

"And pay some attention to his daughter, Marion. Unless your heart is otherwise engaged?"

"Free as air, sir."

"As I rather supposed. You work too hard, my boy. Marion's a fine girl. A bit on the athletic side, but handsome. Apparently she's had some sort of unhappy love affair which she claims she'll never get over. But women like to make a drama of these things. We know about that. There are two brothers in the London office, fine fellows, charming, but a bit on the playboy side. It's not a sure thing they're partnership material. Leslie might content himself with a partner son-in-law. *Verbum sapienti.*"

I restrained a gasp. Had I really come *that* far? Like a papal nephew in the Renaissance marrying into the old Roman nobility? "But would a girl like that so much as look at a dreary bank clerk who doesn't even play polo?"

He shrugged scornfully. "You don't want me to tell you *how* to do it, do you? Go to. You're not a bad-looking fellow. A bit on the skinny and pale side, but even that can be attractive. Who knows? She may be tired of the brawny brainless. And her old man tells me that she's got a thing about the firm. Wishes she'd been a man so she could be a member of it. It's up to you, my boy!"

4

Mr. Leslie was as handsome, as suave and as unsurprising as his fine, purple brick Tudor mansion with its emerald lawns and shady elms and white-fenced fields and stables. He had thick black-gray hair, a strong, well-shaped nose, a square chin and gleaming white teeth. He had to have had brains to have achieved his position in the firm and his assistant secretaryship of the army under Theodore Roosevelt, but I supposed his mind had been largely and shrewdly focused on using a charming personality to its best advantage. Mr. Dunbar, who was plain to the edge of ugliness, had notoriously converted his envy of good-looking males to a desire to be surrounded by them; it was a distinct tribute to my own intelligence that I had become his intimate without a stalwart build.

When my weekend host offered me golf or tennis and learned that I played neither, he turned me over to his daughter with a pleasant grin that effectively masked any scorn the athlete must have felt. If a protégé of Lees Dunbar could play only tiddledywinks, then tiddledywinks it would be.

Marion, tall, broad of shoulder, with the fine paternal nose and high clear brow, but with moppy rich auburn hair, made no effort to conceal her disgruntlement at my paucity of athletic choice. I soon learned that she made no effort to conceal any of her reactions. The good things of life had been plumped into her lap, where she obviously felt they belonged.

"Well, shall we put on our bathing suits and sit by the pool?" she asked. "We can lend you a suit if you don't have one."

But I had no wish to expose my etiolated figure to the contrast of her brothers' brown muscles. If she was to be won, it would not be that way.

"Why don't you take me for a walk? I'd love to make a tour of this beautiful place."

"Oh, all right." She brightened a bit. "We've got a thousand acres, you know." She glanced at my polished shoes. "Can we provide you with sneakers?"

"No, I have a pair, thank you."

And off we went across the meadows, pausing to watch grazing horses and Black Angus, into the woods to the marshland abutting Long Island Sound. Her enthusiasm waxed when she saw I didn't mind a good pace or getting my sneakers muddy when she put a finger to her lips and beckoned me to follow her for a closer look at a perched hawk. On the way back she became more conversational.

"I suppose you don't have much time for sports. Daddy says you work too hard. But that you're one of the real up-and-comers at the office."

"He flatters me. But it's true about the work. I never seem to have concentrated on games."

"You're not like most of the young men I know. You're more serious. I guess that's a good thing. But haven't you missed them? The sports, I mean."

"I don't think so."

"You don't think they're important?"

"Well, they're not to me. They're important to the wealthy, I suppose. They help kill time. You pointed out yourself that one needed time for them."

"Yes, but not just to *kill* it. I never heard such a strange idea. What *do* you find important?"

"Finance."

"You mean making money?"

"Well, that's certainly a part of it. After all, this lovely place, the horses, the cattle, the opportunities for sport, your whole life here, what does it depend on but money?"

Her nose indicated her distaste. "Mother's always taught us it's vulgar to talk about money."

"That's because our families like to think of themselves as aristocrats. They want to feel they owe their position to birth and not just dough. But they're wrong. As mine found out when they lost theirs."

Marion paused. She had not decided whether or not to take offense at any line of argument.

"You sound like a radical."

"Because I talk about money? I should have thought it was just the opposite."

"But you don't think like other people."

"Maybe that's because I think."

"You're pretty sure of yourself, aren't you?"

I decided it was time to pull up. I had made a sufficient gesture of independence. "Forgive me for being such an ass. I'm not used to talking to attractive and intelligent young women. I'm just not socially experienced, I guess."

Marion smiled. "Oh, you're not doing so badly. We may make something out of you yet."

At dinner that night were just the family and I. I had the feeling it was a rare occasion that induced Marion's two handsome brothers, on leave from London, muscular, thin and bony, one dark and one light, like black and spotted jaguars, to sup at home without female guests. But why? Did Mr. Dunbar's arm reach even into his partners' domestic arrangements?

If so, it had failed to touch Mrs. Leslie. Her attitude towards me had none of the friendly accord of her husband and sons. She was a plain, silent, rather grim little woman who seemed to have nothing in common with her good-looking and cheerful family. She had been an heiress herself, I knew, but surely John Leslie could have made his fortune without the help of hers. Or was there, in his very shining air of assurance, the hint of a nature that would have taken *no* chances? Anyhow, the way she reduced the required acknowledgment of my presence to the briefest of nods showed what use she had for the "likes of me." I supposed she saw me as the son of a kept woman, probably as a kind of *fils complaisant.*

But the "boys," Jack and Bob, my own age, more or less, were another matter. They, like their old man, were charming. They might not have been intellectual, but they had plenty of wit for amiable small talk, and they made pleasant fun of their father and sister (never of Mama!) as they exchanged smiles and knowing glances. They were politely complimentary to me in their questions about my work, perhaps overly so. Were they laughing at me? Very likely. But there might have been another compliment to my perspicacity in their letting me see that they saw I saw it, that they counted on me to appreciate their innate good will in a world where one thing, after all, was pretty much as inconsequential as another: a game of tennis, a bond issue, a polo match, a mortgage foreclosure. It was my first glimpse of the aristocratic point of view.

I found it pleasurably warming, but it also dug an odd little crater of desolation somewhere in the root of my being. For I could never be as they, or really included by them. They shared a fraternity of looks and sports and jokes and easy masculinity of which I could never be a true part. At a later date, Bob, the younger brother, would tell me that he recognized only three types among his male acquaintance: "swell guys, shits and genial shits." He didn't say it, but I knew the only category I could aspire to was the third.

Jack, who was slightly more serious than his younger brother, brought up the subject of Mr. Dunbar's great repute.

"Dad tells us, George, that you know Mr. Dunbar better than anyone else does in the whole firm. Even than Dad. Do you consider him one of the great men of our time?"

"The greatest," I replied stoutly.

"More so than Theodore Roosevelt?"

"Even than him."

There were surprised looks around the table. Mr. Leslie, after all, had been a member of the ex-President's administration.

Mrs. Leslie now spoke for the first time. "Mr. Manville, no doubt, is speaking of financial greatness. Surely he will concede that Mr. Roosevelt is the greater *man*."

"Not even at the risk of disagreeing with my hostess."

"Aren't you forgetting an essential quality in greatness? Theodore proved himself a hero at San Juan."

Was the Christian name meant to subdue me? I was defiant. "You agree then with Brooks Adams, Mrs. Leslie?" What, after all, had I to lose? "That war and faith are the marks of a high culture? And that we live in the dark age of the goldbug?"

She looked at me now with a first flicker of interest. But it was just a flicker. "You and I, Mr. Manville, are surely the only ones of this benighted group who have read *The Law of Civilization and Decay*. Yes, I feel there's something in his theory."

But the glance that she bestowed on her sons robbed me at once of my new consideration. What could she think of a world where such a one as I might outrank two such strapping fellows?

"Lees Dunbar," she continued now in what was almost a growl, "never fought in a war. And he was of an age to have done so."

"My wife has always been a breather of fire and brimstone," Mr. Leslie intervened hastily to divert the discussion from so disloyal a turn. "She would rather have had Mr. Dunbar in uniform even if it would have put him on the wrong side!"

But I felt quite justified now to use my hostess's weapons against her. I declined his polite invitation to make a joke out of it.

"President Roosevelt's father did not fight in that war, either. And what is more, he bought a substitute."

"There you are, Ma!" Bob exclaimed. "He got you on that one!"

His father again changed the subject as his wife indignantly shook her head. I felt, perhaps unreasonably, that I had been almost a success.

When I walked again with Marion the following morning, however, I was much less sure of this, at least as far as she was concerned. She was pensive and responded to my remarks with short replies which effectively killed each new subject offered. At last I challenged her.

"You're different today. Did I say or do something wrong last night?"

"Oh, no, not at all. You were very lively and amusing. And I know that's not so easy with a family like mine."

"But they're charming!"

"You found Mother charming? You interest me."

"Well, perhaps that's not just the right word for her. Deep persons may have little use for charm."

We had come out of the woods to a clearing in the center of which was a pile of rocks which offered inviting seats. At least they invited Marion to pause.

"Shall we stop here for a bit, George? I want to talk to you."

She seated herself on one of the higher rocks. Then she gazed across the meadow for a full minute before she spoke, very articulately and coolly, except for an occasional throb in her tone. She must have prepared her speech. Perhaps she had risen early to do so.

"I had a sense last night that Daddy and the boys were throwing me at you. Now, why should they wish to do that, you will ask. I'm not exactly the last leaf on the tree. I'm only twenty-three and certainly not ugly. No, please don't interrupt. Let me talk. What has happened is that I've been through a wretchedly unhappy time. I fell in love with a man called Malcolm Dudley. He was twenty years older than me and had a problem with drink and something of a poor reputation with women. And he had no job — only enough money for a bachelor's life of sports. Obviously not the beau that Daddy ordered. But oh, George, he had charm! Talk about birds lured from trees! And the sweetest nature in the world. And he loved me. He really loved me!"

I saw by the caged wildness of her eyes how fiercely that love must have been returned. I was even nearly persuaded that the wretched Dudley could not have been altogether a sham. Had he cultivated her for her fortune and been caught himself?

"He saw perfectly that he was a hopeless match. He even shed tears over the fact that he had got us both into such an emotional state. Mother said she'd rather see me in my coffin than wedded to such a man. And then Daddy killed the whole thing. He hired a detective who discovered that Malcolm had an illegitimate child by a girl in Philadelphia. Of a good family, but poor. Daddy confronted us both with this. He offered to make a settlement on Malcolm if he would marry the girl and give his child a name. Malcolm turned to me and said he would do as I told him. What choice did I have?"

What could I say to *that?* I was dumbfounded that any father could have known his daughter so well. For indeed there was a Roman quality to Marion. One could hardly imagine her in any role but the heroine.

"And *did* Dudley marry the girl?"

"He did. He agreed it was his duty. There was a terrible scene. He wept."

"He seems to have done his share of that."

"Don't malign him! He's a man of the deepest feeling."

"But what sort of marriage will his be? And if he had a drinking problem to boot . . ."

"I know, I know!" She clasped her hands in agony. "It may all be god-awful, but at least that child will have a name."

I had no need to probe further into the well-deserved purgatory of Mr. Dudley. I allowed some moments to pass in which I might have been musing on the sadness of her story. Then I asked:

"And what does all this have to do with your being thrown at *me?*"

"Well, you see, I told my family that I could never love again."

"Oh, come now."

"And I can't!" Her tone was passionate. "You must believe that!"

I shrugged. "Anyway, you convinced your family of it." I made my tone bitter. "And they decided you'd better meet a man who wouldn't mind? Who would be satisfied with other considerations? Such as money and social position, not to mention interest in the firm? And while they were at it, hadn't they better pick a comer? Possibly even a future partner?"

"Oh, George, don't," she pleaded. "I'm so ashamed. I didn't see it that way when Daddy asked you down here. It wasn't until I saw how he and the boys made up to you at dinner that I realized what was going on. Oh, please go home now — I'll take you to the train — and in the future try to think of me as kindly as possible."

It was at that moment that I may have fallen in love with Marion. That is, as much in love as my stunted nature allowed. I also saw that she was precisely the wife I needed, from every point of view I could *then* imagine. How could my clear mind not take that in? That I might, for the asking, have everything: love, position, wealth! Everything, I might have added had I not been so green, but this young woman's love.

"Let me propose something, Marion. I shall go back to town now, as you suggest. But can we meet again with the promise that neither of us will ever mention Malcolm Dudley or your father's little project vis-à-vis myself again?"

"You like me well enough to want to do that?"

"Why don't you give me the chance to find out? There'd be no commitment on either side."

Oh, how her large brown eyes peered and peered at me! Marion knew that she hadn't fathomed me at all.

"Well, why not?" she demanded, almost wearily, at last. "What does either of us really have to lose?"

5

My courtship of Marion was a curious one. I could have asked, like Richard III, if ever woman had been that way won. It was all based on the premise that she was no longer capable of loving, that her emotional capital had been too lavishly spent on Mr. Dudley to have left more than a trickle of income to water, with a bare adequacy, any romance conjured up to avoid the aridity of old-maidhood. I did not for a minute believe that her capital had been so depleted, but it suited my purpose that *she* should believe it and that I offered the best practical solution to escaping the pity of a too loving family.

She liked, on our now regular meetings, to inaugurate serious discussions. She would even suggest a topic for each of our walks: could women be bankers; was divorce the only answer to an unhappy union; was charity demeaning to the recipient; should we get into the war in Europe. I did wish at times that she would be less blunt in facing what she deemed to be the bleak status of her emotional options. I had never before been as close as this to a young woman, and the idea of romance as a partner or even a possible competitor to my infatuation with work was beginning to titillate me. But Marion did little to enhance this feeling.

I was now invited to spend an occasional weekend with the Leslies on Long Island. Mrs. Leslie had consented to tolerate me — barely. Marion and I took long — rather too long — rambles across the countryside. She seemed never to tire and showed a preference for thick woods and even brambles over paths. When we rested — always at my request — on some rocky seat, she would not even let me take her hand in mine.

"Let us be sensible, George. We needn't go in for anything like that until we know just where we're headed."

"But where *are* we headed? You must remember, please, that *I* have not been the victim of an unhappy love affair. It's not so easy for me to be cool and detached. My heart was free. Until I met you, of course."

"I like your 'of course.' " Her mildly amused smile seemed to define the distance she had placed between us. "I see perfectly that you *want* to be in love with me. But that doesn't have to mean that you are. Or even that you ought to be. *Have* you ever been in love, George?"

"Never."

"Then maybe you never will be. And maybe that's not a bad thing. Lots of people never fall in love, I'm sure. Probably many more than is generally suspected."

"I wonder if your mother isn't one of them."

"Oh, no," she replied quickly. "I'm sure Mother's very much in love with Daddy. The shoe's on the other foot there."

She didn't pursue this interesting idea, but it struck me suddenly that she might well be right. There could have been a coolness under her handsome father's cheer and a passion behind her plain mother's moodiness. And could *this* be why Marion was tolerating my uneasy courtship? Because she wanted a mate who would not importune her? A partner in the firm, like her father, who would be a credit to her name and not a bore about her body? And now that the horrid idea had surfaced, I had to know.

"Marion, just what is it that you have in mind? Why are you putting up with me at all?"

She met this calmly. "That's a fair question. I think we should both be weighing the pros and cons of marriage."

"But what sort of a marriage? What the French call a white one?"

She flushed slightly and looked away. She had not been quite ready yet for such candor. But she met the challenge. "Yes, do you really care? Please don't be a hypocrite, George. I have this idea that you're not a very passionate man. And what you did on the side would be no business of mine. I suppose a lot of people would think it cold-blooded that we should be having this discussion at all, but I don't really see why. Marriages have been 'arranged' throughout history. The only difference is that we'd be doing the arranging, not our parents."

"But yours, I gather, would go along with it."

"Daddy, certainly."

"And your mother?"

"Oh, one can never be sure with Mother. But at least she hasn't said she'd rather see me in my coffin, as she did with poor Malcolm."

"Thanks!"

"Well, *you* asked. You and I might be a great team in running Dunbar Leslie one day. Daddy always says that Mrs. Dunbar and Mother didn't do their share of the social side. Well, I wouldn't be like that!"

I sighed. "And I suppose you won't even allow that love might come after marriage."

"It's better not to count on it. I *do* like you, George. I like your honesty and your seriousness. And I think we might get on very well together. There. That's enough for now. Let's walk on."

I think we both felt that matters had been accelerated by the great event that now befell me. At least a year before I had deemed it possible, I was elected a partner in Dunbar, Leslie & Co. Mr. Leslie came himself to my office to congratulate me warmly. Then he rose to close my door. Speaking in a lower tone, he added:

"And if this brings another pot to boil, you will find no objections from one John T. Leslie, Esquire."

What could a young man do but blush, jump to his feet and grasp the hand of the eminent gentleman who consented so graciously to be his father-in-law?

The flatness which I undeniably felt would surely not have been an aspect of my reaction a year before. Not having met the Leslies, I should have been as close to ecstasy as was possible for one of my temperament. But now that I had seen in them the life of the successful banker *combined* with the joys of family love and solidarity, I could recognize a fuller and more rewarding existence than any I had ever visualized. I had qualified as a husband for a Leslie, but only on a stipulated condition. Like the Byzantine general Marcian, I would be elevated to share the throne with Empress Pulcheria, but not her bed.

The prospect tarnished the glitter of my new position in the office. A membership in the firm, which had once seemed to me the peak of worldly ambition, now threatened to be a lonely rank, even (to any who suspected the truth) a shameful one. Yet, as I took new stock of my assets and liabilities, I could see no valid alternative to proceeding in the direction in which I had so long been headed. A junior partnership was one thing, but I had my eyes on becoming the senior of all, and if Mr. Dunbar should die, I would surely need the Leslies to achieve the highest rung.

When I called at their town house later that same day, Marion received me alone in the parlor. She had already heard about my partnership. Her elation seemed to be strangely mixed with a sudden misgiving.

"Are you as happy as you should be, George? There are moments when I feel that I don't really know you. I guess this is one of them."

"Oh, I'm thrilled, of course. How would I not be?"

"But would you tell me if you weren't?"

I hesitated. "Why do you ask that?"

"Don't most married couples tell each other everything?"

"Some may think they do."

"But they deceive themselves?"

"If they believe the impossible, yes."

"Wouldn't you want to know everything your wife was thinking?"

"In the name of God, no!"

There was a long, rather tense pause before she laughed. Loudly, and at last almost cheerfully. I had the sense that some lurking reservation had been thrown, perhaps recklessly, to the winds.

That evening we became engaged.

❦

Mrs. Leslie was supposed to be as unforgiving as she was righteous. Had she ever, it was said, even once surprised her husband with a pretty housemaid on his knee, she would have left him forever. The mere apprehension of such a crisis was reputed to have kept him permanently faithful. But she seemed to have condemned me on the subject of my parents without the need of evidence. This came out in our discussions of plans for the wedding.

We met, Marion and I and her unsmiling parent, in the latter's chaste pale second-floor sitting room in the Long Island house, with its pastels of the children in their youth and its small glass bookcases filled with the leather-bound volumes of poetry which its grim occupant so unaccountably loved. Banned from its white walls was any suggestion of the trophies that her game-hunting spouse placed over the halls below. No horn, claw, tusk or antler was allowed to sully the purity of the atmosphere.

"A wedding without a single member of the groom's family is an anomaly, George." Her use of my Christian name had been her sole acknowledgment of the engagement. "It looks as if we refused to have them, which isn't true, or as if they held something very strongly against you. I'm afraid I must ask you what that is."

"Mother, hadn't you better talk to George alone?"

"Certainly not, Marion. If there *is* something, surely it's as much your concern as mine."

"But I don't *care*. I trust George for that. I don't want to know anything about his family quarrels. That's his affair. Besides, he has two aunts who will be happy to attend the wedding."

"Aunts aren't enough. Well, George? Are you going to tell us?"

Of course, I was ready for her. It would be my first important lie, but I had weighed all the circumstances, and I was convinced that I had moral justification. "It invokes delicate matters, Mrs. Leslie."

"I expected that."

"You are aware, I'm sure, of my mother's past relationship with Mr. Dunbar."

"Perfectly."

"Mother, I don't want to stay to hear this!"

"Sit down, Marion, and don't be a fool. You can't play the innocent with me. Do you think I don't know what you and your girlfriends gossip about? Go on, George."

"You can imagine that the situation was not agreeable to me. To have my mother so involved, and my father, whether from weakness or love, willing to look the other way! It made it all the worse that Mr. Dunbar, whom I worshiped, should be responsible for the degradation of my family. At last I resolved to have it out with him. I pleaded with him to break off with my mother. I went so far as to urge him never to see or even speak to her again. At first he was furious. I expected to be fired on the spot. But in the end he was too great a man not to be affected by my candor. After due consideration he decided to end the intrigue. My mother learned of my role and has never forgiven me. She has turned my father and sister against me. And she is quite remorseless. There is nothing I can do to bring her around."

Mrs. Leslie's face was a study. I wonder if she had ever been more perplexed in her life. Sexual misconduct has been pretty much the same through the ages, and society has usually been resigned to leaving it under the rug where common sense had customarily swept it. But if the dogma of a particular era requires condemnation if the rug happens to be pulled back, then all must join in that condemnation. In a Victorian or puritanical age my reasons would have been publicly accepted as the justification of my alleged interference, even by those who would have privately regarded me as a prig and a busybody. But was that true in 1916? By then my alleged sanctimoniousness might have been considered almost as low as adultery itself. But not quite. It was obvious that Mrs. Leslie found distasteful my account of the Galahad son, but her feelings would have been much stronger had she known my true role. And she was not sufficiently liberated from puritan doctrine to criticize me openly. Oh, I had her! I was no longer the *fils complaisant.* She would have to go through not only with the wedding but with the large reception that I had in mind.

As she still, however, did not speak, I urged her to check my story with Mr. Dunbar himself. This was a bold stroke. I was pretty sure that even she would lack the gall to do this, but I figured that if she did, the great man would at once deduce what I was up to and, chuckling inwardly, confirm my story.

"No, that won't be necessary, George," she replied with a sigh. "I don't doubt your word. Well, that's it, then. We'll have the wedding without the Manvilles."

6

America's entry into the Great War followed shortly upon our marriage, but there was no idea of my joining the colors. I was significantly involved in the loans to Britain, and even as fierce a war-horse as my mother-in-law had reluctantly to agree that the firm was justified in applying for my draft exemption. But Marion's brothers were both engaged as infantry officers in the trenches, and Jack, the elder and the more promising, was killed in action. When Bob returned from the carnage, he had no further taste for banking, and he bought a large cattle ranch in Argentina which he colorfully and unprofitably operated thereafter at the family's willingly defrayed expense.

As I was the only relative of John Leslie's left in the firm, as well as the continuing intimate of the now sadly aging Lees Dunbar, it might have been thought that my succession to the leadership was assured, and for a time this appeared to be the case. But I could nonetheless perceive behind the faultless good manners of my father-in-law and the perfunctory civility of his spouse that the tragic events of wartime had not improved their opinion of me. The slaughtered youth at Château-Thierry and the hard-riding gaucho of the Argentine pampas had set a standard of virility that a mere economic whiz kid could never hope to attain. It may have seemed, even to the eyes of the nonrelated partners, that I had taken some obscure advantage of my gallant brothers-in-law, who in any case would have more graced the aristocratic corridors of Dunbar, Leslie & Co. than the pale creature in dark civilian garb who seemed to be thinking only of profits while his betters were dying.

Marion herself was not immune to this attitude. She had not, however, seemed to have felt it at first. Our marriage had got off to a better start than might have been expected. Her equable disposition enabled us to live together like two college roommates. She was frankly bored by my political and economic theorizing and didn't even pretend to listen if I held forth on these subjects, but she took, as she always had, the greatest interest in the social side of my business life and loved to entertain the members of the firm and their wives in the commodious houses that she built in town and country. Indeed, her father used to twit her for deeming herself the Agrippina of Dunbar Leslie, being the daughter, wife and (he vainly hoped) future mother of "emperors." I daresay some of the partners' wives thought she put on airs and scoffed at her rousing cheerleader tones, her tossed head and noisy good will, but no doubt they were careful to do so behind her back.

But the loss of Jack and the absence of Bob had, by 1920 anyway, begun to affect our relationship. It might have been because those friendly fellows were no longer around to take my side and back me up. I believe that they had always been rueful about the way they and their father had conspired to give me a loveless wife (they did not know *how* loveless) and that they kept an eye on their sister to be sure she was nice to me. But now their loss served only to remind Marion of how little I seemed a male Leslie. She never said so, but she was cooler with me, at times irritable. I suspected that she had forgotten Malcolm Dudley at last and was beginning to wonder why she had doomed herself to a *mariage blanc*.

And indeed it was not long before she appeared to be taking steps to mitigate the rigor of this doom. In Old Westbury she went fox hunting or golfing every weekend with Hugh Norman, my partner and our neighbor. Hugh, my exact contemporary, was generally considered my nearest rival in the firm. He was certainly not like me in any respect, with his strong build, his slicked-back dark hair, his long stern countenance and eyes which could somehow twinkle and reprove at almost the same time. He gave a remarkable impression of strength, both in character and physique; one suspected that he had been a polo player or something equally stylish and arduous. And to top it off, he had what the military call "command presence"; he could dominate a meeting without raising his hand or his voice. Needless to say, I detested him.

Hugh was married to a wonderful woman of great character, but Aggie Norman had been stricken with a terrible polio five years before and was confined to a wheelchair. Hugh was supposed by the office to have had occasional discreet affairs, and for a time I naïvely took it for granted that these satisfied the rutting male in him and that he and Marion were united primarily by their love of sport and their joint passion for the firm. For Hugh, quite as much as I, lived essentially for Dunbar Leslie.

I had also thought that Marion was not the type to appeal to his senses. Were not men as cold and grave as he notoriously attracted to gamier morsels? But I had underestimated the subservience of his baser appetites to his ambition. If he could subject an infatuated Marion to his will, he might dominate, through her, her adoring father — and John Leslie's share of the firm's capital was second only to Mr. Dunbar's. And if John Leslie became the trustee under Dunbar's will . . . well, what would *that* mean to the future of George Manville?

When I was fool enough to twit Marion with the rumors of her hunting companion's extracurricular sex life, she warmly defended him.

"And if it were true, what's the harm? He's a man, isn't he? Aggie Norman understands that. She and I have become the greatest friends, you know. She wouldn't want him to be frustrated. It might make him difficult in the home. It might even affect his work at the office."

"Because all that loose semen knocking around inside him might clog a he-man's business judgment?"

"George! I've never heard you be so vulgar. What's come over you?"

"Jealousy, perhaps."

"Jealousy? You can't expect me to take *that* seriously?"

Really, was it possible for a woman to be so insensitive? Even granting what our marriage was, or wasn't, couldn't she see that I might still be uncomfortable?

"While we're on the subject of Hugh, don't you think your seeing so much of him may cause people to talk?"

Her firm answer made me suspect that she had been waiting for this. "Let them. And now let me ask *you* something. Hugh and I think we ought to do even more things together. He thinks we ought to take over the firm's entertainments. The receptions, staff parties and so on. Aggie's simply too ill to do more than have a few friends for supper at home, and we all know how you've always hated any kind of office socializing."

"But haven't I always done my part?"

"Yes, dear, but *so* reluctantly. I've always had to drag you! And Hugh has a great flair for public relations. He needs a hostess, and I've always regarded the social side of business as my particular forte. So people are just going to have to get used to seeing us act as a team. I'm sure they'll come to view it as a business relationship. I assume you have no real objection?"

"None whatever," I replied bitterly. "You'll both do it to the queen's taste."

Marion wasted no time in putting her plan into effect. At office gatherings in the following months she and Hugh acted as host and hostess, and as this appeared to have the total sanction of their spouses, Aggie's illness and my solitary preferences being known, the firm seemed to accept it. At a reception at the Waldorf which the partners gave for a delegation of Japanese industrialists, I was told that they made a handsome, almost a royal, couple, receiving together at the head of the grand stairway.

But the woman who told me this, the catty wife of a younger partner, the sort of person who would sacrifice her husband's very future for the pleasure of making a disagreeable remark, added: "One would have thought them Princess Flavia and Rudolph Rassendyl in *The Prisoner of Zenda*. So romantic!"

I realized then that I could no longer go on fooling myself. Except what would I really gain by facing the truth?

7

That same year saw a congressional committee's investigation of monopolies, and Mr. Dunbar himself was called as a witness. I accompanied him to Washington, indignant at the idea that he was being summoned, not because the testimony of an old man of now obviously declining memory would be helpful to proposed legislation, but because his famous name might provide a football to be kicked about for political advantage. And so indeed it turned out.

Mr. Dunbar had difficulty with some of the questions. He showed a vagueness as to the identity of certain corporate mergers that he could have recited in his sleep a few years before. But Rex Florham, counsel for the committee, a former assistant attorney general known for his aggressive enforcement of the Sherman Act, had been quick to sense that the old man might be induced to express a philosophy of economic laissez-faire so extreme as to bring ridicule on the whole banking community, and he pressed his final questions with an air of assumed respectfulness that led his witness deep into the trap.

"To a banker of your vast experience, Mr. Dunbar, the experiments of legislators less versed in economics must often be trying."

"Well, sir, you might say that politicians, like the poor, we have always with us."

"Just so. And no doubt in your time you have seen our elected well-wishers come up with some pretty strange ideas."

"I could a tale unfold!"

"Might it not then have been helpful to the nation, sir, if more of your fellow bankers had seen fit to seek seats in Congress to help in the drafting of regulatory legislation?"

"Only on the premise that such regulatory laws are needed."

"And they are not, sir?"

"No, sir, they are not. I believe in a free market."

"Absolutely free?"

"Absolutely free, sir."

"You believe the Congress should exercise no control whatever over our giant corporations?"

"I believe that control should remain where it still largely is: in the chief executive officers of our greater businesses and in the heads of the major banking institutions. Competition tends to eliminate the inept, and the vital importance of a gentleman's word in any market transaction weeds out the dishonest. Of course, you are going to find rascals in any walk of life, but that includes the Congress as well."

Florham grew bolder now. "But does that not place power in the hands of our magnates comparable to the power of the Congress?"

"And what of that, sir? Are they not more qualified?"

"Tell me, sir. Are you yourself not one of the financial leaders of the country?"

"That is not for me to say, Mr. Florham."

"But if you are — and let us suppose, for the purposes of this discussion, that you are the greatest of such — would you not have a power comparable to that of the President himself?"

"Granting your hypothesis, yes, sir, I should."

I groaned inwardly. I had a vision of what the newspapers would surely make of this. They would shout from coast to coast that Lees Dunbar deemed himself more powerful than Warren G. Harding. And wasn't it true that he *did* believe it, even if he had not said it in so many words? It was not so much that my hero had made himself into a sounding brass or a tinkling cymbal; anything could be forgiven the senescent. What split my heart was that I was now beginning to see that this streak of megalomania had always been there. I had been fighting off my suspicions for some time, but now my vision had been horridly cleared. The Dunbar on the stand was not so different from the one I had worshiped in my mother's salon. Had he not always harbored the illusion that he was running his little world, like Napoleon in Tolstoy's *War and Peace*, pulling the straps and cords in the back of his plunging carriage in the belief that he was making it go? What was Wall Street in the obsessed imagination of Lees Dunbar but a parade ground where regiments in close-order drill executed his barked commands of "Squads left!" and "Left by squadrons!"? And what was I but the dazzled child who had believed it all?

Mr. Dunbar did not long survive the congressional hearing or the embarrassing publicity that followed it, though the worst of the latter I was able to spare him. His last days were marked by delirium, and

I hardly left his bedside. His ravings about a Brazilian rain forest made little sense to me until at last he gave this seeming cohesion to them:

"That company we had on the Amazon. Do you remember, George? We had to clear a great area for rubber farming. And then that crazy manager chucked the work. After the men tried to kill him, do you remember? And how fast the jungle filled it all in. In *weeks*, George! In just *weeks!*"

I supposed this was his way of expressing the futility of trying to make any permanent clearing in the jungle of economic life and that the poor old boy was experiencing some of the same sour disillusionment that I was facing. I attempted to console him, but he did not seem to hear me. Soon after he became entirely incoherent. When at last his heavy breathing ceased, and I contemplated that strangely still body, I was seized with a wild despair. Marion, hearing my cry in the next room, hurried in with the doctor. I shall never forget the shocked look on her countenance as she contemplated mine.

I can appreciate now that what had shocked her was not my grief but its cause. How could a woman, brought up to admire the strong and superior in the male sex, feel anything but distaste for a man who sobbed over the death of an old gentleman who was not even kin to him? And how could such a man take up the scepter that old Dunbar had meant for warlords? Hadn't I just proved myself inept?

With Lees Dunbar's death I seemed to have lost my purpose in life; I began even to wonder if I might not as well have lost life itself. For three weeks I did not go to the office at all. I stayed alone in the house in Old Westbury, leaving Marion and her father to cope with the problems of the estate of which he and I were executors. I wondered at times if my depression would not congeal into a permanent state.

Marion telephoned every other day to see how I was doing. Her attitude was that of a nurse to a child whose illness might have been feigned; she showed a businesslike concern, but little sympathy.

"I suppose you must be aware there are important questions to be decided in the firm. Do you really think it's wise to be away?"

Of course, she meant the question of succession. Marion's conscience required her to warn me. But I had a distinct sense that she was just as glad to have me where I was.

"I can always be reached by telephone."

"All right, George. If that's the way you want to play it."

Mr. Dunbar, even approaching senility, had retained the function as well as the title of managing partner. His replacement would now have to be proposed by a nominating committee on which I, as a likely successor, did not sit. The only other serious candidate was Hugh Norman, and everyone knew that Mr. Dunbar had given me his preference.

It was my embarrassed father-in-law who drove out to Long Island to inform me of the firm's choice.

"I needn't tell you, George, how esteemed you are by all your partners," he assured me, after several throat-clearings. "But there does seem to be a feeling that your talents do not include a taste for the petty details of day-to-day management. Why should they? We have partners who even like that sort of thing. You're too valuable to be wasted on questions of promotion and demotion, or hiring and firing, or whether the reception hall needs redecoration or should we put urinals in the old washrooms."

"In other words, I should stay in my ivory tower."

"Now, George, you mustn't take it that way. This is all very well meant. You can say your partners are greedy if you like. They want to squeeze the last drop out of what you're best at. Leave administration to Hugh Norman. Nothing's too petty for Hugh. He's that *rara avis* who can see both the forest and every damn tree in it."

It was thus I first learned that, without either my advice or consent, Hugh Norman had been chosen to succeed Lees Dunbar as managing partner of the firm. John Leslie was too old, and I . . . well, it was obvious that the membership did not see in me the image they wished to present to the world. It was also obvious that Marion had conspired with her father to promote her lover ahead of her husband. But wasn't the lover more of a husband than I?

The crisis for me was simply that the elaborately wrought inner scaffolding on which I had gingerly positioned my entire emotional life had been swept away overnight by the roaring cataract of Hugh Norman. At dreary dawn I found myself forlornly stranded on the gray banks of his relentless river. Where now was the long envisaged role of the arbiter of Wall Street? Oh, no, not quite of Wall Street — I was never such a fool as to think I could attain that, though in dizzy dreams such a pinnacle might have seemed almost achievable. But I had certainly visualized myself in a position of power comparable to that of Lees Dunbar, though without his hallucinations of national dominance. I had seen myself, much more modestly, as the umpire of corporate conflict within my chosen bailiwick, as a man who could bring some degree of governance into the chaos of my immediate economic vicinity, who could impose the order of the balance sheet on clients of messy thinking and even messier emotions. All I had wanted was to create a little civilization in my own back yard.

But now! Now I was only the expert diagnostician of corporate ailments. My analyses would still be sought by my partners, but how they would use them was no longer my affair. They would, of course, be concerned only with profit. In other words, my firm would be just like all the others. Some would ask: had it not always been? Who cared about George Manville's dreams? Did anyone even know about them? Whom had I ever told but the unlistening Marion?

8

I had never liked Hugh Norman, even before his affair with Marion. Not because he was cold; I have never minded coldness. It was more that I suspected he was at heart unscrupulous. Oh, he would do everything according to the rules, yes. But if he should ever learn that a form of profitable wrongdoing had become at least tolerated by the "better sort," I had little doubt that he would engage in it. His morals, so to speak, depended on his private poll of the marketplace. Like a courtier of Henry VIII, as interpreted by Holbein, he would nurse no ideals. His courage consisted simply in his willingness to risk the headsman's ax in his pursuit of power.

He and I had always got on well enough, outwardly anyway, and he probably assumed we would continue to. He undoubtedly despised me as a cuckold, but this was not a matter that much concerned him. He exactly appreciated my value to the firm, and now he had the satisfaction of knowing I was no longer a rival.

How long his contempt and my resentment would have jogged along uneventfully together without the incident of the "pool" for the cornering of a certain stock, I do not know, but that changed everything. Hugh asked me to attend a small gathering of bankers and brokers at his house in Old Westbury one Sunday afternoon. It was not a firm matter, and it was not my custom to go in for such games, but I had no wish to offend him without good cause, so I went, to be polite.

It was three o'clock on a peerless June afternoon. Most of the dozen gentlemen gathered in that dark library, surrounded by English hunting prints and standard sets of unread classics, would have been on the golf course had not a sharper game attracted them. They had lunched with their host; brandy and whiskey glasses were on the tables, and the air was heavy with cigar smoke. Having walked over from my own place in the glorious air, I felt an immediate revulsion.

"Ah, George, good, we can start," my host greeted me. I declined both drink and weed a bit brusquely and took a seat in the corner. "I think you gentlemen will all agree that this is a very pretty little scheme. I miss my guess if even the great George isn't tempted."

He proceeded, without interruption, to outline his plan to corner the stock of a vulnerable food-store chain of whose precarious financing he had had a careful study made. It was a simple and classic scheme. A graduated purchase of the company's common stock would drive the market price to an unrealistic high, at which point the pool would dump its holdings, leaving a gullible public to pick up the pieces in the subsequent crash. It was the same old game played half a century before by Jim Fisk and Jay Gould except on a smaller and less market-threatening scale, a kind of gentlemen's cockfight, disastrous largely to gambling short sellers with whose welfare the loftier bankers and brokers had little concern. It was not my practice to take part in such ventures, but I had never expressed disapproval of them. I had followed the lead of that greatest of stoics, Marcus Aurelius, who deemed it his duty to attend the bloody but popular games at the Colosseum which even he was powerless to ban, but, seated in the imperial box, kept his eyes fixed on some learned scroll.

"How about it, George? Can we count you in?"

"I think I'll pass, thank you."

I received some surprised looks, even a couple of critical ones, and a general discussion began in which I took no part. But I was confused by my own unrest. Where was the emperor, calmly perusing a tract of Zeno while the gladiators dueled below? I should have been above it all instead of being angry. Was it my function to interfere with bread and circuses? No! But I didn't have to stay and listen. I rose.

"Gentlemen, I leave you to your little frolics."

Hugh followed me out of the room to the front door. "You won't play with us, George?" he asked in his usual quiet tone. But there was a hint of a rasp in it now.

"No, I find I have put away childish things. Particularly when the other children are playing such dirty pool."

"Dirty pool! It wasn't too dirty for your sacred Mr. Dunbar to play!"

"That's a lie! He never did!"

"Really, George, you're too naive. This business of the one god being Lees Dunbar and Manville being his prophet has got to have an end. Dunbar himself didn't dare tell you all he was up to!"

I went on my way without another word, but fury and sickness ate at my heart.

That night Marion accosted me in my study, where I was sipping a strong but single predinner martini.

"Aggie Norman just called me. She said you were shockingly rude to Hugh this afternoon. They're both very upset. She thought you must have been feeling ill or perhaps had had some piece of bad news."

"No, I'm feeling fine. And the only bad news I've had is that Hugh and his little gang are planning a vicious stock market raid. But the good news is that I've taken a resolution which has given me the greatest satisfaction. I intend never to set foot in Hugh Norman's house again. Seeing him in the office will be quite enough."

"George!" Marion looked aghast. "Hugh and Aggie are my closest friends!"

"Oh, you may go there as often as you like. My good resolutions apply only to myself."

"But what on earth has Hugh done to you?"

"Nothing to me. And nothing to anyone else that he hasn't done a dozen times before. It's simply that now at last I *see* him. And I find I don't like what I see."

"But that's crazy!"

"Will you kindly then allow a lunatic to finish his cocktail in peace? I have nothing more to say on the subject of Hugh Norman."

Marion left me at this, but the following day, finding me still adamant, she proposed — and I, after some musing, accepted — this practical compromise. She would continue to go to the Normans', attributing my absence to a need of evening hours for the composition of an economic thesis, and Hugh and Aggie would come to us only for larger parties where he and I need exchange only a few formalities.

To tell the truth, I was surprised at my own obstinacy in refusing to cross Hugh's threshold. I suppose it was my only way of expressing my hostility to everything he represented to me. Other than that, I had no recourse but in the dreamland of fantasized violence. But what a hotbed that was! I imagined myself as a fiery U.S. attorney, brilliantly reinterpreting old cases and laws to criminalize his pools. I saw him abjectly pleading for mercy before a stern, gavel-wielding judge. I even saw . . . but a truce to this childishness. The only benefit I conceivably derived from my rage and helplessness may have been in a dim, dawning sense of what I still might accomplish with my wrecked life.

Some such glimmer, anyway, may have prompted me to come to better terms with Marion. After all, our absurd and unnatural design for living had been as much my doing as hers. I invited her to my study at cocktail time to discuss how our compromise was working.

"Don't you really think, Marion, that under the circumstances my distancing myself from Hugh may have made all our relationships easier? Not only his and mine, but yours and mine and even yours and his?"

She examined the back of her outstretched left hand as if she were appraising her ring. "You and I have never really discussed my relationship with Hugh."

"What would have been the point? Obviously, I have accepted it. It was quite clear to me, long before you took up with Hugh, that your heart had not died with Malcolm Dudley."

"I was an awful goose about that, George."

"But I *knew* you were. Not a goose, but deluded. I knew you'd get over him, and I took advantage of that. That's why I have no moral right to object to Hugh. As *your* friend. He need not, of course, be mine."

"That's really very handsome of you. And if at any time you want a friend, a lady friend I mean, you will find me equally understanding."

"Oh, I'm sure it might even be a relief to you. But I shan't be needing one."

"You don't ever have the needs of other men?"

"Let's put it that I'm neuter. That avoids odious speculations."

But Marion did not want even her husband-in-name-only to be that. "I'd rather put it that you're virtuous."

"Thank you, my dear. I accept the mask." In fact, I was virgin to both sexes, as ascetic as a priest. But only in priests was this considered admirable. "Let me put something more serious to you. Isn't divorce the obvious solution to our bizarre situation? You married me to become the consort of the future sovereign of Dunbar Leslie. You overestimated my claim to the succession. Why not marry King Hugh?"

Marion's expression was fixed now as she concentrated on the problem. "Hugh and I have discussed that, and we had guessed you wouldn't stand in our way. But there are two compelling reasons against it. First, a double divorce under the circumstances, followed immediately by the marriage of a partner's wife to the senior partner, would damage the reputation of the firm. And secondly, Hugh and I could not bear to hurt Aggie Norman, who has been so wonderfully understanding about us."

"More so than I've been?"

"Oh, yes. Because I haven't been giving Hugh anything that you really wanted. And Aggie has wanted Hugh to have the kind of love she hasn't been able to give him since her illness. I can't take anything more from her than I already have. She must remain Mrs. Hugh Norman."

I wondered if this generosity did not spring more from Marion than from Hugh. But anyway I approved it. "Aggie has told me herself that the polio gravely damaged her heart. She doesn't believe she has long to live."

"All the more reason not to hurt her! And of course she might live for years. I sincerely hope she does. But that brings me — plunk — to a very, very delicate question. One that I've been wondering if I'd ever have the courage to ask you."

"You mean, how good is *my* health?"

"Oh, my God, no! For what do you take me? I'm sure you'll bury us all. And I shouldn't blame you if you did it with some satisfaction. No, what I was going to ask you . . ."

She paused. "Really, I wonder if I can."

"I think I'm beginning to guess. Marion, are you by any chance pregnant?"

"No!" she exclaimed excitedly. "But you're very warm. Thank you, George, now I think I *can* tell you. I want to bear Hugh's child. Only one, if it should be a boy. Or more, until a boy came. Call me crazy if you will, but I have this strange feeling that a son of Hugh's and mine would one day be head of the firm! Oh, I'm sure of it! Try to believe at least in my sincerity, George."

"I should think the boy would indeed have an excellent chance. Your father would probably leave him his entire interest in the firm, and with that, added to Hugh's, he'd have to be retarded not to go far."

"Oh, George, don't make mock of it, please."

"I'm entirely serious. You and Hugh, I assume, would be counting on me not to deny paternity."

"Would that be asking for the moon?" But she held up a quick hand to keep me from answering and hurried on in an almost breathless voice. "Please, George, listen to me carefully before you decide against it. I know it's a tricky business, but I'm sure we can work it out if we all agree. Hugh, like you, has never had much interest in children. He'd only be doing this for me. He's perfectly willing to have you be the putative father. He promises he'd never interfere or embarrass you with claims about the child. And I'd see that you're never troubled with it. Oh, if you will see me through this, George, I'll be your staunch ally! We haven't been very friendly since I fell in love with Hugh, but you will find there's a lot I can do to make your life pleasant and agreeable. You'll see!"

I got up and walked to the window. I found myself unexpectedly touched. There was always something rather noble about Marion; she showed it even with her present proposition. And, really, why should I not oblige her in this? I had been, like my father, a *mari complaisant*. Before that I had been, at least in Marion's mother's eyes, a *fils complaisant*. It seemed only logical that I should now become a *père complaisant*.

"So you've found love at last, Marion." I turned back to face her. "And Hugh is really lovable?"

"I love him anyway."

"And he you?"

She paused. She was always honest! "Ah, don't ask too many questions. He loves me as Hugh can love."

Could she have realized that this was the one way to save my pride? No, she was not so subtle.

"Have your baby, Marion. I'll go along."

◆

These things are always known, or at least suspected. We four put on a very good act, but I fear nonetheless that at least a faint odor, something *un peu malsain*, emanated from our performance. Certainly Marion's mother sniffed us out. And it was I, of course, who bore the brunt of her unspoken contempt. If Aggie Norman could be considered generous in her self-effacement, and Hugh romantic even in an adulterous part, and Marion at least forgivable for a gripping passion, what word could mitigate the scorn that might be justly heaped on my role?

Perhaps most confusing to the prying observer was the genuine devotion I felt for John Leslie Manville, born ten months after my fateful conversation with his mother. He was an enchanting little boy full of smiles, and when he stretched out his arms to me I hoped indeed that he might one day occupy Mr. Dunbar's chair. I'm afraid that Marion found my fondness for the child somewhat embarrassing, even showing a lack of taste, but Hugh, cold fish that he was, did not seem in the least to care.

I spent much of my free time now aboard my sixty-foot motor yacht, the *Arctic Tern*, which gave me all the haven I needed from worldly distractions. Whenever I could, I would head out to the ocean, sitting contentedly on the bridge by my skipper, a pair of binoculars hanging from my neck, as satisfied with foul weather as with fair. I eschewed the new habit of fitting out these beautiful vessels with period furniture and master paintings. I insisted that mine be shipshape in every respect: nothing placed on the gleaming bulkheads but charts, and all chairs and divans upholstered in spotless white leather. Whiteness indeed was everywhere on board except in the shining mahogany of table legs, rail tops and instrument covers; it enhanced my sense of the nothing from which we come and to which we shall surely return. It was white that made my boat almost disappear against the alabaster of the horizon. Only at sea was I truly alone with my aloneness.

And what of my stoic hero? What would Marcus Aurelius have said? That I had borne too much? Been too much a stoic? But had he not looked the other way from Empress Faustina's notorious love affairs? Nor had he objected to the naming of Commodus as his heir, although he might with a clear conscience have denied paternity of that cruel and dissolute youth. John Leslie Manville, at least, appeared to be a promising child. No, I concluded that the great emperor would have sanctioned my stand.

9

What finally aroused me from what I might term the spiritual hibernation of these years was the lunatic market boom of 1929. If my social relations with my fellow men had almost ceased, the activity of my mind had not. Indeed, it had taken advantage of my solitude to be more active than ever. The excuse that Marion had used to explain my absence from the Norman soirées — namely, that I was working on some economic thesis — had become true. I *did* now spend my evenings, as well as a good part of my days, in the office studying market trends, past and present, and seeking to determine what principles, if any, guided them. My goal was to place a finger on the very pulse of free trade. Were the rules which Mr. Dunbar and I had sought to apply to a tiny fraction of the general market extendable in any way to the whole? He had had a dream of accomplishing this by himself, but it had been the dream, at least in his senescence, of a megalomaniac.

It was perfectly evident to me, by the spring of that fateful year, that stocks had reached prices which could not be maintained. I was later to be deemed a great prophet, but in fact there had been many men of equal perspicacity. I adjusted my own portfolio to my dour prognostications, investing it in government obligations and the soundest blue chips, but I was much concerned with the firm's capital in which I, both as a partner and as co-trustee with Marion of her trusts, had a substantial interest. Hugh, who was primarily in charge of the Dunbar Leslie funds, was an all-out bull.

When I went to his office to discuss this, he pooh-poohed my doubts.

"Do what you want with your own, George, but don't fuss about the firm's. What we have, and what we're *going* to have, should make us more a power in the land than we've ever been."

"But you see, I don't believe that. Are you prepared to buy me out?"

He frowned. "Well, if you insist. Though it's a bit awkward, with everything invested right up to the hilt. I suppose we *could* raise the cash."

"And for Marion, too."

"Marion! Does Marion want out?"

"I haven't asked her. But I think she will when she hears my reasons."

"Marion doesn't know anything about the market, for Pete's sake!"

"She can learn. I owe it to her to safeguard her fortune. And that of our son."

"*Your* son?" Hugh peered at me with squinty eyes.

"Our son," I repeated firmly. "John Leslie Manville."

"Oh." He might have been reflecting that my reclusive life had affected my reason. "I see. Of course. Well, talk to Marion if you think you must. But I should warn you that I intend to talk to her, too. With sums like this involved, it becomes a serious firm matter. And Marion has always put the firm first."

"A New York heiress never puts anything ahead of what has made her that" was my parting shot.

I had been able to persuade two other major partners of the peril to the firm's portfolio, and I surmised that, if I could add Marion's voice to theirs and mine, Hugh might be forced to some compromise.

With this in mind, I approached Marion that same evening. She was home for a change, and after dinner, in the library, I outlined my plan. She only half listened until it broke upon her what it entailed.

"You mean you and I would join forces *against* Hugh?"

Life in this period had been perplexing for Marion. She had begun to put on weight, and this, with her increased social activity that now extended well beyond the firm (she was the queen of the charity ball), had probably diminished her interest, or at least her dependence, on romance. I had heard rumors in the office that Hugh had a lady friend from a very different social zone, and I had made it my business (always prepared) to verify this. I did not know whether or not Marion was aware of the affair, but if she had her suspicions, I wondered if a person as honest as she basically was might not have questioned her own continued right to call her lover to account.

"Does your loyalty to Hugh require you to place your fortune at risk?"

"But how can I be sure that it is? How can I know which of you two is right?"

"You can't. You may have to toss a coin. At least that would give you a fifty-fifty chance of not going down the drain with Hugh."

"Oh, George, don't be horrid! Explain it all to me!"

"I can't turn you into an economist overnight, my dear. You'll have to play your hunch."

"Can't you do *something* to help me?"

"I can do this. I can at least try to persuade you that honor doesn't call you to be more loyal to Hugh than he is to you." I handed her a card on which was typed a name, address and telephone number. "This is where you can reach Mrs. Ella Lane. I doubt that she will have an interest in refusing you any information you request. Her liaison with Hugh is well known in the social circles in which she moves."

Poor Marion held the card away from her as if it emitted a bad odor. "Why are you doing this to me, George?"

"I've told you why."

Her eyes slowly filled with tears. "I've known there was someone. But I didn't want to know who. Are you sure you're not doing this because you hate me?"

"I don't hate you in the least. I'm very fond of you, and I always have been. I'm doing this for you. *And* for your son."

She was silent for a minute. "Let me go upstairs now. I'll let you know in the morning what I decide."

At breakfast Marion's maid came down to deliver me a note from her mistress which simply read: "Go ahead with your plan." That morning I was able to induce Hugh to agree to reinvest in safer securities one half of the firm's capital. Thus are the major events of history often brought about.

❧

When the great crash came that fall, Dunbar Leslie lost only fifty percent of its principal and escaped what might have otherwise been a receivership. My status in the firm was enormously enhanced, and a much humbled Hugh at partnership lunches was now careful to seat me at his right and to consult me on every question of importance. I never said "I told you so." There was no need.

Marion was much bewildered by these events. The re-emergence of her husband from, so to speak, the back chambers of the firm, whither he had been relegated by the wisdom of the old guard, seemed to defy the rules of the game as she had learned them. True, she had originally picked me as her candidate for the first spot, but had she not been proved wrong by her father and lover? And now here was the old struggle all over again! I was amused by her quandary, likening her in my mind to a sea lioness basking on a rock until the victor of two battling bulls should flop over to claim her.

Except she wasn't basking. She was making cautious overtures to me suggesting that we had drifted too far apart and perhaps should do more things together again. She even asked me if I would join her at the table which the firm had taken at the Waldorf-Astoria ballroom for a dinner honoring the secretary of the treasury. I firmly declined.

"In the first place, there's nothing to honor. Neither the secretary nor any of his party has done a thing to ameliorate the national disaster. In the second, I wouldn't be seen dead at a hotel banquet. We have established our pragmatic sanction, my dear Marion. Let us abide by it."

This may sound cruel. Marion was having her troubles. I knew that Hugh's Mrs. Lane had abandoned him for a corporate tycoon too great to be openly resented and that he was doing his best to reinstate himself in Marion's good graces. I was probably thrusting her back in his arms. But I didn't care. I had no further interest in the politics of the firm, or who was senior partner, and, having lived my life without the complications of sexual involvement, I had little patience for the heartaches and jealousies of people obsessed with their own genitalia and what to do or not to do with them.

Actually, I was probably helping Marion. She did patch things up with Hugh, and this may have been the best thing she could have done with her emotional life, or what was left of it. He probably continued to divert himself on the sly, but if he did, he took greater pains to conceal it. And in a year's time he had already started to take some of the credit, at least with the younger partners, for the investment policy which had saved the firm. The fact that I never bothered to contradict him lent credence to his claim, and by 1933 he was as strongly in the saddle as if his wisdom and leadership had never been questioned.

I have been accused of enjoying the Depression. There is some truth in that. I did not enjoy, certainly, the human suffering entailed, although I have never much concerned myself with human misery that I was powerless to allay. Pain and agony beyond my reach, at home or abroad or even on other planets, in the past, present or future — how could my sentimental wails mend matters? What I did enjoy was the interest of watching a national catastrophe unfold in very much the fashion I had foreseen, with the added excitement of feeling that the same mind which had seen it coming might offer some small clue in the problem of preventing its repetition.

For the years which followed the crash, bringing no return of our fevered prosperity, but, on the contrary, revealing even darker abysses, had begun to open up to many persons, like myself, the vision of radical changes in the management of our securities markets. The time might have come not merely to say "I told you so" to Hugh Norman but to add: "And here is what I'm *going* to tell you!" My life might not, after all, be a failure. There might still be a way to find consistency and even purpose in the career which had started in my mother's salon, discussing the Medici with its principal ornament, and had seemed to end with my relegation from the status of second partner to that of a mere economic consultant.

I had been working, off and on for two years, on a short text about the need for government regulation of the issuance and marketing of stocks and bonds. It had had its origin in my indignation at Hugh's little pool games. But now, with the new confidence engendered by my role in the firm's survival, I decided to expand it into a full-length book and offer it for publication. What I had once conceived as the policing role of the banking community I now realized had to become one of the many functions of Uncle Sam.

Principles of Market Regulation was published in 1932. It was read only by a small public, but that public was precisely the audience I had wished to reach: those economists who hoped to assist the new government if Hoover should be defeated and the banking world of downtown New York. The former hailed me; the latter decried me as a false prophet and, worse, a false friend.

Marion was thoroughly bewildered. She had tried to read my book and hadn't been able to make head or tail of it. But she had talked to her mentor.

"Hugh says you're trying to undermine the whole capitalist system!"

"On the contrary, I'm trying to save it."

"No one in the firm seems to think that."

"Have any of them any better ideas?"

"I don't know. It's all beyond me. I wish my father were alive to talk to you."

"Who knows? He might have agreed with me."

But it was only too clear, in any division between the firm and myself, which side Marion would be on. She was a tribal creature, and if necessary she would carry even the severed head of her spouse to the real chief. She had offered me my chance to be that, first in marrying me, then, when Mr. Dunbar had died, in trying to rouse me from my apathy, and, more lately, in offering me the resumption of a kind of partnership marriage, and I had failed her, and Hugh was king. But I was free of all this. I had my new thing. Detached, superior, in my box of observation, I could watch the inevitable unfolding of the drama below.

Marion's real trial came the following year, after the change of administration in Washington, when I was invited to go down to the capital and help with the drafting of the bill which was to become the Securities Act of 1933. This was the law which, more than any other, would open up the real struggle between right and left. My firm's executive committee came in a body to my office to beg me not to associate the name of Dunbar Leslie with such radical legislation, and when I calmly and politely declined even to debate the matter with them and requested them to leave me in peace, they departed in high dudgeon, but later delegated Hugh to appeal to Marion to intercede with me.

I was thus prepared on the night that she made her dramatic appearance at my study door, more than ever the Roman matron. Dressed for the reception at the Metropolitan Museum of Art whither she was bound, accompanied by the again faithful Hugh, to the opening of an exhibit of Hindu art sponsored by the firm, she was arrayed in red velvet with a necklace of large emeralds, and her fine auburn hair was for once neatly combed and set. Her full figure, erect in the doorway, was almost imperial in its static pose, and across her breast she was wearing the blue ribbon of a pompous Indian decoration which I had privately and ribaldly dubbed "the Order of Chastity, second class."

"I suppose it's true?" she began in a sad, lofty tone.

"Oh, Marion, sit down and have a drink. I'll tell you all about it."

"I don't care to sit, thank you. It's true, then, that you are going to betray the firm to which you owe everything and the class to which you have aspired."

"Aspired? My family was quite as good as yours, Marion."

"I am not speaking of blood. I am speaking of accomplishment and responsibility. Your father was a nobody. And we know too well what your mother was."

"Very much what you are, wasn't she?"

Marion looked more surprised than indignant. Her imagination was not capable of equating her relationship with Hugh, which she probably saw as a mating of gods on Olympus, with the humbler copulations of my mother and Mr. Dunbar.

"Your parents, I meant, were not leaders of the financial community. Which may explain why you have so little sense of loyalty. But have you stopped to consider in what light the captain of a great ship in a storm must view the man who jumps overboard to join the wreckers flashing a false beacon on the rocks?"

Really, Marion was magnificent. She must have written that out on her dressing table before coming down. But my amusement subsided when I recalled how much she resembled the aging Lees Dunbar before the congressional committee. None of those she called our financial leaders, or even the wives who had no real part in the game, were able to play it without waving banners and chanting martial songs. My momentary pity for Marion vanished when I considered that nothing would ever convince her that her values might be false.

"My dear, you are to Wall Street what Julia Ward Howe was to the Union. And your eyes will never admit that they have seen the glory of the going of the Lord. What I'm doing will no doubt raise the hackles of the old guard. I'm sure I shall be called some very nasty names. But not everyone feels that way. Even in the office some of the younger men think I'm doing a very interesting thing."

"I'm sure you're very persuasive. No one's ever doubted that. But Hugh questions whether our John, after this, will be accepted at Groton."

I laughed in sheer surprise. "But President Roosevelt went to Groton!"

"And the school is not proud of it, I'm told."

"Really, Marion, you and Hugh are being too absurd. Even the stuffiest people aren't going to hold what I do against a child. The boy may have to suffer a few cracks, but if he's worth his salt, he'll crack right back."

"Not everyone has your independence, George. Not everyone could take so lightly the bitter feelings that you have aroused."

"Lightly! I *welcome* the resentment of people like that! It actually exhilarates me."

This was too much. Marion seemed now to reach for a hidden weapon she had so far been reluctant to use. "Do you know what Hugh says your real motive is?"

"Oh, do tell me! I delight in Hugh's theories."

"He says you've always hated our world. That you've been biding your time for the chance to bring it down in ruins about our ears."

"And to what, pray, does he attribute this fervid rancor?"

"To your lifelong resentment of what Mr. Dunbar did to your mother! Nothing less than the destruction of his entire life work would make up to you for that humiliation!"

"I *see*. It's not unclever. For Hugh. But what about himself? Might not his reckless investment policies have concealed an inner drive to bankrupt the firm?"

Marion stared. "But what would have been his motive?"

"Ah, the id, my dear, the id. Who can penetrate its murky depths? But no, I shan't press that theory too far. And as to his of me, well, it might be as true as heaven or as false as hell. I don't think I really care. What difference do motives make? If they're unconscious, they're beyond our control. And even if they're conscious, are they our true motives?" I smiled in pleasure at the liberating idea. "Isn't there always a me-me-me behind the fair face of the do-gooder?"

"Is *that* what you think you are, a do-gooder?"

"Well, there you are, my dear. I do. Skip the gold stars. Skip the demerits and black marks. Just look to the *effect* of what I do. If this new law will bring any kind of order to the marketplace, does it matter that I may be getting a jag out of kicking your old world in the teeth?"

"It should matter to *you*. It would degrade you."

"Let it degrade me, then. All that matters is the new law. Young John Leslie Manville may have a better Wall Street to work in. Even though he may have a few genes that will make him hanker for the old pirate days."

"George, please! That's a low one."

"Oh, Marion, you and I have been through too much not to be occasionally honest with each other. And anyway, we shan't be meeting too often, as I shall be moving to Washington. And when poor Aggie Norman dies — which can't be far off now — we'll get a quiet divorce, and you and Hugh can marry." I held up my hand to interrupt whatever comment she might have. "No, please, my dear, let's not discuss that. We both know it's always been in the cards. There'll be less scandal in that than in what everyone suspects now. And my heresy will ease whatever shock is left."

"Oh, George." Marion's voice was lower now, and she put her hand on a table as if to support herself. But she was always transparent. There was a deep gratification for her in my proposed solution. She could be sorry for George Manville and welcome the exclusion of this odd nonconformer from her life. "Will you let me help with the decoration of whatever house you take in Washington?"

"Oh, a hotel will do me. I have no idea how long I'll be there. And now you must get on to your party. But tell me one thing before you go. Do you remember the three categories into which your brother Bob used to divide his friends?"

"No. Why?"

"They had to be either swell guys, shits or genial shits. I'm wondering if I haven't at last qualified for the third category."

"What on earth are you talking about? I never heard such barnyard language!"

But I had no need to answer her. I was content. I felt fully the equal of all the Leslies and Dunbars and Normans now. And I was too proud to be proud of it.

They That Have Power to Hurt

to Hurt

1994

1

I HAD DREAMED that an old age in Paris would be just what suited me. Oscar Wilde wrote that good Americans go to Paris when they die; I had decided not to wait. I had sucked from the fruit of my native land all it had to offer to one even as greedy as I, and now, as a bachelor of seventy-five who had survived his dearest friends (they had all been my seniors, some by many years), I hoped to sit out a tranquil senility on the porch of a café under a chestnut tree, watching the sprucely clad Gauls go briskly by, intent, as are the truly civilized, on the immediate present, oblivious of the glories and shames of the past and certainly oblivious of a small antique American gentleman, however nattily attired, however much possessed of a certain "air," who would not have disturbed them for the world, content as he was to dwell only in his memories of an undistinguished but amusing past.

I am not being modest. Modesty has never been a virtue I admired. If I did not achieve anything great as the assistant art critic of a major New York daily, or as a contributor of urbane tales to popular magazines, or even as an easily identified minor character in a couple of important American novels, I have nonetheless written one short story which achieved something like fame and is still included in anthologies of the "best," and I recently (and fatally, as it turned out) published a little record of my friendships with some of the major artists and writers of our time which I had thought might provide our academicians with some new insights into the intellectual life of Manhattan in the years immediately following the second war. These nineteen-eighties, in which I write, have witnessed a new interest in our American artistic past (perhaps to balance the fashionable shame at our American political present), and it was this which I had hoped to tap.

I should have remained silent. My memoir enjoyed only a modest sale, but it proved manna from heaven (or hell) to the English departments of some of our major universities, where the "psychobiographies" of dead writers are manufactured with total immunity from moral as well as legal retaliation. I found myself the subject of many Ph.D. theses which probed with relentless speculations into the nature of my relations with Arlina Randolph, Dan Carmichael and Hiram Scudder, and when one of my references led to the uncovering of Arlina's letters to me (she had asked me to return them to her to be "destroyed"!) in the unsifted archives of Sulka University (today the great "discoveries" are made, not in attics but in the files and storage spaces of public institutions), there was an explosion of comment that would have led one to suppose it a cache equivalent to the Boswell papers in Malahide Castle. Arlina, the *grande dame* of American letters, the aristocratic soul supposedly faithful to an elderly spouse rendered impotent by arthritis, had, on the contrary, received her "fulfillment" at the ripe age of forty-three in an adulterous affair! Great news!

My stomach turned over as I read the fulsome extravagances of smutty-minded professors entranced at uncovering the copulations of their idol. I thought of the duc de Lauzun in Saint-Simon's memoirs, concealed under the bed of the Montespan and chuckling gleefully to himself as the springs bounced to the thrustings of the Sun King. *That* is scholarship in our day! We have seen in the fantasies of our learned friends the narrow couch of Emily Dickinson groan under the added weight of a lesbian visitor, and the aging Henry James reaching a trembling hand toward the private parts of a young male admirer. And as if to excuse itself from the charge of mere pornography, Academia insists that these postulated encounters were the source of even greater art. Is not a warmer and more human note detectable in the great Arlina's prose after Venus's belated visit? I, anyway, could not detect it. I found her most convincingly described love affair in a story written not only before *me*, but even before her marriage to "Red" Suydam (who was certainly not impotent in that early day).

But why, a stranger to these professorial raptures may ask, do I object so? Is it not something for the obscure Martin Babcock to see himself elevated to the status of a priapic muse? Should I not be grateful to supply even a phallic footnote to the history of American letters? And to know that erudite teachers now divide the fiction of Arlina Randolph into pre- and post-Babcock sperm?

Perhaps I might have succumbed to some such shameful complaisance had I been awarded any credit for my share in Arlina's "renaissance." But I have not been. Not a jot. Her so-called passion is depicted as a purely unilateral affair. If one partner was raised to the glory of a cerulean sky, the other was debased to an underworld of smoky fires glinting in the darkness. Dan Carmichael's clever but malicious drawing of a young satyr, his tiny horns just emerging from his clustered curls, with an impish leer on his deceptively angelic features as he pipes a seductive tune to a group of ludicrously swooning gods and goddesses, has been reproduced in the pages of learned periodicals and interpreted as the great artist's rendering of me and my "victims."

Oh, yes, gods as well as goddesses. Hear what that grand old ham of Yankee fiction, Hiram Scudder, had to say of me in the correspondence dug out of the dead pile of his papers at Gainsville Tech:

"I agree with you about Babcock. Few of Arlina's friends felt that he was worthy of the affection she lavished on him. It is always sad to see a person of the first order chained to one of a baser tier. Martin undeniably had charm and a kind of elfin beauty. He seemed to be trying, by a sort of osmosis, to imbibe from more gifted souls some of the talent with which he had not been endowed. But *his* soul, like his personal stature, was small; he was a busy little animal who played below the belt with both sexes and had no real concept of what went on in their minds or hearts."

Certainly not below *your* belt, horrid old man, embracing young men in homoerotic hugs and extolling their youth and vigor with your stale breath!

Well, where, anyway, do I come out of all this? With the idea, certainly, that if sex be the clue to unravelling the mystery of artistic creation (and I must assume, I suppose, that it *is* a mystery), then sex had better not be viewed through the haze of romanticism which obscures even the vision of pornographers. I can provide my own lens in the form of this memorandum which may one day be found among *my* papers in some university library that accepts *any* bequest (microfilm, after all, takes up so little space) by a graduate student looking desperately for a novel aspect in the sex life of an American writer.

2

—

卐

I was born in 1912, a so-called afterthought, actually a mistake, ten years after the birth of the last of four siblings born to my parents in the first four years of their marriage, so that I was raised essentially as an only child. My father was a sturdy, hearty gentleman of shallow feelings and fixed ideas. As a stockbroker on Wall Street he had managed to lose the bulk of a not inconsiderable fortune, starting even before the 1929 crash, but he would never acknowledge that it was more than a transitory piece of bad luck, and he continued to haunt his clubs, giving vent, to all who would listen, to his market theories as if he were another Bernard Baruch, and leaving the management of his brownstone and his shingle cottage in Bar Harbor, Maine, to the small income and hard-pressed imagination of his plain and feverishly resourceful wife.

I say "plain," but there was an air of undoubted nobility in Mother's long, sad, brown face and tumbled, prematurely gray hair. She took the reverses of fortune as a judgment on a frivolous society and distanced herself from those friends and relatives who had better survived the crash, as if her new poverty were a monastic garb to be worn with a dignified humility, but in semi-isolation. When I was sent on a scholarship to Saint Stephen's, a fashionable New England boarding school, and protested bitterly to Mother (Father was a mere cipher in my life) that my clothes and allowance were horridly inferior to those of my classmates, she retorted that it would build my character to endure the sneers of the "purse proud." And she made the same answer when I begged her not to scandalize the Bar Harbor summer community and cost me my invitations to the swanker children's parties by taking in boarders.

I loved Mother and wanted to help her, but I decided early that we would never recover our position by her formula, and certainly not by Father's, and I learned to grit my teeth and do things my own way. I assessed my cherubic looks and my art of pleasing, and I saw, clearly enough, that the rich dangerous world which Father fatuously thought he still belonged to, and that Mother so fiercely scorned, could, however precariously, be won. The members of the Bar Harbor Swimming Club might disdain one of my parents and dislike the other, but, after all, they had always known them, and they could be cajoled into welcoming "charming young Martin," who had such a "tough time" at home.

Mother saw that I was becoming a toady and, worse, a successful one, and she minced no words in telling me so. At last, in my passionate resistance to what I considered her smothering influence, I said things to her that she could not forgive. Ah, that was it; that was what did it! Mothers should always forgive; the gate to redemption should be ever ajar. I thought, when she at last gave me up and accepted my dedication to Mammon with a shrug of contempt, that I was relieved, but of course I wasn't. The iron had entered into my soul, and no amount of surface gaiety could ever quite cover it. I hated Mother because I loved her.

At boarding school when, at age fourteen or thereabouts, the boys had begun to lift their heads out of the dusty cellar of wanton blows and wisecracks and to see one another dimly as fellow humans, I was able to make friends with the more prominent and popular of my classmates, compensating for my lack of heftiness with amiability and wit. Teenage boys are not accustomed to sympathy and interest from their contemporaries, and a little precocity in this field can do wonders for a social climber. I also knew how to turn a crowd against an enemy with a deadly but smilingly delivered commentary on some particularly vulnerable aspect of his personality. It is good to be sometimes feared.

My good looks were usually an important asset, but not always. They were on one occasion a decided liability. In the annual school play I was cast as the heroine with a blond wig, and so striking was my beauty and coyness of manner that two school prefects, one the captain of our football team, fell in love with me and abducted me to the cellar of the chapel, where they took turns necking with me. I will not say that this experience was the origin of a mild taste for homoerotic pleasures which has never entirely deserted me, but it certainly did not contribute to a normal development. The worst part of it was that word got out, and I achieved a reputation that followed me to Yale and was almost surely responsible for my failure to be tapped by the senior society which I had passionately coveted, the dapper and urbane Scroll & Key. Even today, when I think of this and remember our old headmaster, the holy of holies, drivelling on in his God-drunk sermons about purity and manliness while *that* had gone on beneath his pulpit, I feel a wild rage at the hysterical hypocrisy of those times.

Thus the pattern of my life was set, changing very little from college to my thirty-fifth year, when I first met Arlina Randolph. I was always well liked, even at times the "life of the party," but never the *most* popular, never truly respected by the puritanically serious, suffering a bit from the taint of the clown. In the navy, in the second war, I started as an ensign on an admiral's staff in Washington and ended there as a senior lieutenant. My imagination and diplomatic skills rendered me indispensable to the old boy, who refused to release me for sea duty, but I coaxed him to send me on safe missions to dangerous war zones and was thus able to sport all three area ribbons and even one battle star on my lapel to at least *look* like a combat veteran. But of course these never fooled a real one.

Following the war, I used my service insurance money to give me a year in Italy studying painting, after which I became a newspaper art critic covering the secondary shows (my boss took the primary), gaining an audience more through my style and wit than my insight. But the thing that made me known was the single hit of the short story I have already mentioned. It was the tale of a man who suffered from a lifelong terror that his immunity from the hideous executions of history — the hangings and quarterings, the racks, the floggings, the burnings alive — would have to be paid for in some future existence. But when he dies, he finds that he is not a victim but an executioner. He must, with full awareness of the agony he is inflicting, wield the axe, pull the cord, light the faggots. It is true hell at last.

My many friends expected great things of me after the acclaim that greeted this much reprinted tale. But it seemed I was doomed to be a "one story" man. I never hit the same note again. At thirty-five I was like the man in Mallock's *The New Republic*, of whom it was said, first, that he had a great future, and later that he *might* have one, and finally that he might have had.

But that was not the whole "me." I have not been a mere leech on the fair skin of a prosperous society. I have always wanted to give as well as take. I am too much of a true epicure not to realize that the good life involves the hand that comforts as well as that which takes. If I have practiced some harmless wiles to open doors not at first thrust wide to greet me, I have still wanted everyone in the interiors attained to be happy there. If I have had affairs with beautiful and elegant women, ever ready to smile on a pleasant unattached young man with a literary flavor, I have always ended them, I hope, with tact and kindness. I have entertained an odd little faith in my own ability — sometimes conceived almost as a duty, perhaps even as a kind of mission in (or excuse for) my life — to augment the well-being of every person with whom I found myself in any serious relationship. And never did opportunities for such augmentation more abound than in the salon of Arlina Randolph.

3
——

It was Dan Carmichael who introduced me to that august circle. He was then, in 1947, at age fifty, just past the peak of his great reputation as the last exponent of the Ashcan School, but if he had begun to decline, no one would have anticipated the low esteem in which his name is held today. He was a big, bony, black-haired, hirsute, oleaginous man whose angry canvases of Coney Island bathers, drunken sailors and crowded urban streets on hot summer nights had been considered appropriately powerful and radical in the Depression years. Ordinarily my editor would have reviewed his last show, but he happened to be ill, and I had the chance to write the column which pleased the great man and earned me an invitation to visit him in his studio on the top of his brownstone in Chelsea.

His ego, I found, was insatiable, but I knew how to satisfy it, and I was soon accorded the privilege of dropping in whenever I chose for a drink and a chat, of which I took full advantage, as I saw a longer and perhaps important article in it for me.

One afternoon I met him at his front door about to go out. "This is well met, young fellow! I'm off to the Suydams'. It's one of their Wednesdays. Come along. You'll like them, and I think they'll like you."

I followed him down the street in docile compliance. "Who are the Suydams?"

"I thought you knew everything. She's Arlina Randolph."

Well, of course I knew who *that* was. Like Carmichael's, her reputation was then near its peak, but it was not, despite some rather slick later novels, to dip thereafter as low as his. The feminist movement may have sustained it a bit, but her best books, I feel sure, will bear the test of time. I had read and loved all she had written to the date of that first visit. I knew she had been born in Richmond of an old Virginia family, one member of which had married a daughter of Jefferson's, and that she had been a passionate student of the Reconstruction. Her finest novels — historical ones, I suppose, as their action occurs in the decades immediately preceding her birth — deal with the travails of war-impoverished tobacco planters rebuilding their shattered world, but at the same time virtually reenslaving their blacks. More recently she had turned her lights on the current New York scene, and although her satire was keen, her prose luminous and her plots deft, these later fictions were not bathed in the nostalgia which, at least in my view, gave to their predecessors their peculiar moral beauty.

She was married, Dan informed me as we rode east in a taxi, to a rich older man, Red Suydam, now an arthritic victim confined to a wheelchair, who, although high-toned and high-handed with others, was yet content to regard himself as a privileged high priest in charge of the temple of his wife's art. He maintained her in a beautiful red brick Federal mansion in Gramercy Park, where they provided a buffet supper for a weekly salon of mixed artistic and social folk.

When Dan and I arrived, the great lady was not yet down. It was her habit to wait until most of what Proust's Madame Verdurin would have called her "faithful" had assembled. Dan led me up to where our host was sitting in his chair by the fire.

"I read your little piece on Dan's last show," Suydam informed me with snapping, malignant eyes as Dan retreated out of earshot. "He certainly must like you for *that* one."

I took a moment to assess his tone before answering. He had a long, oblong, cadaverous countenance with steely gray hair, presumably once red, and reddish eyeballs.

"You think I went too far?"

"Oh, not so far as I should have gone! I should have compared him with Michelangelo."

"Indeed? You don't think that would have flattered him?"

"I said compare, not equate, young man. Dan shares a fault if not a virtue with the Tuscan master."

"And what may that be?"

"He can't paint women. His are all brawny men with tits."

I laughed. "But his men are very male, you will admit."

"Oh, they are that! Those sailors with muscular thighs bursting their tight pants." Here the old boy winked at me. "Scrumptious, don't you think? Can you imagine them in bed with Dan's scrawny females?"

"Do you imply they go to bed with each other?"

"*I* don't. Dan does. At least in his pictures. Have you ever met Mrs. Carmichael?"

"Actually, I haven't."

"He won't be apt to introduce you. He never brings her here, poor woman. I guess she sits at home and looks at the sailors."

Another guest came up to greet him, and I was able to make my escape to look at the pictures on the high white walls. They were all American, the finest examples of Hassam, Robinson, Glackens, Sloan, Innes and, of course, Carmichael. I was too enthralled with these to bother with the other guests until I caught sight of my hostess pausing on a landing of the stairway and glancing down at the crowd.

I think I knew right away that a change had come into my life. It was not anything as banal as falling in love at first sight; it was rather the appearance in my too familiar sky of a new planet, a fine glowing orb of still undetermined influence but with an effect on the gravity of minor astral bodies that was bound to be felt. Her tall, full, firm figure, clad in blue velvet, her fine firm nose and strong chin, her alabaster skin and large pensive dark eyes gave her the air of a priestess of classic times, a Norma erect before an altar. Her hair was long and blond. I assumed it was dyed. It wasn't. Descending the stairs, she noted the staring new guest and came directly over to me.

"Who is this nice new friend?" she asked gravely as she extended her hand.

When I told her and explained my auspices, she nodded, complimented me on my "hell" story and led me to a corner, where we both sat. A maid brought her a glass of white wine. I later learned that she was not to be interrupted by others in that corner. Her rules were simple but definite.

We talked about writing, and she treated me charmingly as an equal. I asked her why she had never written about the antebellum South, the old planters in their heyday.

"Because it was too long ago. Henry James said in one of his wonderful prefaces that the charm of the past as used in fiction depended on its proximity."

"And I suppose in your childhood the memory of Reconstruction was still vivid."

"And still bitter!" she exclaimed. "My grandparents were very far from reconstructed. Oh, very far! Yet there were some rare souls who saw it as a period of something like redemption. My father was one of those. He used to say that slavery was the cancer of the Old South."

Her articulation was astonishingly precise. She might almost have been reading aloud, without an *er* or an *ah*. And she seemed to have lost all trace of a Southern accent. Her tones were high and sharp, more the voice of New York than of Richmond.

"You don't mean he saw the war as a spiritual one? Like the crusades?"

"My dear young man, he ran away from home at the age of sixteen in the last year of the war to fight for General Lee. The Yankees had nothing to do with his moral struggles. He loathed them!"

"Would you have fought for Lee had *you* been a young man then?"

"Of course I would!" Her laugh was hearty and infectious. "Do you see me as a fatuous Mrs. Howe scribbling down the inane verses of her battle hymn as she watched a review of the Army of the Potomac? No, Mr. Babcock, I would have been like our sainted general. With a heavy heart I would have shouldered a musket and gone to die for my native state!"

As she clapped her hands together, I had a vision of Boadicea, of Zenobia, of Joan of Arc. And I wondered how heavy that heart would have been. There might have been too much joy in battle.

It was time for her to join her other guests. But I had made the grade. When I left that night, she said, "Come back, Mr. Babcock. Come back to us, please."

And I did. I became the most faithful of her faithful. Arlina's salon had probably the best conversation in New York. The people who came for cocktails and supper, and stayed to talk (unless it was a musical evening) until midnight (Arlina always retired on the stroke of twelve), were a mixture of writers, journalists, painters and musicians, with a goodly number of the more enlightened members of the banking and legal communities. They talked in groups, unless a particularly burning topic united the chamber in a general discussion, moderated by Red Suydam.

Otherwise, he took an almost violent interest in every subject, wheeling his chair furiously from group to group, cackling with sometimes cruel laughter, for he loved to pounce on the ridiculous, even when a half-decent compassion would have spared it.

My enthusiasm for Arlina's salon did not blind me to the fact that she paid a certain price for her high sense of decorum. Because she would not tolerate drunkenness, bad language, too heated arguments or too casual dress, some of the major artists and writers of the day, including too many of the younger ones, made no appearance under her roof. She was quite aware of this herself, but she pointed out to me, with some truth, that geniuses were rarely as good talkers as near geniuses and that conversation, after all, was more the point of her gatherings than the furnishing of food and alcohol even to the sublime. I had to agree with this, but I did not go on to tell her that convention and respectability lent a faint tinge of things *passés* to her salon. Hiram Scudder, the hoary old veteran of an earlier radicalism, whose "big" novel about steel strikers in 1905 had aroused the literary world, seemed, with his hoarse croaking and false teeth, a bit of a museum piece, while Dan Carmichael's shrill denunciations of the new abstract impressionists betrayed a senescent imagination. Time, so to speak, had dressed the old pioneers in dinner jackets.

Yet the milieu formed the perfect background for Arlina herself. She was at her best and brightest with a certain formality in the conversational give-and-take, where a witticism was never lost in a babble of conflicting voices and where a pause could signify reflection on what one's interlocutor had just said and not simply the rehearsal of one's own next *mot*. And her laugh, her wonderful laugh, could unite any group in good humor. She had the remarkable gift of making reserve seem almost intimate.

Sometimes, inevitably, to so frequent a guest as myself, her machinery showed from under its smooth cover. In spring, when she planned excursions out of the city for a select few — for a picnic on the Palisades or a visit to her Westchester "farm" — there was a slight strain in the very perfection of her arrangements and in the precision of her instructions to guests: who was to bring what or wear what or take whom. Some even breathed the word *bossy*, though it would have been kinder to say that she could never quite take in the fact that many people would rather be wrong in their own way than right in hers. The only person to whom she consistently deferred was Red. Hiram Scudder, who had known her the longest, told me that her husband, and he alone, had inherited the subservience with which she had honored her late parents.

I was soon her particular favorite. At picnics she assigned me to most tasks, and I fetched and carried for her like a faithful dog. She was certainly not one to suffer fools gladly, but once admitted to her inner circle one could relax and even indulge in an occasional bad pun. And she was a good sport, too. She could take sallies at her own expense from the initiated. Once on a country outing, where we played a word game of associations (I would say "dog," and you had to say the first word that came into your head, like "cat") and I had totaled up Arlina's responses, I announced to the group that her primary concerns appeared to be "clothes and men."

"Youth, youth," she murmured. "You are so cruel."

She took a personal interest in my life and work and did not hesitate to scold me.

"Your trouble, Martin, is that you are lazy. You should *make* yourself write. You should assign certain hours of the week to composition and stick to your program no matter what."

"Do *you* do that?"

"No, because I don't have to. I can afford to wait for the mood, because I now know that the mood will come. But when it does come I give it full sway. Even if Red and I are traveling in Europe on a fixed schedule, and I feel the mood, then I must stay where I am and write. Red is an angel about changing accommodations."

"But he's still a taskmaster. He *makes* you write."

"He doesn't make me do a thing. He simply insists that I follow my bent. I tell him we should hang a sign on our door: 'Arlina and Red, Makers of Fine Fiction.' "

What *was* their relationship? It was obvious that it couldn't have been a physical one for several years. And before that? They had no children, which was no proof of anything, but it struck me that there was something virginal in Arlina's air. Dan Carmichael, who delighted in sexual speculations, claimed to have had it from Red himself that Arlina had been so frigid and inexperienced at the time of their wedding that it had taken him three months to consummate the marriage. But Dan's imagination was an embroidering one; I did not trust it.

The first time Arlina and I discussed the relation between the sexes was when we were seated on a bench in Bryant Park, whither we had strolled on a mild early spring afternoon following a matinée of *Tristan und Isolde*. I had been asked to fill Red's subscription seat because he hated Wagner. He had missed, however, one of the great performances of all time — Flagstad and Melchior — and Arlina, who had been deeply affected, was moved to speak of the "tragedy" of illicit love.

"Is there anything in art more shattering than the surprising of the lovers in Act Two? They have almost escaped the harsh dry world of daylight — the meanness of things too clearly delineated — into the enchantment of night — death, if you will — I don't care — and bang! Melot breaks in. Marke breaks in. All hell breaks in."

"Just before their orgasm."

Arlina paused — judicially — as if to consider whether I was being crude or merely explicit. "Well, yes, if you choose to construe the music that way."

"Isn't it unmistakable? Those rhythms?"

"I know what you mean, of course. But to me Wagner is expressing more than just that. The lovers have reached a point where their relationship is the only reality. Marke and Melot and even the warning Brangäne are irrelevancies. The terrible thing about unsanctified love — unsanctified, that is, by law or religion or mores or even by a decent regard for one's spouse or betrothed — is that these irrelevancies are always bound to intrude. Even if they're not actually intruding, they may be intruding in the lovers' minds. The lovers are never *free*."

"But isn't that just what makes their love so great? The difficulty? Even the danger?"

"Oh, Martin, what a superficial view! How *can* you?"

"Because it's true! Look what's happening today. People everywhere are obsessed with removing the impediments to love. Easy divorce threatens the very existence of adultery. Our most respectable debutantes are permitted love affairs, and every kind of sexual perversion is freely tolerated, at least in the best society. And is anyone happier? Of course not! Because the pleasure of love is diluted with its availability. The nun in a convent who nurses a guilty passion for the priest who officiates at mass gets as much kick out of it as the busiest Don Juan on Park Avenue!"

"You can't be serious!"

"Never more so. If King Marke, stumbling on the lovers, had said, 'Go to it, kids. I only quit the hunt for a date with Brangäne,' there'd have been a terrible let-down. I bet they wouldn't have got going again until they'd quaffed the rest of that love potion."

"Don't be so disgusting." But the reproach in her voice was mild. The topic intrigued her. "It's all very well for *you* to talk that way. There are no impediments for a bachelor."

"Are there not, Arlina?" I turned to look into her eyes with an expression of mock ardor.

"Don't be silly."

And she rose to walk on.

But the sudden rigor in her tone gave me my first notion that perhaps what she minded was that the ardor was mock.

And was it? My feelings about the wonderful Arlina were mixed indeed. On the lowest level — and that was where I always started — there was the itching yen of a small randy male for a fine large female figure, the lust of a Nibelung to pollute a Rhine maiden, or, translated into terms of literary competition, the drive of a scribbler to equate himself in the only way he could think of with a novelist of the first rank.

But that was far from the whole. By my own half-serious philosophy of love, just enunciated, I might have diluted such intensity as I was capable of in a series of easy affairs, but I still know that I was more devoted to Arlina than to any other woman in my life. She had become the warmest of friends, a kind of sisterly mentor to a man rejected by his own mother, and I cannot think of her even today without a return of something like the old heartache.

At any rate, after our Bryant Park chat, I began seriously to entertain the idea that it might be one of the delightful functions of my idle life to make some contribution to her deeper happiness.

It was Hiram Scudder who first hinted to me that my project was not entirely unfeasible. I had become a great favorite of the paunchy, bald old boy, who was always asking me to lunch, ostensibly to discuss my writing but really to hold forth about his own, and he would walk slowly down the avenue afterwards, his arm entwined with mine, while he chanted about what he would do if he had again, like me, "a manly vigor and youth." In parting he would seize my head with both his hands and plant a wet kiss, presumably of benediction, upon my forehead. Perhaps he thought of the emotion I aroused in him as paternal. Unlike Dan, who, though married, was a notorious wooer of young men, Hiram was a bachelor and very possibly a virgin to both sexes. Such things were not uncommon to his generation. Arlina's court had a decidedly androgynous note, although Red himself was given to tasteless antipederast jokes. But then Red, perhaps out of bitterness at his own incapacities, was anti everything. Except, of course, Arlina.

On one of our postprandial promenades Hiram referred to the obvious problem in Arlina's life.

"A handsome woman like that needs a different kind of love from what poor old Red can give her."

"You don't believe she's sublimated all that into something higher?" I raised my eyebrows in jest.

He chuckled. "No more than you do, young man. What she needs is a warm body two nights a week."

"What a disgusting old satyr you are, Hiram. How do you know she hasn't got one?"

"Because I know Arlina. And I know the body she might pick if she had her choice." Here he pressed his arm closer to mine. I pulled away from him.

"Well, I know no such thing. So far as I'm concerned she's entirely devoted to her old Red. Who strikes me, by the way, as a man who might not hesitate to put a bullet through her if he caught her out. And one in her lover as well."

"You see him bursting in on them in his wheelchair? Besides, he wouldn't object. He's told me as much."

"Really?" I didn't want to encourage the old bawd, but I *was* interested.

"Oh, yes. He told me he hadn't been any good to her in that department for several years. And that he wouldn't mind if she took a lover, so long as she was discreet about it."

"And has he told her so?"

"Oh, no. That would outrage her. If it came at all, it would have to come as a passion strong enough to overcome her sense of duty. I agreed with Red. If it wasn't big enough to do that, it wasn't worth having."

I said no more on the subject, but I gave it careful thought. The removal of Red as a jealous husband certainly cleared the field. I had little zest for violence.

One Saturday afternoon when Arlina and I were walking on the fields of her Bedford farm, she suddenly put a question to me which seemed to be aimed at a very personal aspect of my own life.

"My new novel involves an adultery in Gotham which the characters must keep very secret. My heroine is a Park Avenue matron, and her lover is a law partner of her husband's. They wouldn't go to a hotel, would they?"

"They might. A second-class one on the West Side. But she'd hate that, and if she were ever spotted on the street in that part of town, it would be fatal. No, they'd be more apt to meet in a rented apartment, still on the West Side but south of Central Park, near the shopping district, so her presence in that area, if noted, would seem natural."

"And they'd arrive and leave, of course, separately."

"Of course."

"Would she have a cleaning woman for the flat?"

"He would arrange that. The woman would never see her, and she'd leave nothing in the room that could identify her."

"And when the lovers met socially, they'd be careful to act naturally."

"Unnaturally! The thing to avoid would be any appearance of avoiding each other. That's always a sure giveaway."

"I suppose if my heroine had an unmarried lover, they could meet in his flat."

"Depending on where it is. Elevators are dangerous."

"You *do* seem to know the ins and outs."

Ah, that was what I had been waiting for! *That* had nothing to do with her novel.

"Well, you don't suppose I've been living like a monk all these years, do you?"

"Far from it."

"Would you have wished me to?"

"I?" She seemed startled. "Why, no, I don't suppose I should. What right have I to be your censor?"

"The right I freely give you. The right of a friend I love and respect above all others."

"But, dear Martin, your private life is your own affair!"

"Not anymore. Now that that life is under discussion, I want you to know I've been pure as Hippolytus since the day we met."

We had been walking by the stile that separated the field from her neighbor's. She turned now to lean against it, facing me, but with clenched fists raised to her eyes.

"What are you trying to tell me, Martin?"

"It's pretty obvious, isn't it?"

"Oh, dear friend, please don't play games with me. I'm not up to that kind of thing."

"It isn't playing games to be in love with you."

"Love!" She dropped her hands, and I saw something like terror in her eyes. "You can't love me. You're a mere boy compared to me. A dear, beautiful boy who should be loving some dear, beautiful girl. Do you want to drive me out of my mind? *Do* you?"

"That's just what I want to do." I stepped forward and seized both her hands in mine. I stared at her averted eyes until they turned to me. "There are eight years between us, which is nothing at our ages. Let *me* decide about that 'dear, beautiful girl.' The only woman I want is *you*, and I'm not too humble to claim we can give each other something that's better than anything either of us ever had."

Her eyes now wandered in what seemed an almost childlike confusion. "What about my husband?"

"He needn't ever know a thing. Leave all that to me. If I can do it for your novel, I can do it for you." I allowed a grave pause. "Let me kiss you, Arlina." When she said nothing, I repeated the request. "I don't want you to think I ever grabbed anything you didn't freely accord."

"Very well. Kiss me, Martin."

Whereupon I did so. Her response was all I could have wished. When we got back to the house, Hiram Scudder leered at me disgustingly. He too had been walking, and I supposed he had espied us.

4

When Arlina surrendered to love, it was without reservation. She came to my little apartment in the Village quite openly, disdaining the maneuvers of her fictional characters, on certain weekday afternoons, and we had rapturous times together. At first. But I could not quite accustom myself to the almost reverential aftermaths to our lovemaking of which she made much point. She insisted that we read aloud famous love poems to each other. As she was planning to publish an anthology of these, I could not but note that the time was not, at least in her case, entirely wasted.

I sound like a cad, but what man wouldn't who told the whole truth? The fact was that Arlina's lovemaking, at first delicious, as she shyly and then rapidly more boldly accustomed herself to every intimacy, began at last to be the least bit smothering. She was too articulately romantic, too anxious to possess every aspect of my nature. She wanted me to agree on certain times of the day or night, when we were not together, when we would think passionately of each other. She wanted to penetrate into every chapter of my past, to learn about my old love affairs, to question me about the exact quality of my feeling for her, reaching rather too greedily, it seemed to me, for the smallest evidence that she represented a unique experience in my emotional life.

I had to fabricate almost all my responses. She would have been horrified by the truth. I was only too sure that the fantasies in which all lovers indulge to keep their libidos keen were very different in our two cases. Whereas she may have made love to the remembered rhythms of *Tristan*, I enhanced my lust with images of a proud Roman dame submitting helplessly to the rape of a barbarian, her aroused appetite actually whetted by humiliation and shame. At other times I likened myself to the villain Maskwell in Congreve's *Double Dealer*, boasting how he "had wantoned in the rich circle" of Lady Touchwood's love. That was more my inner style.

It was therefore not without a feeling of a needed recess that I greeted the news that Arlina was departing with Red on a two months' lecture tour across the country to promote her new book. She was very emotional about our separation and made me promise to write her daily to the care of her trusted female agent, who would be traveling with her. I was only intermittently faithful to the task, but the many florid epistles that she indited to me were the ones that turned up in the "cache" at Sulka U.

In her absence I dropped in more often on Dan Carmichael in his studio. If I was not averse to being freed for a while from Arlina's sometimes fatiguing attentions, I missed almost at once the reassuring glow of her approbation, which had given me a novel but gratifying sense of success in life. I knew that I had aroused strong feelings in Dan, and I should have left him alone, but there you have me. My nature craved this new incense of admiration from the great.

His studio was reached by a back stairway descending to the service entrance, so I did not have to encounter his bleak and saturnine spouse, who, in Red Suydam's mocking description, brooded about male models in the floor above discarding their raiment least of all to be sketched. I found Dan in a depressed mood; he complained that he could neither paint nor draw, and wanted only to talk and drink.

He did, however, one afternoon a sketch of me, executed with remarkable speed. It was a very fine likeness, and I flushed with pleasure when he said I could have it.

"But it's too valuable for a gift," I protested, more to please him than to offer it back.

"I can give what I like to my friends," he growled. "Only promise me one thing. Don't give it to Arlina."

"Why should I do that?"

"Oh, some silly notion of how a lover should behave."

"So you know about me and Arlina."

"Everybody knows about you and Arlina."

"Even Red?"

"Oh, Red indeed. He's positively obscene about you being the smaller. He says you have to sling a bucket over her head and hang on to the handle for dear life."

I was horribly mortified, but it was not my habit to show it. There had to be other ways of getting back at Arlina's sneering court.

"You say you can't draw these days." I rolled up my sketch and put a rubber band around it. I wanted to be sure to take it away with me before he changed his mind, of which he was all too capable. "But this," I added, holding it up, "is surely no example of artist's cramp."

He viewed me obliquely. "Maybe you're my only inspiration now."

My stare was cool. Had I really aroused a major passion? If so, I felt little sympathy. I needed to pay him off for the bucket crack. As I turned to go, I asked, "Is there anything I can do for *you* in return for my handsome present?"

He looked up at once. "Yes! Pose for me in the nude."

I laughed. "Dan, you old lecher. You know I'm too modest for that."

"You goddamn little prick teaser!" he exploded. "You're afraid if you stripped you might give yourself away. You're not half as straight as you like to make out. Oh, I've heard about you. Now get your hot little ass out of here!"

I laughed, with genuine good nature, and departed, taking my sketch.

But I returned only three days later, behaving as if nothing had happened. At this poor Dan broke down completely. He pleaded with me desperately to respond to his love; he blabbered about his obsession with me; he even wept as he threatened me with being the cause of the extinction of his art. It was appalling to see a great man reduced to such a state of uncontrol.

Now what was I up to? Was I still smarting about Red's cruel image of me and Arlina? Did I suspect that it was really Dan's invention and not Red's at all? A little, perhaps. But couldn't there be an understandable pride in seeing an artist of the first order (at least so he was still considered by many) grovel before you? And tell you that it was in *your* power and yours alone to enable him to pick up his brush?

Yes, but that was not all. There was still the idea of my pleasant little function in life to give some pleasure where I had received so much. And I had owed in the past year most of my pleasure to the circle to which he had introduced me.

Anyway, I did not keep Dan long on tenterhooks. I accorded him what he wanted, to my very mild and to his too furious satisfaction. Indeed, so ecstatic did he wax that, had I desired it, he would have kicked his poor old wife out of the house and established me in her stead. But of course I wanted no such thing, nor had I the least intention of continuing the liaison after Arlina's return.

Arlina's return, however, was to result in the end of both affairs. I had agreed now to pose for Dan as he had requested, and in doing so I had actually expected to be the subject of the greatest painting of his career, a nude portrait imbued with all the feeling that Dan poured into the love which, at least in his younger days, had not dared to reveal its nomenclature. But one afternoon, while I was posing, the back doorbell rang, and Dan pressed the buzzer to open it, expecting a delivery which could be left downstairs. Instead, two minutes later, Hiram Scudder pushed open the studio door without knocking and walked in.

The mistake I made was to grab a shirt and cover myself. Hiram's beady eyes leered at me; his tone was malignant.

"Oh, go on, please, go on. Let me not interrupt so charming a séance. Or are such beauties to be revealed only to the artist?"

Of course I should have brazened it out, as if it had been a routine posing, and allowed the jealous Hiram's lecherous eyes to feast on my bodily parts as we all three casually chatted. Instead, I protested that the session was over anyway and that I was already late for an appointment. Dressing hastily behind a screen, I took my leave.

Five days later I received this epistle from Arlina:

"I have had a revolting letter from hateful Hiram which has made it impossible for me to continue my tour. I have told Red that I am suffering from migraines and cannot speak in public. And so indeed I am. I cannot find it in my heart to believe it of you, dearest, dearest Martin, though Hiram says that Dan actually boasted to him of his 'conquest.' I shall, of course, hear what you have to say. I will come to you on the afternoon of the 25th. My plane gets in that morning. Oh, God, God! Have I been a fool?"

5

Arlina stood before me in my small living room whose only first-rate objects of art were the three Whistler etchings of Venice which she had given me. She was very pale and sad and grave. I remembered my initial impression of her as a pagan priestess. I had not attempted to deny or even to palliate Scudder's charge.

"You tell me it meant nothing to you. I cannot imagine a human being to whom such things mean nothing. Certainly not one with whom I have been so intimate. A man I loved!" At this she gave a little cry. "Oh, Martin, how *could* you? The moment I was gone! Did I mean nothing to you?"

"You know that's not true."

"How can I know?"

"Don't you feel it? In the deepest part of you?"

"No!"

"Then how can I help you?"

"You can't! Oh, I must face this alone. I see that." She clasped her hands and shook them in her distress. "There's no use talking. You're simply not the man I took you for. That's not your fault. There's no reason you should have been. You never claimed to be. It was my folly to erect a pedestal and put you up on it. It would have been better for me if we'd never met."

"Oh, don't say that. We had good times."

"Maybe *you* did. In your own way. Mine were illusions."

"Isn't love an illusion?"

"Ah, no cheap platitudes, please."

"Look, Arlina. Give this time to heal. You say I wasn't the man you thought me. But the man I am isn't so bad a guy. Get to know him. He and you might still be friends."

"So that's it." She shook her head sadly. "Friendship. It's your *métier*, isn't it? I suppose it's all very well. *If* you've never known the other thing."

And with this she left me.

But we did in time become friends again, mild friends perhaps, but still friends, and we remained such until the day she died.

And now let me put the question. Did I do her any real harm? If, as the critics claim, the affair deepened her insight into the passions that "consume mankind," was she not the gainer and I a significant contributor to American letters? What did her suffering, or even Dan's, amount to? Weren't they both still on top of their worlds?

But the truth is that I had nothing to do with the nourishment of their art. Passion in great artists is as much the product of their imagination as it is of their hearts. As a skilled paleontologist can reconstruct the skeleton of a dinosaur from a single bone in its toe, so could Arlina resurrect the love of Antony and Cleopatra from the mere memory of our poor fling of an affair. Nor, if the truth be told, did she need even that. Jane Austen could create Elizabeth and Darcy, and Emily Brontë, Heathcliff and Cathy, out of daydreams strolling in a garden or a moor.

And so they go, the great Arlinas, supreme in the delights and consolations of their celestial visions, deriving occasional niblets of nutriment from the lesser humans on whom they occasionally feed, yet receiving the lachrymose sympathy of academic researchers for every supposed pang of "disprized love" they may incur, which love is actually only further grist for their busy mills. While as for the poor partner of this "love," well, out upon him! Who was he to play gross tunes upon the heartstrings of genius?

With scrupulous fairness, however, I append the lines which Arlina had underlined in the morocco-bound copy of Shakespeare's sonnets which she gave me one Christmas:

> They that have power to hurt and will do none,
> That do not do the thing they most do show,
> Who, moving others, are themselves as stone,

Unmoved, cold and to temptation slow;
They rightly do inherit heaven's graces
And husband nature's riches from expense;
They are the lords and owners of their faces,
Others but stewards of their excellence.

But you know what the sestet tells of these lords and owners. They are also lilies which, when festering, smell far worse than weeds! Trust the artist to have the last word.